Paper Flowers

Paper Flowers

Paper Memories
Book One

J. L. Jackola

livshe

ALSO BY J. L. JACKOLA

Fantasy Romance

Unbound Prophecy Universe

<u>*Unbound Prophecy*</u>

Ascension

Descent

Surfacing

Submerged

Riven

Adrift

<u>*Unbound Kingdom*</u>

Severed Kingdom

Cursed Kingdom

Prophesied Kingdom

Unbound Kingdom (the trilogy omnibus)

<u>*Unbound Prophecy Prequels*</u>

Orlaina

<u>*Wicked Hues Series*</u>

The Forgotten Hues of Skye

The Coveted Hues of Skye

The Shattered Shades of Crimson

The Impossible Shades of Crimson

The Endless Shadows of Pete

Wicked and Fated Universe

<u>*Wicked Gods Duet*</u>

Trial of the Gods

Tournament of the Gods

<u>*Wicked Warlocks Duet*</u>

Curse of the Broken Prince

Fate of the Broken Queen

<u>*Wicked Shadows Duet*</u>

Mark of the Shadow

Touch of the Torch

Fairytale Inspired

Of Candy and Betrayal

Of Petals and Lies

Of Giants and Betrayal

Mafia Romance

<u>*Wicked Cravings Series*</u>

Obsessive Cravings

Forbidden Cravings

Hostile Cravings

Unhinged Cravings

Contemporary Romance

<u>*Paper Memories Series*</u>

Paper Flowers

ISBN 978-1-960784-63-6 (Trade Paperback)

Published by Tivshe Publishing

Printed in the United States of America

Cover design by Aljune Designs

Visit www.jljackola.com

AUTHOR'S NOTE

While the love story in Paper Flowers is sweet and fragile, Gabe's past holds trauma that may be triggering to some readers. Please note that there are references to physical abuse, suicide, and sexual abuse. All situations are off page.

For those who wish they had a second chance.

CHAPTER 1

TORI

Beads of sweat rolled down my chest, and I cursed the Florida heat. Sure it was July, but it seemed like I was walking through hell instead of a parking lot. I picked up my pace, hoping I wouldn't look like I'd been out for a run rather than heading to my first day of training. Three months to train for a job that would be the foundation of my career...if they didn't turn me away at the door for smelling like sweat.

"Yes, Dad, I'll behave," I told my father, holding my phone to my ear and adjusting my purse. "I'm sure it will be fine, and you and Mom will survive without me there."

"I know, Tor, but you're so far away now."

"Florida is a three-hour plane ride from Connecticut, Dad. It's not that far. Look, I'm about to go into the building, so I need to go." *And hose myself down after dipping my head in a tub of ice water.* "I'll text you later."

"Good luck today, honey. You're going to be amazing."

My goodbye was quick, and I cursed my stubborn need to park at the back of the parking lot for the extra steps as I pulled the glass door open. The building of the brokerage firm looked unassuming. To anyone driving by, it was an office park, not a full-service call center for one of the largest firms in the country.

The guard at the counter greeted me with a warm smile and, after I explained I was part of the new training class, he checked me in and directed me to a door to my left. A loud click signaled he had released the lock, and I walked through, seeing that I wasn't the first to arrive and would have no way to inconspicuously fan the sweat dry.

I took a seat and gave a quiet hello to the woman next to me, who introduced herself as Mary before turning back to nervously type on her phone. About ten other people were in the room, awkward silence filling the space. I fanned my face as the door clicked open again.

My fingers hit my nose as my motion faltered, and I quickly tucked my hand away. The man who walked in had to be the most gorgeous man I'd laid eyes on. Thick wavy brown hair, hazel eyes that could drown me, and an expensive suit that made my off-brand dress look cheap. He caught my eye, and I smiled, not sure what else to do since he'd busted me staring at him. I was half tempted to see if drool had pooled in the corner of my mouth.

He took a seat beside me, towering over my five-nine frame.

"It's so quiet in here," he said, adjusting his suit jacket, my eyes following as if it was some riveting action. I felt his eyes on me and looked up. If ever I wanted to crawl under a seat, it was now. First, I'd gaped at him when he came in, and now I was stalking his hand movements.

Get a grip, Tori.

Thoughtful hazel orbs peered back at me as a lock of hair fell on his forehead. I had the sudden urge to brush it back and balled my fingers into my hand to stop them.

"I'm Gabe," he said, holding his hand out to me.

"Victoria," I replied, my voice sounding like I was a three-year-old child instead of a twenty-four-year-old woman. "But I go by Tori."

When our hands touched, a rush went through me, like a current that snapped and fizzled. My eyes flicked down then back to his, and I drew my hand away as he studied me.

"Tori, huh?"

"Yup." I almost rolled my eyes at my lack of vocabulary.

A door on the other side of the room opened, and a woman entered, introducing herself as our new trainer before guiding us out of the room. I stuck by Gabe, telling myself it was because he'd been so friendly when I knew it was just to smell his cologne. As we waited for security to call us in one by one for our badges, I leaned on the wall.

"Where did you work before this?" Gabe asked me, but a pretty woman a few years older than me stepped into our space and introduced herself as Allison. Her eyes lingered on Gabe, and an unreasonable streak of jealousy had me wishing I could shove her away and continue gazing into his eyes.

You're at work, Tori. A new job you want to keep.

"I worked at Goldman," she said, her blond hair bouncing as she adjusted her stance in her spiked heels.

I was having trouble standing for so long in just my two-inch heels, so I didn't know how she was still upright.

"But this was too good of an opportunity to pass up," she continued. "I'll have to start from the bottom again, but you know how that goes."

"Interesting." Gabe turned back to me. "And you, Tori?"

My eyes flew from Allison, with her perfect makeup and hair, to Gabe, and I stuttered, "I didn't." Geez, I needed to connect my brain to my mouth. "I mean, I ran the finances for my family's business for two years after I graduated."

"Oh, how sweet," Allison said, and the condescending tone crawled over my skin.

Gabe didn't bother looking at her, his attention only on me, and I didn't know what to make of that. I rubbed my cheek, feeling out of my element. I'd spent the last two years in the snowy hills of Connecticut where I returned home after college. Choosing to get real-life experience before plunging into the workforce.

"Out of college?" Gabe asked, and I nodded. "That's smart. I wish I'd taken some time off, but I jumped right into getting my MBA and then worked. Spent four years doing time at another firm before I came here."

"Victoria Hent?"

"That's me," I answered, giving Gabe a goodbye glance before following the man in and leaving Gabe alone with Allison. I wondered how long it would take for her to dig her manicured nails into him.

At home I had never felt out of place, but here I did. I needed to adjust to the business world—the heels and dresses, the skirts and silk shirts. After two years of wearing jeans and T-shirts, I was out of my element. And women like Allison knew that.

I feigned a smile at the camera as they shot my picture for my badge, hating how I couldn't shake the shadow that was hovering over my confidence. After receiving my badge, I was directed to exit the room and take a seat in the room across the hall.

A classroom. I sat, nervously wondering if that was the last attention I'd receive from Gabe until he pulled out the chair next to me and sat. Badge in hand, he said, "So where were we?"

I peered over my shoulder, looking for Allison to come trailing in.

"Hughes," he said, and I scrunched my brow. "My last name follows yours."

There was something bashful about the way he said it, and I couldn't hide my smile.

"That's convenient," I said, finally finding my voice.

"Very."

A confident answer that had my insides twisting into knots. But this wasn't a bar. It was work, and I needed to stop, or I'd be in an HR nightmare.

"You were saying you wished you'd taken time off before working," I said, trying not to get lost in his gaze.

His features took on a faraway look before he focused back on me. Rubbing his jaw, he said, "Yeah, that would have been nice."

More people came in, filling the space around the U-shaped table. My nemesis missed her chance at Gabe's right side, much to my relief. Not that my reaction made any sense. For all I knew, he had a girlfriend. He was entirely too good-looking to be single.

As the man next to him diverted his attention, I looked around the room, taking in all the unfamiliar faces until the trainer entered to start the first class. After a round of introductions, she singled out Gabe, who had since taken his jacket off, leaving him even more distracting.

"Gabriel—"

"Gabe," he corrected her, receiving a nod as she made a note on her paper.

"Noted. Gabe, you'll be with us for the first few weeks to acclimate yourself to the company, then you'll head to the floor. The analyst team is particular about scooping their new hires up fast and putting them to work, especially one with your experience."

"Understood."

My gaze dropped to my hands. So, he wouldn't be spending the next three months with me. I supposed it was a good thing since I had licenses to study for, and he would continue to be a distraction if my drooling over him didn't get me fired first.

Allison raised her hand, a smug look on her face. "I have plenty of experience as well. Shouldn't I be heading to the floor instead of staying here? I'm licensed, after all."

Gabe sat back in his seat, and I glanced over at him, seeing how his eyes had narrowed. Then again, there were several dagger stares being directed her way.

"I'm afraid not. Traders start here and stay here until you've mastered the system and the firm's standards. Don't worry, you'll be on the floor soon enough."

As our trainer asked if there were any more questions, I snuck a peek at Allison. Her lips were pouty, but her eyes were on Gabe. As happy as I was that our trainer had put her in her place, I still didn't think I could compete with her. She seemed too perfect, even if she was annoying and obvious.

I smoothed my hand over my skirt, wishing I was in jeans and a sweatshirt, bundled up in my parents' office with a cup of coffee, until I glanced at Gabe and saw that his focus was nowhere but on me. He gave me a flirty smile, which caused my stomach to somersault, and suddenly, I wasn't so worried about Allison.

***

"Do you want to grab lunch with me?" Gabe asked as I rose, stretching after a three-hour session that made my eyes droop. "I mean, since we have to leave the property to get something."

"Sure," I answered, my heart reminding me it was there.

"Great, you can tell me more about this business your parents own, and I'll drive. In the mood for anything?"

I shrugged. "I don't know the area yet. I just moved here this weekend. I'm still shuffling boxes around to find things."

"I'd love to join." My head made a beeline to where Allison had plopped herself on the table next to me, her skirt riding up to reveal amazing legs. She was too unreal to believe, and she was quickly becoming a pain in my ass.

"Sorry, my car only seats two." Gabe motioned with his head for me to follow, and I didn't bother looking back at her, although I could feel the sting as her eyes bore into my back.

"Is it me or is she a little desperate?" he asked, holding the door for me as we walked out of the building. The heat hit me, singeing my throat and draining my energy. "Don't worry, you'll get used to it."

"Maybe. And will I?"

He chuckled, a sound that reverberated across my skin. "She definitely is, and yes, you will."

I bounced on my feet, a spring in my step at his words, but I didn't dare get my hopes up. This was a work lunch with two colleagues getting to know each other. Nothing more.

His car was two spots down from mine, and he must have read my confusion. "I like to park as far away as I can for the exercise," he said. "Especially on days I don't hit the gym."

I wasn't certain my crush meter could climb any higher, but it did. He held the door of his car open and closed it when I had comfortably tucked myself in. Peering into the backseat, I gave him a questioning look as he got in.

"She wasn't the one I wanted to go to lunch with," he stated, giving me a bashful smile that had me thankful I was sitting.

My mouth dropped, and I slammed it shut, my teeth complaining about the impact.

The car started, the AC rushing out in a warm gust that took a few minutes to turn cold.

"There's a sandwich shop around the corner," Gabe said. "They have the best homemade chips if you're up to it."

"Sounds perfect," I said, soaking in the air and wishing I could pick my armpits up to dry them.

Gabe chatted with me about Florida, telling me he had moved there for school even though it had driven his father mad because he hadn't gone to school closer to home. We didn't stop talking the entire hour we had for our break, and by the time we were back in his car, my crush had warped into something I doubted I could control.

Chapter 2

Gabe

Don't get involved, stay focused, do the job, and get the experience. That had been my motto since leaving home. No distractions. Even in college, I'd rarely splurged on a fling with a girl. They were distractions I didn't need, and I had a mission. The same one that had driven me since I'd left home. But the woman now buckling herself into my car had blindsided me.

Tori was too amazing to ignore. I'd been drawn to her the moment I opened the door to that room, seeing her there with her ebony hair running down her back, her dress flattering her curves and stopping at long, toned legs. She'd turned her navy eyes on me, and I'd stood no chance. I had to talk to her, ignoring the desperate move from Allison, who clearly hadn't gotten the hint that I wasn't looking for that kind of experience. I knew her type, and I knew she'd be a one-night stand at most. When I splurged, which was rare, she was the type I would have gravitated to, someone I knew I would have no attachment to and would only offer the necessary pleasure to get me through a few months before I gave in again.

But Tori. She was a distraction that meant more. This was the kind of woman who would draw my attention from my goal, divert me, and destroy me. And I wasn't strong enough to stop myself from falling under her spell.

I started the car, letting it idle for a moment and debating whether I should say what I was thinking. It was risky, but seeing as she wouldn't be working directly with me, it seemed harmless, even if it was presumptuous and bold. But that was who I was. I didn't overthink, and I took chances.

Her blue eyes crinkled when I turned to her.

Good God, are you really doing this, Gabe?

It was insanity, but there was something about this woman that had me thinking it was worth it.

"I know we just met," I said. Her eyes grew larger as I continued. "But I'd love to take you out for dinner after work."

Smart and contemplative. I could see her thinking over my words, not making a rushed decision. That was what drew me to her, not just her beauty. There was something bold about her I wanted to discover.

"You're asking me on a date?"

"I am. I really like you, Tori."

Her cheeks flushed as she smiled. "You barely know me, Gabe."

"Then let me get to know you better."

She drew in a breath, her lips parting, and I wondered what it would be like to kiss them.

"Okay."

"Really?" I asked, my throat going dry. I wasn't sure what I had expected, but her yes made me dizzy with excitement.

She laughed, a smile filling her full lips. "Yes."

I stared at her for another moment before I turned back to the steering wheel, containing the whoop that wanted to escape. Clearing my throat, I drove us out of the parking lot, glancing over at her.

Her smile hadn't faded, and my stomach flipped. I didn't

know what it was about Tori, but she had my hands clammy, my words scattered, and my confidence obliterated. And those things made asking her out necessary.

"Do you like Italian?" I asked her, my focus back on the road. "There's a place in the city that makes the best gnocchi."

"Gnocchi alla Sorrentina?"

I snatched a glance at her, unable to hide my surprise. She couldn't be this perfect.

"The best."

"Sold." She shifted in her seat, and I peeked over to meet her eyes. Blue like a summer day. "It's my favorite."

Definitely perfect.

Looking back at the road, I hit my brakes, my hand flying out to secure her as I avoided hitting the stopped car in front of me.

"Although we have to make it there first," she teased.

My hand was still across her stomach, and I pulled it away quickly. "Sorry. I don't know why I did that." I scratched my head, trying to figure out where the protective instinct had come from.

"It's okay. My ribs are only a little bruised." My eyes jumped to hers, horror coiling in my chest, but her laugh obliterated it. "I'm just kidding. I'm fine. I don't mind a protective man."

Rubbing my cheek, I returned her smile, feeling once again like a kid who had just asked a girl out for the first time.

The remainder of the ride back held less excitement, but Tori's voice filled the space, and I found it was space I hadn't realized had been so empty.

I tugged my tie off, looking in my closet for something less stuffy but still decent for a date.

"So, your first day," my sister, Olivia, said through the phone. "That's one step closer, Gabe."

"I know, Liv." I pulled a polo shirt out and threw the tie to the side.

"We're close. Two years left and then you come home."

My hands froze on the buttons of my shirt. The expiration date that had been hitting me in the head the entire day. One of several that had ruled my life since I was sixteen. Each date marking another step to our end goal.

"Gabe?"

"Yeah, two years, then I'm stuck working for Dad until we pull this off. Sounds fantastic." I didn't mean to sound so sarcastic. This plan had been mine, and Liv had followed me on it for years. But today had offered a diversion in Tori. A step off the path that had been my motivation since the day my mother had died.

"I've been stuck here while you've been off playing in sunny Florida since you finished grad school," Liv responded. "Dealing with his rants about how you're avoiding your destiny and dicking around. So, yeah. Two years and you return so I don't have to hear about it anymore."

Sighing, I pulled my button-down off and worked the polo over my head. School was just another lie I'd given Tori. Telling her I'd moved here for grad school when I'd attended school up north, taking an accelerated course load to graduate early and finish my MBA when I was twenty-three. Only then had I moved to Florida, after convincing my father to let me live in anonymity while gaining valuable experience. An excuse to get away for as long as I could. One that had left Liv to deal with the aftermath.

"I'll be back to take my place just like I promised him. Don't worry." Although if things went well with Tori, I wasn't certain how I could follow through.

"You're not wavering, are you?"

I squeezed the bridge of my nose, unsure why I was thinking of Tori as something that could undo years of work when I had only met her. "No. Of course not."

"Good, little brother, because we're close. Two years until you return, then three more until we're at the end, Gabe. That's only five years. How many years have you dedicated to this?"

"Too many," I said, thinking of all the planning. Pissing my father off by moving to Florida after grad school. Not returning home to work for him like he had demanded. Convincing him I needed to work at the financial firms to get a fully rounded understanding of the finance world before I came on board at his company. Years of Liv playing daddy's girl and staying in New York, working for him until he finally rewarded her with the COO position. It was as far as she would go. CEO was mine when he retired, whether or not I wanted it.

And all the while, we were conspiring. Building our own empire piece by piece with one goal in mind: watching him fall.

"Then whatever is going on with you, shut it down. We've put everything aside for this, Gabe. Don't let our sacrifices be for nothing."

"God, you're too dramatic, Liv. I'm fine and still on track. Have a glass of wine and take that damn edge off."

"One of us needs the edge because you're lacking it today." I held the phone against my shoulder while I tucked my shirt in as she continued. "Is there something I need to worry about?"

Only the black-haired beauty who stole my attention today. "No, it's under control. I should be in the trenches in a few weeks at the most. That gives us two more years to build before I'm back in New York."

"Then it's the last mile, Gabe. Momma would be proud."

I closed my eyes, hating how she jabbed me with moments of softness like that. Waiting to see if they would weaken me.

"Night, Liv. I'm serious. Go have a drink. Maybe get laid. It might loosen you up."

"You're nasty." But I could hear the smile in her words. "Night, little brother."

Disconnecting, I checked the time before tucking my phone into my pocket. I ran a hand through my hair, questioning what I was doing. Getting involved with Tori when I was so close to seeing the end of my efforts was risky. I'd had one goal for eleven years: to end my father's dynasty. To watch him fall, just like my mother had fallen. But the nervous butterflies in the pit of my stomach told me moving forward with Tori was something I couldn't avoid.

Liv's reminders played through my mind the entire ride to Tori's. She lived farther inland on the side of town where the firm was located. It took about twenty minutes to get there, and in that time, I fortified myself to return to the reserved, emotionally stunted man my father had made me into. The one Tori had unraveled within seconds. Another reason I knew she was the one.

I pulled into her apartment complex and parked in front of her building. Gripping the steering wheel, I chastised myself for that last thought. There could not be a "one." The gamble we were taking was too big, and Liv and I had made a pact that romance wouldn't interfere. Until today, I had honored that pact. But then those big blue eyes had risen to meet mine.

My head dropped onto the steering wheel. "What are you doing, Gabe? Pull away and let her think you stood her up. Avoid her until you no longer have to see her." No amount of those demands had me moving because the thought of seeing her devastated in the morning was akin to the time Liv had jabbed a fork in my thigh to see if I would bleed.

Stepping from the car, I adjusted the jacket I'd thrown over my polo and made my way up to her apartment. Three flights. Of course she would live on the third floor. I shook my head, thinking of how alike we were even though I barely knew her.

The door swung open just after I knocked, and there she was, shoving all doubts away. She looked stunning in a sundress that came to her mid-thighs and showed her glorious legs. Charcoal gray dusted her eyelids, accentuating the darker hues of blue in them. And her smile...I didn't think I wanted to share that smile with anyone else. I wanted it for myself.

Words tumbled in my mind as I fought the need to kiss her lips that were stained with a deep blush. "Hi," I sputtered.

"Hi," she replied, beaming. "Come on in, but I'll warn you, it looks like a storage unit." She walked away, saying, "I just need to grab my shoes."

The apartment was a small one-bedroom. Boxes filled the place, some open like she'd been searching for specific things.

"You weren't kidding," I said, closing the door behind me.

She came back around the corner of her room and leaned on the doorframe while she pulled on a short-heeled sandal. "I warned you."

"Where do you sit?" I asked, peering over a pile of boxes.

"There's a tiny corner on the couch that's free," she answered with a laugh. Switching feet, she continued, "I got my clothes unpacked at least."

Sandals on, she grabbed her purse from atop a box and came to stand in front of me.

"I guess I know what you'll be doing this weekend."

She tossed her head back and laughed, exposing her graceful neck. In her heels, she stood closer to my six-three height, and it would have only taken a quick lean to have her lips against mine.

"I think that's what I'll be doing for the next few weekends." She looked over at the boxes in the kitchen, giving me the perfect view of her side profile. I tucked my hands into my pockets to resist pushing her hair back from her cheek. "I suppose if this date goes well, it might be nice to have help."

My brow quirked as her eyes nervously flitted to me like she regretted the suggestion.

"If beer and pizza are involved, count me in."

Her smile returned. "Pepperoni?"

"Of course. Is there any other way?"

"Only if you add in a marathon of *Lord of the Rings* in the background."

Good God, she was too perfect. "Start with *The Hobbit,* and I'm yours for the weekend."

Crystal blue orbs shimmered with happiness, and I thought I could dive into them and never resurface.

"Ready to stuff our faces with gnocchi?" I asked, putting my arm out for her to take.

"More than ready."

I led her out of the apartment and to my car. After closing the car door for her, I made my way to the driver's side. With each step, all thoughts of the years I'd devoted to my cause and spent hardening myself to everything that might stand in my way floated away like leaves in the wind.

Chapter 3

Tori

I had never laughed as much or smiled as often as I did with Gabe. The food was just as delicious as he'd said, but it was his company that made my night. We talked long after the server took the food away. Long after Gabe paid the bill and ignored my attempt to split it.

The breeze ruffled my hair but did little to cool my skin. Even at night, it was still eighty degrees. Gabe had left his jacket in the car, his muscular arms doing nothing to help me think straight. He was like a walking piece of eye candy. His attention remained solely on me as we walked, like his world revolved around me.

"Don't tell me you're cold," he said, leaning on the rail that overlooked the river.

I dropped my hands from my arms, realizing I'd been rubbing them. "Far from it. Does it ever cool down here?"

A sexy shrug followed by, "Eh, depends on what you call cool. The locals will pull their winter coats out about November when it dips into the sixties. And you might get a handful of winter days in January."

He turned to face me, his hazel eyes almost amber in the moonlight.

"Do you ever miss it?" I asked, my fingers awkwardly playing with the fabric of my dress.

"What?" he asked, his head tilting.

"Being home? I mean, Florida is so different from up north."

Another shrug. "Sometimes, but I left New York for a reason, and I don't regret that."

His expression was so serious, I wondered what burdens he carried. His head lifted, and there was a tug at the corner of his mouth. "Especially not now."

Butterflies crashed like a torrent through my belly.

"Tori?"

"Yes," I breathed as he stepped closer to me.

"I really want to kiss you right now." And those butterflies turned into vicious dragons, heating me to my core. "I know we'll be working together for the next few weeks, and it could be awkward, but…"

"Yes," I answered.

His eyes lit, and I swallowed back the emotion that simmered in my heated body.

"Yes?" His throat bobbed, and he seemed so unsure suddenly when he'd been nothing but confident since I'd met him.

I nodded. "Yes."

He closed the distance between us and tipped my chin, his eyes searching mine before his fingers smoothed over my neck and into my hair. It was the sexiest start to a kiss I'd ever experienced, and the crush that had twisted to attraction twisted into something that I knew I wouldn't be able to restrain once it fully formed. He leaned down, his lips brushing mine before they completely captured them. The breath fled me, and blood pulsed through my veins. My world seemed to turn, my feet no longer on the ground.

Our lips parted, but his hand remained, cupping my neck and keeping my eyes focused on him when they opened. Something passed between us, a spark of recognition, a tug of consciousness.

That kiss had been more like the solidifying of something that had been building since the moment he entered that room.

"I'm gonna need more of those," he said, his voice hoarse. "Plenty more."

"That depends on what kind of beer you bring this weekend," I teased, giving him a coy grin.

His chuckle vibrated through my body. "Noted. Good beer equals more kisses."

I joined his laugh, something that was too easy to do with him. He untangled his hand and dropped it to take mine, keeping it in his firm grasp while we walked back to his car. The drive to my apartment held no awkwardness, only ease as Gabe asked me questions about my time in college. By the time we arrived at my apartment, I was certain he knew everything about me, yet there was still so much I had yet to learn about him.

"As much as I don't want this night to end," he said as we stood at the door to my apartment, "at least I know I'll see you in the morning."

"Mmm, a work date. That's romantic."

"What? You don't like a little flirting after mutual funds and stock foreplay?" And his confidence had returned, making me a mess of hormones.

"Sounds sexy, but I'll stick to romantic kisses by the river."

He smiled, the move lighting his eyes to a dusty golden brown. "Then how about we compromise with a goodnight kiss?"

My lips tingled in anticipation. "I'd like that."

Our first kiss had been debilitating, but this one set my body on fire. I didn't want it to end because it was so perfect. Gentle and sweet with a tethered passion that left me curious to know what it would be like once we set it free.

My lips were still tingling when they separated from his.

"Good night, Tori," he said, brushing my hair back from my cheek before he left me.

I watched as he turned back one last time, throwing me a

crooked grin. Bringing my fingers to my lips, I remained there, hearing him take the steps and, after a few seconds, the start of his car before he drove away.

Entering my apartment, I threw my purse on a box and drifted into the bedroom, my heart still swooning, my head still spinning. After collapsing onto my bed, I listened to the furious beat of my pulse and stared at the ceiling. Gabe was too perfect to be true, and the giddy way I was acting warned me I was likely to get hurt. That didn't stop me from counting down the hours until I would see him again, nor did it stop me from thinking about him before I finally fell asleep.

"Now that's the kind of beer that will earn you another kiss," I teased Gabe.

He swiped his hand over his forehead, feigning relief as I moved so he could enter my apartment. Placing the beer on the tiny corner of counter I'd cleared earlier that morning, he turned back to me.

"Mind if I take my reward now?" Polite and devastatingly handsome.

My head hadn't finished nodding when he cupped my cheek and kissed me. Swooning was becoming a regular part of my life because every kiss he gave me had my body questioning its ability to function. Although we were keeping it professional at work, he had taken me to lunch every day and to dinner two more nights. Each evening began and ended with kisses that left me incapable of thinking.

With much reluctance, we ended the kiss. Dropping his forehead to mine, Gabe muttered, "You and those lips are going to be the death of me."

I swallowed a moan as his hand caressed my neck.

"I promise my intention is to do anything but kill you," I said, wishing my heart would stop beating so furiously. After three dates, he had done no more than kiss me, but each kiss was reverent, like he was savoring each one.

"That's a relief," he said, lifting his head and giving me a kiss on the forehead. Stepping away from me, his eyes skimmed my body. "You look beautiful, Tori."

I glanced down at my ripped jean shorts and UConn T-shirt. Arching my brow, I gave him a disbelieving frown. "Did you start drinking before you got here?"

He let out a laugh before scooping me back into his arms. It was the first time he hadn't waited for permission and the first he'd touched any more than my face or neck. Sparks sizzled like the wings of a million butterflies were alighting in my body. As if he realized he'd moved too fast, he released me, running a hand through his hair.

"Sorry," he said, lowering his eyes.

I picked his face back up, spreading my arms around his neck and noting the strength of his muscles. His kisses left me so lost that I had a hard time moving when caught in the moment, so this was the first time I'd touched him. Pulling his head down and trying not to react at how thick and soft his hair was, I brought his sight to mine.

"You are seriously the sweetest man I've ever met. You have my irrevocable permission to kiss me and hold me any time you want."

His amber irises turned a lush golden brown as they searched mine. "I don't want to mess this up, Tori. You do something to me." He swallowed, looking so uncomfortable that I wanted to erase it from him. "I'm not myself with you."

My heart dropped. "Oh." I let my hands fall from him, but he caught them.

"That's a good thing."

Eyes shooting to him, I saw the conflict in the twisting of his brows.

"I'm not usually like this." His jaw tightened. "I'm hard and driven. I don't let emotions or women in."

Worry hammered me, and I dreaded his words because the man I knew was not the one he was describing.

"But with you...with you, Tori, I want to be different. I don't want to be hard and unfeeling, and that...well, that terrifies me."

I'd suspected he was hiding something from me, and hearing his confession led me to believe something in his past had shaped him into the man he was talking about. A man he hadn't let me see.

"So, I want to treat you like you're fragile. Like I could break you if I move too fast. And I don't want something fast with you, Tori. I don't want us to burn and fade. I want more."

My mouth parted as the air fled my body. I freed my hands from his and threw them around his neck, pulling his mouth to mine. "Then we won't fade," I said against his lips. "But I want you to kiss me when you want to, to take me in your arms when you have the urge, and to hold me when you need to."

The tension in his body relaxed, and I felt his smile as his arms wrapped around my waist again. The kiss solidified the moment, warming my soul with its tenderness.

"Us," I said as our lips separated. "You said us like we're..." I didn't want to make assumptions, but he confirmed my thoughts quickly.

"A couple," he said. There was no question in his statement, only an affirmation.

"Exclusive?" I asked, unsure why. Although this was so new that it seemed fast, even if it also seemed right.

He pulled back, his eyes narrowed, and in that look, I could see the man he'd described, the one he didn't let into what we had.

"I won't do any other way," he said. His tone held possessiveness with an undertone of aggression, and I tilted my head trying to figure out this new side of him. As if he noticed, the darkness left his eyes. "Be my girlfriend, Tori. I don't want any chance of another man tempting you away from me."

I threw my head back and laughed, freezing when he kissed my neck. "Please," he added as his mouth glided to my ear.

"Yes," I answered. He wrapped his hand around the base of my neck and brought me back to look at him. "And you don't have to worry about anyone tempting me, Gabe." I didn't think there was anyone who could compete. "Now, me, on the other hand…" I narrowed my eyes, pretending to be as confident as he was, which only made his grin grow.

"There's nothing that tempts me but you. I thought you knew that considering you stole my attention the second I saw you."

And I did know it because Allison had given up her attempts after day two when his focus remained on me. She'd moved on to flirting with another man in our class, and there were days I wished I had a bag of popcorn with me while I watched the impending disaster.

"I did, but it helps to hear you say it."

He gave me another kiss before releasing me. "If I remember correctly, you promised me a *Lord of the Rings* marathon and pizza."

My heart somersaulted. Regaining my composure, I glanced at my watch. "It's only ten in the morning."

"Then we have two hours of the first movie before we order. Let's get these boxes unpacked so there's room on that couch for us to eat and watch the last part before you make me do more manual labor."

My smile must have been wide enough to deform my face. I watched as he put the beer in my fridge. He had on a pair of khaki shorts that hung over his knees but gave me a perfect view of his sexy calves. The T-shirt he wore was dark navy and brought out the darker tones in his eyes. When he bent, I had to stop my hands from reaching out to trace the pattern the muscles of his back made. He was gorgeous, and he was mine. A giddy excitement bubbled inside me.

Turning back to me, he gave me a questioning look. I threw a smile at him and swiveled to face the piles of boxes, not wanting him to know I'd been checking him out. When I reached up to get the top box from the stack, he was at my back, taking it down before I could get my hands on it.

"Let me do the heavy lifting."

"You know I'm not weak, right? I work out," I complained, putting my hands on my hips.

He flashed me a sly grin. "I know, but remember, I want to treat you as if you're fragile, and that means picking up the boxes."

Shaking my head, I grabbed my knife and opened a box.

"You sure you don't mind my being here while you unpack?" he asked as I started pulling things out. "I mean, there might be some things you don't want me to see."

I crossed my arms, put my chin on my hand, and pretended to think. "You mean like the box of mementos from all my ex-boyfriends?"

His eyes flashed a dangerous shade before they went wide, and I couldn't help questioning if I should worry about that other side of him, the one he didn't want me to see.

"You keep that stuff?" he asked, scratching his cheek.

With a shrug, I turned back to the box and said, "Only the bones of their pinky fingers."

I peeked over to see his reaction.

He chuckled, saying, "So you keep souvenirs from your victims?"

"Only the ones who treated me well."

"Then we'll need to trash that box immediately because there won't be any who treated you better than I will."

I stood staring at him, seeing the honesty reflected in his expression. "Then shouldn't I keep it so I can add yours to it?"

His face dropped, that faraway expression he often got took

over, and again I wondered what haunted him. It was gone as fast as it came, and the confidence returned. "Nah, I won't ever leave you, so there's no need to keep it."

There was so much surety in that statement that I believed it. I couldn't find the words to respond. One week together and he knew with certainty. As if he realized the power of those words and worried that he'd scared me, he rubbed the back of his neck and glanced down.

"Then I'll make sure it goes in the dumpster today."

His sight jumped to mine, and our gazes lingered until the heat was too much, and I looked away.

"You know some men might have worried that I had a box of bones in my apartment, but you were more concerned with being better than the men before you," I couldn't help but tease as I pulled a stack of books from my box.

"Never said I wasn't competitive," he said, humor in his voice. He took the stack of books from me, studying the titles. "You don't really have a box of bones, right?" He peeked an eye up at me.

"No." I tried snatching the books away, but he moved too fast.

"That's a relief. Now I can check serial killer off the list of potential turnoffs." He lifted a book to show me the title. "Your reading choices, however, need to be considered."

I snatched the book away and lunged for the others. He moved just in time to avoid me, and I stumbled. Blowing a strand of hair from my eyes, I crossed my arms.

"You invited me to help, Tori. If you didn't want me to judge your reading habits, then you shouldn't have." He held another book up, and my cheeks grew warm. "So I need to be better than your book boyfriends, too?"

Grabbing the pile from him, I snapped, "Yup."

I took them into my room, where I tossed them on my bed. When I turned, I jumped. He was resting in the doorway, his arm draped on the archway as he leaned into the bedroom.

Good God, he was sexy. I wanted him to pull me into his arms and do naughty things to me. As if he read my mind, his lip twitched. I tried barreling past him because I knew my cheeks had to be a bright crimson by now, but he didn't move. His arm came out, and he dragged me into his chest, just like I'd imagined, never moving so that he hovered over me. If it were possible to physically melt, I did.

He lowered his head, his gaze so penetrating that I wanted to look away, but he had me too entranced. "I can guarantee I'll treat you better than any ex and any book boyfriend. They'll all pale in comparison, Tori."

His voice was so heated it left my body blazing. I didn't know what to make of the sides to Gabe, but I suspected this was the side who would take me to oblivion and leave me destroyed when we moved forward in our relationship. The Gabe who nervously rubbed his neck and kissed me like I would turn to dust if he was too rough was the one I would fall in love with, but this man was the one who would obliterate me.

CHAPTER 4

GABE

Tori took another bite of pizza, the cheese stretching as she pulled the slice back. I didn't know what I was doing, but I wouldn't turn back. Not now. She was amazing, and I would make this work. Somehow. Because even after just a week, I knew I couldn't lose her.

She wiped her mouth with the back of her hand as the movie continued to play.

"You know they make napkins for that?" I said, handing her one.

"Is that what this is? I thought it was for decoration."

I took another sip of beer, shaking my head at her joke. She flopped back on the couch and put her feet up on the coffee table, moving the pizza box over with her bare foot. She was so different from anything in my world, from everything I had escaped and everything that waited in the distance to claim me again. Years of prep schools, expensive clothes and cars, mansions, housekeepers, and parties with the top one percent, yet all I wanted was to be with the woman who gave me none of that. Relaxed, unreserved, informal, down to earth, and from roots that were grounded in family and love. Not death and disdain, resentment and revenge.

Tori made me feel alive, like the withered part of my soul was coming back to life.

Her forehead creased as she studied me. "Where do you go?" she asked.

I could be myself with her, the person I'd once been before my father's hand had hardened me and my mother's death had carved out my heart.

I leaned back next to her, staring at the television. "I get in my head sometimes," I admitted.

Quiet eclipsed us for a few moments before she said, "I know there are things that you have yet to tell me. And we're still new, so I get that. But if you ever want to talk about it, I'll be here."

I turned my head, seeing the sincerity in her bright eyes. Taking her hand, I rubbed my thumb over her fingers. "Tell me more about your family," I said, needing to hear about a normal family.

I kept my sight on her hand but sensed her eyes on me, like she was trying to figure out why I had changed the subject. There were things I couldn't tell her. Not yet. Not until I could determine the best way to move forward with my mission and keep her. An inkling that I would lose her in the process, lose her trust by not admitting the truth, snuck into my mind. I couldn't ignore it because I was risking everything by falling for her, and I risked losing her by not telling her about my intentions in the next five years or the things I'd been building since I was sixteen.

"There's not much more to tell. It's just my parents, me, and my brother Cash."

"He's older, right?"

"Yeah, by six years. I think I was an oops," she said, humor in her tone.

"A good oops." I looked back over at her, seeing her smile. It was something I never wanted to lose.

"Cash likes to say I was an annoying addition who stole his toys and irritated him when he was a teenager, but he loves me. Even if he hates telling me."

"Sounds like a big brother to me."

"Do you have any siblings?" she asked, resting her head on my shoulder. I brought my arm around her and pulled her to my side, loving how it felt to have her in my embrace.

"I have an older sister. We don't talk often. She lives in California." The lies came too easily. I'd been lying since I moved from home, pretending to be someone else. Taking my paternal grandmother's last name to hide my identity, something that my father had surprisingly approved of for security. Having the heir to the Icinda fortune and next CEO so far from home would be dangerous. Having him work for investment firms to wet his feet before he stepped into the CFO position wouldn't look good for business. And my father was all about image and pleasing his shareholders.

I disappeared off the radar, leaving my sister to the wolves while I enjoyed a few years of anonymity. It didn't mean his men hadn't watched me for the years I'd been away. I hadn't caught them following me lately, but that didn't mean they weren't out there, ensuring I stayed protected.

"So, you're not close?" she asked.

"No, not really." Another lie because Liv had been my fortress since we were young. The safe place I crawled to when things got bad and my father's temper had meant cruelty. He'd never hurt her, deciding to take his aggression out on me. To toughen me up, to make me a man. The man I now was. The one who didn't show himself often around Tori. She was a safe place, just like Liv had always been.

"I'm sorry." I hated the sadness in her voice because my lie had caused it. "I can't imagine not having Cash. We talk at least once a week."

Guilt weighing heavily on me, I gave her a shrug and picked her pizza up. "Eat," I said, feeding her a bite.

"Are you trying to stop me from asking questions?" she asked between chews.

Giving her a wink, I offered another shrug with a "Maybe."

Those keen eyes surveyed me, and I wondered if she could see the lies I was building for her. It was a shaky foundation to start us on, and there was a high probability that when the truth came out, she would hate me. Not for what I was planning but for the lies.

"So, your parents own a bed-and-breakfast?"

Blue orbs narrowed before she released a sigh. It was still early enough in our relationship to have secrets, but if this continued in the direction I thought it was heading, I'd have to tell her everything. If I could dig myself out from under my mountain of lies. Confess that I was the son of a billionaire business owner who had abused his status as my father until my mother had taken her life. That had been the first day I had stopped his hand from coming down on me. The day I started fighting back. But it was a day too late, and for that, he would lose it all by my hands and Liv's.

"I may have fibbed a little on that," Tori said, sitting up and tucking her legs under her.

My attention piqued, I waited for her to explain. Maybe we were both keeping secrets.

"They own a resort in Piedmont. The Haven."

I gaped at her, the confession like a punch to the gut.

She scratched her arm. "I didn't realize it was that big of a deal, Gabe."

Finding my voice, I said, "No, it's not at all. It's just that I know that resort. We stayed there when I was young and," I swallowed back the pain of the memory, "my mother loved it there."

So much so that my father had expanded the hotel arm of his business based on that resort. Starting in upstate New York, he had slowly bought out private owners and added each to his collection. The Haven was the one he really wanted, but my mother had made him swear not to touch it. She'd loved it too much. The only redeeming quality of my father was that he loved my mother. Had never raised a hand to her, only me, and that along with his greed had driven her into a depression she couldn't overcome.

"Really?" Tori's voice rose an octave. "When did you stay there?"

"I don't know," I answered, rubbing my temple to take the image of my mother's smile from my mind. "I think I was maybe seven."

She folded her legs under her, and the memory of the lobby flickered in my mind. My parents checking in while Liv and I snuck into the sitting area with the massive stone fireplace. A little girl sprawled out on the rug in front of the fire, coloring. Her black pigtails had bounced when she'd lifted her navy eyes to me and smiled, handing me a crayon. Right before my father's hand had dug into my shoulder and he'd dragged me back to the check-in counter.

Stunned, I stared at Tori. Our paths had crossed long before now, and I couldn't help but think our second meeting had been a destined one.

"Then I would have been four. I wonder if I saw you." She took another bite of her pizza. "How cool would that have been? Like we were meant to be." Her smile sent those blue irises sparkling.

"Maybe you did," I said, resting back on the couch and motioning for her to sit back with me. She scooted closer and laid against me. My fingers played in her hair as I contemplated her words.

The movie continued to play, and I enjoyed the quiet of having her in my arms. It didn't last. She was a demanding boss, and as soon as I finished my beer, we were back to unpacking, a reprieve from questions that dug too far. Given that my father owned two rival lodges further south of Piedmont, the answers to those questions had me even more worried.

Two weeks passed and I was in so deep, I didn't know if I'd ever resurface. Tori scooped the pile of licensing books they'd handed out in class, and I picked up my bag, ready to spend the evening decompressing with her.

"Gabe, I'd like to speak with you before you head out," our trainer, Beth said.

I glanced at Tori, and she mouthed, "I'll meet you at the car."

I'd taken to driving her the last week, so desperate to see her that even the few minutes in the car refueled me. Gracing me with a smile, she adjusted her books and headed out of the room, chatting with another trainee.

"I have good news," Beth told me when I approached her. "On Monday, you'll report to your new team. Sixth floor. Craig, your manager, will meet you at the guard station to take you up. You remember Craig, right?"

"Sure, from the interview."

"Great. It was nice to meet you, Gabe. Reach out if you need anything, and good luck."

It should have been good news. The next step in acquiring the skills I was honing by further entrenching myself in this business. But it meant not seeing Tori all day. She'd become a fixture in my daily routine. As I exited the building, I saw her across the parking lot. A breeze played in her ebony hair, and she lifted her face and laughed. She was so beautiful it left me speechless.

Taking the books from her, I gave her a coy grin. "I guess I have competition now?"

"Is there competition for you, Gabe?" she said, blue eyes that reflected the sky above questioning me.

"Not if this is what I'm competing against," I said, lifting the books. But studying for her licenses would encompass most of her time.

I opened the door for her, and she sat in the seat, looking up at me and saying, "You can help me study. That means even more time together, right?"

My grin turned to a full smile. "Definitely, but don't think I'm going easy on you. Those exams are difficult, and I'll be the drill sergeant to make sure you pass."

Brow quirking, she replied, "Is that a threat?"

"Sure is." I closed her door, shaking my head as I made my way to the other side of the car. "And since my plans were to make dinner for you tonight, you can start reading while I cook," I said, buckling in.

"That's no fun."

"It'll be fun for me."

She gave me an attempt at a lethal glare that made me chuckle. "That's because you already have your licenses."

"Exactly." I gave her a wink and pulled out of the spot. "They're sending me onto the floor on Monday. Sixth floor, to be precise."

I glanced over to gauge her reaction. We'd both known it was coming. She was here for a trader position, to get her feet wet before she moved to a more specialized department, but I'd come for one of the coveted roles as an analyst. And given my prior experience in the role, I didn't have to start at the bottom this time.

Her smile dipped, and she played with her fingers. "I guess that means I'll need to find a new lunch partner."

Eyes back on the road, I tried to contain my jealousy at the thought. "Let's see if my lunch schedule coincides with yours."

"If not, then our dinners will be even more special."

Casting a peek at her, I saw the smile return, the sight easing my strain.

"Definitely will."

"So, you're cooking dinner for me tonight. What's on the menu, Chef Gabe?"

Chuckling, I said, "It's a surprise."

This was the first time we were going to my place, and I wasn't sure what she would think of it. It was a blank slate, a temporary blip in my life that needed nothing more than basic furnishings.

"Don't expect much," I said, unlocking the door when we arrived. "I'm not a knickknack guy."

Throwing the door open, I gestured for her to go in before me. I hit the lights, watching her reaction.

"You surely are not," she said. "Do you own anything but furniture?"

My keys clanked when I dropped them on the counter. "Not really." But I couldn't tell her this was only a stop in my life, that important things didn't need to be part of my life here. Just my computer and a bed. And now, Tori.

She spun to me, evaluating me again, something she did frequently. Tori was a thinker, deep in her head, thoughtful and taking her time with decisions and judgments. She was smarter than she let on, and I saw her trying to figure me out again.

"At least I have furniture," I said, hitting the kitchen light.

"So I should be thankful for the couch?" Humor tinted her question.

"Yup. It was almost a futon."

She put her hands on her hips. "You don't strike me as a futon guy. And considering how high-end this furniture is, I can't imagine one was ever really on your list."

I creased my eyes, trying to figure out how she knew my furniture was high-end. Nothing but the best for William Icinda's son. I'd had to argue for days to buy an inexpensive car instead of taking the Jaguar, arguing that it would make me stand out. The conversation went over as well as my decision to move to Florida. Something that had taken convincing, but after spinning it as a way to help the company, he had relented. I'd bought the car, much to his aggravation, because someone at my level didn't make Jag money.

She was waiting for an explanation, and I could have just told her I made enough. But the lies kept compounding, and I needed to give her some truth. Given how I was planning to spoil her, I ran my hand through my hair and said, "My mother died when I was sixteen." Her face morphed, the sorrow in her eyes enough to make me hate myself for sharing.

"I'm so sorry, Gabe."

"Don't be." *It's my father who should be sorry.* "It was a long time ago. But when she died, she left a trust fund for me and Liv. It provides well above my means every month. I invest most of my payments, but sometimes, I splurge, and I prefer a soft couch to a stiff futon."

It wasn't a direct lie. My mother had died, and there had been a trust fund. One that paid out to me when I turned twenty. She'd also left one to Liv, who had received hers three years earlier than I had. But the money I spent on things like furniture was from the spending account my father had established for me. Our mother's money I had invested in our plan to unravel him. The startup money for the company that was now hidden under layers of LLCs and whose equity would be enough to rival our father's when we made our ultimate move in five years.

"So, you're a trust fund baby?" she teased me. "That was your big secret?"

"Almost as big as the fact that your family owns one of the most popular resorts in Connecticut?"

The corner of her lip tugged, and I knew I had her.

"Get those books out and start studying. You can test out the couch to see if it meets your standards, Goldilocks."

She gave me a peck on the cheek and grabbed her study guide.

"If I fall asleep while reading this, don't wake me," she said, flipping through the pages. "I don't know if I want to be dragged back to this hell."

I chuckled as she took a highlighter out of her bag. She sat on the couch, her skirt bunching to show more of her sexy thighs. Dragging my sight from them, I started prepping dinner. A recipe my mother had taught me, handed down through her family since before her grandparents had moved from Italy.

By the time I finished making the chicken piccata, Tori had

stretched out on my couch, book between her hands. She had her feet in the air, legs crossed at the ankles, and had pulled her hair back. I couldn't help but stare at how adorable she looked, unguarded and relaxed. Navy irises peeked over the book at me.

"How's the studying going?" I asked, bringing two plates of food to the table.

"My head hurts if that tells you anything."

"It does, and trust me, it'll hurt worse. Wait until you get to bonds."

She groaned and dropped her head into the book. Walking over to her, I pulled it away, marked the page with her highlighter, and helped her up. I drew her into my arms, pushing a strand of hair back that had fallen from her ponytail.

"If this happens at the end of each chapter, I'm willing to keep studying." She laced her arms around my neck, and I leaned in to capture her mouth. Kissing Tori was like soaking in the sun on a summer day. It warmed my veins and left my body tingling.

"Come eat, and we'll watch a movie since you've been a good girl."

She shivered deliciously, and I nibbled on her neck, breathing in the scent of vanilla and cherry blossoms.

"Told you I could top your book boyfriends," I said, dragging my cheek over hers and stealing another kiss. Her body went limp, and I wondered why I hadn't taken this farther yet. It was torture living on just her kisses when I wanted to devour every inch of her.

Our lips separated slowly, her eyes opening to meet mine. They were dusty, and I wanted to ingrain their color in my mind forever. This was why I was taking my time. Because everything about Tori was special, every minuscule gesture and look. And I wanted to take all those moments and cement them in my memory before I made love to her.

Tori talked through what she'd learned while we ate, asking questions which I readily answered. I'd immersed myself in the finance world since I was sixteen, a necessity for building our fortune through portfolio and real estate investments. All legitimate and with a proper paper trail. Once we'd had enough, I had scoured business opportunities and Liv had vetted them. We'd accumulated enough businesses over the past four years to become a threat to businesses like my father's, but we weren't ready for that step.

"Where did you learn to cook like that?" Tori asked as she loaded her dish into the dishwasher after insisting on cleaning up.

"My mother. Her family immigrated from Italy a few generations back. She loved cooking the recipes her mother taught her and would bring me and my sister in to cook with her any time she could." Any time my father didn't drag me back out by the ear, bitching that it was woman's work and he wouldn't have his son doing domestic duties. I could still see the pain in her eyes and feel the sting of his belt. From then on, she invited me into the kitchen only when he was away on business.

"Well, she did a good job. It was excellent." She dropped onto the couch, rubbing her stomach. "I'll have to unhook my skirt if I eat anything else."

Her eyes met mine, and I couldn't stop myself from taking three strides to her and kissing her. The kiss deepened, and I leaned further over, catching myself on the back of the sofa. Her hands skirted up my chest, fisting my shirt and the urge to take more from her, to taste every inch of her and discover what those hands felt like on my bare skin roared through my veins.

My knee hit the cushion, and I pushed her back on the couch. Hand moving up her waist, I curled it below her and brought her chest to mine. Her hands threaded through my hair, and my resolve almost faltered. The need to discover every facet of Tori before I explored her body and claimed it screamed for me to stop, and I drew back, letting our kiss end.

Her lips were red from the kiss, her cheeks flushed.

"You're gorgeous, Tori, and you make it extremely difficult to be a gentleman," I confessed.

She rubbed her hand over my jaw. "I don't remember ever telling you to be a gentleman."

"No, I suppose you didn't, but I am," I admitted, dropping my head into her neck.

Kissing her collarbone, I gently lowered her body and released my hold on her.

"It's the stock exchange talk, isn't it?"

I squinted, trying to figure out what she was saying.

"That's the turn-on."

My laugh burst from me, and I dropped to the other side of the couch, scooting her legs over and putting them on my lap.

"I can promise you that was not the turn-on." Her soft skin was smooth as my hand rubbed her calf. "You up for a horror movie or action?"

"Horror, but don't laugh when I hide my eyes."

Patting my chest, I said, "It's here when you need someplace to bury them."

"Good to know. Is there a fee for using your chest to shield my innocent eyes?"

I feigned thinking. "A kiss."

"Done."

She repositioned herself so that she was tucked into my side and proceeded to kiss me with each scary moment before burying her head in my chest and asking me if the scene was over through the entire movie. By the time it ended, I was ready to kiss her for the rest of my life.

CHAPTER 5

TORI

You've been in Jacksonville for three weeks, and you're already seeing someone?" my brother, Cash, asked.

I held the phone against my shoulder and tied my sneaker. "Yes, and before you hound me, he's a good guy. Proper gentleman, good upbringing." Even if I suspected there was something more that he wasn't telling me. "He treats me really well, Cash."

"Better," he grumbled. "I don't want to have to fly down there to hurt him."

My eyes rolled as I sat back up. "You're so overprotective. I'm twenty-four, not eighteen."

"Still young," he mumbled.

"I'm fine, Cash. He's taking me to the zoo today."

"Jacksonville has a zoo?"

I checked my hair one more time and headed into my living room. "Yes. I'm told it's really nice. Although I'm not sure how nice walking around in hundred-degree weather will be."

"That sounds miserable," he groused. "I think I'd rather spend the day getting a root canal."

"Dramatic much?" I teased.

Gabe's knock had excitement stirring in my stomach. "I gotta go, Cash. He's here."

"You tell him he better keep his hands to himself," he threatened as I opened the door and accidentally hung up on him without saying goodbye.

My breath caught as Gabe's hazel eyes met mine. Dressed in black shorts and a tan polo shirt that emphasized his sculpted arms, he was almost too hot. He had his hands tucked in his pockets like he was nervous, and it added an adorable touch to the hotness. If this had been the seventeen hundreds, I would have swooned. As it was, my knees didn't seem too steady.

"Morning," he said, his eyes dropping to peruse my body in a heated gaze. "You look entirely too sexy to share."

He took a step in and gathered me into his arms the way only Gabe could. "I didn't know sharing was on the table," I said, smoothing my hands over his chest.

"It isn't." Terse and deep, that response was like a claim of ownership. His mouth was on mine before I could respond, and his kiss rushed through me like a rogue wave. I may have swooned because I swore if he released me, I would have tumbled to the floor.

Kissing was all we'd done, but Gabe's kisses were enough to leave me satiated for hours. Still after three weeks, he hadn't made a move to go further, and as much as I wanted him to, it endeared him to me more. It almost seemed like he was holding himself back, but I didn't know why.

"I'm tempted to keep you home, so no one sees how delicious you look," he said as our lips untangled. His hand skirted over my bare back, causing goosebumps to rise on my skin. "Did you put sunscreen on?"

I scrunched my eyes trying to figure out if his change in focus was for his benefit or mine. I would have preferred it remained on my skin.

"Yes, all but my back where I couldn't reach."

Giving me a kiss on the nose, he left me there after spotting the sunscreen on the counter. Squeezing some onto his hand, he tugged on one of my braids before pushing it over my shoulder. I'd wrangled my hair into two French braids that unfortunately aged me down so that I was certain I looked like I was still in college or worse, high school.

I inhaled when he kissed the back of my neck. "You need to protect this delicate northern skin," he said, dragging his mouth down my shoulder.

"We can't all have that 'I live at the beach' tan like you do," I quipped, trying my best not to melt at his feet as he bit my shoulder gently.

"I haven't been to the beach in years."

I tried to turn, but he stopped me with a caress of his hand down my back. Shivering, I replied, "How do you live so close to the beach and never go?" And that meant his gorgeous, tanned skin was natural. I remembered him saying his mother had Italian roots, a heritage passed down to him in more than her cooking.

"Never had a beautiful woman to go with me." A slide of his finger down my spine as he applied the sunscreen had my pulse racing.

His mouth traced the back of my neck as another finger slid down my exposed skin.

"So maybe it's time to change that since I have one now," he continued, causing a blaze of heat in me that sent an icy-hot sensation over my body.

Another finger slid over my shoulder blade. If he kept this up, there was no way I'd be able to make my legs function enough to walk out the door. His palm smoothed over my back, turning to a light pressure when he passed over the space between my shoulder blades. I couldn't stop my sigh as fingers skimmed just below the back of the shirt, and I thanked God I had worn the halter because this was heavenly.

He pressed a kiss to the nape of my neck as his hands passed over my shoulders and followed a path down my arms.

"Should we try the beach next weekend?" he said, his breath warm on my neck.

It took me a moment to wake my brain up and answer. "Please." And that had not been what I'd meant to say, but his hands were so close to leaving my skin, that it blurted out.

They traced their path back up, and I felt his lips on my ear. "Please, what, Tori?"

Good God, where had the sweet, bashful man I was falling for gone? This version of him was even more impossible to resist, and I suspected he could ruin me for any other man.

"Can we go to the beach next weekend?" I breathed as his lips dragged over my neck.

"I think I can arrange that." He nipped my skin, his hands dropping from me. "But for now, let's go check out the zoo."

He walked to the door, rolling his neck before he glanced back at me. I threw him a frown, which only elicited a deep chuckle from him. This man was going to be the death of me, and he knew it.

"You're torture," I said, willing my legs to move and praying they didn't give out on me.

He gave me a cute shrug, no sign of the seductive man who had just given new meaning to applying suntan lotion there to see. I snatched my purse, tucking the sunscreen into it before grabbing my keys and walking past him.

"If you don't want me to touch you, then don't leave me an opening."

I stopped and swiveled toward him. He wore a smirk that unraveled me.

"I never said I didn't want you to." My voice was barely a whisper.

He stepped into my space, letting my door close behind him,

and scooped me into his arms. Serious and smoldering. A combination that left what remained of my voice fleeing.

Brushing his thumb over my cheek, he said, "Do you want me to, Tori?"

A nod was all I could manage, the words escaping me like petals on the wind. He lowered his forehead to mine. "Not yet." His voice was hoarse. "You're too special to rush, luna mia." And this time, I really did swoon. His arms held me tight as he stole my breath with a kiss that devastated me. I would have waited an eternity for more touches if this was what waiting brought me.

"Okay," I mumbled against his lips. He smiled, drawing back from me. Hazel with shades of amber searched my face before he took my hand and led me to his car.

I took my phone out while he climbed into the seat, intent on searching for the words luna mia.

"My moon," he said before I could pull it up. "Technically, it's la luna mia, but I took the liberty of shortening it." His focus remained on the street as he pulled out of the parking spot. His throat bobbed, and he gripped the steering wheel as if admitting it had left him conflicted. "It means you're the light in my dark nights."

I searched for words, wondering why he left me so speechless so often. I swallowed, my throat burning. "Do you have many dark nights?"

His eyes flitted to me, his lip twitching to hold back a grin. "Not anymore."

Leaving me stunned, he turned his attention back to the road. Hands wringing in my lap, I studied his profile, wondering how someone who brought so much happiness to my life could have darkness in his. Secrets he had yet to reveal, ones I worried he would never tell me.

"Did you know bald eagles mate for life?" I asked Gabe as I shoved another piece of popcorn in my mouth.

He was leaning over the railing, observing the two eagles in the cage in front of us.

"Can't say I did." He turned his face toward me, a question in his eyes, and I felt the color climb in my cheeks. His sight returned to the cage. "But I admire that. It's how it should be. You find the one and you stick with that one...no matter how hard it gets."

My heart thudded, a noisy, irritating sound I hoped he didn't hear. He reached down and took my hand, guiding me to the next exhibit as his thumb rubbed over mine. We were only three weeks in. It was too soon to feel this way. This certain. But it was there, below the hesitation. A thought that this wasn't just a summer fling. This was something more that would last.

"Got any more fun facts about animals you can educate me with?" he asked, giving me a cute smile.

"Not off the top of my head, but you can feed the giraffes here. I read about it on their website."

His gaze fell on me. "Did you research the zoo, Tori?"

"Maybe," I said, dropping my eyes, but his laugh had them jumping back to him.

"I thought I was the only one who was that obsessive."

I joined in his laugh, relieved he hadn't been teasing me. "I couldn't help it. I was too curious."

"And I wanted to make sure you wouldn't be disappointed," he admitted.

I squeezed his hand. "You could never disappoint me, Gabe."

His response wasn't what I expected. The smile faltered, and his grip on my hand loosened. I tugged it, forcing his body to veer closer to mine.

"Don't do that," I told him.

The space between his eyes crinkled. "Do what?"

"Get in your head and leave me like you do."

His eyes widened before they scrunched. "How do you—"

"Because I just do."

Pulling our hands so they were behind my back, he guided us to a spot in the shade and off the main path. His expression had turned so serious, I couldn't tell what he was thinking.

He took my face in his hands. "I get in my head sometimes, Tori. There are dark spaces there, ones I can't share with you yet. Ones I don't want to bring into what we have for fear of infecting it. But trust me on this, I never leave you in those moments. And I never will."

There was such certainty in those words that I believed them. Maybe I should have been leerier since what we had was so new, but it was hard to doubt him when there was no room in his words to do so.

I reached around his neck and forced his head down, kissing him. He grabbed my waist and yanked my body into his, deepening the kiss. The world fell away, all awareness that we were standing in the middle of the zoo with families walking past us disappeared. All that mattered was the way Gabe clung to me as if he needed me and letting me go would break him.

"We should stop before they add us as an exhibit," I mumbled between kisses.

A smile formed, and his lips separated from mine, lifting to kiss my head. "Let's go feed some giraffes," he said.

I stopped him from moving, and he glanced down at my hand on his forearm before he looked back at me. Reaching up, I swept a tuft of his auburn hair back from his forehead. "I'll be your moon in the darkness, Gabe, and when you're ready to bring me into that darkness, I'll be there, holding your hand."

A swell of emotion flashed in his hazel eyes before his mouth crashed into mine again. I clutched his shirt, afraid of tumbling over with the intensity. Free-falling and unable to stop myself, I spent the rest of the day floating as if clouds cushioned my feet.

"Did you learn Italian from your mother?" I asked later that night as Gabe pulled a movie up for us to watch.

My fingers worked through my hair, freeing it from the tight braids. The grinders he picked up on our way back from the zoo sat on the coffee table with his beer and my bottle of water.

"Yeah. Only a few words, though. Things she picked up from her grandparents, who had come over to the States when they were first married," he said, picking his beer up. "We traveled to Italy every year when I was young, but my father..."

I waited. Gabe barely spoke of his father, and I'd surmised that they didn't get along well, thinking he was part of the secrets Gabe kept from me.

He took a swig of beer, his eyes taking a far-off look. "My father hated her family, so we always went without him." He stared down at where his hand clutched the bottle. "We stopped going when she died. He forbade it just like he forbade speaking the language."

My chest burned with the pain that had seized it. He took another long drink. "She still snuck words in when he was at work," he said, the darkness clearing from his eyes. "One day I'll take you there." Again, the surety erased any doubt that should have been there.

I took his face in my hands, sweeping my fingers over the corners of his eyes. "I'd like that very much. I've never traveled outside of the country."

"No?" He looked surprised, and I couldn't help but be curious about his assumption that I had.

"Nope. My parents are workaholics. The resort is their passion. The most exotic thing we did was travel to Quebec one year."

This had him snickering. "Quebec may be beautiful, but it is not exotic."

Elbowing him, I gave him my fiercest scowl, but all it did was encourage him to drag me into his chest. He planted a kiss on my head and wrapped his arm around my shoulder. "I'll take you to any exotic location you want, Tori. The world is yours. Give me five years, and I'll hand it to you on a platter."

I peeked up at him, brows crinkling. "Five? What's so significant about five years?"

He went stiff, just enough for me to notice before he recovered. "It's enough time for you to finish studying for those exams."

Mouth dropping, I tried to escape his hold and defend myself. "I will pass those exams within the next two months and on the first try."

His laugh broke free just as the movie started. "I have no doubt, and I'll spend the next five years making up for teasing you about it."

"You'd better," I said, relaxing and finding a comfortable spot on his firm chest. Tucking the five-year comment away with the other pieces I didn't understand about Gabe, I watched the movie, letting the sensation of his fingers as they drifted through my hair soothe away any concern.

CHAPTER 6

—————————

GABE

The beach trip didn't happen the following weekend. Rain kept us inside, and I was content to spend the two days working on my computer, furthering my business endeavors while Tori sprawled out across my bed with her study guides and highlighter. My evenings remained hers as did my mornings when I drove her to work. I knew it would change as soon as training was over and they handed her a new schedule, but I planned to enjoy every moment I could.

The following weekend, I took her to a show at the theater in the city, and we spent Sunday in Saint Augustine, where we wandered the forts, took a trolley tour, and ended the day at an alligator farm. Seeing her delight at everything she saw and learned was worth every second of history I had to tolerate.

Keeping myself from touching her for more than the brief petting and multitude of kisses was becoming painful, but I was determined to make this last, even if I hadn't figured out how to contend my need for Tori in my life with my mission and my father's steadfast requirements. I had yet to tell Liv about her, knowing it was hypocritical after all she had sacrificed for this.

How could I tell her I was in a relationship when she'd broken off the one she'd been in just to ensure her focus was on infiltrating our father's empire and helping me build ours?

I couldn't, and there was the crux of my dilemma. No attachments had been our motto since that time. I hadn't asked her to break it off with Hudson. She had made the decision, citing the conflict and distractions it caused. Besides, our father's rule was no marriage before we turned thirty-two. A stupid rule, but one we followed because it matched our own stipulations, and we risked him cutting us off if we went against it. Liv was two years from reaching that age, but I knew if she had already reached it, she still wouldn't indulge, not when we were so close to punishing our father. And that meant she wouldn't approve of Tori.

"Wow," Tori said, stopping as we reached the sand. The waves pounded the surf as seagulls squawked above us. "This is gorgeous." She took a few steps in, adjusting her beach bag before grabbing my arm and reaching to remove her flip-flops.

"I wouldn't do that if I were you," I warned, remembering the first time I'd been to a Florida beach in the summer. It had been so miserably hot the last time that I'd vowed never to return. I could already feel the sweat dripping down my back, and I'd spent four years in this blasted heat. Tori had only been here for a little over a month. She was likely to shrivel up from heat exposure.

With our regular outings, she had a nice base tan developing, but I had still insisted she slather herself with sunscreen before we left. I was looking forward to adding the finishing touch on her back again. The last time, I had almost lost control and ravaged her.

"Why not... Ouch!" Her flip-flop went right back on her foot, and I let out a loud belly laugh.

Throwing daggers at me, she put her chin in the air and continued walking.

"Pouting will only make me laugh harder," I teased her.

"I'm not pouting. Why is the sand as hot as lava?"

"I doubt it's that hot, but it's close. Welcome to Florida."

She stayed quiet as we searched for a spot to spread the blanket she had packed. Two kids ran between us, spraying sand everywhere, and I suddenly questioned my decision to subject myself to this hell. But when she picked a spot, spread the blanket out, and removed the sundress she'd worn, I was glad I had. I thought she was sexy before, but in a bikini...I doubted I'd have the control to keep my hands to myself. She was all curves and long limbs. I almost dropped the cooler and umbrella when she bent over.

I decided strings were going to be my downfall, as was Victoria Hent. Strings that exposed parts of her I had only imagined and as I glanced around the beach and saw eyes on her that she didn't seem aware of, I suddenly had the need to cover her up.

"Are you going to put that up or just stand there all day?" she asked me, a sparkle of humor in her eyes. She knew exactly what she was doing to me...killing me with every step she made as she came over to me. Extending her hand to me, she gestured to the sunscreen she was holding. "Can you do my back?"

Good God, could I ever. *Calm down, Gabe.*

"With pleasure," I said, depositing the cooler and lowering the umbrella to the ground. "Like last time?"

The flush on her cheeks was not from the sun. "Umm, maybe...I mean, no..."

"Turn," I said, scooting her around so her back was facing me. I groaned, trying not to ogle her perky bottom. Could she be any more perfect and devilishly tempting?

Her head whipped around to look over her shoulder, and I pushed it back to face forward. I contained myself as she lifted her hair while I squirted the lotion in my hand and smoothed it over her skin instead of tormenting her like I had last time. This was not the place for me to do something like that, or I'd have to throw her over my shoulder and make good use of the backseat of my car. I rubbed my temple with my clean hand, trying to think of anything but the soft skin under my fingers and the tiny pieces of material separating her body from me.

"Is this revenge for the last time I put sunscreen on you?" I asked, rubbing in the remaining white spot before closing the lid on the bottle.

"Maybe," she said, turning to face me. I took a step back and tossed the bottle onto the blanket. No kissing today and no touching. Not here, not like this. She gave me a devious smile, and I shook my head, realizing she wasn't as sweet as I'd thought she was.

"That's cruel," I said, picking the umbrella up and positioning it over the blanket.

"I can put the dress back on," she offered, her voice too playful for me to take the suggestion seriously.

"No," I groused. "I can behave. Besides, you look hot as hell, and I like it." I tugged my shirt off, seeing her mouth drop before she slammed it closed. "It's the other eyes on you I don't like."

I tossed the shirt where she'd put her dress and met her azure eyes. Hunger sat in them, and it matched what was stalking through me. Maybe it was time to give in to my need to take this slow. It had been six weeks. I strolled over to her and threaded my fingers through her hair, yanking her against me. Skin to skin. Fire flaring, I smashed my lips to hers, letting my desire burn through the kiss and feeling her go limp in my hold.

"Payback, luna mia," I said, dragging her bottom lip with my teeth before walking away and dropping onto the blanket with my book. Yeah, there was no way I could continue to keep my hands to myself. It surprised me that she hadn't pushed for more yet.

She planted herself next to me, crossing her legs and putting her hands under her chin while her elbows rested on her knees. Piercing blue eyes met mine when I looked up.

"What?" I asked, doing a crappy job of containing my smile at how cute she looked.

She jerked her head toward the ocean, her eyes large with

expectation. I flicked my gaze to the rolling waves. Lowering my book, I scratched my head.

"Are you trying to ask me something?"

Not answering, she continued to stare me down, excitement flickering in her features as she fought to keep her frown in place. I stood quickly and, before she could join me, bent and scooped her into my arms.

"Gabe!" Her legs kicked as I walked her to the water, but her giggle lit every shadowed crevice in my chest.

She was clinging to my neck while I walked us in waist deep and dropped her legs. She let out a happy shriek when she hit the water, dragging my neck down with her.

"You wanted to go in the water," I told her, holding onto her as a wave hit us, pushing us back a few steps. "Or did I read those puppy dog eyes wrong?"

"I did," she admitted, pulling my head down further to kiss me.

A mistake because I couldn't just kiss her. Our kisses were like an exchange of souls, an experience that lingered long after the kiss ended.

Disentangling her from me, I stopped the kiss. "None of that, Tori, or I'll take you back to shore and put you in time-out."

"You can't put me in time-out," she pouted, crossing her arms, something that only accentuated the curve of her breasts. "I'm not a child."

"Never said you were." Pushing my hand through the water, I splashed her.

The pout morphed to surprise before it became a determined fury of revenge. A battle of splashes ensued until we were both soaked and laughing.

"I crown myself victor of that fight," she said between laughs.

"I don't think so. I crushed you. You're drenched."

"Because your hands are bigger. I still won."

Just as competitive as I was. I should have known from how

determined she was to ace each of her practice exams and pace ahead of her classmates with studying.

"And what do I get if I let you win?"

Movement behind her caught my attention, and I reached out to pull her away. Creased brows questioned me.

"Jellyfish," I explained.

My hands fumbled to catch her as she jumped into my arms, her hands so tight around my neck that it pulled my posture down.

"What are you doing, Tori?" I scooped up her legs as she curled into a fetal position.

"You didn't tell me there were jellyfish in here."

"It's the ocean. I thought it was a given. Just avoid them; they won't hurt you."

Her eyes darted around, her expression pinched in fear.

"I would have expected this reaction if I'd said there was a shark behind you, but a jellyfish?" I teased, adjusting my hold on her.

"I don't like jellyfish," she hissed, her arms tightening around my neck.

"Any tighter, Tori, and I won't be able to breathe." The grip didn't relent. "So, I'm guessing this is the last of our beach trips?"

Head turning to me, she frowned. "No, it's not."

My brow quirked as I waited for her explanation.

"We can stay on the sand." Her voice was a high-pitched question that had me grinning.

"We can do that." I repositioned my arm so that her butt dipped into the water, and she rolled her body further into mine to avoid it. "We'll stick to the pool at my place or yours for the swimming."

"We have pools?" she asked as I made my way back to shore.

"Did you bother to even look at your apartment complex when you rented there?"

"Cash found it for me," she admitted, giving me a bashful

look. "I was too busy putting things in place for my parents, interviewing a new bookkeeper and prepping to leave."

"So, your brother found the place, and that was it?" I lowered her onto the blanket, fighting the image of climbing over her as I removed my hands from her skin.

With a shrug, she replied, "I trust Cash."

I tipped the umbrella back to let the sun hit her and dropped next to her. She wiggled her toes and dipped her neck back while she rested on her elbows, and I couldn't help but stare at how alluring she was.

"Tomorrow, we explore your complex." I averted my eyes and stared at the pounding waves.

"That sounds good to me. Where is the pool in your complex?"

"Further in. It's nice, but I've never used it."

A gaze weighed on me, but I didn't turn to meet it.

"You're complicated, aren't you, Gabe?"

My chuckle came freely. "That's the best way to describe it. Although that's coming from the woman who is terrified to go into the ocean because of jellyfish."

"They're nasty things, and they hurt," she said with a shudder.

"Has one ever stung you?" I glanced at her, waiting for her explanation.

"Well, no. But one stung Cash when he was on a trip in middle school. He told me it was horrible. They had to peel it off of him, but its suckers stuck in his skin, and it kept electrocuting him..."

I was laughing so hard by then that I had to hold my stomach. Bewilderment had her brows stitched and an expression of indignation sat on her face.

"How can you laugh? It was horrible."

"How many years older did you say Cash is?" I asked, trying to calm my laughter.

"Six. Why?"

"So you were what? Maybe six or seven?"

She sat up and crossed her arms. "I don't think this is funny, Gabe."

"It's hysterical. Jellyfish don't do that, Tori. He played you. I'm guessing you don't get to the beach often?"

Brows drawn, she said, "No. We went to the lake. The shore was too far." She scratched her nose. "Cash went to the Jersey shore with his best friend's family that summer."

"And came back with a horror story to traumatize his little sister."

Her mouth dropped, understanding lighting her eyes. "That bastard. You wait until I talk to him again. He's so dead."

"Ready to go back in the water?" I asked her.

Her head swiveled to the water, then back to me. "Let's enjoy the sun for a while, maybe read some like you wanted?"

"Ha, chicken."

I knew she was too competitive to let me get away with that insult. Blue eyes darkened to navy, and she was on her feet, running to the water before I could catch her. We spent the rest of the day between the water and the blanket, and my adoration for her shifted further to something I didn't want to admit yet but couldn't deny.

***

Rain pounded on the windshield as I pulled into a spot at Tori's complex. She leaned forward and looked up at the sky.

"I think we have to make a run for it," I told her. We'd fled the beach just in time to avoid the storm, but it hadn't ceased.

She glanced over at me.

"Leave your bag and I'll get it when the rain stops," I told her, unbuckling. "Race you there."

Her irises sparkled with amusement as she unbuckled and put her hand on the door handle. I readied myself, knowing she wouldn't let me off easy. She ran for it, and I followed right behind, my long strides catching up to her as she lost a flip-flop. I caught her when she stopped to grab it, bringing her against me and laughing as I kissed the rain from her nose. Giggling, she wiggled out of my arms and took off again. I hadn't felt this free and unburdened in years. Rain-soaked, I chased her up her stairs, pinning her against her door before she could get inside.

"I still won," she said, turning to face me. Hair drenched, raindrops running down her face, and panting, she was beguiling, and I lost my hold on myself. Threading my hand into her hair, I pushed her head toward me and captured her mouth. All the resistance I'd been giving myself to take this at a pace that ensured I wouldn't lose her and gave me time to come up with a plan to keep her crumbled, and I let it go. Freedom had never tasted so good.

My hands roved over her body, pushing at the straps of her sundress as hers slipped below my T-shirt. Currents shot through me at the contact, and I gripped her hip, pulling her into me so she could feel how badly I wanted her. She moaned, and my lips slipped down her chin to her neck.

"Open the door, Tori."

"Gabe," she breathed.

I tore my mouth from her skin and looked at her, seeing the lust in those baby blues. "Open the damn door, Tori, or I'll take you right here."

Her lips parted, a sexy exhale escaping her.

Dragging my hands up her body, I said, "Unless you don't want that, and we can go back to waiting."

Fire lit her irises, and she grabbed my shirt, jerking me closer. "I never said we had to wait. That was your thing, and I respected it, but if you're done waiting, Gabe, then so am I."

That was all the permission I needed. Mouth crashing into hers, I bunched her dress in my hand, desperate to take it off her. "Open the damn door before I pin you against it and ravage you."

Her inhale was sharp against my lips, and I stopped it with my kiss as she struggled to get the key in the lock. The door opened, and we fell into her apartment, our feet fighting to keep us upright. I slammed it shut with my foot, hearing her key fall to the ground right before I had her sundress joining it. She shoved my shirt off, and it landed with a thump steps away from her dress as I walked us to her bedroom. My hands smoothed over all the open skin her bikini wasn't covering until they found the ties to her top. With two quick movements, I had it untied and was pushing it from her body. Her bare chest met mine, and any semblance of control I had disappeared like a summer storm. I lifted her and pressed her against the wall before I could even get her to the room.

Her legs circled my back, and I pressed into her, need throbbing through me. I was moving too fast, lost in the feel of her, and I wanted to relish every moment of our first time together, to memorize every inch of her body, every birthmark, every moan. I didn't want fast and hard; I wanted more with Tori. It was the reason I'd waited so long.

Dropping my head, I kissed her neck, loving how her hands roved my muscles, causing goosebumps. Drawing back, I met her hazy eyes.

"This isn't how I want to take you," I told her.

Her lips pursed, and I gave them a gentle kiss. Adjusting her, I walked us into her room.

"And how do you want to take me?" she asked, her fingers running through my wet hair.

I lowered her onto her bed and hovered over her. Nudging her neck, I dipped in to kiss it, dragging my lips down to her collarbone as I cupped her breast and ran my thumb over her nipple. "Like I'm worshipping you, luna mia," I said, sucking her nipple into my mouth.

Her hands tightened in my hair as her back arched.

"Every inch of this gorgeous body." I dragged my teeth over her nipple and untied the string on her bottoms. My hand drifted over her stomach as I kissed the sweet flesh of her breast, flicking my tongue over her nipple. Her hands dug into my scalp as she whimpered.

I bumped her legs apart, slipping my hand between them and palming her warmth. Within moments, my only focus in life became Tori and having her fall apart for me. I brushed my lips up her neck and stole her lips again, sliding my finger through her and groaning at the sensation.

"Gabe," she purred.

"Do you still want this, Tori?" I asked as I slipped my thumb over the spot that had her legs twitching.

"God, yes."

I drove my finger into her, watching as she threw her head back, her fingers digging into my shoulders.

"Good," I said, kissing my way down her neck again. "Because stopping right now would kill me." I kissed my way down her stomach. "Time for me to worship you, luna mia."

Her sigh turned to a cry as I added another finger. My lips slid down her stomach, the scent of vanilla and cherry blossoms invading my senses. Pushing her legs further apart, I watched my fingers fill her, taking in the beauty that she was as I slid my tongue up her thigh. Back bowing, she moaned, a sound that sent sparks through me. Replacing my fingers with my tongue, I continued to feast on her until she was so close, her legs were quaking around my shoulders. Wrapping my arms around her thighs, I yanked her closer and took her over the edge. I peered up to see the gorgeous display as her body shook around me.

Swiping my tongue over her while she descended from her climax, I trailed my kisses up her thigh, her hip, over her stomach, taking time to taunt her nipples, then up her neck until I hovered over her again.

"Tell me how you want it, Tori, because I'm about to lose it after that sight."

Her eyes were misty, the effects of her orgasm rife in her vivid irises. She pulled my head down and devoured my mouth.

"I want you so bad," I muttered between kisses. My hardness grinding into her.

Lithe legs wrapped around me.

"I'm on the pill," she said, and I drew back to look at her. I never went without a condom, but those words gave me an opening I didn't think I'd refuse. Everything about Tori had me throwing aside my judgment and my rules. "I trust you, Gabe."

Those words pounded through me, evoking guilt for the secrets I still harbored. Swallowing it back, I said, "I have a condom in my wallet."

She shook her head. "It's okay. I want you without it."

My brow pinched, my eyes narrowed, but she thinned her lips and smacked my shoulder. "Don't make it a jealousy thing. I've only ever gone without it in one serious relationship."

That didn't help, and I tipped my head as I waited for more.

"Really? You jealous ass," she teased. "It ended four years ago."

"That's not the answer I was waiting for," I said, nipping her lip.

She cocked her head, squinting as she tried to understand.

"Are we in a serious relationship?"

Her lips parted with her deep inhale. "Very."

The answer was what I'd wanted. I didn't care what she'd done in the past. She was mine now, and I planned to keep it that way. Lips crashing into hers, I kissed her again, pulling her body further into mine when I slid my arm below her. Our brief interruption had done nothing to calm my yearning for her, and I peeled her legs from me and stood.

"Scoot back," I said, standing over her.

She questioned me with her eyes as she moved further onto the bed. "Shit, you are the most ravishing creature I've ever seen," I told her as my eyes perused her body. "And I'm about to claim every piece of you."

Her shiver was violent, and I couldn't help but grin as I

dropped my pants. She didn't shy away from taking a long look at my body before I climbed over her.

"It's all yours," I said, resting at her entrance.

"Good, because I'm all yours, Gabriel Hughes."

A shot of guilt surfaced that she didn't even know my real last name and wouldn't until I could tell her the truth. I shoved it aside and found her lips again, sliding further into her until I could no longer be patient. I kept my eyes on her, observing the expression of ecstasy as I filled her completely. Heaven couldn't compare to what it was like being inside of Tori, and as she wrapped her legs around me, I knew there was no other place I wanted to be than with her.

Our bodies moved as one, our kisses deep enough to drive me to the edge. I dropped my head to her neck, my teeth gritting as my release threatened to pounce. Hand sliding over her breast, I teased her nipple, rubbing it between my thumb and my finger and slowing my thrusts. She trembled, her body bowing as another climax teetered on the precipice.

"That's it, luna mia, fall apart for me again."

She dug her heels into me, sending me so deep she cried out. Sucking her nipple, I shoved my hand into her hair, fisting her locks as I fought my impending orgasm. The move sent her over the edge, and she broke, her muscles bearing down on me and causing me to lose control. Slamming into her, my climax exploded through me. Like an avalanche collapsing, it buried me.

I lowered my head to her chest as the remnants of my orgasm rolled through me. She shivered and moved her hands to my head, her fingers drifting through my hair as my body calmed.

"That was...amazing," she breathed.

I picked my head up to meet cornfield blue glazed with satisfaction. Giving her a gentle kiss, I slid from her, hating to leave her warmth.

"Worth the wait?" I asked.

"Definitely, but no more waiting."

I laughed, kissing her nose before disentangling our limbs. "I've had a taste of you, Tori. There's no stopping me now."

Her laughter joined mine, and I pulled her to my chest, burying my face in her hair before she pushed away and went to clean up. As I lay there, I stared at her ceiling. The sensation in my chest that had been building over the past weeks pressed to be acknowledged, and with it, the understanding that I could never give Tori up.

The book flopped onto my head after I released it, and I groaned in frustration.

"Hey, I'm the only one who gets to evoke that sound from you," Gabe said, rubbing my calves and setting his book aside. Today it was a memoir about a Fortune 500 man who built his company from the ground up and made billions.

Gabe was always reading books like that, telling me he liked to keep his focus on business even when he wasn't at work. It was one reason I didn't mind that he often sat at his computer for hours reading articles and doing research. At least that's what I assumed he did since any time I checked on him when he was entrenched, there was always something business related on the screen.

"That bad?" he asked, taking the book from my face and checking out the source of my frustration. "Oh, bonds. Yup, those will get you every time."

He dogeared the corner of my study guide, and I tried not to cringe at the mishandling of my book. Placing it on the coffee table, he added his own to the stack before looking at his watch.

"What do you say I take you out for dinner? Maybe the Italian place in the city?"

"Won't it be busy?" I asked, stretching my arms out. His hand smoothed over my stomach where my shirt rose, and goosebumps trailed it. His touch was the death of me every time. It had been a month since we first had sex, and every time was like the first, devastating and erotic. But emotion clouded it the longer we dated, and there were times it was akin to making love, my heart and soul open for his taking.

"Nah. It's a Sunday night and we're past the dinner crowd." He picked my legs up and scooted them off the couch, forcing my body into a sitting position. "Besides, your exam is in three days. You've taken every practice test and aced each one. I doubt bonds will cause you to fail."

I rolled my eyes, but his look remained stern. "Fine, but I'm not dressed for a nice dinner."

"Then we'll stop at your place so you can change." He hopped up and headed to his room, pulling his T-shirt over his head. I couldn't help but ogle the muscles in his back. He was just too sexy not to. He threw a look over his shoulder, giving me a smirk that told me he enjoyed busting me. "Keep that up, Tori, and we won't make it to dinner."

"Keep taking your clothes off and you won't make it out of your room," I yelled back after him. His chuckle was his only reply.

Standing, I stretched out my back and straightened my shirt. Gabe returned a few minutes later, pulling on a green polo shirt that brought out the green hues in his hazel eyes. He tucked his shirt into the pair of slacks he'd changed into before fixing his belt. His thick auburn hair dusted his forehead, and I strolled over to him and swept it back as he lifted his eyes to mine.

Catching my hand, he brought it to his lips and kissed it.

"What are you thinking?" he asked, keeping it in his hold.

"How devastatingly handsome my boyfriend is. I'm not sure I want to share you with the world."

His arm wrapped around my waist, and he brought me into his chest. "No sharing necessary. I'm all yours."

He planted a kiss on my lips. Even now, a kiss from Gabe was never just a kiss. It was a time-stopping, earth-shattering moment, like something out of a romance novel. When he released me, I teetered, which only caused his grin to grow even more debilitating.

"Come on, before I decide I'm hungry for something else."

Swooning had become the norm for me now, and I wasn't sure I wanted it to go away. He strolled to the door, and I followed, about to walk out when he halted my steps. A nod to my feet had me looking down to see that my feet were still bare. That smirk was enough to break me.

"Helps to wear shoes," he teased.

I tried to think of a witty comeback, but he had me too dazed, and after studying for the past two hours, my head was mush. Trudging back in, I grabbed my flip-flops and returned with a delayed response. "I thought you liked them bare."

His body shook with his laughter. "That's all you could think of? You're off your game today, Tori."

He held my purse out to me, something else I'd forgotten, and I snatched it from him, sticking my tongue out before walking past him. His laughter didn't stop the entire way to the car.

I tried to pout on the way to my apartment, but it was too hard to be irritated with Gabe. Within minutes he had me smiling again. By the time I'd run upstairs and changed, my cheeks hurt from the action. He made me too happy to ever be mad at him. Being with him was a constant state of bliss that I never wanted to fade.

When we pulled into a parking spot, he hopped out of the car, opened my door, and extended his hand. "We're about thirty minutes early for our reservation," he told me as he helped me from the car.

"I thought we didn't need reservations?"

He shrugged. "I may have called while you were getting ready."

The buzz of his phone distracted him, and he pulled it out of his pocket to look at it. A frown formed before he tucked the phone away.

"All good?" I asked.

It was strange for him not to answer a text. His phone buzzed often, and a serious look would cast over his features while he read and replied. He never talked about them, brushing them off as business, but I was growing curious about what kind of business meant texts on the weekend and at night. If he hadn't devoted his time entirely to me, I would have suspected another woman, but Gabe spent every waking free hour with me and, lately, his sleeping hours.

"Yeah, nothing important," he answered, his brows knitted. "Let's go down to the river while we wait."

With a squeeze of my hand, his expression softened.

"That sounds good. Just like our first date."

"And our first kiss," he added, taking my mind back to that moment. My stomach somersaulted when I thought of how he'd told me he wanted to kiss me, then proceeded to leave me wrecked.

We walked in silence to the riverside, and I could see the text was still on his mind. The river was quiet, the lights reflecting in the calm water.

"Gabe," I started, and he turned his gaze to me. "Is there something wrong? Something you're not telling me?"

He stopped us and repositioned my body so I was facing him. Concern lined his eyes, and my fingers traced the creases it left.

His throat bobbed, and he took my hand in his. "There are things...things I haven't told you. Some of which I can't, not yet. But one day I will, I promise you."

"I know you have secrets." His cringe confirmed they were ones he would continue to hold on to. "And I'm okay with you keeping them if you must, but can you give me some hint? Some confirmation that you don't have another family in Kansas you're hiding from me?"

His head went back with a laugh that lasted until he took my face in his hands. "I can promise you, there is no one but you, Tori. There isn't room in my heart for anyone else because you take up every crevice." The air struggled to reach my lungs as he closed the remaining distance between us. "I love you, Victoria Hent, and I never want to love another woman again. If you were to leave me today, I would continue to love you until the day my heart shrivels and dies."

Tears pushed behind my eyes. He loved me. We had left the words unspoken. There had been moments and actions, a look in his eyes as he made love to me, but never had we spoken them.

A tear slid down my cheek, and he brushed it away. "Please don't cry, luna mia. I didn't mean to make you cry."

I sniffed and threw my arms around him. He held me close, his embrace warming my soul. "I love you, Gabe. From the moment you walked into that room with your flirty grin and sat next to me, I fell for you, and every day since, I've fallen deeper."

Fingers in my hair, he brought my face to his. Hazel eyes left me breathless before his mouth crashed into mine with a kiss that seared a brand on my soul. Claiming me again and asserting ownership of the other half of it.

I clung to him, my emotions an erupting volcano I could no longer contain.

"Maybe we should skip dinner?" he asked, his lips seducing mine further.

No answer came. I was too caught up in the magic of the moment, the revelation of his confession, the strength of his hold. When I thought my body had gone too limp to stand, his lips drew away. Dragging his mouth over my forehead, he continued to hold me.

"Maybe we'll eat and save this for dessert," I said, still panting.

His lips curved on my skin. "I like that idea, and I know exactly what I want to taste for my first dessert."

Heat blossomed in my chest. "First?"

His kisses traced a path down my face. "Mm. First, I devour you. Second, I taste every inch of this tanned skin." Fingers skimmed my arms, causing goosebumps to follow them. "And finally, I make love to you for the rest of the night."

An exhale accompanied my shiver, and he smiled against my lips as he kissed me again.

He took my hands in his, resting his nose on mine. Amber eyes peered at me, and I could see his mind working.

"My sister," he said.

Brows furrowed, I waited for more.

"That was the phone call. I told you we don't get along." He cleared his throat as he stepped from me, keeping my hand in his. "She's on my case. Remember how I told you I invested most of the money from my trust fund?"

"Yeah."

He tucked me into his side and started walking us back to the restaurant. "Well, it was only a partial truth. We both invested the money in..." I could see him struggling to find the words and wondered why this was so hard for him. His jaw clenched, that darkness that periodically surfaced overtook his eyes. "...an investment to honor our mother. It causes friction sometimes, and she's been on my case about it and other things."

I was trying to piece together why that would have been so hard to tell me, deciding he was still only giving me partial truths. There was more to it he wasn't ready to divulge.

"Other things? Like me?" I wasn't certain where the thought had come from, but his reaction confirmed it.

His head swiveled to me, his eyes so dark they almost looked chestnut. They searched mine as his jaw ticked. He reminded me of one of those dark romance characters, and as out of character as it was, it fascinated me. I wanted to know who that man was, the man he kept from me along with his secrets.

"Yes," he admitted before looking away. "She doesn't know about you. It's better that way."

"Why? What could possibly be so bad about me that you wouldn't tell her about me?"

I pulled my hand from his and crossed my arms, stopping to await his answer.

An exasperated sigh came from him as he ran a hand through his hair. Stuffing his hands in his pockets, he looked up at me, his eyes riven with pain, and my anger faded.

"Let me in, Gabe," I said. "Please."

He looked so torn that it was killing me. I wanted to take the burden from him, whatever that burden was that he didn't think I could bear. Dropping my arms, I moved to him, tipping his chin up with my finger.

"I can't. Not yet. Not until I figure this out."

"What out?"

"Everything. My past isn't as simple as yours, Tori. It's..." He looked away, his brow pinched. "...complicated, and I'm not sure I can untangle it. But I'm trying."

"These secrets you carry, are they dangerous?" I fought back my fear, praying I hadn't fallen in love with a serial killer.

A tug at his lips told me I wasn't even close to guessing. "No, nothing dangerous. Just personal and rife with...with lines. Some I drew, some others drew. And it's those lines that I have to untangle in order to keep you."

My heart sputtered. "Keep me? Like you could lose me?"

"I...God, Tori, I can't do this. We just confessed our love to each other. Let's enjoy that and deal with this when I figure it out."

"Gabe, you won't lose me. Whatever you're not telling me, I can handle it."

He closed his eyes. "I know you can." Opening them, he took my hand. "We're going to lose our reservation."

I studied him, seeing the resolve there. The conversation was over. He had shut it down, and he was asking me to let him. I did, even if it nudged at me the entire time we were at dinner.

As we lay in bed later that night, my head on his chest, his fingers stroking my hair, he murmured, "There's a lot of pain in my past, Tori. My childhood wasn't like yours."

I picked my head up to look at him. He stared at the ceiling, his fingers continuing their pattern in my hair. Pain pinched his face, and guilt hammered me that I had pushed him too much.

Palming his cheek, I forced his eyes to mine. "I'm sorry I pushed," I said. "I'm here when you're ready, and I won't love you any less if you're not."

The intensity of his gaze left me breathless as he pulled me in for a kiss. It ignited a fire in me, and soon our kisses led to touches. I climbed onto him, letting his hands work my body into a frenzy I couldn't tame, and enveloped him. The steel intensity of his gaze remained on me while he watched me fall apart. Those hazel eyes were so full of adoration and love that I no longer cared that he held secrets from me. All that mattered was Gabe and the way our bodies moved in tandem. As he grew closer to release, he threaded his fingers into my hair, dragging my mouth to his. My climax tore through me, eviscerating me just as he succumbed to his.

Filling me, he murmured, "Ti amo, luna mia."

And I clung to those words and the emotion they held as I rode out the waves of my ecstasy and fell so far for him that I knew there was no going back, no matter what complications his secrets held.

Chapter 8

Gabe

The clink of Tori's keys informed me she was ready to leave. Now that she'd passed her exams, the company had assigned her a permanent schedule, one that included Saturdays and second shift weekdays. It left me more time to work on my businesses and plan the next steps, but it kept her from me when I'd grown attached to having her with me so much.

"I'm leaving," she shouted from the living room.

Rushing from the bedroom in just my boxers, I scooped her up and swung her around before kissing her goodbye. She teetered, grabbing my shoulder when I put her down.

"No leaving without a goodbye. Remember?" I said, loving the smile that lit her eyes.

"How could I forget?" She brought my head down and gave me a peck before heading out. "Dinner when I get back?"

"I'll have it made and waiting."

"You're cooking tonight?" she asked, holding the door open.

"Gotta keep you spoiled."

With a laugh, she shook her head. "That's all you do, Gabe. You spoil me nonstop."

"Good."

"I love you," she said.

I pressed my hand to my chest. "Love you, too. Go put those clients in their place."

"Can't wait. Another day of talking people through pin resets and giving stock quotes."

"You'll get there, Tori. Give it time, and you'll be running the company one day."

Her laugh echoed long after she closed the door. There was always an emptiness to the apartment when she left. Five months had passed. Five months since the day she had entered my life and changed it completely. I rubbed my neck, making my way to the shower to get ready for a day of work. Without Tori there, I could work freely. There was no need to hide browsers from her when she came to look over my shoulder. Hiding the spreadsheets and internal workings of my LLCs. The business emails and dark web searches. Given the multiple screens involved in my day job, she never questioned why I had so many monitors and screens open at once.

I peered out the window, seeing her climb into her car. We'd been spending more nights with each other, and I was contemplating taking the next step and asking her to move in with me. Scratching the back of my neck, I returned to starting my day. Her shift would last until four, and I had plenty to do until then.

As I dressed, my phone buzzed. Liv. There wasn't anyone else it could be this early on a Saturday morning. I'd been ignoring her calls for the last two days, and I knew she was pissed and worried.

"Morning," I said, waiting for her to rip into me.

"Morning? Where the hell have you been, Gabe? I've been trying to reach you for two days, and before then you could barely spare me five minutes. I was about to send one of Dad's men down to make sure you were still alive."

Pissed was an understatement. I walked into the kitchen and filled a glass with orange juice.

"Don't be dramatic. I'm fine. Just busy with work."

She stayed quiet, and I could just picture her gnashing her teeth. "Talk."

"I told you work—"

"There's something going on, Gabe. I'm not stupid. We've been checking in consistently for years, and suddenly, you're AWOL. What are you up to?"

The couch cushioned the drop of my body, and I leaned on my knees.

"Gabe."

"I met someone."

"Good for you. Glad you're finally getting laid. What the hell does that have to do with ignoring me?"

"Don't be a bitch, Liv. I didn't hook up with someone. I met her and..."

I heard something drop before she snarled, "Don't, Gabe."

"Liv, listen to me. She's the one. I can't walk away from this."

"Are you shitting me? We have one rule. No relationships past a one-night stand. No attachments, Gabe. That's what we've always done. You can walk away from this, and you will."

I raked my hand through my hair. "No, I can't."

"You can. Just like I did. Or are you forgetting that I had my *one* when we started this thing? We were planning to get married. I walked away from that for us, and you promised it would be worth it."

I caught the emotional break in her words. She had never admitted it, but I suspected she had never gotten over Hudson, the man she'd dated for four years and turned her back on when she graduated college.

"That wasn't just us. That was Dad, too. You can't put all that on me."

"Yeah, Dad. Think about that one. There is no future with this girl, not if you want to keep your inheritance. Break it off with her. If Dad catches wind of it, he'll crush it."

I heard the threat in her voice and picked my head up. "He

won't find out. Let me have this, Liv. I've been down here running the business off his radar all these years. Keeping our plan out of his sight. I left everything behind so we could make this happen. Let me have this much."

As much as she loved to tease me about my living the sunny beach life, Florida had provided enough distance to allow me to stay out of our father's sight while I continued to build the network of shell companies that hid our identities. Acquiring smaller companies and using them to cover my steps as I strategically set us up to crush my father. With Liv on the inside and me prepping to join in less than two years, we were in place to start demolition. A strategic unraveling of his companies, one by one until we left him no choice but to sell to any bidder willing to risk their neck on his failing business.

"Please, Liv."

Her sigh came through, and in it, I detected her frustration. "Fine. You can play until it's time to come home. That's it. Don't get serious with her." *Too late.* "Don't think this is anything more than a fling. When your time is up, you return home and leave her in Florida."

The thought sent a blade through my chest. My silence caused her to continue. "If you can't do that, Gabe. End it now. Trust me, you don't want her to get attached. It will haunt you forever." Her voice cracked, her pain still raw after all these years. Just like I imagined mine would be if I had to leave Tori. "I need to go. Dad has me working on a new project. He's researching a resort in New Hampshire he wants to bring under his control. Don't do anything stupid, Gabe. End it if it's going to hurt too much."

I clutched the phone in my hands long after she had hung up. I'd gone into this knowing it would crush me. After one day with Tori, I was lost, and I had known there was no coming back from it. Placing the phone on the coffee table, I slumped back into the couch. I couldn't leave her, couldn't walk out. I was too far gone. One year and seven months. That was how much time I had left before my father's deadline for me to return to New York and work for him. One year and seven months to figure out how to make this work. To be selfish and hypocritical. To choose Tori and break my sister's trust.

"Damn it." I threw the closest thing, the couch pillow, sending my juice tumbling and spilling all over the carpet. There went my deposit. Storming to the kitchen, I tore a handful of paper towels off the roll. I rested my hands on the counter, fighting the wave of exasperation and anger that battered me. This was my father's fault. Just like everything in my life had been. It didn't matter how far I was from him, his shadow lingered, infecting everything I touched.

If it weren't for Liv, I would have given up the inheritance. I had enough, and the business ventures and investments had made us both millionaires on our own. I didn't need his money. But Liv and I had made a promise to each other. On the day of my mother's funeral, with the rain pouring down on us, we had sworn our revenge. I couldn't turn my back on her, not after all we'd done to get to this point.

My phone buzzed, and I returned to it, tossing the paper towels onto my mess. A text from Tori.

If I have to explain what a browser is to one more person, I'm going to scream.

I chuckled as I texted her back, the stress lifting with just the thought of her.

Patience. In six months, you'll be on to a better role. You're earning your stripes.

Easy for you to say.

Yup, get back to work, and I'll erase the annoyance of the day from you when you get home. I'm thinking spaghetti and meatballs with a side of The Hobbit?

No response, and I knew she'd taken another call. I focused on cleaning up the juice, and the answer came when I was tossing the soaked paper towels into the trash.

With your homemade sauce?

Of course. Nothing but the best for my girl.

It's a date. Ugh, another call. Love you!

And that was why I couldn't give her up. Just thinking about her was a balm to my spirit.

Placing my conundrum to the side, I spent the rest of the day buried in my computer until it was time to make dinner for the woman whose very presence would erase everything else from existence.

Tori's fingers ran a pattern over my stomach before tracing the scar on my side as she often did. I knew she was curious, could sense her hesitation every time she touched it. With another month having passed, I'd continued to separate my heart from my mission. Refused to give Tori my secrets and avoided speaking of her when I talked to Liv. Keeping the two parts of my life separate gave me a semblance of peace. A way to pretend the inevitable wasn't waiting for the right time to send my house of cards tumbling. When I was with Tori, it was easy to live in the fairy tale, to believe I could have my happily ever after, and I lived every moment with her like I would, denying the reality that sat outside of that bubble.

"Glass," I said, thinking I could let her in just a little to appease her curiosity.

She lifted her head, but I continued to stare at the ceiling.

"I fell through a glass window when I was sixteen. Mostly superficial wounds, but one piece got me good."

"How did you fall through a window?"

I sucked in a breath, not sure I was as ready as I'd thought I was. She scooted up and turned my face to hers. Cornfield blue questioned me, and I brushed my fingers over the corner of her eye.

"It was more of a push," I admitted. Her brows scrunched as

she waited for my explanation. "I told you my past holds darkness." I turned my body to hers, pushing a strand of hair from her face. "That you are the light in my dark nights, luna mia."

She gave me a small smile, her gaze expectant.

"I was four when my father raised his hand to my sister for leaving her dolls in his office. He didn't allow us to play in his office, and she had snuck in, forgetting to bring her dolls out when my mother called her for lunch." Going back to that time only reminded me of the hatred that had festered for years. "I jumped in front of her. She was older, so it was stupid, but I hated how hard he was on her. Even at that age. And when I saw it, I reacted." Dropping my sight to her neck, I forced myself to relive the moment, to go back to the start of it all. "He punished me instead. Smacked me so hard, I hit my head on the table and ended up with stitches."

The horror reflected in her eyes when I met them was why I had never admitted it to her. I'd never told anyone. Only Liv knew the truth.

"From then on, I received punishment for every infraction Liv did as well as my own. Bruises were commonplace. I was a boy, so others brushed them off as rough play. The scar on my side is the last one he gave me. I was sixteen. It was a month before my mother died." Before he had driven her to take her life. Unable to protect me, she had slowly spiraled, and he had ignored the signs of her depression until it was too late.

"I talked back to him, told him how much I hated him. He lost his temper and punched me. We had these long windows in our living room. Floor to ceiling. My mother loved to stand and look out of them in the winter. To watch the snow fall on the deck." It hurt to talk about her still. She'd been gone eleven years, but I could still picture her standing there, wrapped in her shawl and telling me how winter was the way God cleansed the earth while I played at her feet. "He kept yelling for me to get up and fight back, and I wanted to. I wanted to so badly that I didn't dare move or I would have killed him. He still saw me as the little boy who had stood up to him, but I wasn't. I was bigger than him, had been playing sports for years and had muscle. When I didn't move, he dragged me up and shoved me so hard I broke through the window and ended up in the hospital getting stitched up again."

Tears had gathered in her eyes, and I hated it. They weren't pity tears, not from Tori. She was soft-hearted, and the thought of my pain drove those tears. It only made me love her more. She smoothed her hand over my cheek, and I turned my mouth to kiss it.

"He only lifted his hand to me once more before I stopped him." It was after our mother's funeral. When I blamed him for her death and his reaction had been to smack me. I'd caught his hand, telling him if he ever lifted a hand to me again, I would walk away from him and never return. I was his heir apparent, my only saving grace. "He never raised a hand to me again. I just wish I'd stood up to him earlier." It might have saved my mother, lessened her heartache.

A tear fell from Tori's eye, and I wiped it away. "Please don't cry, luna mia. It was years ago. In the past."

"I'm so sorry, Gabe. You told me you kept your secrets for a reason, but I never imagined...no child should go through that."

"Shhh." I stopped her with a finger to her lips. "It's in the past where I need to leave it." Otherwise, that darkness threatened to drown me. It flickered in my periphery, threatening to escape, but Tori kept it content to keep away.

Her eyes flitted between mine, and I took her face in my hands. "Now you know one of my secrets. I promised I would tell you when I was ready. Eventually, you'll know them all."

"Are they all this bad?"

"Some, yes." Her mouth twisted, and I wanted to wipe away the concern she now carried for me. Tipping her chin with my finger, I told her, "But you turn them all to ash when I'm with you. I have no worries, no past. Only a future with you and your smiles." I kissed the corners of her eyes, kissing away the rest of her salty tears. "No more tears."

My mouth traveled down her face until I reached her lips. "Get some sleep, and I'll take you out to breakfast in the morning."

"Or we could stay in bed all morning." She gave me a ruthless grin.

Pulling her into my arms, I kissed the top of her head. "I like that idea. I'll never turn down breakfast in bed."

She snuggled further into my hold, her hand resting on my waist. "I love you, Gabriel Hughes."

"I know and I love you, luna mia."

It didn't take long for her soft breaths to fall into a pattern that told me she was asleep. I held tight to her, knowing there might come a time when I wouldn't have her there and knowing I would never be the same if she weren't.

CHAPTER 9

TORI

My phone rang just as Gabe came through the door.

"That's all of it," he said, walking to my room with an armful of dress shirts and slacks.

I picked my phone up and answered. "Hold on, Mom. That's all you have?" I shouted to him, guessing he was in my closet.

"Yeah. The furniture came with the apartment."

My brows knitted while I thought about that. The furniture in his apartment had seemed to fit him, and I vaguely remembered him saying something about buying the couch.

"Victoria?" My mother's voice came through the phone, distracting my thoughts.

"Shoot, sorry, Mom. Gabe's moving in today, and he was bringing in the rest of his stuff."

With Gabe's lease running out in a month, we decided to take the plunge and have him move in with me. It made the most sense, and with us already spending the night between apartments, it was already like we were living together.

"Today? Oh my, that's so exciting and perfectly timed for my call. Dad and I want you to bring him home for Christmas so we can meet him."

There was a high probability she heard my grimace through the phone. Gabe peeked his head out of the bedroom door, his auburn hair messy. I chewed my lip, knowing I was going to crush my mother. I'd already let her down by telling her Thanksgiving was off the table.

"Umm, I don't think we can."

"Can what?" Gabe mouthed, entering the room, his hazel eyes scrunched with worry.

"Why not? It's Christmas. We always do Christmas together."

"It's not that simple, Mom. I'm still new, and I don't have vacation time accrued yet. I only get the one day off, and there won't be enough time to warrant a plane ticket, especially at holiday rates."

"Your dad and I will pay, Tori."

"We will!" I heard my dad yell in the background.

"I just can't, Mom. I'm sorry."

"But Cash will be home and, well, we've never had a Christmas without you."

My heart dropped, and the pressure at the back of my eyes had me looking for an excuse to hang up. Gabe took the phone from me before I could stop him.

"I'll have her there, Mrs. Hent."

"Gabe!" I heard my mother exclaim, followed by a shout from my father.

My parents loved Gabe. After the first time he talked to them, it was like they had another son.

"What are you doing?" I asked him, trying to grab the phone from him. He put his hand out and held me at a distance.

"Don't worry. She'll be home for Christmas."

"Are you crazy? We won't have time." I was still fighting to get the phone back, but his damned long arms had me too far back.

"Sure will. Of course I can come."

A pause while my mother spoke.

A shadow of darkness passed through his eyes. "No, my family won't mind."

Quiet again, and I gave up my fight, flopping onto the sofa and crossing my arms.

"I'll make the arrangements, and she'll let you know the flight information. Gotta go. She's pouting."

A few seconds of silence followed with my mother's farewells before he said goodbye and hung up.

"What are you doing?" I asked.

He sat on the coffee table across from me, a smile tugging at his mouth. "You're really adorable when you're pouting."

"Don't suck up to me. I can't go home for Christmas. I'm working that Friday, which means I only get Saturday off for the holiday and Sunday. That's two days and not worth it."

"It's worth it. Your family means the world to you, and Christmas is important." A faraway look crossed his eyes before it disappeared, like all his mysterious moments. Another of those memories he hadn't let me in on. I hadn't pushed him since he'd told me about his father's abuse. He had trusted me with that pain, and I carried it with him, understanding now why he didn't like his father, never spoke about him, never talked to him. I still didn't know what had divided him and his sister, but I knew in time he would tell me.

"But..."

"No buts. Let me handle this."

I sighed, knowing he was too stubborn and determined to argue with.

"Come help me make space in your closet. I didn't know women had so many clothes." He stood and held his hand out to me. When I took it, he yanked me into his arms and kissed me.

"I changed my mind," he said, picking me up and pushing my legs around his waist. I giggled as I wrapped my arms around him. "I think we'll christen the closet first, then we'll reorganize it after we've made a mess of it."

I clung to him, yelping when he misjudged and my back hit the doorway while he was busy biting at my neck. Lowering me to the floor, he hovered over me, concern crinkling his eyes.

"Shoot, are you okay?" he asked.

Hands bunching his shirt, I tugged him to me, catching his mouth with a raise of my head.

"Apparently," he muttered against my lips.

He pushed away and kneeled over me, pulling his shirt off and giving me a naughty smile. So many times, I looked at him and couldn't fathom how I'd gotten so lucky. I ran my hands up his muscles, knowing how hard he worked for them, the early morning hours he spent at the gym. I wasn't complaining because I wasn't awake that early, and the result was sexy as hell.

In a heated rush, he shoved my shirt off, tugging my bra strap down and worshipping my breasts in the way only Gabe could. As if I were his queen. His hand slipped below the waist of my shorts and hit the spot that melted me each time. Between his fingers and his tongue, I was in a constant state of bliss.

His fingers slid further, and he lowered his head to my neck, groaning. "Damn, luna mia, what have you been thinking about?" He pushed a finger into me, causing my back to arch.

"You," I purred. His finger was keeping a rhythm, his mouth pulling my breast in and when combined with my nickname, my climax built.

His tongue flicked at my nipple before he took it between his teeth and scraped them over it. When he sucked it back into his mouth, I lost it, clamping down on his hand and riding out my release.

"Oh, luna mia, you are the most exquisite creature when you're coming for me."

My body convulsed as he freed his hand, sat back, and licked his fingers clean. His sight remained locked on mine, the intensity causing my skin to pebble. When he finished, he groaned and worked my shorts off before removing his. I watched as he stroked himself, his eyes devouring me until my chest was heaving. He gave me a cocky smile, moved his hands to my legs, and adjusted them so my feet were on his pecs. My lips parted as he nudged me with his tip.

"Ready?" he asked, his eyes mischievous.

"Always."

His eyes darkened, and the grin turned to a sexy smirk that had me salivating. He took my mouth hostage before thrusting into me. Back bowing, I let out a cry, scraping my hands over his neck. He freed my mouth and leaned on his hands as he continued to drive into me. Muscles stretching, body heaving, I pulled his head down to deepen our kiss. Each thrust sent him so deep I grunted with every one until he slowed his pace.

Hand cupping my breast, he murmured, "I need you to come undone again for me, Tori."

I moaned, but his mouth dampened the sound, his tongue entangling with mine. Another sweep of his thumb over my nipple had the climax he'd summoned readying itself. Mouth lowering to my breast again, he turned his attention to the other nipple just as his thumb traced a path between our bodies and tormented me. I dug my fingers into his hair as my release prepared to heed his command. My body tingled, the air locked in my chest, and I fell apart.

Gabe threw his hand to the other side of my head, his pace a steady pounding of his body into mine as he chased my release. His features twisted, and he smashed his mouth onto mine, filling me as his body weighed on me.

Going limp, he rubbed his cheek over mine, burying his face in my hair. The strain in my leg muscles burst through my lingering rapture, and I lowered them, trying not to wince from their stiffness. I really needed to haul my butt out of bed earlier and join Gabe at the gym.

Lifting his head, he gave me a smile. "Any other spots we haven't christened yet?"

With a laugh, I flung my hands back around his neck. "I think there's a spot on the kitchen counter we haven't hit."

"Good, we can put it on the list with the one on the bathroom counter."

The heat in my cheeks rose, but his kiss soothed it. Gabe had no problem taking me whenever and wherever the urge to touch me hit him. And I couldn't resist him, so I never stopped him. Knowing Gabe, he would have backed off if I'd told him it was the wrong time. He was too sweet not to, but I was too addicted to his touch to ever say no.

"I love your blush," he said. "And your neck." He gave it a kiss. "And your ears." A bite to my earlobe. "And these shoulders." A lick that kicked my libido back into gear. "These breasts."

The list of places continued to grow, his love nips and kisses following each until I was a mess again. By the time we left the closet, the day was over.

Gabe's fingers tapped the steering wheel, excitement buzzing from him and infecting me.

"Where are we going?" I asked, scanning the road for any hint.

After leaving me completely weakened when I woke, he'd announced that he had the day planned for us. A day that called for me to dress nice but wear comfortable shoes, a combination that didn't match up.

"It's a surprise," he said, taking my hand and kissing it while he waited for the light to change. He continued to drive into the city, passing over the Blue Bridge with the morning sun sparkling on the water below.

When we pulled into the parking garage, I eyed him, thinking how cute his devious smile was and still clueless as to where he was taking me. He led me out of the garage, and only when we were heading with others into the theater did I gasp and jerk him to a stop.

I looked up at him with wide eyes. "Is it *The Nutcracker*?"

His smile widened until it lit his face.

With a squeal, I threw my arms around his neck. He picked me up as I kissed him and gently lowered my feet to the ground. This man amazed me more every day. He caught everything I said and did, storing that information for moments like this. My family had attended *The Nutcracker* at the local theater every year since I could remember, and I'd lamented the fact that I would miss it this year. But Gabe had ensured I wouldn't, once again reminding me why I loved him so intensely.

Hand in mine, he took us inside, buying me hot chocolate before leading me to the best seats in the house. My heart was bursting by the time we left, and I couldn't imagine the day getting any better until it did.

"Why are we stopping at the mall?" I asked as he opened my door for me and held a hand out to help me out of the car.

"Another surprise," he said.

Shoppers packed the mall with bags and packages, but Gabe kept me tucked next to him, guiding me through the crowd to his destination. Stopping in front of the Christmas store, he turned to me. Confidence faltering, he gazed down at his feet and palmed the back of his neck.

"My mother loved Christmas. She would decorate the entire house, and my sister and I would help. But..." He dropped his hand and shoved it into his pocket. "My father hated it. And after a time, his shadow infected it. Every year there was less until it just stopped when I was thirteen." Hazel eyes, misty and dark, met my sight, and my heart broke a little more for him. "You reminded me of what it was like before that, Tori. Your excitement, the traditions you and your family have. I want that with you. Can we—"

"Gabriel Hughes, are you asking me to decorate for Christmas with you?"

He chuckled, the stress fading from his features. "Yeah."

"Hmm," I feigned concern. "That's a big step."

His sheepish grin had me grabbing his hand and dragging him into the store. We filled basket after basket until we walked out with four giant bags of decorations.

"I don't know where we're going to put all this stuff come January," I said as he closed his trunk.

"We'll make room. Ready for some lunch? I have one more surprise after that."

I rubbed my stomach. "I could definitely use some food."

Over lunch, I pressed him for more details about Christmas in the Hughes household, but his walls were back in place. There were so many moments when he closed up that I still didn't know what to make of it. We'd been dating for six months, and I still barely knew anything about his past. He seemed to live through my memories, and it hurt to think his were so bad that he wanted someone else's. Maybe in time he would open up more like he had the night he'd told me about his father. I suspected whatever demons he carried they would hurt me to hear. I loved him too much for them not to.

This was life with Gabe. Secrets and mysteries, surprises and sweetness. A dichotomy that had me in a fairy tale most days, with the darkness pushing at my periphery. I couldn't help but worry that it would invade my happiness and turn my fairy tale into a nightmare. Only the knowledge that Gabe was too sweet to let that happen, to let anything hurt me, kept my anxiety in check. I allowed the secrets to persist, knowing he had his reasons and that as someone who loved him unconditionally, I had no choice.

"It's not a day trudging through the snow to get the perfect tree, but it's the best I could find."

My jaw went slack when we pulled in. Christmas trees of all sizes filled the lot of the farm.

"We can cut one down or take a pre-cut one home," he said, scratching his cheek. "I think they have a small store, too."

Speechless, I continued to stare out the window.

"Too much?" he asked.

With tears pressing behind my eyes, I turned to him. "No," I said, shaking my head. "Perfect."

His worry transformed to excitement, and he hopped out of the car, making it to my side just as I was exiting. Hand in mine, he pushed my hair from my face, his eyes flitting between mine as if searching for my approval.

"I love it, Gabe. I love everything about this day, and I love you." I pulled him toward me, our lips meeting in a passionate kiss that ignited my body. "Let's go pick out our first tree."

His grin spread wide, and he hurried us off to the trees. Dragged from tree to tree, I tried not to laugh at how adorable he was. At every tree, he stopped to evaluate it and get my opinion. None seemed to meet his expectations of perfection.

As we trudged through the tree farm, I was glad I'd worn a pair of dress boots with low heels. The weather was still in the sixties, but I pulled my sweater around my chest, trying to keep up with his long strides. I had long legs, but his steps were ridiculously large.

"Did you have real trees when you were little?" I braved, hoping I wouldn't drag his mood down.

"Always," he answered, musing over a thick evergreen that stood a few inches taller than him.

"Were you always this excited about picking one?"

Pulling at branches, he said, "I never got to pick one. My father always had them delivered."

I mulled that over as he stooped to look at the trunk.

"You had someone deliver your tree?"

"My father had someone who did it for him and..." His head shot up, his eyes wide as if he realized he'd said too much. He swallowed, and I could see him scrambling to cover his admission.

"Part of the past you'll tell me about one day?" I said, hating how angry I sounded.

"Tori, I—"

I put a hand up. "It's okay. I know I need to be patient, but a little at a time would be helpful rather than something every few months."

Guilt shadowed his irises as he stood. Brows knitted, he tucked his hands in his pockets. "We had money. Well...we have money. I told you about the trust fund, but..." His jaw clenched, that shadow spreading to turn his hazel eyes closer to brown. "My father is successful, and we had more advantages than ordinary families."

He turned and stomped away, and I couldn't help but wonder why it had been so hard to tell me that. There was nothing in it other than that he came from money. It wasn't a surprise to me. I recognized it in the way he dressed, the way he insisted on paying for everything even though I made a good salary. And my family wasn't poor. They did well running the resort, and we had never gone without. So what was it about Gabe that made it something he had to keep from me?

I ran after him, grasping his elbow and forcing him to stop. The sparkle had disappeared from his eyes, and I wanted it back. Taking his face in my hands, I lowered his head to mine. "Come back to me, Gabe."

"I'm right here, Tori." There was a harshness in his tone and an authoritative quality that surprised me.

"No, you're not. You went wherever you go when you think about your past. Do you not understand that I love you no matter what? I don't care if you have money, I don't care if you have ghosts, I don't care that your mood shifts when you talk about those ghosts. I love you, Gabe. Don't you see that? There's nothing you could do to make me stop loving you."

"I'm terrified of losing you." His words were a whisper of fear that shredded any lingering irritation.

"You won't lose me. I promise you."

Eyes dropping to the ground, shoulders drooping, he looked so wounded. Vulnerable and not the strong man I knew. He yanked me into his body and buried his face in my hair. His hands clung so tight to me it almost seemed like a tornado would drop on us and rip me from him if he didn't hold on.

"I will," he murmured, and my chest lurched because I knew in my heart that something in those secrets he kept led him to believe this. How did I compete with something I didn't understand and couldn't see? I dug my face into his chest, a sense of foreboding chasing away the light in my day.

"I'm yours, Gabe. I will forever be yours." The words came freely from me. An admission that I was certain was true.

His soft declaration followed. "I won't ever stop loving you, luna mia. Never."

I sank further into his hold. The safety of his arms too comfortable to leave, that sense that some impending event was lurking in the distance to shatter our happy ending not allowing me to leave it. Whatever was coming, Gabe feared it, and while I refused to let it damage what we had, I couldn't deny that I was beginning to fear it as well.

CHAPTER 10

GABE

What am I doing? The question replayed in my head repeatedly as I followed Tori through the airport. I was in too deep, and there was no way to remove myself. She was a part of me now. The weight of the ring box in my coat pocket made me even more aware of that.

A storm was building, and I was behind it, churning it up and preparing for it to swallow me whole and destroy the only thing I cared about more than revenge and my sister: Tori. While the truth continued to drag at my heels, it wasn't slowing me down from the train wreck that waited in the distance.

I continued to tell myself I would find a way to make this work. To take my father down and keep the woman I loved more than life itself. But within the storm lurked the truth, that the trust fund my father established for me was contingent on two things: that I didn't marry before I was thirty-two and that I held the CFO position in his company by that age. And the plan my sister and I had set in motion twelve years ago was contingent on me assuming the CFO position my father had promised was mine once I earned my dues and nothing else came before it, including love.

But within six months, I had derailed that plan, and it was threatening to implode by my hand.

Tori had stopped pressing for answers, and I had none to give her. Liv chastised me every day, so I had started ignoring her calls. There was no way I could tell her I was spending Christmas weekend with Tori's family, or that I planned to propose to her. I'd already decided I would give the money up for Tori. She was worth so much more. It was giving up on revenge and my sister that had me fighting my heart's pull.

"There she is." Distinct blue eyes and thick black hair made it impossible to think the man greeting Tori could be anyone but her brother. The similarities were uncanny, and if I didn't know he was six years older, I would have thought them twins.

"Cash!" She dropped her bag and ran into his arms.

Gathering the bag, I watched as he picked her up and swung her around. Giving her a kiss on the head, he put her back on her feet. The display of affection was in striking contrast to the strained and distant contact that occurred when my family was in the same room. Without my mother, my father's restraint had infected me and Liv. Hugs were not a thing in my family.

"And this must be the infamous Gabe." He extended his hand to me and with some bag shuffling I took it.

"You would be correct. Nice to meet you, Cash. I've heard a lot about you."

"All good, I hope."

"Eh, most."

She elbowed me as he popped the bags in the trunk of his SUV. "All good," she said.

"Better be, sis. Otherwise, I'll have to put you in a headlock and give you a noogie."

The banter continued with me fielding questions in between until we pulled down a tree-lined lane that led to a massive house sitting along a frozen lake. Snow made the scene picturesque, and I suddenly missed being up north. It had been too many years away, with infrequent visits back home composed of awkward conversation and icy stares. My father was nothing like Tori's family, and as her mother folded me into her arms like she'd known me all her life and her father pulled me in for a hug, I suddenly saw how broken my family was. I'd always known, but seeing how perfect we could have been if my father hadn't destroyed us opened my eyes to how wrong it had all been. Reminding me of why Liv and I had been plotting against him all these years.

I tucked the ring box in the side of my suitcase when Tori was taking her heavy coat off and her parents were fussing over her. I put my coat on the hook next to hers, kicked my boots off, and followed her into the house. It was inviting and cozy, even though it was spacious. Every bit of space was filled with pictures of Tori and Cash as kids, family vacations, and graduations. Cinnamon candles left the air with a sweet holiday scent. Decorations covered everything, from the fireplace mantel to the stair railing. This wasn't just a house; it was love and safety, a place of acceptance and support.

It was everything I had found in my mother, the shield from the storm that was my father, until she had found her way out and left us alone with him. There was so much joy that it spread, and the worries of takeovers and business faded to the back of my mind.

The feeling continued through the late Christmas Eve dinner, scheduled to accommodate our late flight. While Tori and Cash helped their mother clear the table, her father gestured for me to follow him. I didn't know what to expect. The only fatherly talks I had ever experienced were stern and had often ended with pain. Even now they remained cold, business transactions.

"Sit," he said, gesturing to the couch in the main room. He took a seat in the recliner, his sharp blue eyes sizing me up. "So, Gabe, this is serious."

I sat up straighter, expecting the criticism my father would have given me. "Yes, sir, it is."

He rubbed his beard, then let out a belly laugh. "Relax, I'm not going to do anything. Victoria is happy. I can hear it in her voice when she calls us. She's shining, and I think we both know you're the cause."

"I like to think so," I admitted. "The only thing I care about is keeping her smiling."

"Good. So what's next?"

This was my chance, and the voice in my head that should have been telling me this was the first step in sealing my fate remained quiet. "Well, with your permission, I'd like to ask her to marry me."

His mouth gaped before he closed it and leaned forward in his seat. "I was thinking maybe a Christmas movie, but that's a plan, too."

Strain leaving my shoulders, I rubbed my temple, feeling like an idiot but glad I'd said it.

"You want to marry our Tori?"

I dropped my hand and held his gaze. "Very much so."

"Then ask her. You don't need my permission, but I appreciate you asking. Proper upbringing is a plus."

I sat back, thinking of how my father had drilled proper into me from my earliest days.

"It was the way I was raised," I admitted.

"Sounds like your parents did a good job."

I tried not to wince at his words, but I couldn't stop it. "I suppose," I said, looking out at the snow accumulating on the balcony. "Looks like we're getting a white Christmas."

"Dad, are you torturing Gabe in here?" Tori's voice saved me from any questions.

"Not torturing, sweetheart, just talking."

She sat next to me, pulling her feet up to her side and handing me a glass that looked like milk but smelled too sweet and spiked.

Lifting a brow, I questioned her.

"Eggnog with a little something extra to warm you up."

"Do I need warming up?" I asked, taking a tentative sip and thinking she could keep the eggnog to herself. Turning my nose up, I handed the glass back to her.

"My kind of guy," Cash said. "That stuff is nasty, Tor."

"Well, Mom and I love it," she snapped, taking a sip and sticking her white tongue out at him.

The debate about eggnog continued with no defined winner until we reconsidered the movie and turned in. Tori surprised me by dropping to her knees when she closed the door, and unable to turn down the treat, I pushed her hair back as her big blue eyes held mine until her mouth took me over the edge.

***

Christmas with the Hent family was unforgettable. There were moments when it reminded of my mother and her bright smile as she watched us open our presents. A smile that had diminished with every passing year so that by the time I was a teenager, it was difficult to find. My father's ever-present glare was nowhere to be found, his presence not overshadowing the festivities with his irritation and impatience. The nerves that were always on edge, waiting for a blow or an insult meant to harden me, were absent.

This was family, and that realization had me determined to make this a reality. To have my future consist of the laughter and joy that filled Tori's family home.

When the wrapping paper was cleaned up, I raised the new scarf Tori had made for me in UConn navy and gray because as they reminded me repeatedly, I was now in Huskie territory and although my girl 'tolerated' my Harvard roots, she was a Huskie girl whose blood ran navy and gray.

"Wanna take a walk and test this out?" I asked her. She was fingering the bracelet I'd bought her. Delicate silver with charms that represented the moments in our relationship. A nutcracker for our first show, a bridge like the one in the background of our first kiss, a book for the hours we'd spent reading together while she studied, a meatball for our favorite restaurant, and intertwined hearts.

After learning that she'd spent her downtime at work knitting me the scarf so I wouldn't know, I was glad I'd had every charm handmade. It had been worth every penny to see her expression.

"Go," her father said. "Cash and I will help your mother in the kitchen. Take Gabe out to the lake and show him the property."

"Okay." She tugged my hand, leading me toward our room to get changed. He threw me a wink when her back was to him, and my nerves lit like electric sparks.

What was I doing? This couldn't happen. Every rational side of me knew that, but the irrational side that was drowning in love didn't listen. I snuck the ring into my pocket as I pulled a sweater from my bag. Tori was changing out of her pajamas, and I couldn't stop my eyes from grazing over her body when I stood.

"With that look, I'd think you were ready to devour me."

Pushing her shirt from her hand, I pulled her into my arms. My lips brushed her bare shoulder. "I'm being respectful to your parents." Hands soaking in the softness of her skin, I regretted the decision to touch her. "And a room lined with UConn pendants isn't exactly a turn-on." Even if I hadn't noticed them the prior night when she'd taken me to oblivion. I nipped her neck, and she squealed.

Tugging on my scarf, she said, "I'll convert you, Harvard boy."

With a laugh, I dipped her body and dragged my mouth down her chest. "We'll see." I released her, loving how she stumbled slightly and color filled her cheeks. "And when we get home, I plan to devour every inch of you multiple times."

Rolling my neck to calm myself, I walked from her, taking a spot against the wall to watch her dress. Tormenting myself even more. If the ring in my pocket didn't have me rigid with stress, I may have played more, but the thing had my nerves strained. She wouldn't know the true significance of what I planned, how I risked losing everything to keep her. Especially if I couldn't convince her to wait five years for the wedding. Who was I kidding? I didn't want to wait. I would have married her that day if I could have. Screw it all. She was all I wanted, and I knew I was being selfish, that my decision would hurt Liv, but Tori was worth it.

"Hey." Her voice brought me back, and I realized she had already dressed. "You okay?"

Light fingers drifted over my jaw, worry lining her eyes. I took her hand, kissing her palm. "I'm fine. Just thinking about how lucky I am to have you."

"Even after meeting my family?"

"Especially after meeting your family."

Her smile lit her eyes, and I gave her forehead a kiss.

After tugging our boots on and wrapping up in our coats, we walked through the snow. Holding her hand in mine, I listened as she told me about the property, how Cash would chase her around it, how she'd adopted a turtle she found crawling from the woods until it bit her, and about the snake Cash had put in her sandbox. Memories of a childhood that had shaped her into the amazing woman she was. Ones not marred with the things that had shaped me.

I stopped her, turning her body to mine. Eyes the color of a summer day looked up at me brightly with joy that was infectious. Would I destroy that joy? Twist it into something unrecognizable by attempting to hold on to it? The fear made me hesitant.

"Gabe?"

"You're beautiful, luna mia."

Her smile returned, adding to her beauty. Snowflakes landed in her hair and on her cheeks as she looked at me with love shining in her eyes. The train had started derailing the moment I met her, and now it cleared its tracks, disaster imminent.

"I love you, Victoria Hent, and I know there will never be anyone but you who fills the space in my heart. Every crevice belongs to you." The train wheels shook with a last-minute attempt to return to the track, but they lost their fight. "I want to spend every day of the rest of my life with you."

Tears welled in her eyes, and the train burst into flames as I dropped to my knee and held the ring out.

"Marry me, Tori. Let me spend the rest of my life spoiling you and loving you. I promise you, a day won't go by when I won't love and worship you."

Her tears fell as the ashes of years of planning and building joined them.

"Yes. Yes. Yes. I'll marry you, Gabe."

She jumped into my arms, and I rose, lifting her and spinning her around as a jubilation I'd never experienced overtook me. This felt right, like destiny falling into place, no matter how a voice screamed in the back of my mind that it would all fall apart. I wouldn't let it. She loved me, and she was mine. If I came clean, told her everything, she would forgive the secrets and wait for the wedding. And if it was too much to ask, then I would give it up. All of it, regardless of the cost.

My plans came crashing around me, and the runaway train that was my life rose from the ashes to explode a second time as we ate Christmas dinner. The excitement over our engagement left me in a chaotic storm of anxiety that only increased the more Tori and her mother talked.

"We'll have it at the resort," her mother said. "It's so pretty in the spring."

"That would be perfect," Tori gushed, dashing my hope to delay the ceremony.

"Why don't you do it this spring?" her father offered. "There's nothing booked in April."

My fork dug into my skin as another train derailed to shatter my life.

"This spring?" I croaked.

Tori turned to me, her features twisted in concern. "Is that too soon? It's so pretty that time of year."

"He probably needs time to tell his family, Tor," Cash offered, sending me a sympathetic look.

"My family won't come," I blurted, the words short.

An awkward silence hung over the table. Tori turned my face, lifting it from where my eyes focused on a slice of ham.

"We can wait," she said. "I got excited, and we should have talked about it first."

She was too good to be true, and I saw then that she would wait if I asked, but did I want to wait? I wanted her, all of her, completely and unreservedly, to be mine. Taking her hand, I brushed her fingers with my thumb. "April sounds fantastic." Why not go for the kill right away? Destroy my sister, shatter her hopes, and leave her hating me for the rest of our lives. Let my father off, never make him pay for what he had done. Dismantle the LLCs, sell the businesses and live off the profits while I lived the white picket fence life with the woman who would make it all okay.

Her blue eyes studied me. "Are you sure?"

Giving her a smile, I said, "More than sure. As long as planning a wedding in four months isn't too much to take on."

A tilt of her head, then a smile that lifted my spirits and soothed the ache.

"April it is," her father said, bringing us from our private exchange that hadn't been so private. "And, Gabe, you're part of our family now, so yes, your family will be there."

I swallowed back the wave of emotion that threatened to undo me completely and gave him a nod. I'd never known a father so devoted to his family. Mine had only ever shown that to his money. Greed and power drove my father, and that's all I'd known.

"Catering is on us, and I'm sure our pastry chef can make the cake," her mother went on as if her husband hadn't just unraveled years of abuse and cruelty in one sentence.

The talk continued for the rest of the day, and by the time we left Connecticut, all we had left to plan were the invitations and tuxedos. I squeezed the bridge of my nose as the plane took off.

"Was that too much?" Tori asked me, and I looked over to see the worry return to her features.

"No. Your family is a blessing. They're wonderful."

She nudged me with her shoulder. "No, I meant the wedding plans."

"Are you two getting married?" the flight attendant asked as she shut the overhead compartment. She handed Tori a blanket, a perk of the first-class seats I'd gotten us.

"Yes," Tori answered, excitement bursting over in her voice. "He asked me yesterday."

I almost rolled my eyes because telling people about my personal business was something I never did. It was hard enough to make friends, and I only had a handful from college and one from prep school. They knew I wasn't a social person, so texts were usually enough, although I knew once I shared this news in the group chat that my phone would start ringing.

After a few minutes of wedding talk that I ignored by keeping my nose in my book, the flight attendant disappeared.

"How did I not realize how antisocial you are?" Tori teased me.

I peeked over my book at her. "I mask it well."

She snuggled closer to me. "So then, going to meet my parents..."

"A struggle for social normalcy," I replied, giving her a half grin.

"Damn, you had me fooled, Gabriel Hughes. Maybe I need to rethink this wedding thing."

I dropped my book and took her chin in my hand. "I don't

think so, luna mia. You already promised yourself to me, and I'm going to hold you to it."

"There's my book boyfriend," she murmured as I brought her lips to mine, giving her a searing kiss to affirm my statement.

That kiss burned away any doubt about my decision to marry her. As the flight continued and Tori curled up against me, I resolved to confess my plans to Liv when we returned.

A vow I didn't keep, avoiding the conversation as the sense that something waited in the shadows to destroy my imaginary life of happiness grew. And with it, the suspicion that I would never recover if it did.

CHAPTER 11

TORI

The bags thudded to the floor when Gabe dropped them at the door. I followed him into the apartment, glad to be back but homesick at the same time. The whirlwind trip had me exhausted, and both of us needed to work the next day.

"Chinese?" Gabe said, stretching. His long arms almost touched the ceiling, and I followed the rise of his shirt as it freed from where he had tucked it in his pants.

"Sounds fantastic," I answered, grabbing my bag and dragging it to the bedroom. Opening it on the bed, I began unpacking. I heard him call in the order, one he knew well enough not to ask what I wanted.

So much had happened in the last two days. The engagement ring shimmered as I carried my makeup bag into the bathroom. I was getting married. To the man of my dreams. An amazing man who made me happier every day. Whom I loved beyond anything I thought possible.

A man I was still discovering, his pieces slowly coming together. Another secret, that he wasn't social after months of thinking he was an outgoing, sexy, heartthrob type. How wrong I'd been. Granted, the sexy, heartthrob part had been right, and that side of him was all mine. But the outgoing side had been a façade, and I'd never realized it because with me he wasn't that way.

Perhaps I should have seen it in the bashful looks he sometimes had, the nervous way he rubbed his neck and struggled for words, but I factored those adorable traits as those of a man in love. They were moments reserved for me, and I loved them.

"Ordered," he said, coming into the room and tossing his bag next to mine. "About twenty minutes." His eyes perused me as I stood in the doorway of the bathroom. "Dinner in bed? Followed by dessert?"

Throwing my head back with a laugh, I replied, "Sounds like a plan, but maybe we could start with dessert?" I was craving his touch. He hadn't done more than kiss me the entire trip, a sweet need to be respectful to my parents. His surprise at them letting us share a bed told me more about his upbringing than I thought he wanted me to know. He was proper, polite, well-mannered, something I'd always known, but it was even more evident around my parents.

"Why is it you never told me you don't like social situations?"

His expression dropped, and I gnawed my cheek, hating that I'd been the cause. Sitting on the side of the bed, he folded the shirt he was holding. "I prefer to be solitary, but I function fine because..." That faraway look crossed his features, the one that told me he was in the past, facing haunting memories. My chest ached at the thought, and I crossed the room, scooting the suitcase over and sitting next to him. "I had to be social. There was no choice, and if I complained, it meant punishment." He rubbed his face, that distant expression still there. "My father hosted parties, and his children were on display, examples of proper upbringing. Spine straight, mouth shut unless addressed, hands tucked to the side, behavior on point. Nothing to embarrass him."

He fidgeted with the shirt, and I brought my hands over his to stop the motion. When his eyes turned to me, there was so much pain in them that I wanted to erase it, to wipe his memory of the past, but I couldn't. "I always preferred being alone until you came along." His hand moved to encompass mine. "When you came into my life, I never wanted to be alone again. You filled a space I hadn't realized was there, an emptiness that had been waiting for you all this time. I can function, and I do it well, but my preference is to be away from people and now, to be with you."

"And your friends?" I knew he had a text group of college buddies, and he'd told me about his friend from high school with whom he still talked.

"They know how I am and respect it. I wasn't much fun at the parties in college."

"So you were the one in the corner looking sexy and broody?"

He gave me a mischievous grin and didn't have to tell me he wasn't always alone. I rolled my eyes and elbowed him. Catching my elbow, he pulled me into him.

"I'm your sexy and broody man now, luna mia. Only yours. These hands will never touch another body because yours is the only one I'll ever hunger for."

My insides somersaulted, and I smashed my mouth into his, pushing him back on the bed. Days of barely touching had his hands shoving at my clothes and mine doing the same as our suitcases tumbled to the ground. By the time the food arrived, he'd feasted on me, then taken me, and left me too weak to answer the door. That man's tongue was a deadly weapon, almost as deadly as the rest of him.

***

The reflection in the mirror was that of a fairytale princess, not me. Wrapped in a plethora of white satin, I turned to view the back of the dress. This was the one. I'd known the moment I saw it, but the clerk had insisted on sending me out with ten other dresses before she let me try this one. Simple and elegant, it gave me an hourglass figure and sat softly on my skin. And I knew Gabe would love it, that he would look at me like every man in a romance movie looked at his bride-to-be when she walked down the aisle.

I pushed the curtain aside, and the woman shook her head. "I guess I should have listened to you. This is beautiful on you." She gathered up the train and followed me into the showroom where my mother, my cousin Anne, and my best friend Cindy waited. Their gasps informed me they loved the dress just as much as I did.

The three had invaded our peace two days before, and I knew Gabe was going crazy with all the commotion. Cindy was loud, and with Anne, the volume only increased.

"Victoria, you look so beautiful," my mother said with tears in her eyes.

"You look like a princess," Anne added, with Cindy agreeing with vigorous head nods. She was sniffing, her eyes glossy.

"This is the one," I told them, swiveling to the standing mirrors and looking at the dress again.

The clerk took some measurements to make a few minor adjustments while my mother brought over a handful of veils. It hit me again that I was getting married in three months. A month had passed since Gabe had proposed, and each day passed quicker than the day before. A giddiness set in, and I hopped up and down on my toes.

"I'm getting married, Mom."

She hugged me, squishing the veils, and I heard the clerk huff.

"Come on, you two. It's time to find our dresses," Cindy said. "And I better look as good as you, Tor."

"You can't look better than the bride," Anne scolded.

"I didn't say better, but I can look as good."

My mother and I shared a look before breaking out in laughter. The day continued that way because there was no other way with Anne and Cindy. It was a taste of home I'd missed, not having noticed that Gabe consumed my existence now. I didn't mind because I loved him so much, but it was nice to have other parts of my life coming in to show me how complete he had made me.

"Did you have fun today?" Gabe asked me that night, his fingers draping up my arm.

"I did. Thank you for putting up with them."

He peered down at me. "Put up with them? They're your family."

"I guess so." I'd known Cindy long enough that I considered her family, as did my parents. "But they're a lot to deal with."

Kissing my head, he rested his head back, shifting me so I was looking down at him. Pushing my hair back, he said, "I want you to be happy, Tori. If a group of chatty women makes you happy, then so be it. If a stadium of that made you happy, I would fill every seat just to see you smile."

And my heart swelled further. I didn't think my love for Gabe would ever fade; he took up too much room.

"Wait until the wedding," I said, giving him a kiss. "When my entire family is there."

"Can't wait," he mumbled, a grin tugging at his lips.

Smoothing my hand down his chest, I asked, "Are you sure you don't want to invite your family? The invitations don't go out until next week."

As I'd expected, his mood soured, the grin eclipsed by the shadow that always lurked over him. "No, they won't come, so why waste the ink?"

"Did you tell them?" I hadn't asked, afraid of upsetting him.

"No." His gaze rose to the ceiling. "I'll need to, but...I don't want them to spoil this moment."

His muscles were taut with a tension I'd noticed had been more prominent since we'd returned home from Connecticut. Whatever demons he was struggling with, they had escalated. The only people he had invited were his school friends, whom he'd told me he had informed through their group chat. It seemed sad that he didn't have anyone from his family coming, but it was something I couldn't remedy for him.

"Get some sleep, luna mia. You had a long day." And he had just worn me out further, taking me against the wall the minute I'd returned home and then again in the bathroom when I was getting ready for bed. It was almost like he couldn't get enough of me, and I wasn't complaining. If this was life with Gabe, I would gladly take the brooding moments for all the amazing sex that came with it.

CHAPTER 12

GABE

"W hat is that?" I asked when Tori entered the apartment, a white dress bag in her hands.

"That is my wedding dress."

My heart thudded at yet another nail in my coffin—invitations, cake, and flower selections, and now a dress. There was no turning back, and yet I still hadn't broken the news to Liv.

"That didn't take long. I thought dress shopping took months." As if I knew anything about it other than what I'd seen in the plethora of bridal magazines that now took up the length of the coffee table and her bedside table.

"I found it when I went shopping with Mom and the girls," she said, hanging it in the back of the closet.

I leaned on the doorframe as she exited, kicking her heels off. "I picked it up on my way home after they called me today to let me know it was ready." Reaching up on her toes, she gave me a kiss. "I can't wait for you to see me in it."

"Well, try it on now."

A look of horror crossed her features. "I can't do that," she exclaimed as if I'd suggested we rob the local bank.

Laughing, I snagged her waist and pulled her into my chest. "And why can't you?"

"Because it's bad luck. You must wait until I'm walking down the aisle for the big reveal."

I nuzzled her neck, pulling her blouse from her skirt. "Damn. Well, if I can't see you in the dress, then I guess I'll have to settle for you in nothing at all."

She giggled just as my phone rang. Ignoring it, I scraped my teeth over her neck.

"Don't you want to get that?" she asked, trying to free herself from my hold.

"Over a chance to have you come undone around me? I don't think that's even a choice."

Laughing, she tipped her neck back further. The call went to voicemail, and I backed her into the room. Not two seconds later, the phone started again. Dropping my head to her neck, I groaned.

"Go. Someone wants you."

"Not as much as I want you," I said, reluctantly releasing her. I had a suspicion it was Liv, and I wasn't ready to tell her about the wedding yet. I'd been dodging her calls, and she was losing patience, irritated that I'd stuck to email and texting.

"Go," Tori said, pushing me out of the room. With an exaggerated sigh, I snatched the phone from the table, seeing that I'd been spot on.

"It's my sister," I told her.

"Then answer it, Gabe."

"I'm going to take it outside. Make sure you're naked when I get back."

But her playfulness had faded, and I had a hunch mine would be nonexistent after this call.

"Yeah," I answered, giving Tori a wink as I left the apartment. She would assume it was because of the rift between me and Liv, the fake rift, but I knew this discussion would be heated and involve information I still hadn't given her.

"That's the way you answer me, jerk?" Liv sneered on the other end. "After two weeks of avoiding me?"

"I've been busy, Liv." I ran my hand through my hair and put more distance between me and the apartment, following the sidewalk toward the pond.

"What the hell is going on, Gabe? You've got me worried. Is this about that woman?"

Pinching the bridge of my nose, I knew I had no choice but to come clean. "Yes. And yes, I've been avoiding you."

"What happened?" Suspicion layered the question.

Tucking my hand in my pocket, I stared at the fountain in the middle of the pond. "I asked her to marry me."

"You what?" she erupted. I held the phone away from my ear as she spouted colorful words that emphasized her anger.

"She's the one, Liv. I want to marry her."

"You've gone mad. For eleven years we've been planning, Gabe. Eleven damn years and you're going to blow it all on her?"

"I can let her in. I'll tell her the truth, and we can still do this."

Although every day closer to the wedding had buried me under more lies. Invitations that listed a false name, a planned trip to the courthouse in two weeks where I would present a driver's license that wouldn't match my birth certificate because my father had used his influence to get me an alternate ID when I'd moved. Making calls to his buddies to get me into the companies under my pseudonym. Sure, they had my correct information for their records and reporting, but in company systems I was a Hughes and not an Icinda. All of that was about to blow up on me, and I had yet to tell Tori the truth.

The silence on the other end of the phone was the reason, and I could picture the pinched expression on Liv's face.

"We made a promise to each other, little brother. A promise that we would let nothing come between us taking him down. We're so close and you pull this shit? You selfish ass."

"Come on, Liv. When have I ever done something for myself? I spent years working for this. For us. Taking accelerated paths to get my business degree in three years, spending two years getting my MBA, more years of working for financial firms to earn Dad's approval and get experience."

"And you're going to throw it all away for some bimbo—"

"Shut up, Liv. You don't even know her. She's not a bimbo. She's intelligent and sweet. She's amazing, and you know it because I would never risk this for someone who wasn't."

Her sigh resonated through the phone. "I gave things up, too. Things I can never get back. We had a plan."

I palmed the back of my neck, guilt hammering me. After a few moments of silence, she said, "At least tell me you're not going through with it until after this is over. That you're waiting."

My grimace was severe. "Well, I was planning to, but she got excited, and it's..." Shit, how was I going to tell her this. She was already pissed at me. "It's in April."

"This April? In two months?"

"Yes."

"Damn it, Gabe. You really have lost your mind. Not only are you betraying me, but Dad will disinherit you. You know the conditions. The trust doesn't kick in until you're thirty-two and you can't be married. That's still over four years away."

"I know, and I don't care. I'll give it all up for her. We have enough from the other businesses. If I unwind them—"

"I'll be out, too, Gabe."

My step faltered. "What do you mean?"

She drew in a ragged breath. "The conditions of the trust are that you hit thirty-two."

"But you're almost there."

"No, Gabe. It's not contingent on me. It's on you. My trust requires you to meet the requirements. The asshole only cares about you. He doesn't care if his selfishness leaves me alone and miserable the rest of my life."

"So if I break the terms of the trust, you get nothing?"

"Yes, and I'm out of a job. I'm sure that in his vindictiveness he'll ensure I'm blocked from any other company." And he would, because I may have stopped him from hitting Liv that day, but that didn't mean he hadn't punished her repeatedly since then in ways like this.

"Shit."

"Yeah. You can't marry her, Gabe. I know you love her, but you need to walk away. Break it off with her before he finds out. If he hasn't already. You know his men still watch you, right? So, whatever you're doing down there that isn't behind closed doors and under your massive computer firewalls, he knows."

My eyes flicked up as I canvassed the area. I'd gone lax in the months Tori had kept me distracted, no longer looking for evidence that his men were tracking me. Protection he had insisted on when I'd first left for college and in the years following, but they'd gotten good at hiding from me before Tori walked into my life. After that, they'd become another piece of my past that she muted.

"I can't leave her, Liv. She's my everything now."

"I had my everything once, and I left him behind. It's your turn. Focus on the plan, Gabe. You'll be twenty-eight in three months, then it's only four years and you can find her again. You'll be a billionaire and CEO of what's left of our father's dynasty after we send it crumbling to the ground. Our chance to rebuild it the way Mama would have wanted and in her name. Remember why we started this."

She disconnected, and the silence was deafening.

I continued my walk around the pond, debating what to do. Coming clean to Tori made the most sense. This had gotten out of hand. I'd gotten caught up in her excitement and the thrill of knowing she would be mine forever. The wedding was in two months; she'd sent the invitations and bought her dress. All the while I'd justified it, telling myself I could give up the inheritance, the vengeance, the work I'd done for the last eleven years of my life. But I couldn't.

My father had leashed me, just as he had my entire life. No matter how many secret businesses Liv and I had built, no matter the fortune we had amassed and stashed in secret offshore accounts, no matter how many companies we'd swallowed under our umbrella, I would always be under his finger. Only when I could walk into that conference room and watch him sell off the last piece of his dynasty, see his expression when he realized it was his children who had pushed him to the brink of bankruptcy would I ever be free of him.

My phone rang again, and dread strangled me. No one else called me. Liv was it. My friends knew to text. With hesitation, I pulled it from my pocket, my fear validated when I saw my father's name.

As if the dashing of my happy ending hadn't already ruined my day. I was clinging to the thought that if I confessed everything to Tori, she would forgive me and stay with me until I could give her the wedding I'd promised. That if I walked back into that apartment and told her the truth, she would willingly wait for me. I stared at the phone, each ring like a sledgehammer to that last piece of hope.

"Father," I answered.

"William." I hated that name. The reminder that I would always be his son, his namesake.

"I'm in the middle of something."

"No, you're not. You're walking around the pond of your apartment complex."

My eyes flew up, looking for the source of his information but not finding it.

"Correction, your girlfriend's apartment. You've been busy down there, William. Maybe you can explain why my men saw her taking a wedding dress home today?"

Ire surged in my veins. "Are you having her followed?"

"Of course, I am. Now answer the fucking question."

My teeth gnashed as my mind searched for the correct answer, Liv's confession halting any admission.

"Awfully quiet now, aren't you? Always quick to come back at me, yet you have nothing because you've broken my rule."

I scraped my hand down my face as he continued.

"Almost broken. I want you home. No more playing around in Florida. I expect you in my office on Monday morning."

"Are you delusional? I can't do that, and that wasn't the agreement. My time at the firm isn't over."

"You broke the agreement when you proposed to that girl."

"She's not a girl," I snapped.

"It doesn't matter. You know the rules. No attachments. The company is your focus."

"I'm not doing anything that jeopardizes your precious company, Father."

"Love, attachments, relationships. They jeopardize everything I have built and everything you will inherit from me. You are my heir, William. That comes with expectations."

"Your expectations."

"Exactly. The only way you can run this company is by remaining cold, calculated, and unattached. I realized too late that your mother was a weakness. I won't let the same thing happen to you. Get your ass home."

"Mother was a weakness?" I wanted to reach through the phone and punch him. My hatred for him continued to grow every time he opened his mouth.

"Yes. All women are."

"God, you're a prick."

I could feel the tension through the line, envisioning his scowl. He hated when I talked back or called him out. Those were the times he reined in the leash tighter, cutting off my oxygen until I could only get back in line.

"Pack your shit and return home."

"And if I don't? If I give it all up?"

"Then I'll show you what a prick I can really be. Since you spent the holidays with the Hent family, I'm sure you realized they own a successful resort in the western part of Connecticut. The one your mother loved so much."

My body tensed, my grip on my phone so tight it was leaving indents in my skin.

"I have plans for that resort that include demolishing the original structure and building a multi-level hotel catering to the more elite skiers."

"You'll never do it. That resort is successful, and they already have an elite clientele. They would never sell to you. Besides, you promised Mom."

"She's been dead for almost twelve years. I don't give a fuck about promises that no longer hold meaning." My hatred singed me, and I strained not to throw my phone in the lake. "It would be a shame if they suddenly started having problems. Unhappy lodgers? Failed inspections? Faulty equipment? God forbid they have a tragic accident on their property."

And the true depth of my father's viciousness was there for me to see.

"You wouldn't." But I knew he would. When my father had an eye on a company or a location for one of his hotels, he got it. His hands had been dirty long before I'd even been a thought.

"I would. Did you know her mother was diagnosed with cancer seven years ago? That their medical bills drained their savings? That they paid for her college with loans they didn't tell her about because there was nothing left?"

Tori had told me about her mother, how she'd been in remission after battling breast cancer, but nothing of the finances. She'd spent two years working on their books for them and running the finances of the resort, but that didn't mean they'd given her insight into their personal finances.

I rubbed the space between my eyes. My father was boxing me in, giving me no way to escape.

"Leave her, and if you don't and decide she's worth the risk, not only will I take her parents down, I'll ensure her career spirals. I'll lock her out of every firm and ensure she never makes it further than answering service calls for the rest of her life."

He'd blocked any chance of me finding that escape because I would do nothing to hurt Tori, and he knew it.

"And if you dare tell her about any of this, I'll ensure it happens at the same time as I change the stipulations in your trust to make you wait even longer to find her again. I'm sure that by then she'll have moved on." The thought had me struggling to breathe. "Love is a weakness, William. I told you that years ago. It blinds you and leaves you vulnerable. Hard and uncaring, cruel and vindictive. It's the only way you'll ever step into my shoes."

I didn't want to step into his shoes. It was something I had never asked for but that he had expected since the day his only son was born. He wanted my obedience while he molded me into another version of himself.

"I hate you," I snarled.

"I never asked for anything different. Hate fuels. Love destroys. Pack your things. I expect you in my office ready to work on Monday morning. Your outside training is over. It's time to return to the fold and accept your destiny."

He was gone before I could say anything else. There was nothing to say. No way I could stop the train that had derailed again. I had done this to myself. To Tori. And she would be the one who suffered because of my selfishness.

CHAPTER 13

TORI

The elation of picking up my wedding dress had diminished through the evening. Gabe had returned from his walk and, upon finding me naked in bed just like he'd requested, had torn his clothes off and taken me with a passion that had left me riding wave after wave of ecstasy. He hadn't let up until my body was putty in his hands. It almost seemed like he would never touch me again and needed to fill himself.

I stood in the doorway, watching as he stared blankly at his phone while he sat shirtless on the couch. Something was wrong, and I was certain it had to do with the call from his sister. The pizza he'd ordered for us sat untouched in front of him, his half-empty beer bottle next to it. I'd never seen him so distant and worry gnawed at me. Determined to bring him back to the present, I went back into the bedroom and searched through the bins at the bottom of my closet. Pulling out a pack of colored paper and two pairs of scissors, I returned to the living room.

The pack thudded onto the coffee table, jerking him from his thoughts. Hazel eyes that no longer held their sparkle looked back at me. They roamed my body before lifting back to mine. A quirk of a smile formed, giving me some hope that he was still in there.

"You know you look entirely too sexy when you walk around in my T-shirts."

I dropped next to him, my hip bumping his thigh. "Don't get any ideas. You just wore me out for the next week."

"Too bad because I was planning to bury my face between your legs the rest of the night."

"You're naughty," I said, noting how even his playfulness seemed off.

He took my hand and rubbed his thumb over my knuckles.

"I love you, Tori, please never question that. I will always love you." His expression was so serious that fear crawled up my spine.

"Gabe, what's wrong? Ever since you talked to your sister, you've been acting off."

His eyes flicked from mine, a grimace drawing his lips down. "Nothing. It's fine." He turned his body toward me and cupped my face in his hands. "Tori, I need..." I watched as he slowly unraveled, and I couldn't help him because I had no idea what was wrong.

"What? Is there something you want to tell me? Another secret?"

Darkness crossed his eyes, the change pronounced. "No, it's nothing," he muttered, dropping his hands. "What are you planning to do with the paper and scissors?" Another mood shift and a sexy tug at his lips. "Something kinky?"

I stared at him, trying to read the man I loved, who was so hard to read sometimes. Who still kept secrets from me that I allowed because I knew he loved me too much to let those secrets ever hurt me. He glanced back at me, the hardness that had been there moments before gone. There was something in that look that pleaded with me not to push him, and I relented.

Smiling, I said, "Get your mind out of the gutter," playfully nudging him. "We're making paper flowers for the wedding."

I leaned over and picked the paper and scissors up. Handing him a pair and a few sheets of paper, I tried to ignore how he had flinched when I'd mentioned the wedding.

"You know, we can afford real flowers, right?" he asked, his brow raised.

"Of course, I do. These are to decorate the tables. A little something special to represent our love."

"Wait, we're going to make bouquets of paper flowers for every table?"

I laughed at his horror. "Not all at once. We have two months. So we make a little every night, and we'll have enough by April."

Again, the slight drop in his mood. Something was bothering him about the wedding, and I suspected his sister was behind it.

"Watch and learn," I told him, folding my paper like my mother had taught me when I was young and we would spend rainy days making crafts.

Gabe kept his focus on making the flowers, avoiding my eyes and keeping silent. By the time my fingers were sore, we had a pile of various colors and types. I picked up a pink one shaped like a daisy and handed it to him.

"This one will go on our table. Now pick one."

He took the daisy from me, his eyes suddenly so sad that it caused my chest to hurt. He clung to it while he picked up a yellow daisy he had made. It was a mirror of mine, and I took it from him, tears pricking at my eyes.

"Two halves of a shared heart," he said. "You will always own my heart, luna mia. There will never be a time when it doesn't belong to you. I promise you that."

My chest tightened, something nudging me that this moment was one I would look back at forever, that our paper flowers would be with us until they grew faded and worn.

"I love you, Gabe."

"I know." Hand wrapping around my neck, he brought me forward, our lips touching and reigniting the fire in me. Our flowers fell as he scooped me up and took me back to the bedroom, where he spent the rest of the night worshiping me.

I worried about Gabe during my entire shift the next day. He'd barely let me leave that morning, ravaging me before I could get out of bed and then grabbing me as I left the apartment, kissing me like the world was ending. His stamina had always been amazing, but I couldn't help but think he was desperately trying to get as much of me as he could before some expiration date.

I texted him repeatedly throughout the day, but his replies seemed forced, especially when I called and asked about what he'd been up to when I was on my lunch break.

"Just working," he said, his voice distant.

"Are you sitting in front of those computer screens again?" I asked.

He didn't answer right away, but when he did, I couldn't hide my shock. "They won't be here when you get home." There was regret in his tone along with guilt.

"Why? What happened?"

He worked nonstop. Even on his days off, he would spend time on his computer. Monitoring his investments was the only answer he gave when I questioned him.

"I... I should spend more time with you and not on my computer." The answer sounded false, and I scratched my head trying to figure out what he was doing. "I sold the monitors today, and I've got the hard drive loaded in my car to drop off at a recycle center."

I knew my mouth was gaping, but I was at a loss for words.

"It's fine, Tori. It takes up too much of my time anyway, and you deserve more of it." His voice cracked on the last words. "I need to go. I'll see you when you get home."

"Okay. Gabe..."

"Yeah."

"I love you."

"I know. I love you, too."

The conversation replayed in my mind as I finished my shift, and when I walked into the apartment, the empty spot in the corner of our room confirmed he had indeed removed his computer as well as his desk and chair. The only things besides his clothes he had brought with him when he'd moved in.

I tossed my shoes into the closet, relieved when I saw his clothes were still there and chastising myself for letting that doubt creep into my mind. Changing into a T-shirt, I left my jeans on, glad Saturdays were casual days. I tied my hair into a ponytail and walked into the other room, just as Gabe was walking in.

His smile was like a summer shower, reinvigorating me and erasing the unsettling sense of foreboding that had crawled over my skin.

"I tried to beat you home," he said, dropping a shopping bag on the counter and scooping me into his arms. His kiss left me in a puddle before he turned back to the bag. Emptying it, he said, "I'm cooking tonight. You're going to sit and put your feet up. My only request is that you load up *Lord of the Rings* so we can watch while we eat."

"*LOTR* tonight? What's the special occasion?" I teased, resting my elbows on the counter while I watched him.

Hazel with shades of amber met my eyes. His smile dropped but returned just as quickly, leaving me to puzzle over where it had gone.

"I want to spoil you tonight." He sized up my jeans and T-shirt, his brows crinkling. "I'm adding a request. I want you in your underwear and my T-shirt again. That look is enough to drive me mad."

I shook my head as I laughed. "And you want me to drive you mad?"

"Definitely." He turned to the stove, rattling around in the pans. "Go on, get that ass moving and plant it on the couch. If you're standing here with it sticking out like that when you're in nothing but my T-shirt, I'm gonna burn the food while I use this counter in ways I don't think the builders anticipated."

And my cocky, sexy man was back. Heat warmed my cheeks as I ran into the bedroom. Slipping my clothes and my bra off, I grabbed the T-shirt I'd had on the night before.

"You sure you want me over here?" I asked, walking toward the sofa.

"Damn it," he muttered, and I heard a can drop on the counter. His hands were lifting me and dragging me back to the kitchen before I could even let out a squeal. Planting me on it, he shoved my legs apart and stood between them, ensuring I could feel how turned on he was. "Guess I'll need an appetizer before dinner."

I fisted his shirt and pulled him to me, our lips meeting in a heated kiss that set my body on fire. His hands were greedy, his kisses hungry, just like he'd been the night before. Desperate and frenzied. He tore my shirt from me, flinging it across the kitchen before lighting sparks in me with his touches. Working his shirt off, I smoothed my hand over his chest, relishing his strength as he jerked me forward and his fingers drilled into me. My head went back, his fingers working their magic while his mouth devoured my breasts. I stood no chance. He had my body at his command, and my climax shredded me. Capturing my cry with his kiss, he removed his fingers, tangling them in my hair just as he penetrated me.

I rode the remnants of my climax as he tore into me, eclipsing me with his desire. His body moved with forceful thrusts and needy touches until my release soared, washing through me just as he broke, filling me with a growl that rumbled through his chest and claimed any remaining pieces that had slipped past his original claim.

Head dipping, his hand encased the back of my neck as if in an assertion of ownership. His eyes met mine, and in them I saw a myriad of emotions I couldn't pinpoint. His kiss left me devastated. There was so much emotion in it that I clung to his arms.

Planting a peck on my forehead, he said, "Take that sexy body into the other room before I skip dinner and make you my main course the rest of the night."

My breath caught at the power of his words, the dominating tone that had my insides knotting. He backed away, tucking himself back into his pants while his eyes skimmed over my naked body. "You're too perfect, Tori. Too fucking perfect."

He picked my shirt up and helped me put it back on, his touches tender again. Holding my cheek, his gaze was intense. No words, just a look that told me everything he needed to. Helping me off the counter, he returned to prepping dinner, watching me from the kitchen when I came back out from cleaning up. His sight remained on me the entire time he cooked and even when he brought my favorite gnocchi dish over so we could eat, they never left me.

Again, the sensation that he was soaking in all he could from me was there. We ate on the couch and curled up afterwards to watch the movie. Our paper flowers were now in a vase on the coffee table, a touch he must have added when I'd been at work. A symbol of us, two halves of the same heart, sharing space in our love for one another. An unbreakable love that I knew would never die.

That night, he made love to me. His touches slow, the frenzied need gone and in its place deliberate and reverent touches. As I came undone around him, he joined me, his climax chasing mine while he murmured, "Ti amo, luna mia," in my ear. The whispered words echoed through my mind long after.

Chapter 14

Gabe

The room was dark, the only sound Tori's steady breaths that told me she was sleeping soundly. I hadn't slept, instead holding her through the night, afraid to let go because once I did, I knew I'd never hold her again. What I was about to do would crush her, and she would hate me forever. There would never be a chance of finding her again, of confessing my mistakes or the secrets I'd kept from her. There would be no second chance for me.

I looked at my watch. Four thirty in the morning. My usual gym time, but this was Sunday, and she knew I didn't go to the gym on Sundays. I ran outside, but not this early. So, I'd snuck a sleeping pill into the glass of wine I'd brought her after making love to her. Insisting I wanted to watch the rest of the movie in bed while I held her. I'd really wanted to take her again, needing to memorize every inch of her over and over until I would never forget how it felt to touch her, never forget that she had once been mine. A constant reminder of what I'd lost when I returned home.

Moving her from my chest, I noted how she was still sound asleep. I sat on the edge of the bed, resting my head in my hands as agony ripped through my chest. I didn't want to do this to her.

Didn't want to leave her, and it was pure anguish to even think about what I was doing. Rising, I dressed.

Within a few trips, I had emptied my side of the closet and cleared my things from the bathroom. All traces of my existence were gone, packed up in my car. I'd broken the desk down and dropped it in the dumpster the day before, donating the monitors and chair, and putting the hard drive in my car. All that was left I had just packed.

Standing in the closet, I unzipped the bag with her wedding dress. It was elegant and simple, and I could only imagine how beautiful she would have looked. But it wouldn't be me she would walk down the aisle for. I was giving that up, and someone else would steal it from me. It would be foolish to think I could find her again when this was over. That she would ever want me back after this.

I knew I would hold on to that hope. If I didn't, I wouldn't survive. I removed the note from my pocket—one small gesture to hold on to her, to assure her that I loved her—and placed it in the dress pocket. A smile tried to form when I thought of how typical it was that Tori would have a dress with pockets. But it faded as I zipped the bag back up, sealing away our happy ending.

I took one last look around the apartment to ensure I had removed all traces of me. A clean break would help her get over me. I would never get over her, but I wanted her to be happy again, and with traces of me in her life, she wouldn't ever get there. Ebony locks draped over her pillow, her soft features tucked into it as she slept. I pushed a lock back and kissed her cheek, emotion threatening to undo me. Pressure formed behind my eyes as I slipped the engagement ring from her finger. I clenched it in my hand as my heart cleaved in two.

I needed to leave before I changed my mind. I was doing this to protect her and her family. It was something I kept reminding myself. I'd been selfish, and I wouldn't be anymore. Not if it risked her future and her family's.

"Ti amo, luna mia." I love you, my moon.

I walked out, not looking back at her, because looking back would destroy me. The paper flowers we'd made sat in the vase where I'd placed them last night. Tucking the ring in my pocket, I took the flower she'd made for me, leaving the other one. A piece of her to take with me since I could no longer have the rest of her.

Leaving my key on the counter, I left the apartment, locking the door behind me and knowing there was no going back now. Overcome with grief, I dropped my hands to my knees and held back the retching sob that was strangling me.

"Men don't cry," my father had told me on the day of my mother's funeral. I could still feel the sting of his hand from the slap I hadn't stopped.

Pushing back the emotion, I wiped my eyes with the back of my hand and took forced steps away from the heart I was leaving behind. Readying myself for the long ride home and a life where love would never find me again. Tori was the only one I had ever let have a place in my heart, and no one else would ever take it from her. She had branded it with her claim, and I would never remove that claim, even if she gave it up after my actions.

The morning sun bled through the floor to ceiling windows that lined the family room of my childhood home. It had taken me sixteen hours with minimal breaks to arrive, and each minute that had passed had fractured me further. I touched my finger to the pane I had fallen through so many years ago, remembering how it had shattered, just like I currently was. Broken into too many shards to recognize it had once been whole.

It didn't look like anyone had been to our home in the Hamptons for years. The house was eerily quiet, with the furniture draped in cloth sheets. My father had a penthouse in the city. Liv had one at the hotel we owned in the city.

"So, the prodigal son returns."

I saw Liv's reflection in the window as she entered the room but didn't bother turning around. I had texted her to let her know I was back in New York.

Hands in my pockets, I continued to focus my gaze on the dunes.

"For what it's worth, I'm sorry," she said. "I know what it took to leave her."

"Do you?" I asked, my voice too harsh considering I knew she had a sliver of knowledge. An inkling of the pain that held my body hostage.

"I do."

She moved next to me. I hadn't seen her in two years, and the distance weighed heavily between us. I glanced over at her. She had cut her long chestnut hair to her shoulders, giving her a more mature look. Her hazel eyes, twin to mine, had hardened from too many years of dealing with our father, of carrying the burden of the one he scrutinized the most and never hating me for it.

"You look like shit," she said, giving me a sad smile.

"I feel like shit." My voice broke on the last word, and I saw the pity in her eyes. For once, I wished we were a normal family. One like Tori's, where a moment like this demanded a hug that wouldn't ease the pain but would offer some comfort. But we weren't. My mother had been that person, and all hope of it had died with her. I turned my eyes back to the window, bristling against the well of tears that I refused to release.

"There's a penthouse suite for you at the hotel. Dad saved the top floor for you."

"And you?"

"I have the floor below yours. Only the best for his son. You get an entire floor to yourself, while I get only a portion, just like always. My curse for being born female."

It had always chafed me that he didn't see Liv as my equal, didn't recognize her firstborn status because she was female. My father was a sexist who would have been sued ages ago if his people didn't excel at keeping him from the regular staff of his companies. Their nondisclosure agreements—NDAs—guaranteed his biases stayed guarded. His lawyers, all men of course, ensured there was never a chance for a slipup. Discretion ranked as high as his greed.

"I'd forgotten how pretty it is here," I said, searching the sky and watching a bird swoop toward the water.

"Yeah. I never come out here anymore. There's no reason to." She rubbed her arms and turned away from the window. "I left your keycard for the elevator and your room on the table in the vestibule. Is that your piece of shit car out front?"

"It's not a piece of shit; it's only four years old."

"Whatever. Have someone get rid of it. Your Jag is in the parking garage, just let the valet know who you are, and they'll bring it up."

The door slammed behind her, leaving me to my thoughts.

"Welcome home," I muttered, the familiar ache returning to my chest. It was one I knew I would carry for the rest of my life along with the hollow sensation that reminded me I had left half of myself in Jacksonville.

I took a few more minutes to soak in the memories, realizing too many terrible events shadowed them to remain there any longer. Returning to the car, I glanced at the missed calls from Tori, too weak to listen to her messages or read her texts yet. It took me until I had settled into my new home to finally build the courage. Hearing her confusion turn to anguish then anger and back to anguish before the messages stopped drove me to pour a glass of scotch. I'd never been a hard-liquor man, but something told me this wouldn't be my last glass. Especially if it dulled the horrendous ache that left me feeling as if someone had cleaved my chest in two.

I fidgeted with the collar of my dress suit, straightening my jacket as I stepped from the elevator and through the doors. Sleep had been futile, and my eyes felt like cement blocks.

"Welcome home," Paula, my father's secretary, greeted me. "He's waiting for you."

I gave her a nod, the only functional response I could provide. Deep breath, emotions fortified behind a wall that was anything but supportive, I walked down the hall to my father's office. Hesitating for mere moments, I opened the door to his office and entered. The windows behind him offered a magnificent view of the city, the wide office attempting to make my father look small behind his desk. It hadn't worked. Nothing could make my father small. His presence dominated every space he was in.

"William." A terse greeting from a man who hadn't seen his son in years. He'd made an effort to attend my college graduation but hadn't bothered when I'd gotten my master's. Liv was the only one who had attended. Otherwise, it was only my brief and distant trips home that had left our paths crossing. "Nice to see you made the right choice."

"Choice?" I stalked over to his desk, my hands landing on it as I stared him down. "You gave me no choice."

"I gave you another chance, and in return for your obedience I left your plaything alone." He snapped his paper and folded it, still not looking at me. "If you remain loyal to your family and this company, I'll continue to leave her and her family alone."

"Plaything? Is that what you think she was?" His eyes lifted to me. Cold, heartless brown eyes. Emotionless like they'd always been. "Do you even know what love is? What it's like?"

His jaw ticked. The only noticeable change in his blank expression.

"Yeah, I didn't think so, or you would have never asked me to leave her."

He stood and slammed his fist on the desk, his calm cracking. "You knew the rules, the expectations. This is not a blame I shoulder. It's all yours. You led that girl on, knowing you were breaking the rules I established long before she walked into the picture. Don't let your guilty conscience slander me."

"Wouldn't think of it, Father. Your lawyers might come after me, or you might disinherit my sister as punishment for my mistakes. Maybe torment an innocent family because you didn't get your way?"

His eyes evaluated me before he sat back in his seat. "You need new suits. That one looks like it's been in your closet for ten years. I won't have the heir to my empire looking like a pauper. See that you dress appropriately tomorrow."

My fists clenched, and I bit back my retort, thinking of Liv and Tori, both of whom would suffer if I walked out like I wanted.

"Report to Frank in the mailroom."

"Mailroom?"

Dull brown eyes flicked to me like I was nothing more than a pest he wanted out of his sight. "Did you think I'd offer you the CFO position as soon as you walked in here?"

I had, and of course that hadn't been his plan.

"You'll earn your dues like your sister did. You still owe me the time you were supposed to be working at the Jacksonville firm but instead passed your time between a woman's legs."

The air hissed as it dragged through my clenched teeth.

"No more fucking around, William. It's time you accepted that you are my heir, and this company will be yours one day. Until that time, you will do as I expect, and that means making up for the year and five months you lost by leaving the position that would have given you the experience I expected from you."

"God, you're an asshole."

"And you'll be one, too, William. It's the only way men like me succeed. Now get out of my office and get fitted for new suits on your lunch break."

The paper snapped open again, his attention no longer on me. A clear dismissal. An order I would obey only because he had fueled my need to see our plan through again. To dismantle his empire piece by piece until he sat across from me at a conference table and realized I'd been behind it and was now the only one willing to bail him out of it. All while building my own empire and remembering every day why I despised him.

Chapter 15

Tori

A wide stretch had my fingers hitting the empty side of the bed. I looked over to see that Gabe was no longer there. Grogginess lingered as I reached for my phone, bumping into the empty wineglass. It had knocked me right out. I was a lightweight with wine, but it had been a nice topper to a wonderful night. Butterflies skittered through me when I thought of the way Gabe had made love to me. Like he was savoring every moment, memorizing my every curve and freckle.

Ten o'clock. Had I really slept that late? I never slept that late, and Gabe had a way of waking my body in the morning that made it impossible to go back to sleep, especially on my days off. I sat up, kicking my legs over the edge of the bed and wiggling my toes to wake them up.

After using the bathroom, I searched for Gabe's T-shirt, not finding it on the floor where it should have been. Maybe he was washing it.

"Are you doing the wash?" I called, expecting him to be in the other room. When no answer came, I peeked my head out of the bedroom, frowning to see he wasn't there.

Where did you go? I texted.

Still no answer, but if he was driving, his response would be delayed. Heading back to the bathroom, I turned the shower on, only then noticing his shampoo was gone. He must have headed to the store and let me sleep in. Always the sweetheart. My body hummed as I bathed, thoughts of his touches flooding my mind. As I combed my wet hair out, it occurred to me that his side of the sink was empty. No deodorant, no shaving cream. Nothing that had been there the night before.

A sinking sensation grew in my gut as I walked out to the living room, looking for any sign of him. His book was gone, and only my paper flower remained in the vase. I went to twist my engagement ring, my chest seizing as I looked down to see that it was gone. Stumbling back, I put my hand on the counter to catch myself. Below my hand was a key. I brought it up, my hand shaking as every part of me screamed it was Gabe's. Dropping it, I ran to the closet, finding it empty of everything he owned.

A strangled cry clawed its way up my throat. I ran to the window, searching for his car, but it, too, was not there. My heart pounded, every thud like a knife slicing into it.

This couldn't be happening. There was no reason for it. Maybe it was a joke. A horrible joke. Hands trembling, I called him, trying to rationalize the situation, but no matter how I tried, I could find no answer.

My call went to voicemail.

"Gabe, what's going on? Where are you? Why did you move all your stuff out and leave your key? I don't understand what's going on. Please call me."

I lowered the phone, my mind going in a million directions as I tried to come to some conclusion other than the one that was staring me in the face just like the empty closet. He had left me. But why? Rubbing my forehead, I stared at my phone, waiting for a call that never came.

As the day went on, I ran through every second of the last two days. Remembering how off he'd seemed, how he'd taken the call with his sister and insisted on taking it away from me. The thought of another woman crossed my mind, but that made no sense because he spent all his free time with me. We were inseparable... until now.

I remembered the computer and his story of selling it, wondering if that had been his first step to leaving me. Had he really left me? The suspicions and questions continued to barrage my mind until I tried calling him again. Voicemail and another message caused the tears to burn at the back of my eyes. The shock was wearing off, and as if it was a barrier holding my emotions at bay, I lost control. The tears flooded from me, my throat dry as my stomach churned.

He couldn't have left me. It wasn't possible. He loved me too much. He had promised he would always love me. But he had taken the ring and everything else, leaving an empty space like he had never existed. A sob, hoarse and raw, came from me. I curled into a ball, clutching the phone and watching the light fade in my room while I waited for a phone call that never came.

I called in the next morning, unable to move myself from the bed. Curled on Gabe's side, breathing in his scent, I called and texted him over and over. With each passing hour, my mood switched from anguish to anger, then back to utter devastation.

He wasn't coming back. I knew it in my gut, even though I tried to convince myself this was just some horrible dream. It wasn't. The pain was too real, burning through me like he had severed my heart in two, leaving a massive hollow space inside of me.

By nightfall, I hadn't eaten for two days, and my mouth was so parched from the heaving sobs and lack of water that I had to move. I peeled myself from the bed, my will to take steps to the kitchen nonexistent.

My phone rang, and I jumped, looking quickly at it as hope returned only to be dashed when I saw Cash's number. I stared at it, uncertain how to answer but knowing I needed help. Needed someone since the someone I wanted had left me.

I answered, gasping for words, my cry bunched in knots in my throat.

"Tor? Are you there?"

The words came out in a squeak, not forming.

"What's wrong, Tor?"

Holding my stomach, I doubled over as grief drowned me.

"Tori, talk to me. What's going on?"

The worry in his voice only worsened the ache that had burrowed so deep in me I knew I would never lose it.

"He... l... e... f... t...," was all I could sputter out before my tears overwhelmed me.

"Who left?"

I couldn't answer, the wave of emotion imprisoning me so that my organs threatened to seize up just as my limbs had.

"Damn it, Victoria. Who left?"

"Gabe," I said in a sob that wrenched me in two.

"Gabe left?"

I nodded as if he could see me.

"He left you?"

"Yes," I cried, the sound so foreign I didn't recognize it as my own.

Cash remained silent, and I shivered out another sob, my tears flowing freely again. Saying the words had left me riven just as Gabe had.

"Why would he leave? You mean he moved out?"

I sniffed, rubbing my nose on the back of my hand.

"Tor, you have to give me something here. Help me understand," he pleaded, and I could hear the emotion, that this was killing him because he was too far away to help me.

"I don't know," I managed, sniffing again. "He was gone

yesterday. When I woke." I swallowed, the salty taste of my tears hitting my tongue when I licked my lips.

"He wouldn't just leave you. I'm sure there's some explanation."

"My ring is gone and..." Another cry tore from my throat, scraping it like talons. "All of his things. He's gone like he was never here."

But I knew he'd been there because he had left my heart a shattered wreck of carnage.

"God, Tor. What happened? Something must have made him leave. Did you have a fight?"

"No. We had a wonderful night." Memories of his touch returned, and I bent over, fighting the nausea as more tears came. "I can't talk," I said, dropping the phone and running to the bathroom. I slid to the floor, throwing up and crying until I was so exhausted I curled up in a fetal position. I didn't know how to survive this. Nothing I'd ever experienced had hurt this badly. No one had ever hurt me like this, and to know Gabe was the source only worsened the agony because he had made so many promises that were now nothing but lies.

The next day was no better, but at least it was my day off. I tried calling Gabe two more times before I gave up. Before I convinced myself he was really gone. That he would never call me back. That I would never hear his voice again.

The next morning, I had no choice but to go to work. I managed to shower and dress. It wasn't until I forced myself to drink some water and have a piece of toast that I saw my birth control pack sitting with the vitamins I'd forgotten to take for the last four days. My heart pounded as I counted the days I had forgotten to take it. I had never missed a day, always taking it before I went to bed, but Gabe had distracted me the two nights before he left. His sex drive pushing me beyond exhaustion, and the last night, the wine had ensured I'd never made it back to the kitchen to notice I'd missed it. I hadn't set foot in the kitchen since that Friday morning. He had pampered me, getting me drinks and food, making dinner for me, and in my bliss I had forgotten.

And during the two days I'd been too devastated to move, I had missed it. Four days. I swallowed back the fear and quickly researched how to catch up, taking the pill I'd missed the day before and setting an alarm so I wouldn't forget the one tonight.

I shoved away the thought that the mistake could exacerbate my current predicament, ignoring the way my hands wouldn't stop quaking the entire time I drove to work. I lasted three hours before my manager sent me home because I couldn't stop crying on my calls. On my way out, I stopped on Gabe's floor, peeking my head into his manager's office.

"Tori, how... Are you all right?" Craig asked, rising from his desk.

I looked like hell. There was no hiding my red, swollen eyes, and no amount of makeup could conceal the dark circles under my eyes.

"Did you talk to Gabe?" I asked, my voice cracking when I said his name.

"No, he sent me an email on Sunday morning at like five o'clock resigning. His badge was on his desk along with his laptop. I stopped by to see you on Monday, but you were out sick. What's going on?"

"Did he..." Another crack in my voice. "...say why?"

His brows furrowed. "Only that something came up, and he had to quit. I figured you would have an answer as to why he would throw his career down the drain like that. I can't give him a recommendation when he just up and quit like that."

I crinkled my eyes, thinking it odd as well, but then everything about this was unexplainable.

"Okay, thanks." I turned to leave.

"Tori, what happened?"

My step faltered. "He left. That's all I know."

"You?"

I glanced back at him, pressure building behind my eyes again and warning me the dam I'd put in place when I'd left that morning was about to break for the tenth time today. "Yes."

His eyes held pity that broke me, and I wiped my hand under my eye. "I need to go."

I didn't give him time to reply, bolting from the office and getting myself as far from where Gabe had once sat, his beautiful hazel eyes lighting when I would come up to visit him on my break.

I cried the entire ride home, and when I climbed the stairs to my apartment, I found Cindy sitting in front of my door, scrolling on her phone, her suitcase beside her. She jumped up and took me in her arms where I broke completely into so many shards that I knew no one would ever put me back together.

***

Two and a half months had passed, but the gutted sensation hadn't left me. Everywhere I turned was another reminder of Gabe, and I often found myself downtown, staring at the river, wrapping myself in memories of our first kiss and the first time he told me he loved me. Memories I couldn't let go even when I should have. I was still wounded, raw and bleeding from his cruel departure, but I couldn't convince my heart to stop loving him. I wasn't certain it ever would.

I had no one in Florida, only acquaintances from work but no one I could confide in. And so I'd accepted a position in the Boston offices. Closer to home and with more opportunities in specialized areas. The movers would arrive the next day, and I was ready to leave the memories behind. To see if doing so would somehow heal me. Nothing else had.

I sat on the bathroom floor, holding my knees to my chest, and waited. My hands shook even as they clutched my knees. I had missed my period the month before and rationalized it as poor eating and lack of self-care. During that time, I'd lost ten pounds, letting my emotions feed me because I had no appetite for anything more. But when a second month had passed with no sign of it, I knew the truth.

The alarm went off, and I froze, my eyes riveted to the white strip of plastic sitting on the side of the tub. My heart thudded violently as I unlatched my hands and reached over for it.

"Please, please, please be negative," I said, tears breaking the words.

Tears that spilled when I read the result. Positive. Thumping my head against the wall, I sobbed as the anguish of losing Gabe thundered through me. I was pregnant with his child, and he'd left us both. Even if he hadn't known that I'd foolishly missed my pill, he'd still left me and now our child.

I needed to tell him. Maybe he would tell me why he'd put me through this hell if he knew there was another innocent victim. It was a desperate, emotional thought followed by a phone call that went to voicemail. Instead of leaving a message, I texted him.

Please call me. We need to talk.

It was still early. I hadn't been able to sleep and after convincing myself that my period wasn't coming, had gotten up at five. He was probably still at the gym. Strange how I knew his schedule just like I knew him. At least I thought I had.

I tried again at six, leaving a voicemail for him to call me. When I hadn't heard from him by seven, I knew he wouldn't call. For whatever reason, he never called me after he left. He had left me in the dark to crawl around and find my way out of the crushing boulders he'd dropped on me. Dialing him back, I readied myself to leave a scathing voicemail, but it didn't go to voicemail this time.

A woman answered.

"Hello?"

I tried not to drop the phone as the world crumbled under my feet.

"Is Gabe there?" I asked, finding my voice and forcing it to stay steady. Another woman. The one thing he'd promised me hadn't been his big secret.

"He's in the shower."

I held my stomach, trying not to let out the scream that was swelling inside me. What fractured remnants existed of my heart curled up and died.

"Look, I know who you are. Let him go. He doesn't need you clinging to him. Let him go and stop calling him. He won't call you back, and you're only making yourself look desperate. Move on just like he is."

She disconnected, but I didn't move. I stayed curled in a ball with my back against the bathroom wall, the phone still to my ear. He'd left me for another woman, moving on like I was nothing. The phone fell from my hand, cracking against the tile floor as I cried, rolling to the floor and lying there the rest of the morning.

By the time the movers arrived the next day, my eyes were puffy and red, my skin pale.

"Are we taking this or is it going in your car?" a mover asked me.

In his hands was my wedding dress, still bagged and ready for the wedding that I'd had to cancel. The invitations had already gone out, and every acceptance card that had come back to me drove another crack in my chest. The dress I would have worn, but instead I was packing up my life and moving in a futile attempt to free myself of the man who had left a lingering print on my soul that I would never be able to remove, no matter how he had damaged me.

"Can you pack it? Just be gentle with it."

He gave me a nod and walked away with it. I should have sold it, but I couldn't bring myself to. It symbolized a happy time I wasn't ready to leave behind. I rubbed my stomach, thinking of the baby growing inside. There had been moments on that bathroom floor when I wanted to give it up, to have a doctor remove it so I wouldn't have the constant reminder of Gabe in yet another part of my body. But I couldn't bring myself to do it. Even if he had hurt me beyond repair, he had given me months of happiness, and two nights of absolute bliss had created this baby. A child who would remind me that there had been good in all my suffering.

As I stood in the doorway of my empty apartment, I opened myself to the memories again. Moments curled up on the couch watching movies and eating pizza. Gabe cooking me dinner, making witty remarks and sending me melting grins while he tossed pasta, countless hours of our bodies tangled up in my bedroom and every other place he'd taken me. They had been good times. Ones he had ruined the day he'd left me for another woman. I closed the door, locked it for the last time, and left those memories behind.

CHAPTER 16

GABE

Two months, sixteen days, two hours, and three minutes. The amount of time since I'd left Tori and any chance of happiness in my life. I had yet to stop the countdown, each minute driving the dagger further into my chest.

I stepped out of the shower and dried off, pulling on a pair of slacks. Toweling my hair dry, I walked from the bathroom and through my bedroom. The suite my father had secured for me was massive, with two bedrooms and a window-lined view that overlooked the city. A view I never had time to appreciate because he worked me to the bone as punishment for my disobedience. I'd given everything up in his punishment, but it still hadn't been enough.

Intent on grabbing a cup of coffee, I headed into the living room, seeing Liv on my sofa with my phone in her hand.

"What the hell are you doing in here?" I asked, snatching the phone from her. There were two missed calls from Tori and a text. My heart beat frantically at the sight. I hadn't heard from her in over two months, and that had only worsened the guilt of what I'd done.

"I stopped by to tell you Dad wants you in his office by eight." She stood and smoothed her skirt out.

"I don't give a shit what he wants. How did you get into my suite?" I read the text—*call me. We need to talk*—not bothering to look up at her.

Stealing the phone from me, she closed the text out.

"Give me the fucking phone, Liv, and answer the question."

"Nice language, little brother." She puckered her red-stained lips and gave me the look she always did when she thought I had asked a stupid question. "Our father owns the hotel, and I'm the COO of the company. I can get a key to your room easily, and that's what I did."

My molars ground as I reached for the phone again.

"Block her, Gabe."

I stumbled, stunned by her demand. "I'm not blocking her."

"Then I'm not giving the phone back." She danced away from me, her spiked heels too close to digging into my bare feet. "Block her and delete her number. You need to move on and let her go."

"You're such a bitch. Give me the damn phone back."

"That's not news. I've always been a bitch, but you've gone soft, and she's the reason. If you don't block her, you'll continue to regret leaving her."

My motion stopped, and I gaped at her. "I'll never stop regretting it. It won't matter how many years pass or how many missed calls there are. The regret will remain, as will the guilt."

She sighed, her hazel eyes softening for a flash before turning hard just like our father's. Handing me the phone, she said, "Block her. I'm not leaving until you do."

The weight of the phone seemed to double as I stared her down. "I can't."

"You must. This is war, Gabe. You and I are fighting a ruthless, greedy bastard who will prey on your weaknesses."

"He already has."

"Exactly. If you don't let her go completely, you will remain soft, and he'll see it. The CFO position will never be yours, we'll lose the inheritance, and our revenge will fail. You need to be like him, just like I am."

I glanced down at the phone, pulling up Tori's contact information. "I don't want to be like him."

Huffing, she said, "Too bad. I didn't want to lose my mother at nineteen, but I did, and he was the cause. Remember why we're doing this, little brother." She peered over at my phone. "Why do you have a moon as her icon and Luna as her name?"

Because she was my moon, the light in my darkness. But I didn't tell Liv that. "It doesn't matter."

Her stare didn't waver, and I could feel the pressure of it as my hand lingered over the block button.

"Do it. If you keep hesitating, you'll be late for Dad, and he'll leave you in the mailroom for another year."

My finger shook as I hit block, another part of me severing.

"Now, delete her text chain and clear out your missed calls."

Eyes shooting up to her, I waited for an explanation of why I had to remove every reminder of Tori from my life, already knowing the answer. She crossed her arms and waited.

I pulled up Tori's text chain. Anger and anguish until the last calm text. "This last one is different. I really should—"

"No, delete it and be done with her, Gabe."

But I never would be done with her or over her or forget her. She would always be a part of me.

"William Gabriel Icinda."

When Liv used my full name, it was never a good thing. She was just as vindictive as my father, the mirror to him in some ways, especially after the last few years. As much as I knew she was right, it didn't make it any easier.

With a sigh that cut through me, I deleted the chain.

"How do you get anything done?" she complained, grabbing the phone back and quickly deleting my missed calls before jumping into my recent calls. I thought I saw Tori's number, but she deleted the list too fast for me to question it. She was back to Tori's contact information and had it deleted before I could stop her.

The sight shredded me, and I brought my hand to my chest to stop it from cleaving in two. She shoved the phone at me. "Now socials. Unfollow and block."

"Could you be any more cruel? I can't do that to her, she'll know."

"And she'll thank you for it later. You're giving her a clean break. Allowing her to move on. If you're following each other and spying on each other's lives, you won't be able to get over each other."

As much as it hurt, I followed her direction, severing the last of our ties. "It's not like that's your real handle, anyway. Why don't you just delete it?"

"It has been since I left school. Nobody knows my real name, and I prefer it that way. I'm not deleting my handles. It's the only anonymity I have, and I'm keeping them."

And it was my only remaining tie to Tori. A false name, one she would never find if she looked for me but one I didn't want to give up because it was all she knew.

Liv fluffed her auburn curls before smoothing her blouse down. The model of affluence, my sister lived her life in designer labels and expensive tastes. I sometimes wondered if she did it to hide the loneliness. A way to flaunt the appearance of happiness when deep down she was dying, just like I was.

Tori had been a moment of light, leading me out from the shadow of my father for just that brief time, but it had been enough to remind me that there was more. A painful reminder that would ensure I became the mirror to my sister the longer I went without it.

"Get out, Liv."

"You'll appreciate my help one day when you're a billionaire and Daddy's crawling away in shame as his empire crumbles around him."

She sauntered out, leaving me alone with my phone and a void that now encompassed my entire being. I did the only thing I knew would numb the pain, the thing I'd done after every beating and after my mother died. I closed off that wound, carving it into its own space next to the others and hardening myself to it and any emotion that would rupture it again.

CHAPTER 17

TORI

Five years, eight months, twenty-two days later

Fall leaves swirled as the wind picked them up, and I searched the yard.

"He's fine, Tor."

I looked back at Cash, who sat at the table across from me. Taking a sip of my coffee, I looked back out, seeing Reid run as his cousin chased him. It seemed like just yesterday he was a tiny infant, kicking his legs and giggling as I made funny faces at him. Now he was a rambunctious soon to be five-year-old whose curiosity constantly got him into trouble.

"Are you certain about this?"

Tearing my eyes from where my son ran carefree through Cash's yard, I said, "A hundred percent."

"But moving to the city?"

"I haven't gotten the job yet, Cash. It's just an interview. Icinda Holdings is one of the largest companies in the country. The opportunity is too good not to try."

I smoothed my finger down the handle of my mug, staring at the steam coming from it.

"It was, but they've gone downhill. Their stock is in the tank, and they've had to sell off most of their holdings. It's a shell of the powerful company it once was. I've heard talk of a buyout."

I'd read the same things, doing my research when talk of the CFO position opening surfaced. William Icinda's son was stepping down from the role to take another position. As with any interview, I stuck to facts and refused to search images, knowing that drawing the wrong conclusions based on looks would leave me nervous. But I hadn't been able to avoid the picture of the company's owner, William Icinda, Senior. Cruel and cutthroat, he'd built his company by taking over other holdings in a hostile manner. His picture had given me chills, and I was glad I'd be interviewing with his son and not him. The son, William the Second, was reclusive and stayed out of the news. His sister, Olivia, the COO, was just as secretive, so it had been easy to avoid making any assumptions about them because it was the father who dominated the headlines.

"All the more reason for me to come in and clean it up." And it would be work. Scandals at their resort properties, equipment breaking down, and inspection failings had led to the sell-off of all but one hotel in New York City. Their other holdings had also suffered problems, leading to manufacturing issues that led to liquidating them from the portfolio. All that remained were a handful of small real estate holdings and one hotel. It was almost like someone had dismantled the company piece by piece, and I wondered if that was only apparent to someone on the outside.

Cash ran his hands through his hair.

"You always did like a challenge," he muttered. "But you're in for an uphill battle."

"The structure is still there."

"But you've got two spoiled rich kids to work with who clearly don't know what they're doing because the company has fallen apart on their watch."

I shrugged, knowing it would be rough, but I needed the job and the money.

"What happened, Tor?" he asked just as his wife, Brandi, came in. She took the chair next to his, pulling her sweater around her.

I rubbed my wrist, remembering the pressure that had been there. The perfect job at Bradman Holdings, a resort chain that rivaled Icinda's glory days. They had recruited me two years ago after I'd worked my way to the top at a Boston company, restructuring its finances and turning the company around. I'd loved Virginia, but things had turned ugly, and I gave my notice just as the opening at Icinda came up.

The deck doors swung open, and Reid came tumbling in with his cousin, Shelby. His cheeks were pink from running, his thick auburn hair messy. He looked up at me with bright hazel eyes and ran to me.

"What are you two up to?" I asked, brushing leaves from his coat. He was so much like his father that it hurt to look at him sometimes, but I never once regretted having him. He'd been the light in my dark world, a ray of love that healed part of my heart. The rest remained damaged from Gabe and had never healed. I doubted it ever would. It still belonged to him even after all he'd done.

"Shelby got me," he told me, giggling as he talked.

"Come on, Reid. Let's go color."

She tugged his hand, and they were off again.

"Are you sure you don't mind watching him?" I asked Brandi.

"Not at all. Shelby loves having him here, and it will keep her busy while I'm working."

"When are you leaving?" Cash asked.

"I check in tomorrow. I want to take Reid to the FAO Schwarz store and through Central Park."

"Are they really putting you up at the Fiaba?" Brandi asked.

The Fiaba, the last hotel in their portfolio, was world-renowned and one of the most exclusive hotels in the city.

"Yes," I replied, taking another sip of my coffee. "I've heard it's beautiful."

"Take pictures," she said, her excitement shining in her eyes.

Cash rolled his eyes. "Overpriced and gaudy."

I exchanged glances with Brandi, as the same excitement tingled up my arms.

"You two are too much," he said, scooting his chair back. "So, you'll bring Reid back Tuesday morning before the interview? That's a lot of travel."

"I know, but he'll have fun, and I want him to have the experience, especially if I get the job. One of the perks is a suite at the hotel. Free housing and maid service every day. Who can turn that down?"

Brandi leaned forward, her eyes wide. "You need to invite me over. I'll leave Cash with the kids, and we can pamper ourselves."

"Really Brandi? Aren't you late for your weekly manicure? I don't think you need more pampering, sweetheart. I already spoil you enough." He gave her a kiss on the head. "And she hasn't even gotten the job yet."

He walked out of the room, leaving me and Brandi to giggle over all the accommodations we could take advantage of at the hotel.

Reid bounced up and down the entire drive into the city. I nervously clutched the steering wheel, swearing I'd take the train from then on and never drive my car out of the parking garage if I got the position. Dragging his little suitcase behind him, he made me run him through the revolving doors three times before a lady with a poodle in her purse gave me a disapproving look.

I couldn't help but crane my neck as I walked into the lobby. Gorgeous was an understatement. With gold inlay patterns of leaves set in the stained wooden beams, murals of Italian scenes spilling across the walls, and a chandelier that took up the entire space, it screamed decadence. Bellhops bustled with racks of designer luggage while guests leisurely strolled after them with no care in the world.

This was the world I was stepping into, and it was one I could adapt to but one I never felt comfortable in. There were times I missed the casual days of working for my parents. I had traded it for expensive dresses, suits, and heels that gave my feet cramps.

Keeping Reid's hand in mine, I walked up to the concierge desk to check in. I made casual conversation with the woman behind the counter, not indulging my true reason for my visit and assuming the company had been discreet with booking my room.

"You're on the tenth floor," she said, circling my room number. "You'll need the key card to access that level." She went on to explain how to work it before wishing me a pleasant stay and offering to have someone take our luggage to the room.

"That would be wonderful. I'm taking my son out to see the city. Which way should I go to get to the toy store?"

She gave me a big smile, telling me about a candy store that her daughter loved.

"Did you hear that, Reid? A candy store." My heart came to a screeching halt when I looked down to find him gone.

Swiveling my head, I scanned the lobby.

"He's over there," she said, pointing to the left where he was walking around with his head up, gawking at the murals. "I'll have your bags sent up to the room. Have fun."

"Thank you," I said, running to get him. Eyes on him, I snatched him just as he was tugging on a man's pants.

"Reid Nathaniel Hent, what have I told you about wandering away from me?" I turned him toward me, fear still shaking my limbs. "You frightened me."

"He's so tall, Mommy. Will I be tall like that?"

I peered up at the man, my heart slamming into my chest when hazel eyes with specks of amber met mine. My world spun, the pain I'd carried for five years trampling over any healing I'd done and ripping the wounds raw.

CHAPTER 18

GABE

Adjusting my cuff links, I waited for my attorney to tell me the words I'd fought to hear since I was sixteen.

"It's done. He's still in the conference room talking to his attorney."

Relief cascaded through me. It was over, and now I would walk into that conference room and tell my father his downfall had been my doing and Liv's. Sweet revenge that had been too long in the making.

I shook his hand as he told me he would follow up with me later in the day. After I dealt with my father. Rolling my neck, I turned toward the hall that led to the special meeting rooms, but a tug on my pants leg stopped me. I peeked down to see a small boy with large eyes and a mop of brown hair gaping up at me.

"Reid Nathaniel Hent..." That voice and that name had my world turning silent as I watched his mother scold him. Her lush ebony hair slipped over her shoulder when cornfield-blue eyes locked with mine. The heart I'd buried behind layers of foundation and years of cold indifference cracked open again, the fissures spilling liquid lava into my veins. For over five years, I had mounted an attack on it, refusing to set it free again. Ignoring every flirty look, every pretty face, every invitation because there would never be another who held my heart. Another I wanted to touch, to kiss, to hold. To murmur that I loved her as she slept in my arms. There was and always would be only Tori who rose to her feet, her eyes still holding mine.

"Tori." Her name came out in a fractured whisper.

She looked as beautiful as she always had, matured over the last years. Her style sophisticated, her hair loose in long waves that begged me to tangle my fingers in them.

"Gabe." Emotion enveloped the word, and I could see it twisting in her features. The longing was there along with the hurt and anger I suspected she had carried since the night I left.

"Do you know him, Mommy?"

Her eyes flicked to the boy, and mine followed. Agony raked through me with the knowledge that she'd moved on. She'd left her love for me behind and found another man. What had I expected? That she'd wait around for me? After hurting her and leaving her in the middle of the night. But some part of me had. That same part that had clung to the thought as the only way to survive.

"A long time ago."

I stared at the boy. He was young, maybe four or five. My sight jumped to hers, anger and hurt now rife in my blood, the walls refortifying around my heart. The ruthless man I'd become since that day, taking over.

"I see you moved on quickly," I snapped.

She reeled back, her hands tightening around the boy's shoulders.

"How dare you? After what you did, you have no right to even talk to me."

Her words stung, but not as bad as the fact that she'd gotten over me so fast.

"You're right." I adjusted my cufflinks again. "I have a meeting to attend. It was nice to see you, Victoria."

I walked off, knowing if I didn't, I would falter, and it would leave me vulnerable. This was a moment for cold calculation and cruel vindictiveness, not memories and what-ifs. Every step reminded me of the day I'd left her, the pounding of my shoes against the marble jarring my nerves as I fought to leave her again.

My father was still in the conference room, and he looked up when I entered.

"William. I told you there was no need for you to be here."

"It's done?"

He sat back in his chair and dismissed his attorney with a nod. "It is. Forty years of building this empire and now there's nothing left."

"You've got your fortune. The offer was a lucrative one, just like they were for each piece of the business we sold off. Should have you living in retirement no differently than you live now." But I knew it wasn't the money that drove him. It was the business, and with every failure, his mask had slipped. No longer was he the proud, arrogant man who had beaten me to teach me a lesson.

He may not have retained his billionaire status, but he was still a multi-millionaire. Liv and I had ensured that with each buyout. It was more than I'd wanted to give him, but he was too greedy to sell his holdings to a low bidder, and as his CFO, it would have raised suspicion if I'd advised him differently.

I dragged my finger along the table. "How does it feel, Father? To no longer be the one on top? The one who holds the power?"

He stood, placing his hands on the table. "I have more power than you. I just sold off your future and your sister's. Ensuring you'll never get another cent from this business. There will be no CEO position for you. You failed so miserably in your last position, it's a shame I won't get to see you fail at that one."

"Always the asshole, right up to the end."

"And you're still the weak, whiny boy who clung to his mother's skirt."

I clenched my fists, stalking over to him.

"I want you to remember this moment. When you're alone in your dusty penthouse, taking your last breath, I want you to remember that I was the one who brought you to your knees."

His eyes creased.

"Luna Industries bought this hotel, the last piece of your measly holdings. But it falls under an umbrella of companies owned by two people who have despised you their entire lives. Two people who took great satisfaction in seeing you fall from your pedestal, Father."

I pulled the official charter of the very first LLC Liv and I created, from my pocket and slapped it on the table.

"Fiorella Holdings. You might recognize that name since it was my mother's. A company buried so far under others that it's impossible to trace and impossible to identify the founders. Me and Liv. Every company that has scooped up your dying investments is owned by us, including this one."

He ripped the document from my hand and stared at it. "This proves nothing."

"It proves everything. I want your stuff out of my office by noon today. If not, I'll have security see you out."

"You sabotaged me? To what? Make a point?"

I stepped further into his space. "I did no such thing." Even though I had with a team as undercover as my companies. The same men I'd formed a bond with in school and who were now private shareholders in my company, soon to be board members once I cleansed the board of the corrupt and enabling fools who currently dominated it. "And no, not to make a point. Just to make you suffer. Get out of my hotel, Father."

His lips pulled up in a sneer, reminding me of when I was young and he terrified me. I was no longer that young boy. "You are still my son. Still my namesake and an Icinda."

"Much to my frustration. I won't let that stop me from cutting off all communication with you. Now get out."

He threw the document at me and stormed from the room,

slamming the door behind him. I couldn't hide my smile as I gave him time to leave the hotel before I called Liv.

"It's ours," I told her, exiting the conference room.

"Did you tell him?" Her excited voice came through the other end.

I walked into the lobby, my eyes searching instinctively for Tori. Wiping my hand down my face, I said, "Yes. You would have enjoyed the show."

"Ah, I knew I would, but this reward was yours to reap, little brother."

Heading to the check-in desk, I said, "I'll tell you all about it when I get into the office. Gotta go."

I ended the call, gesturing to the woman on duty.

"Good morning, Mr. Icinda. How can I help you?"

"There was a woman in the lobby earlier. Pretty with black hair and blue eyes. She had a young child with her."

"Oh, Ms. Hent. Yes, her son is adorable."

"Mm hm. I need her room number."

I followed her over to her computer, watching as Tori's information loaded.

"She's staying in the tenth-floor suites."

I frowned, wondering why she would be on that floor. My father usually reserved the two floors below mine for special business guests, which included the floor Liv's place was on. Maybe he'd opened them up and not told me.

I thanked her and turned away, stopping as a thought occurred to me. "Did she say what age her son is?"

"No, but we have it since he's staying with her. Let me see." She scrolled another page. "Ah, he's four. He'll turn five at the end of October."

"Thanks." I walked away in a daze, my mind churning through the numbers. Five years, eight months, and twenty-three days since I left Tori. My feet stumbled, and I reached out to the wall to brace myself. It couldn't be possible. The shock on her face when I'd commented on how quickly she'd gotten over me had been for good reason.

Straightening, I swallowed back the emotions that were threatening to break my composure—pain, guilt, fear, disbelief. Following my path outside, I nodded to the valet, who called my driver. It was good I wasn't planning to drive myself to the office. I likely would have crashed.

During the drive, I convinced myself the staff had typed in the wrong date when booking the room. That had to be the case. The alternative was too gut-wrenching to believe. That not only had I left her, but she'd been pregnant when I had.

After a brief recap of my meeting with our father, I left Liv, intending to transfer my office to his. She had already packed up his belongings and left them at the front desk. The guards posted out front would escort him out. I couldn't wait to hear his reaction to that.

"Weird to see you in here and not Dad," Liv said, popping her head in.

"Yeah."

Head cocked, she studied me. "What's wrong?"

"Nothing. It's just been a long day."

She strolled closer to my desk. "No, there's something wrong. You should be celebrating. And I don't mean with a glass of scotch in your hand." I swirled the glass and took a sip. "We should be out toasting his defeat. We finally did it."

I stared out of the office windows, the city skyline looking back at me. "I saw her today."

"Who?"

"Tori."

"Should I know who that is?"

I looked back at her, reading the confusion. I'd forgotten that I had kept everything about Tori from her. Not that she would have asked, but after she'd had me delete Tori's contact information, I'd never mentioned her again. Keeping all my thoughts of her to myself.

"The fiancé I destroyed." Saying the words brought it all back. The excitement of proposing, the moments of happiness that existed despite the storm brewing outside our bubble.

"You did?"

"Yeah." I scratched my neck before taking another drink.

"And?"

"She has a kid." Who might be mine, I wanted to add, but I didn't have confirmation, and without that, I would stay silent.

"Oh, well, that's good. See, she moved on without you. Now you can move on and stop pining over her."

"I'm not pining."

"Whatever you want to call it."

A knock at the open door had my eyes rising to see Tina, our head of Human Resources. "I have the files for tomorrow's candidates."

I rubbed my forehead. "That's tomorrow morning, right?"

"Yes, do you want to review them now?"

"No, just leave them. You and Liv reviewed them. I'll look at them before the interviews."

She dropped the files on the corner of the desk. Liv flicked through them as Tina left.

"Your morning interview is the one I'd go with. Smart, proven track record, worked her way up fast. The afternoon has good credentials, but he has a pattern of leaving positions quickly. Screams red flags and lawsuit threats to me."

"I'll keep that in mind when I talk to him." Rising, I stretched my neck, trying to release the tension that had been sitting there all day. "I need to take a walk." She closed the files and swiveled to me. "Maybe take the rest of the day off."

Brow pinching, she said, "Let her go, Gabe. It's been over five years."

Yet it seemed like only hours ago that I'd left her. Being so close to her again had awakened a yearning in my chest I couldn't ignore. I left the office, my mind on Tori, where it stayed the rest of the day.

My knock echoed through the quiet hall, and I rested my hand on the doorframe while I waited for an answer. Nerves threatened to make me walk away, but I shoved them down just as Tori answered. Her dusty eyes went large before they narrowed.

"Go away." She tried to close the door, but I stopped it with my hand, forcing my way into the suite. Crossing her arms, she glared at me, daggers piercing me with the anger etched in her features. Still, she looked as beautiful as the day I first saw her. Ebony hair clipped up in a messy bun that left thick strands draping down her neck. Her jeans hugged her figure, her sweater engulfing the top half. "What do you want, Gabe?"

"It's the tall man." I turned my attention from her to see the boy in his pajamas staring up at me.

"You've seen tall men before, Reid. Uncle Cash is tall. Now get back into bed." Still, he stared at me, his head tilting, and I wondered if he saw the similarities like I now did. They were striking, and my need to hear Tori admit it, to drive the daggers further into me, had me clenching my fists. "Go." She shooed him off with her hands, and he ran back into the bedroom.

"Whose is he, Tori?"

She whipped her head around toward me. "So fast to accuse me of moving on, yet now you want to know?"

I rubbed my temple. "It was a gut reaction."

"I have several gut reactions to you being in my presence, but I'm not jumping to conclusions." She pressed her hands on her forehead before storming to the coffee table and grabbing her wine. After taking a sip, she said, "He's mine. I'm his mother and his father, the one who carried him for nine months by myself, the one who gave birth to him without his father there, the one who is raising him to be nothing like his father."

It was like a slap in the face, but I deserved it.

"You left me, Gabe. Two months before our wedding. Disappeared without a trace, blocked me, erased all our ties to each other. Without a word. Decided another woman was what you needed—"

"Is that what you thought?" I almost stumbled back with the accusation.

"I didn't have to think it. Get out, Gabe. I owe you nothing."

"Tori, I didn't—"

"Get out and just leave me alone. You hurt me enough. I won't let you hurt him, too."

I pinched the bridge of my nose. Frustrated, I stepped closer to her. "Who is his father, Victoria?" I could hear the anger surface, but it wasn't directed at her. It was self-inflicted because I had let this happen, and it was aimed at my father for forcing my hand, for threatening to damage her.

"Two months before our wedding, Gabe. Why do that to me? Why pretend to love me when you had another woman? Why bother?"

"Damn it, Tori. There was no other woman. I have no idea what you're talking about. Now tell me who the fuck his father is." The ire came out in succinct sound bites and a level of swearing I barely used unless pressed. Her head snapped back, eyes flaring.

"He's yours. There was no other man, and I didn't rebound quickly. I never rebounded because you left too much damage." The crack in her voice simmered my aggression. Her confirmation of what I feared tore me into pieces.

"Why didn't you tell me?" I asked before I realized I'd just added fuel to the fire.

Her features twisted as she snapped, "Tell you? So you could ignore my texts and my calls? Delete my voicemails? I tried to contact you for weeks until I convinced myself you weren't coming back. And when that pregnancy test confirmed that I'd been stupid and too wrapped up in you to use my common sense, I tried again. That's when I realized what a liar and cheat you were. How your word meant nothing. It didn't help the pain, didn't erase the wound you left, but it helped me regain my dignity. I tried to tell you, Gabe, but you were too busy with your life to care."

I took another step toward her, still trying to figure out why she thought I had cheated. The idea made my guilt tenfold because never once had I even thought of anyone but her. To this day, there had been no other that I'd even looked at, let alone touched. No one would compare to her, so I hadn't even bothered to look.

"Stop," she said, putting her hand up. "Leave, Gabe. It took me years to get over you." Tears glistened in her eyes, making the blue sparkle. "Just leave me alone. Please, I can't have this conversation. The wounds are still too raw, and you don't deserve it."

Five years, eight months, twenty-three days, and she had just admitted her wounds were still raw, like mine. As much as I wanted to celebrate it, I hated that she'd suffered for so long. That I had been the reason for that suffering.

"Please." Her plea was a broken string of syllables, and I lowered my head.

Tucking my hands in my pockets, I said, "You're right. I deserve nothing but your anger. I'm sorry...for everything."

I turned and walked away, knowing it was the best for her. All I was doing was causing her pain again, and I didn't want to ever have her suffer at my hands again.

Returning to my room, I sat in the dark, scotch in hand, and thought about all I'd lost that day and all I would never get back. Knowing I had two interviews to prepare for, I flicked my light on and pulled the two folders out Tina had prepared for me. After flipping through the first one, Liv's thoughts on the red flags were now my thoughts. I needed someone who would stick with us because restructuring the pieces of our business that we'd broken up through the past few years wouldn't be easy. I had plans for the company, and that meant a sound financial plan. One I had in place for our part of the business but had slaughtered in my father's company. It was time to merge the resorts and hotels back together and then segment the other branches into an organized flow.

That meant someone who wouldn't leave after a year. I dropped his folder to the floor, thinking his interview would be nothing more than a waste of time. My drink fell from my hand when I opened the second folder and stared at the name on the resume.

Victoria Hent.

Chapter 19

Tori

Sleep was what I needed, but it evaded me. Staring at my reflection, I wondered if even concealer could hide the circles under my eyes.

Gabe. Had I envisioned a day when I would run into him again? Yes, but it had gone much differently in my head the million times I'd played the scene. Seeing him, having him that close, smelling his cologne, looking into those gorgeous hazel eyes, turned every scenario to ash. He had changed. I could see it in the hard edges of his features, the icy looks, the expensive suit, and the scent of scotch on his breath. Hardened and refined.

This was no longer the man who drank beer and ate pizza with me while we binge-watched fantasy movies. This was a shrewd businessman. But underneath were glimpses of the man I'd loved, and I thought it would be better if those didn't exist. If he was the cold man who accused me of having a child with another man, I could easily admit I should never have spent the past years wondering if I could ever forgive him. If there could ever be a second chance for us.

The emotion in those eyes had told me there was. That under the hesitation and steely glances lived the adorable smirk and fiery kisses that had once lit my soul on fire. And that he would give them freely to me again.

"He left you for another woman," I told myself. Although I didn't really know if that was the truth or if he had simply moved on. Either way, it hurt because I had never moved on. My heart had never healed, and I didn't know if it ever would.

Glancing at my watch, I snapped out of it, finishing my hair and makeup. I had taken the train out with Reid and met Brandi earlier in the morning before returning to the city. If I got this job, that round-trip commute would need to continue until I could find childcare for him. He was too young for kindergarten, and the daycares I had contacted all had waiting lists.

One last glance in the mirror had me shrugging my jacket on and grabbing my purse. I considered giving the front desk a piece of my mind for giving Gabe my room number but thought it better to wait until after my interview. I didn't want to go in fired up.

They had sent a car for me, and so I took the time to look at the city while the driver took me to their headquarters. I couldn't get over how busy it was, how many people there were in one city. It would take some adjustment, but maybe I would grow to like it.

"Miss Hent." A woman in her late forties came toward me, and I recognized her from the virtual interview I'd had with her the prior week, Tina.

"Please call me Victoria," I told her as I shook her hand.

"Noted. Have you had a chance to do some sightseeing?" she asked as she led me to a set of elevators.

"A little. I took my son to FAO Schwarz and Central Park yesterday. But there are so many things to see, I'm sure it will take me weeks to see them all."

"True," she said. "The floor we're going to is reserved only for the higher-up positions. Although we now share this building with two other companies, the top six floors are all functions for Icinda Holdings. The floor you were on is designated for the call center."

"Is each floor a different division of the company?"

"Mostly," she said, guiding me out of the elevator onto a floor that screamed luxury. This was not where the employees spent time; this was for the heads of the company. We walked through the glass doors, where a woman answering a phone gave us a smile and a wave.

"That's Paula. Officially our receptionist but she's more like the gel that holds everything together, as is Sean, who is William and Olivia's assistant. He ensures everything runs smoothly."

"Does the new CFO have the same assistant?"

"Yes," she said, leading us around a U-shaped hall with a conference room in the center.

At the end of the hall, open space led to three more offices, these decidedly larger than the ones we'd passed. Ones that were two times bigger than my last office. Two massive offices sat across from each other, one with a beautiful woman who was rolling her eyes at the phone and gesturing with her hands as she talked to whoever she had on speakerphone. She looked so elegant, I subconsciously fixed my suit jacket, thinking I now looked under-dressed until I realized who she was.

"That's Olivia Icinda. You won't meet with her today, but she sometimes takes part in the follow-up interviews."

Rich beyond belief and handed every opportunity. These weren't people who had worked for their positions. Their father had handed them everything. No wonder her clothes looked like she spent ten times what I did on my three-hundred-dollar suit. Because she probably had. I glanced at the other office, which was dark. William Icinda the second, the reclusive one but still a man who had never had to fight for his position or his money.

"Will I still be interviewing with Mr. Icinda's son?" I asked just as we reached the last office, confused about why his office was dark and unoccupied when I'd expected to interview with him.

"Of course, he's just in here."

My eyes left the empty office and focused on the open door

ahead of us. I stumbled, my foot twisting in my heel as my eyes locked with Gabe's.

"Are you all right?" Tina said as Gabe approached the door. His eyes were shadowed, the steely look he'd had yesterday darkening them.

"I'm fine," I said, staring at Gabe. "Just a little thrown off."

"William, this is Victoria Hent."

"Miss Hent," Gabe said, extending his hand as if we were meeting for the first time. I swallowed back the emotion as I played along. Tingles shot up my arm when our hands touched.

What was he doing here? My world was spinning, and my legs were wobbling as I followed him into the office.

"I thought I was meeting with...I mean, I thought..." I didn't know what I thought anymore, and now I sounded like a fool.

"Tina, would you mind getting Miss Hent a bottle of water before we get started? I should have gotten Sean to get it, but I didn't think."

"Of course. I could use one myself. I'll be back in a few."

She bustled out of the office, closing the door behind her.

"What is going on, Gabe? Are you stalking me now? First my hotel room and now this?"

That gorgeous smirk that made my insides melt peeked out at me. "I'm not stalking you. It's a long story." He ran his hand through his hair, and the man I still loved returned.

"Why did she call you William?"

"Because that's my name. William Gabriel Icinda. William Icinda is my father, but I used his mother's maiden name for anonymity when I was in Florida."

My head swirled. "Secrets. This is one of your damned secrets?"

"I told you. It's a long story."

The door opened, and Tina came in with two water bottles.

"I was just explaining to Miss Hent that I took over as CEO as of yesterday, which is the reason my last position is open."

Yesterday, when he'd been standing in the lobby, telling me he had a meeting to attend. When our lives had intersected once again.

"Yes, we've had quite the change in the last twenty-four hours. Please sit."

I hadn't realized Gabe and I were still standing, our eyes on each other and nowhere else. This was a disaster. I couldn't interview with him, pretend I hadn't spent eight months of my life loving him and the next five years in a love/hate relationship with memories of him as I raised our son.

Still, I sat, unsure what my next move would be.

"So, tell me why you left Bradman Holdings, Miss Hent," Gabe asked, entirely too calm and unfazed by this.

"Victoria," I corrected him. I tried not to fidget with my hands. "I spent three years bringing them to financial security, stabilizing their balance sheets, and cutting out frivolous costs. It seemed like the right time to leave and look for a new challenge." I rubbed my wrist, that firm hold still itching under my skin. The memory of the day I'd walked away still fresh in my mind. "We parted on friendly terms, as I'm sure you know from your diligent background checks."

He glanced at Tina, who nodded. That's why he had said nothing yesterday. He had left the vetting up to others and not bothered to look at the candidates until now. More questions followed, typical for this level position and ones for which I had prepared. Listing the ways I could make the company more efficient and build it back to the dynasty it had once been.

"You mentioned a son the last time we spoke," Tina said, and Gabe's spine went straight.

"Yes, Reid. He'll be five later this month. The joy of my life, even if his father abandoned us."

Out of my periphery, I saw Gabe's jaw tighten and thought I heard teeth grinding.

"Oh no, one of those," she said.

"Yes, he was a real winner. I'm glad I don't have to deal with his lies anymore."

"I'm not sure what this has to do with the interview, so let's focus back on the subject."

The level of discomfort in Gabe was well worth derailing the interview.

"I can assure you it's relevant." I faced him, sitting back in my chair. "You see, it made me more resilient being a single mother, raising my son by myself with no help. I could have moved home with my family, but it pushed me to move to Boston, where I climbed my way up the ladder until I was ready for a new challenge, which I took on at Bradman. They saw my potential, and I helped turn the company into one that others see as a model when studying its financials."

That clenched jaw didn't ease up.

"If that bastard, pardon my language, hadn't left me in the middle of the night, I might have been content to spend the rest of my life never reaching my potential."

"And would you have been happy then?" he asked me, folding his hands and leaning onto his desk.

"Yes, I would have. But that's not the way my cards played out."

I detected a flicker of regret in his amber eyes and dropped my sight to my hands, hating how it teased my unruly heart.

Tina turned the conversation, asking a few more questions before the interview ended.

"I'll walk Victoria out," Gabe said, as we stood. I didn't really want to walk out with him or be stuck in an elevator with him, but that's exactly what happened.

"Why did you really leave Bradman?" he asked as the doors closed.

"It doesn't matter. I'm not getting the job, not that I'd want it now."

He turned to me. "I don't care what happened in our past. If you're the more qualified candidate, you'll get the job."

"I'm sure your girlfriend would love to know I'm working with you."

A frustrated growl came from him. "I don't know why you think I left you for another woman, but I didn't."

"Then you got over me fast." The door opened, and I stepped out quickly, not wanting to be that close to him anymore.

"Tori," he said, catching up to me.

"Thank you for the interview, *William*. I'm sure you'll be in touch, but I won't get my hopes up." I put my hand out to shake his, knowing the contact would only remind me of how my heart still belonged to him.

"Tori, there was no other woman. There never has been."

"No more lies. Just shake and say goodbye." I heard the fracture in my last word, the emotion that seeped into it.

He took my hand, the shake lingering as his eyes held mine. The intensity of the moment reminded me of our time together, causing flames to leap in my chest.

"Goodbye, Gabe." Letting go, I left him there, feeling his eyes on me as I made my way out of the building. I didn't look back, didn't stop to think about how everything he'd told me had been a lie and I'd never known him at all, until I was on the train to get Reid.

William Icinda. The billionaire's son. How could he have kept that from me? And why? I hated to go back to that time, to think of him when I was in my delusional state of bliss, planning to walk down the aisle to marry the man of my dreams. But he had been nothing more than an illusion. A carefully crafted lie that I'd fallen for.

"So, did you get it?" Cash asked as I climbed into his car. With the train station so close to their home, he and Brandi had set up a schedule to pick Reid up in the morning and me when the interview was done. We'd set up the same for several days in case I had a second interview. The company had booked the hotel for the week, and I had intended to use it until I'd found out the truth. I should have packed up and checked out when I left the interview, but I hadn't thought it through. Maybe I'd take Reid back to the toy store in the morning and check out in the afternoon.

"That's doubtful."

He glanced at me as he pulled out of the lot. "What happened? You were so confident yesterday."

"William Gabriel Icinda happened." Just saying his name caused my chest to spasm.

"The CEO?"

"His son, the new CEO and the man who might as well have left me at the altar."

Cash slammed on his brakes, narrowly avoiding the car in front of us. "Wait. Gabe? The dick who left you pregnant two months before the wedding is the CEO and Icinda's son? I'm so confused."

"Join the club. Apparently, he didn't use his real name for privacy reasons when he lived in Florida."

He gnashed his teeth, something he did when he was thinking. "That's actually really smart. He goes incognito, falls off everyone's radar, and bides his time in financial firms to gain training and knowledge that ensures he succeeds when he takes over as CFO."

I stared at him, trying not to gawk. Although I'd been the one to take the finance path, my brother was a finance nerd at heart.

"Still doesn't mean I don't hate the man," he added.

"Yeah." I stared out the window, my emotions and thoughts jumbled and confused.

"What are you thinking, Tor?"

"That I'm glad I have enough savings to live on while I look for another job."

Chapter 20

Gabe

The city continued its motion below my office, people going through their days oblivious to the raw ache in my chest and the mess of emotion seeing Tori had stirred. For years I had planned for the day I could find her without the threatening shadow of my father. Waited for our takeover to come to fruition so I could find her again. I had known she would hate me, argued there was a strong possibility she had moved on. Still, hope had driven me. But of all the scenarios I had imagined, this had never been one.

I still couldn't wrap my head around her accusations, and the idea that she'd thought I left her for another woman was one I'd never imagined. It scraped over that ache, gouging it so it was as unbearable as it had been when I'd first left her.

I glanced over at the folders on my desk. The second interview had been miserable, but after Tori, the man stood no chance. Her resume was impeccable, even if she had ten years less experience than he did. I also knew that despite our past, she would be the perfect fit for the company.

Scraping my hand through my hair, I grabbed her folder and headed to Liv's office. She put her finger in the air as she finished up a call. Looking around her office, I realized how bland it was, just like mine. No family pictures, no special moments. Just a piece of expensive art and windows overlooking the city. Sterile and cold, just like we'd both become.

"How did the interviews go?" she asked when she finished the call.

"Spot on with the red flag guy."

"See, I know how to pick them out."

I dropped the folder on her desk. "I need you to meet with her."

Eyes rolling, she leaned back in her chair and crossed her arms. "I don't do interviews by myself."

"The hell you don't. Put her on your schedule and meet with her. I want your opinion."

"I gave you my opinion."

"Damn it, Liv. Meet with her."

Her hazel eyes flicked up from her desk, irritation reflected in them. "You're awfully on edge today."

I didn't answer, crossing my arms and waiting for her to agree. Huffing, she flipped through her calendar. "Fine. I have time at three tomorrow."

"Thank you. I'll have Tina reach out to her."

As I turned to leave, she said, "Is this about your run-in yesterday?"

My step halted long enough for her to read the answer.

"You need to move on, Gabe. Like I did."

I peered over my shoulder at her. "Did you? Because I don't think you did, just like I never will."

The truth of my words stung her as much as it did me. A reminder of what we'd both given up in our pursuit of revenge. I'd been willing to give it all up until the shadow of my father had destroyed everything. And here I was wishing there had been some other way because, if given the chance, I would have done it differently. I would have made the life I wanted with the woman who still owned my heart and the child we would have raised together. But it was too late, and now I made my life with nothing but loneliness, scotch, and more money than I'd ever spend in a lifetime.

I didn't know what I was doing standing outside Tori's door again. Or why I hadn't let Tina tell her about the interview with Liv. A need to explain my reasoning, to convince her to take the job I knew I would offer her, ruled my decision. My reasons for wanting to give her the job were selfish. I wanted her there, to see her every day even if she couldn't be mine. I knew it would be torment, but I deserved it for everything I'd done to her. And then there was our son. A boy I didn't know but wanted to because I had seen myself in his eyes the last time I'd seen him. The younger version of me, before the abuse and trauma had infected my life.

The door opened, and Tori's smile faltered. "I knew I should have checked out earlier. I thought I made it clear this morning was goodbye. It's more than you gave me."

The jab stung, and my hard exterior cracked some. But then, Tori had a way of fracturing it, just like she had when I fell for her. She had brought out the man I wanted to be. Not the one driven with revenge, hard and cold.

"May I come in?"

"Asking this time? So polite. I guess I know how you got my room number. Perks of being the owner?"

"Something like that." I waited for her to open the door further, and for a moment, I didn't think she would.

"Mommy, can I take my cars on the trip?"

Tori turned her attention to the voice. Our son's voice. A tingling sensation formed in my gut.

"Just one. Pack the others up."

"You're packing?" I said, walking into the opening she'd unintentionally given me when she'd moved from the door.

"Hi!" If anything could have soothed the turmoil in me, that tiny voice could.

"Hi there."

Tori looked between us, her eyes growing sad before she said, "Reid, that's enough for tonight. Go brush your teeth and put your pajamas on. I'll be in to tuck you in soon."

"Can I look at my book while I wait?"

She stooped in front of him and brushed his hair from his face, and my heart swelled. This is what I'd missed. What I'd given up, and that hurt more than anything. Giving him a kiss on the head, she answered, "Of course you can."

"Yay! Bye, mister."

He ran off, closing the door behind him and leaving us alone again. I dragged my eyes from where he'd run to and met Tori's.

"We're checking out in the morning."

"No." I blurted the word before even thinking.

Head cocked, she put her hands on her hips. "No? You don't have any say in what I do. You gave that up when you left me two months before our wedding."

She turned her back on me and folded a small blanket with sports cars on it.

"Stay. Please. You have another interview tomorrow with Olivia."

Her gaze snapped to me. "Olivia...your sister? The sister you don't get along with and who lives out west somewhere? Oh, how the lies are coming back to bite you."

I rubbed my temple, knowing I'd done this to myself. "I had no choice but to lie."

"You had a choice, and you chose to lie. Just like you chose to leave me. Was anything we had real?" Her brows scrunched, eyes turning a rich navy as they pleaded for me to say there was.

"Us. We were real. My feelings for you were real, and everything we had together was real. I never lied to you about any of it."

"Yet you did. I don't know who you are, Gabe. William. God, I don't even know what to call you."

"Gabe. I hate William. It's my father's name, and he insisted I use it, but my mother called me Gabe, as does anyone I care about."

Her features softened, but the divide between us was so large I didn't know how to cross it. Or if I had any right to ask to cross it.

"Stay. Liv doesn't know who you are. She never knew your name or anything about you other than that I love you...loved." But the admission had slipped before I could stop it.

I saw the subtle transition in her eyes, the way they jumped when it had come out. Right before they hardened again.

"You didn't tell her about me? Of course, you didn't because I was just some fling to keep you occupied. Biding your time with me. Playing house until you grew bored and moved back to your affluent life. Why would I expect you to have told her about me?"

She threw the blanket onto the couch and ran her hands through her hair. "I don't think I can do this, Gabe. It took me so long to free myself of you, and even then...you left a stain. And it's hard enough every time I look at Reid. I see you in him. In his eyes, his hair, the looks that cross his face, his gestures. He's so much like you that it's like this knife that continues to plunge into me and reopen the stitching on my wounds."

And the walls around my heart continued to crumble, the pain like electrical shocks.

"To even consider working alongside you. I...I can't."

Taking a page out of my father's playbook, I said, "You left Bradman for a reason. Unexpected and unexplained. I think you need this job, Tori."

She stepped back, her eyes wide, before she recovered. "I don't need a handout from you."

"Damn it, it's not a handout, which is why I want Liv to interview you. She's an unbiased third party, so there will be no question about the decision. You're qualified and the best candidate for the job. If Liv agrees, it's yours, but it won't be my decision. It will be hers."

Dusty blue eyes stared back at me before they looked away. The urge to close the distance between us and tip her chin to force her eyes back to me had me palming my neck and dropping my head.

"Just stay, Tori."

"I'll think about it."

"Three o'clock. I'll have a car here for you at two-forty."

Not knowing what else to do, I walked away. As my hand reached the door handle, I heard, "Did you ever love me?"

Gripping the handle, I answered, "I've always loved you, luna mia." The emotion threatened to tear me to pieces, so I left, not turning back as the sound of her inhale penetrated the silence.

A knock on my office door followed its opening to reveal Liv peeking in. I'd stayed locked in my office during the time Tori was talking with her, surprised that she'd changed her mind and accepted the second interview. When I'd left her suite, my confidence had been low, and I'd spent the night tossing and turning until I gave up at three thirty and went to the gym to release the tension.

"She's good. Intelligent, sharp, detail-focused, confident. I wouldn't bother interviewing anyone else. What is this? The sixth candidate you've interviewed?"

I sat back in my seat, putting my hands behind my head. "Yeah, but none seemed like the right fit."

My father and I had been at each other's throats over the last six months, and knowing what was coming, I'd accepted the demotion he'd thrown at me as punishment for questioning him. As if stripping me of my title would make him feel better about his failing company. He'd ensured I was the one interviewing, and while I'd only found one candidate who seemed like he might work, my father had vetoed the suggestion. Liv believed he was planning to hand the role back to me after he made me suffer, and that was his reason for turning the candidate down.

It had given me the chance to have Tina vet candidates for the day I would take him down and take over the company. And I supposed it was good that we'd already told the man I'd considered that he hadn't gotten the position because fate had put Tori back in my life.

"Hire her," Liv said. "I'm leaving. I have a manicure scheduled at four-thirty."

"I can't be the one to offer the position to her."

She scrunched her eyes. "Then have Tina call her, but it makes more sense for you considering the position level. It's not like you're hiring her to manage the hotel. This is your CFO."

Leaning forward, I rested my elbows on the desk. "That's why you need to be the one to call and tell her."

"I'm not in charge of this company. You are."

"It's her, Liv."

More scrunching. "Who?"

"The woman I left in Florida. Tori was her name. You know her as Victoria Hent."

It took a lot to shock my sister, but her mouth gaped, and she almost tumbled as she came over to my desk.

"I didn't know until I reviewed the files the night before the interview. That's why I wanted you to interview her. An impartial decision."

"She's the one?"

"Yes." I didn't want to tell her about Reid. My son. It left me in twisted knots of regret every time I thought about him.

"Why would you even think about hiring her? Are you mad?"

"No. She needs the position, and she's the most qualified for it. You even said so yourself."

"But to work with her after all this time. Why would she even consider it after seeing you yesterday?"

She sat in the chair, studying me intently.

"I think there's something behind her leaving Bradman."

Brow furrowing, she said, "Like what?"

"I don't know, but she left in a hurry just when she had the company financials turned around. Why not stay and enjoy the calm?"

"She said she needed another challenge."

"Maybe." And it sounded like something Tori would do.

Sighing, she looked at her nails. "You're making me late for my appointment."

"I know. Call her in the morning and offer her the job. Full package with private shares, the suite at the hotel, and all the other perks that come with the position. She'll accept if someone other than me makes the offer."

"That should tell you something. If you're doing this as some kind of self-punishment, don't. You've punished yourself enough."

But I hadn't. Especially now that I knew we had a son. No amount of punishment could ever be enough for leaving her pregnant and alone to raise him. For leaving him without a father.

"I haven't, and I'll be fine. Just make the call. Tell her to start on Monday."

She rose and smoothed her skirt out. "That's the day we meet with the board."

"Then it will be an excellent introduction to how I plan on operating this company now that it's in my control."

Chapter 21

Tori

The office was massive, the view incredible. I unpacked the few things I'd brought: the water bottle my parents had given me for Christmas with the UConn logo on it, the stress ball Cash and Brandi had sent with me saying I'd likely need a replacement within days of working with Gabe, and the framed picture of Reid. He was playing with his cars and had lifted his head to give me a magnificent smile before focusing back on them.

I'd spent the last week weeding through the boxes I'd had in storage after the company had paid to have them shipped to my new home. A luxury suite in the hotel that made the one we'd stayed in look like a small apartment. It wasn't the townhouse with the fenced-in backyard I'd had in Virginia, but it came with the job, and with the cost of rent in New York, it made the most sense.

Gabe had given me my space, and I hadn't seen him since his last visit when he'd convinced me to interview with his sister. The next day had been a series of internal debates where I'd finally relented and called to accept the position. And since that day, I had reconsidered my decision hundreds of times until my need for the job outweighed my emotional need to flee. Now I was standing in my new office, facing the reality that I had accepted a job that would have me working side by side with the man who had left his mark on my heart before he had left it in tatters.

"Coffee?"

I looked up to see Olivia standing in my doorway, two cups of coffee in her hand.

"You look like you could use it."

Insult or observation, I couldn't tell. Olivia Icinda was a difficult woman to read. She was gorgeous with long auburn hair, the same color as Gabe's, and hazel eyes that, like his, were fascinating in how they reflected hues. There was an edge to her though, hard and prickly but wrapped in an arrogance that screamed 'I'm rich' in a way that Gabe didn't have about him.

"Thanks. I guess I could."

She placed the coffee on the desk but didn't leave. After putting my purse in my closet, I looked back at her, trying to figure out what she was waiting for. Astute eyes studied me, perceptive and inquisitive.

"He told you, didn't he?" I asked, understanding that look.

"After our interview and after I told him to hire you."

I held my head tall, knowing she was looking for a weakness she could pounce on. Maybe she was doing it to protect her brother, maybe she was just that kind of person.

"We have a meeting with the board at nine. Our first since Gabe took over." So, she called him Gabe as well. Score one point for telling me the truth, but the amount of lies he'd told me still left the tally uneven. She picked up the picture of Reid, and I wanted to grab it from her, feeling protective of him. Her eyes jumped to mine, perfectly groomed brows furrowing. "God, he's Gabe's, isn't he?"

"Did he fail to mention that?" I snapped, biting my cheek because this was my first day and it wouldn't do for her to fire me within the first hour.

Her hard exterior slipped, regret deepening the hues of her

amber eyes. She looked back at the picture. "He looks just like my brother did when he was that age. Before..."

I swallowed, knowing what she was about to say, remembering his story of the abuse. Another truth. And suddenly my view of this woman morphed. The older sister who had wanted to protect her little brother, but he had been the one who had protected her all those years. What had she suffered knowing all he had endured? And had her life been any easier?

She returned the picture to my desk. "Did he know?" she asked. "Before he left?"

Guilt slashed her features, and I wondered what she would have to be guilty about.

"No. I found out two and a half months after he left. I tried to tell him, but..." The agony returned. "He had moved on already, so no, he never knew."

She looked like she wanted to say something but shut her mouth before she set the words free. Pushing her hair off her shoulder, she sauntered out of my office saying, "Welcome to the team," without turning back to me.

Scratching my head, I tried to put the strange conversation to the side. Tina had given me my credentials, and so I logged into the system, amazed that they had my information loaded already. The technology differed from Bradman's, but Gabe's assistant Sean had swung by earlier and scheduled time later that morning to train me on the systems.

It would be a learning curve, but I'd had the same when moving to my last company. I spent the next twenty minutes acquainting myself with the rest of the floor, meeting the other executives in the company. I had just returned to my office when Gabe walked in. The air rushed from my lungs, and suddenly I was in Jacksonville again, twenty-four and in love. It didn't matter how much I hated him, my heart would always be his, and it leaped every time I saw him.

"The board has arrived. We're heading down to the fourth-floor conference room to meet with them."

"You don't use the conference room up here?" I asked, not sure what else to say and surprised I'd found my voice.

"No, that's for our team meetings. The board doesn't get that luxury."

Confusing to say the least since the board was an oversight to any company. Disdain had tainted his words, which left me even more confused.

He stepped further into the office. "Are you all right?"

Eyes squinting, I said, "Am I all right? That's an odd question coming from the man who left me devastated two months before our wedding, left me to clean up the mess of RSVPs and cancel arrangements all while trying to convince myself to keep breathing because the pain would someday cease. Which it did not, by the way. Oh, and then learning I was carrying his child and having him ignore my calls to tell him that." I walked around my desk and right up to him. "And you know the worst part? The one that really drove the knife through what remnants there were of the heart you shredded? That you were with another woman when I was curled up on the bathroom floor clutching the pregnancy test in tears."

His mouth fell open, confusion creasing his eyes.

"Yeah, guess you know now that every time you lied to me about not leaving me for another woman, I knew the truth. Unless you just moved on that fast. I'm not sure which thought hurt more, but they both did. So don't ask me if I'm all right when I now work for that man."

"Tori, I didn't—"

"Don't, Gabe." I turned back to my desk and grabbed my notebook and pen. "Let's just go to the meeting, and then I'll question my sanity as to why I subjected myself to this."

Hazel eyes fractured with color and a wounded look met mine when I turned back around.

"Time's ticking, you two," Olivia said from the hall. "It's your show, William."

Another moment of conflict. She only called him Gabe to those who were close to him, using William for business and the others they worked with. Yet more layers to a man I had thought I knew but in reality, was a mystery to me.

"Sure," he said, running a hand through his hair.

Demeanor morphing, he straightened his suit jacket, his eyes hardening. I had to admit he looked sexy, even if I didn't want to. Suits were his thing, and he made them look good. I bit my lip as he turned and walked out of my office without saying another word.

I remembered how darkness would shadow his features, hiding the playful, sexy man and turning him into something frightening. This was that man. The one he had kept from me but who had slipped in occasionally. And I stood frozen, wondering if this was the expectation and with me he'd been free of it. Able to be himself, the man he wanted to be.

I shook off the thought and the sensation that was burning in my chest. Catching up, I hopped into the elevator with Gabe and Olivia.

"Did you bring the paperwork, Liv?" he asked her.

"Yes. This is going to get ugly, Gabe. Are you ready for it?"

He adjusted his cufflink. "I've been ready. Let's just hope Victoria can stomach the carnage."

The elevator opened, and he walked off. "Welcome to my world, Victoria."

Olivia followed, and the doors started closing. I stopped them just in time, holding my spine straight and proud as my heels clicked on the floor while I wondered what kind of carnage he was talking about. I suspected I was about to see the side of Gabe that he had shielded me from, and I wasn't sure I would like it.

The board had already taken seats around the large conference table when we entered. A startling picture of white men who looked old enough to be my grandfather. There was no diversity whatsoever.

I took my place next to Olivia, noticing we were the only ones from the top floor who were there.

"Gentlemen."

"This is highly inappropriate, William. Where is your father? He called the meeting, not you."

They didn't know about the transition. He hadn't announced it yet. For a private company, that wasn't unusual, but Icinda was large enough for it to matter.

Gabe remained standing, and I noted the changes from when we'd been younger. The tension he held in his jaw, the matured features of his face, the tiny lines at the corner of his eyes. But mostly I noticed the confidence. He'd always had it, but this was more pronounced. A don't mess with me or I'll ruin your life kind of look. He was a threat in a suit, all muscle and power that emanated from him.

"My father is no longer CEO and no longer the owner of the company."

A murmur went around the table.

"As full owner of Icinda Holdings, I have appointed myself CEO and no longer have need for your oversight."

The murmur grew.

"This is ridiculous. Where is William?"

Gabe slammed his hand on the table, and the room went silent.

"Olivia."

She rose and handed everyone a packet.

"This is the official announcement that Luna Holdings now owns Icinda." I tried not to show my reaction to the name. "Icinda will be folded under the umbrella of my corporate holdings, and restructuring will begin this week. That starts with you."

Dead silence and wide eyes.

"You can't fire us. The CEO does not have that power," a man who looked about seventy with thick white hair and dull green eyes said.

"True, as CEO I don't have that power, but as this board has always been more decorative than useful and seeing that I am the majority shareholder in both Luna and Icinda, I do. Terry, you can stay. The rest of you can leave. I'll have my attorney contact you about compensation for the private shares my father rewarded you for doing such a pitiful job."

The room erupted, and I tried not to react. Gabe held his ground as the door opened and two men dressed in black suits with earpieces walked into the room.

"Please escort these gentlemen out of the building."

Gabe stood, arms crossed, his glare not faltering as the men left in a huff. I squeezed my hands in my lap, trying not to show any reaction.

"Well played," the remaining man, Terry, said, sitting back in his seat.

"I don't play," Gabe said, rolling his neck. "No longer is this board a decorative title given to my father's loyalists. There's too much at stake. Olivia will work with you to find replacements. I'm cutting the board down to seven members. I have hand-picked two, and I expect you to fill the remaining seats with diverse members. I will only consider those vetted through Olivia."

Arms unfolding, he continued, "I've brought Victoria Hent on board to fill my former position. With her track record at Bradman, she'll have the financials for Icinda back on track."

"After you let them unravel?" Terry dared. His observant green eyes held Gabe's.

The corner of Gabe's mouth twitched. "That's why I kept you on the board, Terry. You're not afraid to speak up. And no, I didn't unravel my father's business." He glanced at Olivia. "Well, maybe I had a hand in that, but my father's failure is due to his greed and arrogance. Think what you'd like to think, but make sure you understand the success of the company is the only priority from now on, not title dropping and ego smoothing. Good day, Terry, I'll leave you in Olivia's hands."

He motioned for me to follow, and I trailed his brisk steps out of the room, holding my tongue until the elevator closed on us.

"It would have been nice to have a heads-up that you were cleaning house."

"Probably, but seeing as it's your first day, it didn't seem necessary." His eyes remained focused ahead.

The door opened, and he continued his long strides, ones I had trouble catching up with. Dropping my stuff in my office, I ran back out and caught up with him just as he stepped into his office.

"Are you following me for a reason?" he asked, taking his jacket off and laying it over a chair. My eyes jumped around the space, taking in the magnificent view of the city behind him, the liquor bar, the private bathroom, the small sitting area. Things I hadn't noticed during my interview because seeing Gabe had left me shaken. It was an office fit for a king.

"Did you sabotage your father's business?"

He stormed over and slammed the door so quickly that I jumped. "I did a lot to get where I am today, Victoria. Gave up everything and, yes, may have made a few unethical moves. Nothing I did was unnecessary. If you don't like it, then leave."

My pulse quickened as the dark side of Gabe came into full display. I hated that it made me even more attracted to him. He stood there, his eyes steeled, his muscles tense.

"Will I find anything in the financials that is illegal?"

"No. They're clean. The company is clean, as is every company I own."

I tilted my head. "Explain."

Hazel eyes narrowed before they turned away from me. He walked across the room, pouring himself a glass of liquor before taking a sip. I couldn't help but wonder when he'd turned to hard liquor and when he'd started drinking in the morning.

"Fiorella Holdings is the head company, but below it are multiple layers of LLCs, including Luna Holdings. Most are real estate holdings, but certain branches have businesses that complement the main real estate structure. A few limo services, some restaurants, rental properties, the list goes on. Within the main real estate holdings are the pieces of my father's empire. Your job is to piece those back together so Icinda returns to its former glory."

My forehead creased as I tried to understand. "Why, when you were set to become CEO, would you dismantle your own company and buy your father out?"

He took another drink. "That's not something you need to know."

"More secrets." No response, just a gaze that held mine with an intensity that burned me. "You've changed, Gabe. What happened to you?"

Placing his glass on his desk, his long legs closed the distance between us. "This is me, Tori. The person I've always been. The one I was before I met you." Hand scraping through his thick hair, he said, "But who I was with you...was honest. You're the only person with whom I could be someone different, someone I had lost, someone I gave up the day I left you because he was impossible to be with anyone but you."

I didn't know what to say. The emotions his confession had stirred left me confused as sadness and regret swirled along with a longing to go back to that time.

He released a sigh and turned from me. "We have a team meeting at eleven to discuss the restructure and next steps. I expect you to bring your ideas and to speak your mind. I hired you because you're good, Tori. What you did at Bradman shows that. Bring that intelligence to the meeting and don't hold back with your suggestions or your thoughts. But if you accuse me of doing anything illegal or nefarious in front of anyone in this office, I'll replace you."

And those emotions solidified, returning to the hate that had festered for years.

"Understood."

I left the office, the weight of his gaze still on me as I questioned why I had taken this job.

Chapter 22

Gabe

I had thought being a jackass would make this easier, but it hadn't. The look of revulsion that had splattered across Tori's features before she left my office had ensured it was hell. I hated that she'd witnessed that side of me, that she now thought worse of me than she already had. I was tempted to tell her the truth, to let it all spill out, but I doubted my confessions would do anything. There was no taking back the pain I'd brought to her. The fact that I'd left her. What made it worse was that she thought I'd left her for another woman. That piece was driving me mad because it wasn't true, and I didn't know how to make her believe me. She'd sounded like she had confirmation, and that made no sense.

As the day ended, I knew I needed more answers. If she'd give them to me. I knocked on her open door, and her head lifted from where her focus had been on packing up her bag.

"I don't have the figures finished yet," she said as I approached her desk.

"That's fine." I hadn't expected her to have any reports done since she was still learning the systems and the company.

I picked up the picture on her desk, relieved to see that it wasn't of another man but of Reid playing with toy cars. His grin was ear to ear. He reminded me of the times before everything had changed. When I was still innocent and oblivious to pain. I wanted to get to know him, to learn all about him, but I didn't think I had that right yet. Not when I'd been absent in his life all these years.

"I need to catch the train," she said.

My sight jumped to hers. "A car can take you back to the hotel."

"No, Reid is with my brother in Fairfield. His wife, Brandi, is watching him for me until I can find daycare."

So, her brother had married. I wondered if seeing his wedding come to fruition had hurt her as much as I imagined it had. Placing the picture back on the desk, I chose not to torment myself with the thought.

"There's a daycare on the first floor for employees. Why not enroll him there?"

"They're full. I called five other centers, but they all have year-long waiting lists. Until I can find something, I'll continue to run him to Fairfield in the morning and at night to bring him back."

"That's ridiculous. You take the train out and back every morning and afternoon?" It was easily an hour and a half each way.

She shrugged. "I can't bring him into the office." A ghost of a smile formed, and I realized just how much I'd missed her smiles. "He'd have fun running his cars up and down the conference room table, though."

"Might be fun."

Her eyes lit before they dimmed again.

"I'm going to miss the train."

"Take the company car. Just let the driver know your morning and afternoon schedule. No more train. I'll take care of the daycare situation."

"No, we're fine."

"Tori, let me do this. I've done nothing else for him or for you, let me do this."

She nodded, her eyes dropping.

I took my phone out and dialed the car service. "The car for Miss Hent needs a change of route."

"Yes, sir. What's the new destination?"

"Fairfield. She can provide the address when she reaches the car. Going forward, until I tell you otherwise, the route will be Fairfield and back each day."

"I'll let her driver know. He's on his way."

I said my thanks and hung up, meeting cornfield blue eyes that had my heart skipping a beat.

"You didn't have to do that."

"I did." I continued to hold her gaze, unable to think because she left me so rattled.

"Was there something else you needed, Gabe?" Her voice had softened, the angry edge gone.

I moved back to the door and shut it.

"That's not a good sign. What now?" she said, her brow arching.

Clearing my throat, I said, "Tell me why you think I left you for another woman."

A flash of emotion crossed her eyes, turning them a deeper shade of blue. "It's not like you gave me any answers, Gabe. You disappeared from my life, blocked my calls, and unfollowed me on social media. It was like everything we had was something I'd imagined. And it hurt. Sure, you didn't know I was pregnant, but you still left me almost at the altar." She rubbed the bridge of her nose.

"But nothing I did should have led to that conclusion."

With anger contorting her face, she snapped, "You left me after telling me you would always love me. After promising your big secret wasn't another woman. After setting me up for the most devastating thing to ever happen to me. God, I don't want to rehash this anymore."

"But there was no one. Now tell me why you think there was. I deserve an answer, Tori."

"You deserve? You deserve nothing." She stormed around the desk, her anger rolling from her in waves. "You left me. Crushed me. Left me pregnant and alone. And when I tried to tell you, tried to reach out to you to let you know, another woman answered the phone. What was I supposed to believe when she told me you were in the shower and that I needed to put my big-girl pants on and stop calling? Telling me you were better off without me. What else was I supposed to think, Gabe?" Her voice broke, and I scrambled for an answer because I had none.

"I promise you, Tori. There was never another woman. I had my reasons for leaving, but that wasn't one."

"You're impossible." She grabbed her purse and stormed past me.

Grasping her arm, I stopped her right before she opened the door. She looked down at where my hand held her wrist. The contact sent currents through me, but she acted as if I'd scalded her, and I dropped it.

"When did you call me to tell me about Reid?"

"Coming back to you now? Maybe you didn't leave me for another woman, but you sure got over me fast. Two and a half months after you left. Right after I took the pregnancy test. Right before I decided I was better off without an asshole who had deceived me. You know what hurt the most?"

I shook my head, still sifting through that time to find out who had answered my phone.

"Not that I was pregnant, or that you had found someone new, but that you had promised to love me forever, promised there was no other woman, that I was the only one and I wasn't."

She left me standing there, fighting to make sense of what she'd said. Time passed, yet still I remained, the scent of vanilla and cherry blossom lingering in the air.

"This is a creepy new low for you, little brother. Do you always sneak into her office when she's not here?"

Looking over to see Liv in the doorway, a memory returned. The day I'd blocked Tori from my phone, erasing the voicemails that I had constantly replayed to further enhance my guilt, blocking her number, and deleting her texts.

"You answered the phone that morning." I heard the heat in my tone, the edge to it.

"What are you talking about?" She glanced at her nails. "I think I went with the wrong color."

"Fuck the color. Did you answer my phone and tell Tori to stop calling me?"

She froze, her eyes darting back and forth before they landed on mine.

"You told her I was showering? That I was better off without her? What the fuck were you thinking, Liv?"

My voice had risen, and she stepped into the office, closing the door behind her. I was livid, seeing shades of black when I looked at her.

"Look, you needed to move on. It wasn't my fault she called when I was there. If you had been man enough to answer your phone and tell her to stop calling, I wouldn't have had to."

"Man enough?" My hands balled into fists as I resisted punching the wall. "She called to tell me she was pregnant!"

She flinched, and I saw the knowledge in her eyes. She knew about Reid. If she'd seen the picture, she would have known. He looked too much like me not to guess I was his father.

"And what would you have done?" she said.

"I would have gone back to her. Not let her raise our son by herself. Not let her think I was with another woman." I dragged my hand down my face, detesting that Tori had thought that all this time because my sister had let her believe it. "Do you have any idea what you did? She thought I left her for another woman. All this time, that's what she thought."

"So what?" Her cool exterior was snapping, her irritation coming through. "It was better that way. You had a job to do, and we had a task to complete."

"I had a son, Liv. A boy who doesn't know I'm his father. Who is growing up without one."

"It's better than growing up with the one we had." Her shoulders slumped. "You couldn't have gone back to her, and you know it. There was too much at stake."

"I would have risked it."

Her eyes bounced between mine. "You would have stolen my inheritance from me? After all that I sacrificed?"

Defeat sank into my shoulders. "Yes. I loved her. I'll always love her, Liv. And that boy is my son. I don't know him, and I missed almost five years of his life. I would have given everything up for that."

She nodded, but I saw the emotion there, the hurt. Hurting the people I loved seemed to be what I did best.

"We had plenty of money, Liv. The other businesses were thriving. We would have had plenty to live the lifestyle you have."

"It was never about the money," she said, turning her back on me and opening the door. "It was about getting to the end. Avenging Mama. In denying me my inheritance, you would have been denying us the chance to make him pay for what he did."

"Liv, I..."

She was gone before I could even try to make it better. Not that I could. I'd always been caught in the middle, my heart torn between the woman I loved and the promise I'd made the day we buried my mother. A promise that I'd now fulfilled, but that had only left me empty.

I avoided everyone the next day. With no meetings, I worked from my suite. It was really an apartment on the top floor of the hotel, but to me it had never been home. The only time I'd felt like I was home was when I'd been with Tori. Anyplace else was just a place to live.

I poured myself another glass of scotch and looked out at the skyline. Night had fallen, but my thoughts had me too wired to sit. I'd been that way since the previous day. Making good on my promise to Tori about childcare, I had talked to the director at the employee center, authorizing the hiring of two more teachers to accommodate more children. They had the space, but my father was stingy on employee benefits, something I was planning to change and had discussed in our meeting the prior day.

A knock at my door had me crossing the room, opening it to find Tori there. She pushed me aside and walked in.

"Come on in?" I said, scratching my head as I closed the door behind me.

I raised my glass to take another drink, and she grabbed it from me. "Since when do you drink this stuff?" she asked, wrinkling her nose at it.

Since my life went to hell.

She plunked it onto the coffee table and turned to face me, crossing her arms. I fought the tug of my grin at how adorable she looked. She had changed into a pair of leggings and a UConn sweatshirt. Her hair was up in a messy bun, and it reminded me of our days together. Natural and so Tori.

"So, you barge into my place to complain about my drink of choice. Was there anything else you'd like to complain about while you're here?"

"I won't bore you with my list. I'm not sorry, you know."

"What would you have to be sorry about? I'm the asshole who left you."

Plunging my hands into my pockets, I waited for whatever barrage of accusations she was planning to send my way.

"Your sister talked to me today." She freed her arms and rubbed her hand up one.

My eyes shot to hers. "What did she say?" I didn't want Tori to know the truth, how I'd been protecting her. Not yet.

"That she answered the phone that day." She took a few steps toward me. "Did you tell her to say that? Tell her to lie to me, or was she being honest?"

I let out the breath that had gotten stuck in my airway. "It was the truth. I didn't know she had answered. She never told me until yesterday when I confronted her."

The pain that accentuated her blue irises nearly broke me, and I looked away.

"Then why?" A whispered question I couldn't answer. "Why did you leave me, Gabe?" A crack in her voice that I couldn't ignore. "At least the thought that you were cheating or wanted another woman offered me a reason. Is that still the reason? You wanted someone else? You grew bored with me?"

"Damn it, Tori. I didn't want another woman. There has never been anyone but you." The words were out before I could catch them, and she stared at me, tears glistening in her eyes. I dropped my gaze to the floor, tired of fighting with her, tired of having her hate me. "I've never even looked at another woman."

I heard the huff and looked up to see her roll her eyes. "It's been over five years. You can't reasonably expect me to think you haven't dated someone else."

My gaze wavered. "Have you?" I didn't want the answer, but I deserved the hurt it would cause me. I had given her up. To expect that she would stay faithful to me like I had to her was a ridiculous notion.

A defeated sigh preceded her answer. "A handful of first dates." And the knife plunged a few more times. "But no one wants to date a woman with a child and baggage from an ex she can't get over." And the knife receded, leaving only minor wounds. "You're a hard act to follow, even if your departure tainted those times."

I didn't know what to say, so I stayed quiet, letting her words sink in.

"Did you leave me so you could have someone else, Gabe? Have you been living the bachelor life here with all your money and playboy looks?"

"Playboy looks?" I asked quirking my brow.

"Shut up. I'm serious."

I dared to take two steps closer, letting the scent of vanilla and cherry blossoms tickle my nose. "I didn't leave you to live that life, Tori. And no, there has been no one since because there is no other you. I barely look at other women because when I do, all I see is that they aren't you."

Graceful brows knitted, and I watched the myriad of emotions pass through her face.

"Then why did you do it? If you needed space, I would have understood." She rubbed her nose with the back of her wrist. "If we were moving too fast, we could have pushed the wedding back." She went stiff, her eyes growing wide. "Was that it? You regretted proposing and didn't know how to get out?"

I clawed my hand through my hair and eclipsed the remaining distance between us, grasping her arms with my hands. The contact sent a flurry of currents charging through me.

"If it's one thing I have never regretted, it's proposing to you. Don't ever think I didn't want to marry you, Tori."

She jerked her arms free, anger etched in her features. "You are the most confounding man. If you didn't leave me for any of those reasons, then why put me through that hell? Why cause me so much pain?"

The strength leached from my body, and my shoulders sagged. I couldn't give her the reason yet. The ink had just dried on the contracts, and my father was vindictive. While he could no longer destroy her career since she worked for me, he still had the means to go after her family business. Until I knew he wouldn't, I wouldn't risk it.

Hands plunging into my pockets again, I looked away from her. "Because I'm an ass, just like you thought I was. You have every right to hate me, Tori. I hurt you, and nothing you did warranted my actions. Now you know the truth. I'm the selfish bastard you thought I was all those years."

Her head tipped as she studied me. Walking to the bar, I poured myself another glass of scotch before turning back to her.

"Anything else you needed to discuss?" I asked, taking a drink.

"Secrets," she said. "It was always secrets with you, and it still is." She threw her hands in the air and headed to the door. "Your secrets got us where we are today, Gabe. Maybe it's time for honesty."

She swung the door open and glanced back at me.

"I'd like to get to know Reid," I said, expecting the reaction I got.

Her eyes narrowed, and she stormed back over to me, the door slamming behind her. "You have no right to see him. Not until I have some answers. I can't trust you, Gabe. I don't even know who you are anymore." And the pain lanced through me again because she was the only one who truly knew me. "Until you earn my trust, you'll have no contact with my son. I don't need you doing to him what you did to me. I already have to face the questions about why he doesn't have a father. Why the other kids at the daycare have dads and he doesn't. Why his cousin has a mother and a father but he only has me. I don't need to explain why you left him when you decide you've had enough and disappear on me again."

Her steps were quick and angry as she crossed the room and didn't stop this time. The door closed behind her with a loud thud, and I lowered my glass. Her words stung like a hive of aggravated bees attacking me from the inside. The guilt hammered me until I slid down the bar and pulled my knees to my chest. I'd done this. Left her alone. Left my son without a father. Nothing I could ever do would make that better, nor could it ever alleviate the guilt that had festered for over five years and continued to compound with every day Tori was back in my life.

CHAPTER 23

GABE

Two weeks passed, and in that time, the tension between me and Liv didn't cease, and the uncomfortable silence from Tori continued. I was stuck between the two women I loved but who currently hated me.

I stepped into Liv's office, trapping her before she could dodge my attempt to talk.

"I have Pilates at noon. If you make me late, I'll empty every bottle of that high-end scotch you like."

"Ouch, that's uncalled for."

Her mouth twisted as she sat back and crossed her arms.

"I thought I made it clear I wasn't talking to you anymore."

"Come on, Liv."

She stood and rested her hands on the desk. "Go away."

"No." I moved to the desk and placed my hands on the other side, staring her down. "You can't continue to not talk to me. It's bad enough I have to walk on eggshells with Tori, but adding you and your emphasized silence doesn't help."

"Too bad, backstabber."

"Are you kidding me? So I told you I would have gone back to her. I didn't, and things worked out for you. You have your inheritance, and we had our revenge. It worked out."

"But you would have given it all up for her."

"I didn't." Even if it was still killing me.

She lifted her hands and crossed her arms. "But you would have."

"I have a son, Liv. Your nephew. A boy I don't know because I turned my back on them." I let out a sigh. "I know what you gave up to do this, but there was no child involved. If there had been, would you have made the same choice to leave him?"

"It doesn't matter," she said, her sight falling from mine.

"I think it does because I don't think you would have. What you did was difficult, Liv. Just like what I did was. We got what we intended, but I no longer think the payoff was worth what we lost to get here." Straightening, I reached over and moved a curl from her cheek. "Maybe you should look him up. You never know."

She shook her head, giving me a small smile. That was enough to know she forgave me.

"By the way," I said, fixing my shirt where I'd rolled the sleeves. "Thank you for talking to Tori. For telling her the truth. I know how hard it is for you to be humble."

She laughed and threw a pad of paper at me. "Get out of my office, little brother."

I picked up the pad and tossed it on her desk before I headed out.

"Did it help?" she asked as my hand was on the handle.

"For a moment, until she started hating me again."

"Give her time. I see the way she looks at you. She's still in love with you. You'll just have to find a way to win her back."

"Nothing like a challenge I have a zero percent chance of winning," I mumbled as I walked out.

Heading to my office, I heard Tori talking to our assistant, her voice carrying so that it inched its way into my chest, causing an ache I couldn't ignore. Changing direction, I left the office, taking a walk to clear my head. I thought about Liv's observation that Tori still loved me. The idea caused fluctuations in my pulse, and I swallowed back the hope. Paired with the small hints she'd dropped in her frustrated conversations with me, there was hope, but I didn't know how to win her back. It seemed an impossible feat, but the possibility was too exciting to ignore.

After a brisk walk in the late October air, I found myself standing in front of the daycare, watching Reid play with the other kids in his class. The director had informed me that a new teacher had started last week, a rehire whom she had cut when my father had insisted on slowly dismantling the center. Something I had argued against and had now rectified.

Reid was playing cars with a redheaded boy and a very animated girl with braids. His smile warmed a place in my chest that only Tori had ever reached. I wanted to know him, to hear his stories, to learn his likes and dislikes, to watch him continue to grow.

The scent of vanilla and cherry blossoms and the familiar sensation of Tori standing in my presence had my nerves buzzing.

"Give him a car and he can play for hours."

"I was the same way," I said, watching him laugh so hard he was holding his stomach. "Had a collection of miniature cars until..." The memory of my father taking them all away when I'd left one in the kitchen returned. His voice had cut through me like barbed wire as he scolded me and the spanking he'd given me had left my bottom sore for two days.

"I'm hoping he doesn't want to be a racecar driver when he gets older," said Tori, filling the silence. "I don't think I could handle the worry."

"I'll buy the cars he wants to feed the addiction," I blurted, wanting to kick myself for assuming she would let me give him anything. I rubbed the back of my neck. "I bought my first when I was sixteen and still have it in my garage."

"Guess your Jacksonville car isn't part of that collection?" An acidic tone laced the question.

"No. I donated it when I returned home. My father would have disowned me if he had seen me driving that."

Awkward silence let me know it was time to leave. It had hovered over us since the night she'd confronted me.

I turned to leave when she said, "I'm taking Reid to the zoo for his birthday."

"The zoo?" My voice squeaked at the memory of Tori at the zoo. Her smile in the Florida sun, tanned skin, and hidden kisses. I clenched my hands to stave off the need to touch her.

"Yes. This weekend if you'd like to come."

I swiveled around, meeting dusty blue orbs. The air rushed from my lungs, and I struggled to reply. "I'd like that."

She nodded, swallowing. "Saturday morning, before I head to my brother's for the birthday party."

Something I knew I wouldn't be welcome to attend. I was certain her brother hated me even more than she did. Anyone who had hurt my sister the way I'd hurt her I would loathe.

"Sounds like a..." I almost said date but caught myself. "A plan."

She gave me a forced smile, then turned back to watching Reid. It was only Monday, but I headed back out of the building and made my way to the toy store, buying every miniature sports car they had.

Wiping the sweat from my forehead, I stretched my tired muscles. The gym in the building was always empty this early, and having a full bathroom in my office made it easy to get my workout in before turning my focus to the day. I pulled a suit from the small closet in the bathroom and returned to lock my office door only to find my father standing across from me.

"I'll need to have a talk with security if they're still letting you in here. How did you get to this floor?"

"I have my ways." He strolled across the room and took a seat.

"What do you want?" I asked, noting the more laid-back look of khakis and a polo shirt. My father had never been one to go without a three-piece suit.

"I admit it took me some time to understand how you did it. Dismantling my empire piece by piece under my nose. And even more time for my anger to simmer."

I folded my arms and glared at him, waiting for whatever devious plan he had concocted to bring me down.

"I'm impressed, William. All this time I thought you were squandering all I gave you, fooling around with that woman in Florida." I sucked in air between my teeth, holding back my sharp retort. "Insisting on moving there after you finished school when you could have worked at any firm in the city for experience. But you were paying attention, manipulating, scheming, cheating, just like I did."

"I never cheated." Although I had done some underhanded things to make him fall.

"Whatever you want to call it. You learned it all from me."

I snorted, looking down at him. "I learned what not to be from you."

"Maybe," he replied with a shrug, "but that final move and all the ones you played to get me to that closing table, those you learned from me. And I'm proud of you."

My jaw dropped. "I don't need your pride."

"No, you needed me to pay for something you and your sister blamed me for."

"Because you were at fault."

Standing, he stroked his hand over the desk. "Your mother struggled with depression her entire life. She was on anti-depressants when I met her. It was a constant battle, and I supported her through every downturn."

"By beating her son in front of her every chance you had? By berating her daughter and belittling her every chance?"

His head snapped up, eyes going dark. "You needed discipline, and the last thing she needed was your whining and messes. I made you what you are today, William. You and your sister. You're tough, focused, and driven. Without me to guide you to that point, you'd still be in Florida despising your life."

I grabbed him by the collar. "I would be happy. That's what I would be. Not here alone and miserable while the woman I love is no longer mine."

He brushed my hands away. "You were always emotional. That's why you needed discipline. Too soft and clinging to your mother's skirts. She didn't need you underfoot while she was trying to have good days. She needed you quiet and in your place."

"You're delusional. How did I never see that? You drove her to kill herself. You are the reason she's dead."

His features went rigid, a flash of surprise the only sign of emotion. "I loved your mother. She's the only woman I've ever loved, which is why I never remarried. She killed herself because she went off her meds, and I didn't realize until it was too late. Hate me all you want, but it doesn't change the truth."

"Why are you here?" I couldn't take any more of his delusional excuses.

He smoothed out his collar. "Carl Bradman has been talking about your new CFO. I saw him while I was at a dinner last week, and he was his usual arrogant self. Pissing away the liquor and hitting on the staff while his wife tried to keep him contained."

"What does that have to do with Victoria?"

"Seems she left on terms he didn't like. Did Tina do a check with her former employer?"

"Yes, they gave her high praises. I spoke to Carl the day I interviewed her. He gave me the same accolades."

"Watch him. He's someone I've never trusted. If he has something on her, he won't hesitate to use it to his advantage."

I scrunched my forehead, trying to think of what he would have on Tori. My suspicion that she'd left Bradman in a hurry returned. Secrets. She'd accused me of still having them while she had her own.

"Why are you telling me this? I thought you hated me."

He chuckled, looking entirely too relaxed. In fact, I'd never seen him look so relaxed. "Because you may hate me, but you are still my son. The heir to my empire, one I know you'll rebuild because I watched you build your own."

I tried not to stumble back.

"Where do you think you learned everything from, William? Hate me all you want, but I told you I would make you CEO, and I did. Maybe not in the way I intended, but as my company was crumbling around me, you and your sister looked entirely too calm. There were other bidders for the hotel and the last of the holdings, but I made your mother a promise the day you were born, that you would have everything. You and your sister. You may not like the way I went about it, the way I raised you, but I fulfilled my promise to her, just like I imagine you did. Both brought you to where she wanted you. A billionaire with an empire to pass down to your children."

I couldn't grasp the words to respond, too stunned that he'd found us out yet still let us have our victory. "That day in the conference room?"

"I knew it was you, but hearing you admit that you'd betrayed me, that you hated me so much that you wanted to see me fall still hit hard, and my reactions were honest. I suppose we're even now."

"We'll never be even. You abused me and defended it as discipline. I can promise you I will never treat my children the way you treated me, and they'll still grow up to be adults I'll be proud of."

"We all have our ways."

He sauntered to the door. "I'm selling my apartment in the city. The money I accumulated through every sale and this last one is enough to let me travel. What's left will go to a trust for your son. There's already a trust in his name with a substantial amount in it; the rest will pass through to him and any other children you have when I die."

"You knew?" My knees threatened to buckle. "You knew about him and never told me?"

"I wanted to make sure you didn't break your word, so I kept my eye on her. I wasn't sure he was yours until I saw the pictures two years ago. That's when I established the trust."

"You made me leave her and never told me I had a son?"

Steel eyes with no kindness met my astonished gaze. "You had a job to do, and the terms of your trust were still in place. If you had known, it would have jeopardized all I worked for and you worked for. It was better this way."

"Better that he doesn't know who his father is? That I never knew he existed?"

"Yes. This is business, William. That's all it has ever been. One business transaction after another. She was one, and you under-stood that seeing it through would have cost too much."

"Get out."

He shook his head. "You'll thank me one day. Besides, she's working for you now. Yet another business transaction that presents you with an opportunity."

"I'll never thank you. Now get out of my office."

He opened the door, throwing a look at me over his shoulder. "I'll be in Greece for the winter if you need me."

"I won't."

"Of course you won't." The door closed behind him, and I stared dumbfounded at it as my mind attempted to make sense of all he had told me. The most startling piece, that he'd known Tori was pregnant yet he'd kept it quiet, denying me yet another chance of happiness in my life. Taking one more thing from me and replacing it with money and titles I would have traded in a heart-beat to have the two things in my life that I valued more.

Chapter 24

Tori

After tossing and turning all night, I gave up and headed into the office. I had plenty to do to occupy my mind. Gabe's plan to bring the network of resorts and hotels under one company after he had dismantled the original and severed it into a complex maze of holdings was enough to keep me busy for months. Thankfully, the finances for every holding were strong and detailed, unlike what he'd done for his father's company.

I dropped Reid off at the childcare center, glad it opened early. Eyes focused on digging my elevator card from my purse, I didn't notice I was no longer alone in the lobby.

"Miss Hent."

I looked up, trying to place the man before me. He looked so familiar and...similar to an older version of Gabe, something I hadn't noticed in his online photo. William Icinda Senior. Although Gabe held the same intense gaze, the strong jawline, the fierce presence, there were striking differences that led me to believe Gabe favored his mother in appearance.

"Mr. Icinda."

"I see you're settling into your new position quickly."

"Yes."

Hardened edges shaped his jawline, and his eyes lacked the life that Gabe's held, the joy that had once been prominent but now only flickered behind the darkness.

"I hope William's mess isn't proving too difficult to unravel."

I quirked a brow at him. This man didn't call him Gabe, and I remembered the story of abuse, knowing it had been a truthful insight into his childhood.

"Not at all."

He gave me an appraising look. "Convenient," he said, throwing me off with the response that made no sense to me and following it up with one that further confused me. "I suppose my threat no longer holds sway. Although he knows better than to underestimate me, which explains the confusion you're struggling to hide."

"I'm not sure what you're talking about," was the only thing I could think to say.

"Of course you're not. Even when I'm not controlling him, I am. Let's see if he rebels again with you this close. Good day, Miss Hent. I'll be watching to see how it plays out."

He left me standing there, my mind still working out what he was saying.

"Oh, and Miss Hent." I glanced over my shoulder. "Tell my grandson to have a happy birthday."

My world spun as he walked away, his confident swagger so similar to Gabe's. Had Gabe told him about Reid? From everything he'd told me, it didn't seem like he would. And what had he meant by a threat and controlling Gabe?

Key card in hand, I watched the elevator doors close. When they reopened, I jumped, not realizing the floors had passed by so quickly. I dropped my stuff in my office and signed into my computer, attempting to get the conversation from my mind. Secrets. So many secrets defined my relationship with Gabe, and the reason we barely had one now was because those secrets kept compounding.

After staring at my computer with no luck quieting my brain, I needed answers. Gabe's door was closed, so I knocked and peeked my head in. Big mistake because he wasn't sitting at his desk.

"Jesus, Liv, do you ever wait before you barge in?" he grumbled, not looking up as he snatched his dress shirt from where it rested on his desk.

"I'm sorry, I didn't even think you'd..." My words wouldn't form. He was still just as beautiful as he'd been. Muscles defining his chest, his arms powerful and sleek, the V that I'd loved tracing with my fingers still leading to where his pants sat low on his hips.

"Tori? Shit, sorry. I should have known Liv wouldn't be here this early."

I dragged my eyes up his bare chest, memories of all the times I'd laid on it, touched it, kissed it, all the times I'd felt safe wrapped in his arms overwhelming me.

"I can come back," I stuttered.

"No, it's fine. I used the gym here this morning. I should have known my father hadn't locked the door on his way out." He reached for his tie, the shirt still in his hands, and I wondered if he was purposely torturing me. As he grabbed it, I caught the outline of a tattoo on his shoulder blade. My breath stuck in my throat. A half-moon. My knees almost gave out. "Did you need something?"

He pulled the shirt on, resting the tie around his neck while he buttoned it.

"Umm, I... When did you get a tattoo?"

His eyes shot up, a flicker of emotion in the hazel. "It's just something I got a few years ago. What did you need, Tori?"

I wanted to press him, to understand why he would put a moon on his body or why he would name one of his companies Luna. But the answers were in everything he'd told me, and they rubbed at my need to continue to hate him. To keep him at a distance because even with all he'd told me, I still didn't have the one answer I needed. Why he had left me.

Clearing my throat, I said, "I ran into your father in the lobby."

Narrowed eyes and a jaw twitch. "Did he bother you?"

I shook my head. "No, but he said something I didn't understand. He mentioned a threat and how it no longer held sway, but you knew better than to underestimate him. What does that mean?"

His fingers froze, a flash of worry lighting his eyes before he said, "It's nothing."

Shuffling my feet, I studied him, knowing from that reaction that it wasn't 'nothing.' "What aren't you telling me, Gabe?"

His eyes dropped to focus on his buttons. "I said it was nothing. Why are you working so early?"

"Don't change the subject."

Amber eyes jumped to mine. His features altered. It was subtle, but for a moment my Gabe was back, the soft, sweet man I had fallen in love with. And my chest swelled, beating with a steady rhythm that belonged to him. But the moment passed, and the hesitation that had been there disappeared. "There is no subject, and it's nothing you need to worry about."

A ragged sigh scraped from my throat. "I'm so tired of your secrets. I just want the truth for once. I'm not asking that much, but you seem to think I'm asking you for the world."

Hazel with specks of gold lost its darkness, and his mask slipped again. I hated that he thought he had to wear it because I knew what he was like without it. The amazing man he had been.

Until he left you, I reminded myself.

"Fine," I huffed, throwing my hands in the air and storming back to the door.

"I would have given you the world, Tori. It's the rest I can't give." His wounded voice carried the weight of years of regret.

I paused at the threshold, my head dropping. "I never needed the world. I needed you."

Not turning back to see his expression and giving him no time to respond, I closed the door behind me and buried myself in work the rest of the day, avoiding him as much as I could. I questioned what I'd done to myself because every time I was in his presence, it reopened the fractures that remained and had never healed.

People hurried through the hotel lobby where Reid and I waited for Gabe. I couldn't stop the nervous shaking in my hands as I considered if this had been a mistake. Why had I suggested he accompany us to the zoo? A momentary lapse of sanity. One of many lately because being in his presence left me too weak to think.

Reid hopped on the balls of his feet, his fingers tugging at the buttons on his coat.

"Will we see lions, Mommy?"

"Of course we will." I crouched down and wiped a spot of jelly from his mouth. "And lots of other animals. Then we'll go see Uncle Cash and Aunt Brandi."

He squealed, and I couldn't help but laugh. Giving him a kiss on the cheek, I stood back up just as Gabe stepped from the elevator and came our way. Nerves bounded through me like a collapsing pile of plastic balls. He looked so handsome that it tugged at the pressure in my chest. His long black coat covered a pair of jeans and a charcoal gray T-shirt, and I was suddenly back in Jacksonville, in love and completely addicted to the man who owned me.

Swallowing back the sensation, I looked away, seeing a few women in the lobby checking him out. Streaks of jealousy struck those bouncing balls, destroying them.

He's not yours anymore.

But my thought didn't halt the emotion, which only ceased when I met his eyes again and found they were only on me. He gave me a bashful grin that had me gripping Reid's hand tighter.

What was I doing? There was no way I could spend the entire day with this man and not have him crush my resolve to hate him for the rest of my life. A resolve I'd fought with for almost six years because as much as he'd devastated me, I couldn't seem to stop loving him.

"Hey, mister," Reid called to him. "We're going to the zoo because it's my birthday."

Gabe's smile could have repaired my heart ten times over. "So I've heard. Mind if I tag along?" He held out a handled paper bag to him.

Reid glanced up at me, and I nodded. His little hands tore into it as Gabe said, "I'm not one for wrapping." He palmed the back of his neck, and the emotions stirred in me again. How many times had I watched him do that, and how much further had I fallen for him when he had? He seemed so different today, so like he'd been then.

A squeal broke my thoughts, and I glanced around to meet judging eyes. All except Gabe's, which were fixed on Reid, full of adoration.

"Look, Mommy. It's cars," he exclaimed, showing me the bag of sports car replicas. "Lots of cool cars." He pulled one out and started zooming it around like it was on a racetrack. Gabe's chuckle had me turning my sight to him. His smile lit his eyes, turning them a muted green hue.

"What do you say?" I asked Reid.

"Thanks, mister."

"It's Gabe," I corrected. "His name is Gabe."

Reid put his hand out. "I'm Reid," he said, beaming.

Gabe shook it, emotion splashing over his features. "Nice to meet you, Reid."

My heart threatened to stop at seeing them together. How

many times had I dreamed of this for Reid? For something different from answering his questions about his father with 'I'll tell you when you're older' because I didn't have the heart to tell him his father had left us. That he didn't know he existed because he'd left me.

"I invited Gabe to go to the zoo with us. Would that be okay, Reid?"

"Yeah." He put the car back in his bag and took Gabe's hand. "Come on. I can show you my favorite animal. Do you like cars? I love them..." He dragged Gabe toward the doors.

Gabe was staring at their hands, surprise in his eyes. Tears pressed at the back of my eyes, and I bit my lip, reminding myself that he had hurt me. That no matter what this seemed like, our happy ending had died years ago with the heart he'd shattered. His vision flitted to mine, the emotion shifting as his smile dropped.

"I have a car waiting out front," he told me as we walked.

"Okay," I managed, hearing the shake in my voice.

"What kind of car?" Reid asked.

"Nothing exciting," answered Gabe. "That one." He pointed to the black sedan, like the one we took to the office building every morning.

"Oh, that's like the one that takes me to school."

"The same one," he answered, helping Reid in as the driver held the door open for us.

Gabe stood aside to let me in, but I heard Reid say, "Can you sit next to me, Gabe?"

"Uh..." He looked at me, concern lining his forehead.

"It's fine."

We stood there frozen, our eyes locked and my pulse thrumming until the driver cleared his throat. As I climbed in after Gabe, I realized I hadn't been this close to him yet. Our thighs brushed, and shocks raced through me. Panic climbed into my throat. I shouldn't have done this, but there was no going back.

Reid dominated the conversation, enamored with Gabe's presence and knowledge of cars. They talked cars the entire way to the zoo as I stayed rigid, fighting how the sound of Gabe's voice brushed over my soul, waking parts of me that had died the day he'd left.

I fared no better the rest of the morning. While Reid monopolized the conversation, something I was thankful for, there were moments when I cracked and found myself too relaxed with Gabe. Returning to a time when we had spent the day at the Jacksonville Zoo, stealing kisses and holding hands. A time when he had been my everything and his mere touch could melt me. Longing built, pushing aside the anger at his secrets, at what he'd done to me. A longing to go back to those days.

"He's a good kid," Gabe said as we watched Reid run around the play area.

"Yeah." I picked at the popcorn Reid had requested, hating how it took me back to that day with Gabe.

"I'm sorry, Tori. Sorry I let you down. That I left you to raise him by yourself." His voice went quieter. "That I left you."

"Yeah," I repeated, anguish swelling inside me. "But you did, and you can't take it back. The scars will always be there." I glanced at him, meeting pain-etched irises. "He doesn't know who his father is. Doesn't understand why I can't give him answers. Doesn't understand why other kids have fathers but he doesn't. The other kids teased him at his old school. Told him his father didn't love him and that's why he didn't know him." I looked away, knowing I was close to breaking. "Do you have any idea how hard it was to tell him that wasn't the truth when it was?"

"Tori, I..."

I put my hand up. "Don't, Gabe. You left me, not the other way around. You stopped loving me, and you don't love him. I have to lie about that every day. I have to tell him I'll explain when he's older every time he asks about you. Not because I don't want to tell him the truth but because..." My voice cracked, and a tear broke free. "...it hurts too much to admit."

"Tori—"

I got up from the bench, intending to get Reid and leave, but Gabe grabbed my hand and turned me back to him. He had stood and now looked down at me. So much agony misted his eyes that I doubted my words.

"I never stopped loving you, Tori. You must believe that. I didn't leave you because I stopped loving you. I left because I loved you too much, and it…"

"It what, Gabe? Tell me the truth, please. Just this once, stop with the secrets."

"Mommy, are you okay?"

I sucked in a breath, knowing the moment was gone. This had been my chance, and it might never return.

"Please," I pleaded as Reid tugged on my pants.

"I can't."

The strength fled me, and I ripped my hand from his grasp. "Everything is fine," I told Reid, sniffing and rubbing away the tears. "I got a splinter in my hand, and Gabe was getting it out."

"Can I see?" He took my hand, inspecting it.

"There's nothing left to see. It's gone."

He kissed my palm. "All better?"

Laughing, I replied, "All better. But it's time to go. We need to go back and get ready to see Uncle Cash."

"And eat cake?"

"Yup."

He hopped up and down. "Do you like cake, Gabe?"

"I do," answered Gabe as I buttoned Reid's coat back up.

"Can you come with us?"

My hands froze, and my sight flew to Gabe. Sadness etched the corners of his eyes. "No, I don't think that would be a good idea. How about you save a slice for me?"

"Okay." He tugged from my hold and took Gabe's hand again. "Let's go."

I stared at them as Reid led Gabe away, marveling at how alike they looked. Reid was a miniature version of Gabe, and it ached to see. Following, I thought about Gabe's words that he had left me because he loved me too much. It made no sense unless I added it to the run-in with his father. The comment about Gabe rebelling again and being under his control. Had I blamed Gabe all this time when there was more to it? Secrets. Things he refused to tell me.

When we arrived back at the hotel, I waited for Reid to say his goodbyes as he clutched his bag of cars.

"Go sit in the seat over there and play quietly with one of your cars while I talk to Gabe," I told him.

We were in the middle of the lobby with no privacy, so I couldn't press Gabe more, but I needed answers, and I was tired of being in the dark.

"Thank you for inviting me," he said, his eyes trailing Reid. Longing tinged them, and I softened, knowing as much as I blamed him for leaving Reid without a father, he hadn't known about him.

"How did your father know about Reid?" I blurted.

"My father has ways of finding things out. Apparently, he knew about Reid all these years but didn't bother to tell me until today."

That answer had not been the one I expected. "He knew and never said anything?"

Gabe turned his attention back to me. "Yes. I told you my father wasn't a nice man. I never lied to you about that. We don't get along. We never have."

"Tell me why you left me, Gabe."

He swiped his hand through his hair. "This again, Tori? It doesn't matter, and it won't change the fact that I did or that you hate me for leaving you and leaving Reid without a father."

"I don't hate you," I admitted. "It's more of a love/hate thing."

His brow lifted, and surprise lit his eyes.

"I'm tired of secrets, and living life like this is too difficult." I chewed the inside of my cheek, hating what I was about to say but knowing I couldn't continue to do this to myself. It was too emotionally challenging, and I would never heal if it continued. Not that I thought I ever would. "I need answers, Gabe. No more lies, no more secrets. If you can't give them to me, then I'm leaving."

The light dimmed in his eyes. "You can't do that."

"I don't want to, but I will. This hurts too much. Seeing you, being near you, seeing the possibility." I looked back at Reid. "What could have been. It's tearing me apart, and pretending that it isn't hurts just as bad."

"Please, Tori."

I turned back to him. "No. It's not fair to me and not fair to him. It's my job as his mother to protect him, and I will do whatever I need to ensure I do. Even if it means..." My voice splintered, and suddenly, I was back to that day, realizing he was never coming back, that he had left me and never looked back. "You have until Friday. Otherwise, consider this my two weeks' notice."

Looking away, I forced my legs to move toward Reid, gathering him up and taking him back to the elevator. As the doors closed, Gabe remained in the same place, his head bowed, and the dam on my tears broke. I brushed them away before Reid could spot them and pulled the mask on that I'd worn for years. The one that pretended my heart wasn't still a tattered wreck that would never heal. That acted as if I had recovered from the devastation Gabe left behind. That told everyone I hated the man who had left me when I had never truly stopped loving him.

Chapter 25

Gabe

With my head in my hands, I considered my options, unsure if any were viable. Spending the day with Tori and Reid opened my eyes to all I'd lost. And it had torn me in two. I'd spent the rest of the weekend drowning myself in alcohol and memories, locked away in my room.

Tori had ignored me all day Monday, sticking to emails when she needed something. And in our meeting earlier this morning, she'd avoided my eyes, keeping her sight on everyone but me. The tension crawled over my skin until the meeting ended.

A knock at my door had me dragging my head up. Liv peered around the corner before stepping in and closing the door behind her.

"You've looked like shit the last two days and..." She walked around my desk and took my chin in her hands, tipping my head back and forth. "...when was the last time you shaved?"

I swatted her hands away. "I hope you're here because you finished that report I requested."

"Not a chance," she said, sitting on the corner of my desk. "What's going on with you two? It's like I'm caught in one of those reality shows where they're all awkward after they start screwing each other. Are you two fighting again or did you have sex?"

I rolled my eyes and fell back into my chair. "I didn't sleep with her. She gave me an ultimatum."

Her brow arched as she waited for me to explain. I dropped my eyes to my desk.

"I'm waiting," she snapped.

"You're a pain in my ass," I grumbled, looking back up at her.

"I know. Now tell me what she said."

Wiping my face, I said, "If I don't tell her the truth, she'll leave."

"So just tell her. You had responsibilities and the trust guidelines to meet. She can't hate you for that."

"For leaving her for money and never telling her about it? I beg to differ."

"Well, when you put it that way. But you were doing it for me, too. That should count for something."

With a sigh, I turned my attention to the window, watching thick clouds coast overhead. "I did it for both of you."

"What does that mean?"

"Dad called me right before I left. He knew, just like you'd warned, and he threatened her and her family."

Her mouth fell open as she stared at me. "What did he threaten?"

"To destroy her career and ruin her family's business. Remember the resort Mom loved, The Haven? Tori's parents own it."

"The one he was dying to buy but Mom made him promise not to touch it?"

"That one."

"Holy crap. I can't believe he'd go that far...never-mind, I can believe it. What an asshole."

"He knew about Reid. He's been watching her all these years, waiting to see if I went after her. I don't know that he won't do something still."

She scratched her head before pushing off the desk. "What can he do? She works for you. You won't fire her, and he's in no position to do anything to her parents. Tell her. She deserves to know the truth."

My phone buzzed, and I glanced down to see it was Bruce from the lobby front desk. Putting him on speakerphone, I answered.

"There's a Carl Bradman here requesting to see you, sir." His voice went lower, like he didn't want anyone to hear him. "Made a fuss when I told him no. He's still going off about how we should know who he is."

I glanced up at Liv, but she shrugged.

"Thanks, Bruce. Please have someone escort him up."

Standing, I pulled my jacket on, fixing my sleeves as I questioned Liv. "What does Bradman want?"

"No clue, but better yet, what's he doing here? He's a long way from home."

"Guess I'll find out." I opened my office door and gestured for Liv to leave. A hop from the desk and she sauntered out.

"Tell her," she said as she walked by me.

Snapping my lapels, I headed to the elevator, thinking just maybe I would. Liv was right. My father could no longer hurt Tori, and I could protect her this time if he did. But would she believe me? Believe that I'd had no choice but to go, even if I'd continued to look back since that day.

"Carl," I said, extending my hand as he exited the elevator. I gave a nod and a quick 'thank you' to the security guard, who had escorted him.

Carl Bradman was a shrewd businessman in his early sixties with a thick head of black hair streaked with gray. Fit and tall, he stood only about two inches below me. His grip was firm as he greeted me. It was my first time meeting him, but I knew his type, and any show of weakness would be an opening for him.

"William. Do you use your father's name or go by something else to avoid confusion?"

"William." My response was sharp because that was expected with a man like Bradman.

I led him back to my office, discovering he was in town for a business meeting. We had a brief chat about his observations of city life before I closed my office door behind him.

"So, what brings you to see me, Carl?" I asked, unbuttoning my jacket as I sat and offered him a seat.

"I came to congratulate you and introduce myself in person. Since we share business interests, it seemed best to get off on the right foot."

Bradman owned mostly commercial real estate and apartment complexes throughout the East Coast. To say we shared business interests was an oversimplification. He'd been breathing down my father's neck for years, trying to buy the company while I'd been slowly dismantling it. I'd competed with him for most of the properties my father had divested, but he didn't know that since my attorney always worked the agreements and closings for me. And I'd won every bidding war, my assets more profound than his.

"And to let me know your offers to buy the company still stand?"

He chuckled, looking entirely too comfortable. "Of course they do. You've acquired a failing company, William. You've been part of that demise, and now you expect to revitalize something you should have let die."

I stood, fooling with my cufflinks as I came around the desk. "Let me make one thing clear, Carl. I do not intend to sell this company. I intend to rebuild it with the holdings I've collected over the past few years." His eyes grew large. "I don't need an investor, nor do I need to know what you planned to offer me when you walked through those doors this morning. If anything, maybe it's your company that's in danger."

He stood, his face muscles rigid. "My company is not for sale, and you're a fool if you think you can resurrect this dying one."

"My financials say otherwise. I'm happy to maintain a civil relationship as business acquaintances, Carl, but don't threaten my company or disparage what my father built. He turned your offers down every time, as will I. You don't have enough money to even consider buying me out, so next time you're in town, let's have a drink and talk about politics or the market, anything that doesn't insult me like you just did with your assumptions and arrogance."

His head went back, and I could see him weighing his options. Power was a coveted thing, and I had the power here. A shrewd business owner would keep me on his good side.

"I see your father taught you well."

"Did you think otherwise?"

"I did, but I see you're not the inexperienced, naïve pup I thought you were."

"Never make assumptions, Carl. They're bad for business." I smoothed my suit jacket and walked toward the door. "I have a meeting, but let me show you out."

"I'd like to stop by and congratulate Victoria before I leave."

That instinct that had been nudging me about why she'd left, returned. With my hand on the doorknob, I turned to him. "I don't know what happened to cause her to leave, but if I find out and I don't like it, I can promise you'll be hearing from me."

Beady green eyes glared back at me. "She has an NDA, and if she breaks it, I'll have her in court."

"Which makes me even more curious about what happened to make a talented CFO leave just as she brought the company financials into the best spot they've ever been. Bradman Holdings is thriving because of her, and you lost her when you should have been celebrating her. I suppose that's my blessing since I now have her on my team."

The clench of his jaw told me I'd struck a nerve.

"Let me show you to her office," I said, opening the door for him.

His body language told me everything, and I straightened my spine to stand my full height over him as I walked him to Tori's. Her door was open now, her focus intent on her computer. I had to stop my reaction at how fantastic she looked. She wore her hair up in a loose bun, a pen protruding from it, and I remembered how she would tuck pencils in her hair when studying for her licenses. The times she would sprawl across my bed, her ankles crossed and her feet in the air.

"Victoria," Carl said before I could get her attention. Nothing could have been more revealing than her reaction: wide eyes, a sudden jump from her seat, knocking papers from her desk that she disregarded as they fell, the paling of her skin. I wanted to drag him from her office and ease her discomfort because it permeated the air.

Her eyes jumped to me, and I tried to read them before they returned to him.

"Carl," she said, staying behind her desk. "This is unexpected."

"Can we have a few minutes, William?" he asked me.

I continued standing in the doorway waiting for Tori's approval. The tension coming from her body made me hesitant to leave her alone with him, and I decided then that knowing what had happened between them was more important than holding onto my secrets. She had hers, and I had mine, but it was time to come clean.

She gave me a nod, one that was too hesitant for Tori, and I debated saying no and staying right where I was.

"I'll be right outside to walk you out, Carl." I glanced at my watch. "I have a meeting in five minutes, so make it fast."

He threw me an icy glare, and I ignored it, walking out of the office and softly closing the door behind me even though every part of me screamed to leave it open. Something had happened between them, and from Tori's frigid movements, I suspected it was one-sided. I leaned against the wall, catching Liv's attention in the office across from Tori's.

She creased her brows and mouthed, "What are you doing?"

Shaking my head, I loosened my fists, which were balled tightly in my irritation at Carl Bradman. Tori's voice came through the wall, raised and angry, and I fought my need to barge in.

The door opened a few minutes later, and I lifted from the wall.

"Remember what I said, Victoria."

"How could I forget? Goodbye, Carl."

"Let's see you out," I told him, leading him back to the elevators. "Call ahead next time, and I might have more time to chat."

"Of course." He looked back to Tori's office as the elevator opened.

I placed my hands on the doors to keep them from closing and leaned into the elevator. "And we'll leave Victoria out of it next time, understood."

His teeth ground as he eyed me. "Understood."

I stepped back and let the doors close, keeping my eyes locked on his until he was gone.

"That was intense," Paula, our secretary, said.

"Something like that. Do me a favor, call security and have them make sure he leaves." I didn't want him hanging around waiting for Tori to leave.

"Got it," she said, picking up the phone.

I heard her talking to Bruce at the front desk while I walked back to Tori's office.

Tori had her back to the door, her sight on something out the window.

"Mind telling me about that?" I asked, crossing my arms as I leaned on the doorframe.

"Yes," she replied without turning around.

"I'm assuming the NDA isn't for trade secrets."

"Go away, Gabe."

I walked into her office and stood in front of her, leaving her no choice but to look at me.

"What?" she huffed.

"Did he hurt you?"

A flash of emotion confirmed my suspicion, and my urge to hurt the man increased.

"I need to get back to work." She turned her chair and refocused on her computer.

"Secrets?" I asked.

"I guess you know how it feels now."

The remark stung, but I accepted the pain, knowing she had every right to aim her anger at me.

I left her office, muttering, "I suppose I do," as I walked out.

What had I thought? That she'd open up to me when I had denied her the same courtesy? It was time to come clean, to tell her everything and let her decide what she wanted to do with the information. I couldn't force her to believe me, and if she didn't, then that would be the end of it.

Strolling into Liv's office, I said, "What are you doing tonight?"

CHAPTER 26

TORI

The words on the page blurred as my mind slipped again to the events from earlier in the day. I closed my book and stood up from the couch, stretching out my back. It was no use trying to focus.

Seeing Carl Bradman had left me rattled, and Gabe had noticed. He knew me too well not to read my reaction. But I couldn't tell him why or give him any reasons for my icy reception. Nor could I tell him Carl had threatened me again, using the ruse of a friendly visit to ensure I didn't tell anyone his dirty secrets. I rubbed my wrist, the scalding sensation of his hand still present from the night he'd grabbed it. He hadn't touched me this time, but that didn't mean I wanted him in my space ever again.

I was certain if Gabe knew the truth I'd see his darker side, but the NDA gagged me, and then there was the pesky fact that he had his own secrets he refused to tell me. It was nice to have leverage for once.

I carried the book to my room and tossed it on my bed before checking on Reid. Hands clutching the car Gabe had gotten him, he slept soundly. I pulled the blanket over his shoulder and kissed his head. Out of everything I had gone through, he was the bonus.

The piece that made it all worth it. I would relive the heartache repeatedly if it meant I had him.

Closing the door behind me, I walked back into the main part of our suite. Sharp raps at my door had me checking the time. It was nine o'clock, and I hadn't ordered room service. A flash of fear charged through me at the thought that it might be Carl. I didn't trust the man, and if he found out where I lived... I couldn't stop the horrifying images that crept into my mind until I remembered that there was no access to this floor. The front desk would have called me. Calming, I pushed a strand of hair back and pulled my sweatshirt down further.

The door had only opened a fraction when Liv pushed it open, barging in with Gabe following.

"Make yourself comfortable," I said as she sat on the couch and took a fashion magazine from my coffee table.

"Is this all you have?" she said, waving it in the air. "This isn't fashion. It's fashion knock-off, like those off-the-rack blouses you wear."

Gabe gave me a shrug, and I frowned at him before I snapped, "I do not buy off-brand clothes, and not all of us have billions to spend on our wardrobes like you do."

"True," she said, dropping the magazine and throwing me a smile.

"What are you two doing here?" I asked, rubbing my temple.

"I have an offer," Gabe said, and my eyes shot to his. "A secret for a secret."

Tipping my head, I squinted as I tried to figure out what he was saying.

"I want to show you something," he continued, holding his hand out to me.

I looked down at it, remembering all the times his hand had encompassed mine.

"Please, Tori. I'll tell you everything. An exchange of secrets, so there are no more between us."

"There is no us, Gabe." The light in his eyes dimmed, and the cavern in my chest twisted in rebellion.

"Just go with him," Liv said.

My sight remained on Gabe. "I can't leave. Reid is sleeping, and I'm not waking him up this late."

"You don't have to. Auntie Liv is here, and I'll make sure he's safe."

My head swiveled toward her. "I am not leaving my son with you."

She looked offended, her hand coming to her chest. "I'm hurt, Victoria."

"Have you ever been around children?"

"No, but I'm sure it's not difficult."

I snorted, but before I could respond, Gabe said, "Please come with me, Tori. And I promise, no more secrets, no more lies. That's what you wanted, and it's what you deserve."

Hazel with amber hues pleaded for me to take his hand that remained outstretched. I glanced back at Liv, who was flicking through television channels and ignoring us.

"Let me make it up to you."

I met his eyes again. "You never can," I said, my voice quivering.

"I can try."

There was so much hope in his eyes that I put aside the past for just that moment and took his hand. Sparks flickered through me.

"You two have fun. I'll watch over Rick."

My sight snapped back to her as I corrected, "It's Reid."

She gave me a devious grin, but Gabe tugged me out the door.

"She's just playing with you," he said, pushing the elevator button.

"I don't have my coat or my wallet." I tried pulling away, but he kept my hand firmly in his.

"You don't need either."

"But..." I gave up as he pulled me into the elevator.

My pulse thrummed like a beating drum in my head. My hand remained in his, and I looked down at it, hating how perfect it felt and how much I'd missed his touch. Being this close to him always left me jumbled, like the pieces of a jigsaw puzzle spilling from a box.

We passed the lobby level, and the doors opened into the garage.

"Come on," he said, giving me no choice but to follow, his grip tight on my hand like he feared losing me again.

A private gate blocked this part of the garage off. He pressed in his code and walked me through. I had parked my car next to the Jaguar, whose lights flicked as Gabe unlocked it. I frowned at the pattering in my chest when I realized I'd parked next to his car as if even then I'd been drawn to him. There was only one other car in the vicinity with plenty of open spots, yet that's where my body had led me.

Gabe opened the door for me, finally releasing my hand. I gazed into hazel eyes, the colors fractured with emotion.

"Where are we going, Gabe?"

"Just trust me, please. I promise you'll get all the answers. No more secrets." His features were softer, giving me a glimpse of the man I had loved and still loved despite how my mind protested.

After closing my door, he ran to the driver's side and got in. The engine purred as he backed out, and I couldn't stop myself from saying, "I see you upgraded."

After a long pause, he said, "Yeah. I've always had Jags. I've had them since I could drive." We exited the garage, and I stared out the window as the city passed by. "It didn't go with the just out-of-school vibe when I moved, so I bought the other car to keep up pretenses."

"Pretenses," I repeated. "Is that all I was? A pretense?"

He slammed on the brakes to avoid running the red light, but the motion was more pronounced than it should have been. I bit my lip, thinking this had been a bad idea.

"You were never part of the pretense, Tori. Nothing about us was a lie."

Turning to him, I said, "Everything was. You built our relationship on lies that corrupted every part of it."

His eyes grew darker, the light from them fading before a horn had him looking away from me. Silence fell over us and remained as we exited the city. The miles continued with the quiet, and I felt myself nodding off. Sleep had been coming in interrupted segments since taking the job. Having Gabe back in my life disrupted it.

"Tori," I heard as I fought to return to the waking world. I blinked my eyes open to see him leaning over my door, his face too close to mine not to send my chest into mini convulsions. "We're here."

I stretched, looking past him and seeing a magnificent beach house in front of us. It stretched across a manicured lawn, lights forming a path up the walkway and along the front gardens. The breeze brought the smell of salt water to my senses, and I looked back at Gabe, questioning him with my eyes.

He held a hand out for me, and I dropped my eyes to it, hesitating.

"Where are we?" I asked, placing my hand in his. The sparks returned, snapping at my skin and reminding me that my body still answered to him even after all this time.

"The Hamptons," he answered, helping me out and closing the door behind me. A four-car garage faced me with one door already lifted. "This was my parents before my father had to sell it. I bought it under one of my companies so he wouldn't know."

"Why?" The garage door closed behind us, and he opened the inside door. An alarm sounded.

"Because my mother loved it here and because..." He punched in the code, silencing the alarm.

"Because what?" I asked as he lowered his head.

"I wanted to reclaim it, to erase the memories that haunt it and replace them with ones of you."

My inhale plunged into my chest. "When did you buy it?" My voice was barely a whisper.

"Two years ago."

Before I had returned to his life, before he even thought we had a second chance.

With a sigh, he moved through the kitchen. It was like something from a magazine, and I couldn't help gaping at it as he flicked the lights on. Gray cabinets with a blue tint lined the walls, some with glass doors. An island took up the center, five stools against it. Windows lined the seating area, the ocean barely visible in the dark beyond.

Gabe strolled into the attached living room that stretched the length of the bottom floor. Windows formed the wall, long panes of glass that looked out onto a deck and beyond to the shore. He turned on two dim lights that let me see the sheet-draped furniture. A house that no one had used in far too long, like a museum of memories waiting for someone to bring it back to life. And that someone for Gabe was me. I could barely stand, let alone follow him. I stood in the threshold as he walked to a window and stared out.

He touched the glass, his fingers tracing an invisible fracture, and he didn't have to tell me this was the pane his father had pushed him through. How many times had I traced the scar on his chest?

"My mother suffered from depression. It came in waves, the worst when my father's mood would trigger it and far worse when his anger came out in force. When she was well, she was the light in my world. Just like you were. Her smile would take the sting away; her kisses removed the pain. She loved this house and would sit on the beach, staring at the waves while Liv and I played. Our days were filled with joy until they weren't."

He tucked his hands into his pockets, his shoulders drooping, and I wondered at the weight they had carried for so long.

"The older I got, the more I noticed and the longer her lows lingered. My father's aggression toward me, his verbal assaults on Liv, caused her to sink lower. There were days she wouldn't get out of bed. It was like he had stolen the light from her, and no matter how hard Liv and I tried, we couldn't bring it back. And the further she sank, the worse he became. He would blame us." His hand raised, and he rubbed his cheek as if the sting of a hand still lingered. Head leaning on the glass, he shuddered before saying, "I found her that day. My father was on a business trip, and she hadn't come down when I'd come home from school. Liv was home from college but had spent the day with her friends. I was used to cooking my dinner and fending for myself, but something made me check on her. Like this voice in my head that told me something was off."

I moved closer to him, my body rigid with emotion.

"She was on the bathroom floor, bottles of her medications spilled across the floor with a shattered glass of wine."

My chest fractured for him, tears spilling.

"Suicide, they ruled it, but that wasn't how I ruled it. He had driven her to it. Ignoring her mental state, not seeing what his abuse of us was doing to her, never stopping to consider he was sending her to her grave. His money, his company, his ambition were the only things he ever cared about. And as I watched her casket lower into her grave, I vowed to avenge her death."

I sucked in a breath, knowing what was coming because I had seen the result in the complicated infrastructure of businesses he and his sister had acquired. In the unraveling of the financial stability of his father's company.

"Years of strategizing, of investing our inheritance from our mother, of making bets that paid off led me to Jacksonville. It was the next step in my plan. He balked at my suggestion of moving to Florida. There was no reason other than the distance from him, but I made excuses, convincing him the experience would be beneficial to the company. That earning my stripes at various investment firms would give me the knowledge I needed. Staying under the radar of the press and building a resume that would make me worthy of the CFO position and eventually the company."

Lifting his head, he kept his gaze out the window, but I moved closer, waiting for the answers I'd sought for six years, fearful of what I would hear.

"When we met, I had two years left before he expected me to return to New York and take the CFO position and three years more before my plans of revenge would be complete. Five years. That was all that stood between me and victory." A jagged sigh scraped from his throat. "I didn't mean to fall in love with you, Tori. But the day I walked into that room, and you lifted your eyes to me, I knew you were the one. I tried to deny it, but you were too special. Years of avoiding relationships, of keeping emotion from any interaction with women, knowing I had a goal, fell apart that day." He scraped his hand through his hair. "Liv and I made a pact that nothing would come between our revenge, including love. She broke it off with her college sweetheart the year she graduated. It was her statement to me that she was serious about our task. And I took that vow seriously until you."

The pounding of blood as it rushed through my veins was so loud it threatened to drown his words out.

"I couldn't stop myself from falling for you, and I knew you were the one I wanted to marry. The one I would give it all up for. And I almost did. Almost convinced myself I could leave it all behind, break my word to Liv and my vow to my mother. But I couldn't." He let out a defeated sigh. "My father set up a trust for me and Liv when we were young. By the time you and I met, it was worth billions. But there were conditions. We couldn't marry until we reached the age of thirty-two. Liv had to earn the COO position, and I had to earn the CFO position. My father's intent was always to have me take over as CEO, but he wanted me to work for it."

"You left me for money?"

He swiveled to me, his features so twisted in agony, it almost caused my knees to go out.

"No. I had intended to delay our wedding, to tell you the truth, and have us marry when I met the conditions. But then you were so excited, and I wanted you to remain that way. Making you wait five years seemed an impossible hurdle, and I wanted to be selfish and not wait that long."

"Then why?"

His throat bobbed, and he dropped his eyes from mine. "There was another condition to Liv's trust that I didn't know about. She couldn't touch her money until I met my conditions, and if I broke them not only would I lose my trust, but she would lose hers."

I brought my hand to my mouth, hating the man who had done that to them. The obvious favoritism that must have badgered Liv her entire life, the weight that condition placed on Gabe.

"I was ready to give it all up," he said, and my eyes grew large as that uncontrolled pounding returned. "To sell the companies we'd acquired and be content to live off that money. To have Liv hate me for the rest of our lives for robbing her of her inheritance. To let my mother's memory down, to break my promise to her and Liv." He turned from me, looking back out at the shore.

"But you didn't," I whispered.

"No, because my father knew. He had eyes on me. He always did. His men watched me, and when they reported seeing you with a wedding dress, he gave me an ultimatum." He knocked his head against the glass. "I've regretted answering his call since that day. Leaving you was the hardest thing I've ever done, and I pulled my car over a hundred times ready to turn around and go back to you." His voice cracked, and the swell of tears returned, leaking down my cheeks.

"What was the ultimatum?" My voice shook with emotion.

"He knew who you were. I hadn't lied about your parents' hotel. My mother loved it there, and my father promised her he would never buy it to build one of his resorts in its place." Pinching the bridge of his nose, he continued, "He knew about your mother's remission."

I stepped back, hating that he had brought my mother and her battle into this. It was an underhanded move that fortified my view of Gabe's father.

"They were in debt, underwater from the medical bills, and he had a chance to buy them out."

"No, I did their financials for them. They were in good shape."

"The company was, but personally they were struggling. Your father took out a second mortgage on the house, and the debt was building. It was the kind of weak spot my father looked for. He would have made them an offer they couldn't refuse and bulldozed the resort to build one of his in its place." Pausing, he tucked his hands back in his pockets. "He threatened to do it if I didn't leave you and return home. I couldn't let him do that to your parents or to you. And to seal my compliance, he threatened to have you blocked from every firm. To destroy your career before you could even get started. He had the power, and he would have left you suffering in entry-level positions for the remains of your career."

My head was spinning, but within the cluster of information was the realization that Gabe had been protecting me and my family. That all the years I had hated him, thinking he had left me willingly and for another woman Jan, he had been doing what he thought was necessary.

"I started packing the next day." Memories of the fevered times he'd taken me repeatedly like he was getting his fill, like he would never touch me again, returned. "I slipped a sleeping pill into your wine that night to ensure you wouldn't wake while I packed my stuff in my car." Emotion laced his words. "I've never been in so much pain. Knowing you would wake up confused and hurt, knowing you would think I left you because I didn't love you, that I was running from you. It crushed me, and I've lived with that every day since."

Tears were spilling down my cheeks as the grounds I'd built my hate for him on collapsed.

"You left me to protect me?" Syllables broken in fractured pieces.

He gazed over his shoulder, and I saw the broken man there, the one who had left me that night, severing both our hearts because circumstance had left him with no choice.

"Me, my family, your sister. God, Gabe, how long have you been carrying this?"

"Five years, ten months, and four days."

Air rushed into my lungs. He'd counted the days since he'd left me, and that truth hurt me as much as his leaving had. He turned to me, pulling his wallet out.

"I told you, Tori. There has only ever been you. I've never even looked at another woman because you will always own me."

"The tattoo?" I asked, remembering the half-moon on his shoulder blade.

"To remind me of you and all I gave up. A piece of you to carry with me." He opened his wallet. My inhale was a violent shudder when I saw the weathered and flattened paper flower I'd made him. I brought my hand to my mouth, trying to stifle my sob. "I've always loved you, and I always will."

Amber eyes lifted to mine, and a rush of warmth flushed through me, waking my heart and repairing it. I had no words, my center of gravity thrown off, all I'd convinced myself of since that day now a scramble of nothing more than incorrect guesses. And the possibility that I could have my happy ending surfaced before I could squash it.

I swallowed back another sob and brushed the tears from my

cheek. He stepped closer to me, and I didn't stop him as he reached over and cleared my other cheek.

"Don't cry, luna mia." And another fracture repaired. "That was not my intention. I never want to hurt you again, and if you still want to leave, I won't stop you." But I saw the anguish there, shadowing his attempt to shield me from more hurt.

"I wanted to hate you, and for a time I did, but I could never stop myself from loving you," I told him. "It remained, and in time, I gave up fighting it, knowing I would always love you. That there would never be anyone who could take your place because you still owned too much of me, and I couldn't break your hold on me."

He cupped my cheek, and I closed my eyes to his touch, having missed it for so long.

"What do we do now?" I asked him. "Start over?"

Forehead scrunching, he said, "No. I could never start over." I tried to step away from him, my defenses going up, but he tightened his hold on me. "I know you too well. Every curve, every freckle, every sigh, and I've envisioned them for too many years to pretend I don't know them."

I relaxed, my chest growing tight. "You hurt me, Gabe. So badly that it took me days to even leave my bed, months to stop crying, years to temper the ache, and never to fill the hollow space you left."

Anguish slashed across his face, a reflection of the guilt he'd harbored all this time. "I know, and there hasn't been a day that's passed when I haven't regretted the pain I caused. Regretted leaving you. Wished I could go back to that day and make another choice, fight my father like the man I am now."

I sniffed, seeing the predicament he was in for the first time and realizing that both of us had suffered. "But then you would have hurt your sister."

His head dropped, and I moved closer, resting my head against his. Understanding what we'd both lost and all he'd given up for me and his sister.

"Somewhere in the middle?" I asked, and he drew his head up. "If starting over isn't an option, then we start in the middle?"

The crooked grin he gave me swept the rubble from the furthest recesses of my heart. "Does that involve kissing and touching?"

A laugh fled me, and my smile took me back to a time before the damage. When I'd smiled often, laughed regularly, and loved freely. "Yes, and some."

His brow lifted. "Some?"

My smile widened. "Some...for now."

Emotion splashed through his hazel eyes. "I have a lot of groveling to do first."

"Not a lot, but a little would be good."

"I can do that. Any other requirements?"

"No, but can you kiss me now?"

Amber irises searched mine, an expression of wonder settling over them as if he didn't quite believe this was real.

"That I can do." His fingers stretched into my hair, and he brought my face closer to his. My chest thudded, and the past became a nightmare I was waking from as his lips softly brushed mine. The world tilted back into place, and rightness returned, the hollow void suddenly flooded so that it was overflowing. This was what I'd missed, the way he completed me. Resting my hand on his chest, I leaned into the kiss, parting my lips and giving him more access.

His wallet fell when he wrapped his hand around my waist to pull me nearer. A clinking sound had me stopping us. My eyes fell to the floor, seeing the ring that had rolled free with the impact. A glance back at him told me it was okay, and as he released me, I bent to pick it up.

My engagement ring. For a moment I thought he had intended to move faster, and doubt entered, but when I picked up the wallet, I saw the worn spot, the leather rubbed raw with the indent from the ring.

"I can't tell you how many wallets I've gone through in the past five years."

I peered up at him, seeing him palm his neck in that bashful way that had always caused my stomach to somersault. He had carried my ring with him, just like the flower, and the thought had tears prickling behind my eyes again. I tucked the flower back into it and rose. Our gazes locked, and that sensation of being home returned.

Gabe had been my center for months, grounding me and leaving his mark in that short time, and being here with him reminded me of why I'd never gotten over him. This man was like water to a dying plant, a fire on a winter day, an icy glass of lemonade on a summer day, the breeze in the stillness. And I hadn't lived since the day he left.

I threw my arms around him, the ring still on the top of my index finger. Our lips crashed in a heated kiss that restored every wounded crevice in me and woke the places that had been asleep. His hold on me was powerful, and I knew then that he would never let me go again, and I would never let him.

Chapter 27

Gabe

Tori was in my arms, her body curled into mine, her hair smoothing with the strokes of my fingers. I still expected to wake from a dream and find myself back in the nightmare, but the longer this continued, the more certain I became that this was real. Kissing her again had lifted the cages I'd built to hold myself together, freeing the man she brought out in me. I'd reveled in that kiss, soaking in the bliss of it until she drew away, her lips a gorgeous shade of red.

After she insisted I show her around the house, I'd given her a tour, sharing only the pleasant memories. Nothing remained but furniture, yet the ghosts of my past were there. I hadn't lied to her. I'd bought the house from my father with every intention of leaving it empty until the day I brought my father down and could find her again. At the time, it had seemed an impossibility, a reckless dream, but now the thought of her and Reid filling it with new memories no longer seemed like a dream.

Grabbing a blanket from under the sheet covering the couch, I had led Tori onto the deck. Hours of talking, of hearing everything I had missed—all of Reid's firsts, birthdays, holidays, lost teeth, and bruises—left me yearning to go back and experience them.

And I promised myself I would never miss another first. If it took me years to win Tori back completely, I would do it.

"I promise," I said, kissing her head. "I'll be at every first. Reid will never again question where his father is, and you'll never be without me. I will be by your side, Tori. No matter what comes our way."

She peeked up at me, her eyes glossy, and I leaned down and kissed her. We had stretched out on the wide lounger, a fire blazing in the fire pit. The waves crashed in the distance, the moon's reflection stretching across the ocean.

I wanted to do more than kiss her. To remind her how much I worshipped her body, to have her fall apart for me and remind myself why I'd wanted no one but her. But I understood the hesitation. I'd hurt her, left her in anguish to pick up the pieces of a life I'd shattered and to raise our son without me. She could take all the time she wanted because I would continue to wait for her.

Dropping her head back onto my chest, she let out a long sigh. "We should go back. I'm not sure your sister is the best choice to watch our son."

My hand froze, hanging in stasis as strands of hair slipped through my fingers. Our son? Had I heard her correctly? She lifted her head, eyes searching mine until understanding filled them. A small smile offset the emotion in her eyes.

"Prove yourself to me, Gabe, and I'll tell him the truth. He's your son, and he needs to know that."

"And I'll tell him the truth." I had to because the blame was mine. The lost years. As much as I blamed my father, I had made the choice and done the damage. "I'm the one who should. You've done enough. It's my turn."

Her hand smoothed down my shirt. "We've both carried our own burdens, Gabe. I see that now. It's time we stopped."

My fingers returned to sifting through her hair. "And how do we do that?"

"By falling back in love with each other."

I tipped her chin, forcing her eyes back to mine. "I never fell out of love with you."

She moved her body further into mine. "Neither did I."

The truth set my soul ablaze, burning away the pain of leaving her and offering an opening to finally heal. I dragged her mouth to mine, capturing it in a kiss that ricocheted through me. Knowing she didn't want to move fast, I stopped myself from smoothing my hand over her body like I wanted, but when she climbed over me, my hold cracked. I took her hips in my hands to steady her. Sweatshirt lifting, my fingers spread over her skin, and I questioned how I'd ever taken it slow with her when we'd first met.

Her hands pushed at my shirt, tugging it free from my pants, and sliding over my chest. I sucked in a breath, pushing her back and seeing the desire that shadowed her blue eyes.

"Middle," I said, hearing how strained the word came out. As much as I didn't want to stop, I didn't want her to wake up in the morning and regret moving too fast. We had years of history behind us to work through and emotions that needed recognizing. I wouldn't risk losing her again on my body's need to have her.

She crinkled her nose, twisting her lips as she contemplated the word.

"Your boundaries, Tori. Not mine, and I won't risk plowing through them." She ground down on me, and I groaned, the need for her howling through me. "Even though moves like that make me want to be the bad guy."

Her smile broke through as she sat back. I grabbed her hips, giving her a warning look, although I knew she hadn't done it to torment me like it had.

"You've never been the bad guy type, Gabe."

Head tipping, I said, "I've been the bad guy for over five years." Regret and guilt returned with the admission.

Leaning forward, she took my face in her hands. "Because you had to, which means you weren't really the bad guy I thought you were or that you thought you were."

Sweeping a piece of hair behind her ear, I studied her, taking in the small parts of her I'd missed. The gentle smile, the depths of blue in her eyes, the thick lashes that outlined them, the dark locks with hints of brown in them, the small freckle on her left cheek. Lifting her hips, I settled her back to my side, tucking her in as close as I could have her and rubbing my hand up her back.

"I don't want to be that man anymore," I told her, staring out at the ocean. "I want to be who I am when I'm with you. You make me a better man because you make me whole."

She buried her face further into my chest. Silence fell over us, but it was a comfortable quiet, our breathing matched, our bodies calm. After a few minutes, I said, "A secret for a secret." I hadn't forgotten my intention in bringing her here—to stop the secrets between us.

"I told you everything," she said, and I heard the mistruth.

"Tori, you know everything I kept from you. What happened with Bradman?"

She went rigid. "Nothing."

"You were never good at lying. Remember that time we played poker?"

Her head shot up, her eyes narrowing. "I wasn't that bad."

"You were pretty bad," I replied with a chuckle. "Talk."

A roll of her eyes let me know she was going to fight me on this.

"There's an NDA. I can't tell you anything." She sat up, rubbing her wrist, where I'd seen her do the same action when Carl had stopped by her office and another when I'd mentioned the company.

"My lawyers can shred it within minutes. I have more money and power than he has, so don't worry about the NDA."

"It was nothing," she said, her sight on the water.

"Nothing doesn't leave you this rigid and rattled. What did the asshole do?"

Her head turned to me, blue orbs wide.

"I'm not playing, Tori. What happened?"

"But the NDA—"

"Again, my attorneys are better and more expensive."

I sat up further, suspicious that what she was about to tell me would piss me off.

Rubbing her wrist, she said, "He made a pass at me." A slash of anger turned my vision crimson. "We were working late, which wasn't abnormal, but I'd never given it much thought. We'd been working closely for years. He came behind me and put his hands on my hips and tried to push me onto the desk, saying I'd been flirting with him for years and he was ready to take me up on the invitation." She shivered, but the fire raging through me had me heated.

"I broke away, smacked him, and ran from the office. I hid in the lobby, shaking until I had no choice but to return since I'd left everything in my office. Security took me up and let me back onto the floor. He was gone by that time." She pushed a strand of hair back. "I gave my notice the next morning, and he slapped me with the NDA, saying he would smear my name and never give me a recommendation if I didn't sign it."

And his recommendation had been glowing. No wonder he'd stopped by my office. He was checking on her to make sure she hadn't broken the agreement. My teeth ground as I thought of what I wanted to do to the man. I wasn't violent, but the thoughts were enough to let me know I could be.

"What did he do to your wrist?" I asked, taking her hand and gently caressing the soft skin around her wrist.

"He grabbed it when I broke free. I had bruises for a week. Only when I smacked him did he let go."

I let my head fall against the seat. Power and money made men expect they could get away with anything. I'd seen it too often, and many of the companies I'd bought up had been owned by assholes like Bradman.

"You can't do anything, Gabe. Besides, it brought us back

together." That truth still didn't make what he'd done acceptable. "Forget about it."

I turned her to me. "You can't forget about it, so I won't. He'll pay. Trust me. I'll find a way to make him pay."

Cerulean blue set against the night sky had my anger calming. Her fingers draped over my jaw, soothing the tension. "It's late. We should get back."

Nodding, I helped her stand, taking her hand and drawing her in for another kiss. Hesitation turned to hunger, but recognizing it made me keep the kiss short. Until there was no hesitation, no question, I would take it slow. Because the day it faded, there would be no holding me back.

Quiet encompassed the ride home. Tori fell asleep within minutes, and I used the drive to think through the Bradman dilemma until I had a plan. With my mind calming, I looked over at Tori, the corroded chambers of my heart healing with every minute more she was in my presence. She stirred, her hand slipping, and I spied the engagement ring on her right finger. While not on the correct hand, it was a ray of hope that I might remove it one day and place it where it needed to be. I'd held onto it, keeping it and the flower with me as a reminder of what I'd lost. And now I had her back. A tightness took over my chest, and I looked out at the road, unsure of what the future held but confident Tori would be in it.

"Tori," I nudged her awake as I pulled into my spot in the garage.

Dusty eyes peeked open before she rubbed them.

"We're back," I told her, climbing out of the car and opening her door for her.

"That was fast," she said with a yawn.

Laughing, I kissed her on the head, saying, "Maybe for you, sleepyhead."

"Did I sleep the entire ride?"

"Yeah. It was cute. Especially the line of drool I wiped from your chin."

Her jaw went slack before she gave me a mock hit. "You did not."

I drew her into me, feeling more like myself than I had in years. Relaxed again, unburdened, happy. "No, I didn't, but you were still cute."

Grasping my face, she dragged my mouth to hers. Her smile continued through the kiss and remained when I tipped my head back.

"Ready to see if my sister lost our son?" I asked, loving the way it felt to say he was ours.

"Yeah."

I took her hand, closing the door for her and leading her to the elevators.

"She isn't really that bad, is she?"

Shaking my head, I said, "I don't know that Liv has a maternal bone in her body. She hates kids, but he is her nephew, so there's a higher probability he's still safe."

An elbow in my side accompanied the opening of the elevator doors. We found Liv sound asleep on the couch, with the television still running in the background. I left her there while Tori checked on Reid.

"She looks too comfortable to wake," Tori said. "Leave her there. I'll wake her in the morning."

I eyed her. "You really want to deal with the wrath of my sister when she finds out we let her sleep with her makeup on?"

She gave me a brilliant smile. "I can handle it." Taking my hand, she led me over to Reid's room and opened the door a crack. "Look."

I peered over her shoulder, my chest constricting. Reid was wrapped up in the car blanket I'd seen Tori folding the last time I'd been there. Clutched in his hand was the model car I'd bought him. I couldn't help the warmth that filled me at the sight of him. His auburn hair was a messy clump of curls, his tiny hands holding the car tight, his face almost angelic. A sting of pain ricocheted through me. I'd missed so much of his life that seeing him like that was a painful reminder.

Tori's hand touched my cheek, and I looked down at her, realizing my eyes were misty. I turned away, but she brought her other hand up and forced my sight to hers.

"He'll forgive you," she said. "Just like I have."

"Have you?" I asked, still not truly believing it.

A nod and a soft smile. "The hurt is still there, but it's healing and will continue to heal. But I know why now, and that makes it easier."

I wasn't so sure it was that easy. Not after all I'd done. Peering back at Reid once more, I closed his door.

"You really want to leave her there?" I asked, gesturing with my head to where Liv was still dead to the world.

"Let her sleep. I'll have Reid wake her." The mischievous grin she wore had me wondering if this was payback for the phone call all those years ago.

"Don't say I didn't warn you," I joked. "She's a beast when she wakes up."

"I made it through the toddler years. I can deal with your sister."

Again, the thought that I'd missed too much resurfaced, and again, she read my change in emotion. Taking my hand, she reached up and pulled my mouth to hers. The kiss searched out the doubt, obliterating it, and as the ash settled, her teeth scraped over my bottom lip.

"Stop," she said. "We can't move forward if you continue to wallow in guilt. If I can set my pain aside, you can set yours aside. Only then can we make it from the middle to where we left off."

I dropped my head to hers, breathing in vanilla and cherry blossoms. "I'll work on it," I said, giving her forehead a kiss.

"Good night, Gabe."

Hand plunging into her hair, I wrapped my fingers around her neck and dragged her to me, kissing her once more. Heated, needy, and lingering, the kiss reinforced more of the corroded chambers of my heart. "Good night, luna mia."

Her inhale, seductive and tempting, stayed with me long after I returned to my suite. Walking to the bar, I picked up my scotch. The bottle hovered in my hand, the liquid one minuscule movement from filling my cup. Since leaving Tori, it had become my crutch, the only thing that got me through the day. I set the bottle back down, replaced the lid, and turned from it, knowing I no longer needed it to make it through the day or the night. I had hope again, and I had Tori.

Movement outside my office had me lifting my head. I'd come in early to work out then entrenched myself in emails and reports, unaware of the time that had passed.

Liv walked in with a flourish, closing the door behind her. From the quick strides to my desk and the exaggerated drop into the chair, I could tell she wasn't happy with me. I tried to hide my grin.

"That mongrel woke me up this morning using my back as a racetrack."

I stifled my laugh, and it came out as a snort. "He's not a mongrel. He's your nephew."

"Not after this morning. I'm disowning him. Do you have any idea how hard it is to make conversation with a child?"

"For most, not that hard. But you?"

She crossed her arms, pouting at me. "He made me eat some disgusting colorful cereal. It will take me weeks to clean that pollution from my body."

"You're full of crap, Liv. You used to love that stuff when we were young. I distinctly remember boxes of cereal with marshmal-lows in your dorm room."

The roll of her eyes told me she wasn't in a playful mood. She looked down at her nails, picking at one. "So how did it go?"

"Better than I thought it would," I admitted.

Her eyes lifted. "And?"

"We're taking it in steps, but there's hope."

She gave me a smile. "Good. She's here, by the way. We rode in together."

My grin grew. "You shared a car with Tori and Reid?"

"I put up with sharing a car with them. The child never shuts up. I haven't heard so much about cars since you were an annoying brat." A tug at her lips told me she'd enjoyed it more than she would ever admit to me. "Next time you need a babysitter, pay for one."

"I'll make sure Auntie Liv is available," I teased as she walked to the door.

"Don't you dare, or I'll take a pair of scissors to every one of those designer suits you love and shred them."

"Ouch. That's extreme."

"You owe me, Gabe."

"And I know you won't let me forget it."

After she left, I made my way to Tori's office. Her door was open, and she was studying her computer screen, a pencil between her teeth. She wore a navy dress that brought out the hues in her eyes and deepened the ebony in her hair. I watched her, fully aware that it was a creepy move, but she had me mesmerized, and the idea that she could be mine again left me frozen.

Eyes lifting, she jumped slightly before a gorgeous smile lit her face.

"Morning," she said.

I moved from where I'd been leaning on the doorframe and closed the office door before I made my way to her. Leaning over, I tangled my hand in her hair and kissed her. She clutched at my shirt, and I pulled her up, needing to feel her body against mine. A reminder that I hadn't dreamed this, that we were really getting our second chance.

"I'm not sure how appropriate this is for work," she mumbled against my lips, her hand in my hair.

"Since I own the company, I'm making an exception." My hands followed the curve of her waist. After years of yearning for her to be in my arms again, now that she was, it was difficult not to touch her. "Have dinner with me tonight," I said.

"But I have Reid."

"Then we make it pizza and a movie. Just like we used to do."

She tipped her head, giving me a smile. "You'll bring the beer?"

I laughed, trying to think of the last time I'd had a beer. "Definitely."

"Sounds like a date, but I have to warn you, movie time isn't what it used to be."

Shrugging, I said, "Whatever Reid wants. As long as I'm with the two of you, I won't care."

Eyes the color of a clear summer day shimmered. "Why don't you pick him up with me?"

My stomach knotted as the air in my lungs froze. "Really?"

"Yeah. But Gabe," she dropped her arms from my neck, taking a step back, "he can't know yet. Not until..."

Her eyes fell to the floor, but I put my finger under her chin and lifted it, saying, "Until we figure this out?"

A simple nod and melancholy eyes. "I'm sorry."

"Don't be. You need to protect him, and I've already hurt him. You don't want to take the chance of that happening again." It hurt to say, to know she didn't fully trust me, but how could she? One night of confessions couldn't erase years of pain.

"I want to let you back in, but I'm frightened."

I stepped back into her space. "I'm never going away again, Tori. Nothing could make me leave your side or his. If I must spend the rest of my life proving that to you, I will."

"Not the rest of your life. Just a little while."

"Then you have whatever time you need, as long as you let me in enough to prove myself to you." My fingers brushed over her cheek as I tucked a strand of her hair back. "Starting with pizza and a movie."

"That sounds like a good place to start."

While I wanted more, she was right. I needed to prove myself to her. A few kisses and confessions weren't enough to win her back. I needed to earn her trust again, but I had destroyed it so completely that I didn't know if I could ever repair it.

Chapter 28

Tori

The night had been a whirlwind of emotions, and I'd tossed and turned, running everything Gabe had said through my mind repeatedly. I didn't doubt him, but I'd been caught up in the moment, in his kisses, in having him close to me again, in his strength. Too caught up to be rational. We'd agreed to start in the middle, but even that seemed too fast, even though my body craved more.

I didn't know how I was going to take this slow because it felt so right with Gabe. It always had. But picking up where we left off when he left seemed impossible. The divide was still there, as were the memories and the pain.

His knock on the door pulled me from my thoughts. Reid let out an excited sound, clapping his hands where he sat at the table, coloring. He had stayed glued to Gabe from the moment we picked him up, and when Gabe left us on our floor so he could go change, Reid had been devastated. Until he found out Gabe was coming back.

He had already formed an attachment, and that made this even harder.

I opened the door, catching the drop of my mouth. God, he

was sexy. He had on a charcoal gray T-shirt and a pair of jeans. His hazel eyes looked over the pizza box, and I remembered the confident, sexy man who had taken a seat next to me and stolen my heart within minutes.

He held up his other hand to show me the six-pack of IPAs in it.

"No scotch?" I asked, letting him in.

"Eh, my tastes are changing."

"Gabe!" Reid rushed from his chair and tackled Gabe's legs, almost knocking him over.

"Hey buddy. Ready for some pizza?"

"Pepperoni?"

Gabe threw his head back and chuckled. "Just like your mom. Wouldn't be a good slice if it didn't have pepperoni."

I freed his legs from Reid's hold and motioned to the coffee table.

"What's the movie pick?" he asked, setting the pizza down while I handed Reid napkins and grabbed him a juice box.

"*Cars*," Reid said, his excitement spilling over. "Have you seen it?"

He jumped onto the middle of the couch and patted the spot next to him for Gabe to sit. Glancing at me, Gabe's eyes questioned me about the seating order. I gave him a smile and a nod, mouthing, "Go ahead."

I stood there, listening to them as Reid told him all about the movie and Gabe asked questions as if they were best friends. Tears pushed at the back of my eyes. Possibility. That's what this was, and I wouldn't let it go because the outcome was too important to lose.

Taking a seat on the other side of Reid, I turned the movie on. We settled in, the three of us, Reid munching on his pizza, picking his pepperonis off and dropping them into his mouth just like Gabe did. As the movie progressed, I felt Gabe's hand on my shoulder. I glanced over at him, meeting amber irises that shone with satisfaction. Leaning my head on his hand, I let myself relax into the comfort of his touch and the idea of possibility.

By the time the movie ended, Reid was sound asleep, his head resting on Gabe's chest.

"He's a lightweight," Gabe teased, dropping his arm from me and tentatively brushing a lock of hair from Reid's forehead.

I moved to lift him, but Gabe stopped me. "Leave him, please. Just a few more minutes."

Sitting back down, I watched him, seeing the expression of wonder on his face. The same I'd had since I'd given birth to our son. He was a miracle, a light that had come from the darkness Gabe had left.

"He's so beautiful, Tori." His voice held a reverence that shone in his features.

"I know. He was the only good thing you left me."

His eyes shot up, the hurt clear until he covered it. "I'm sorry. I can never take it back, but I promise I'll spend the rest of my life making it up to you."

Swallowing back the emotion, I nodded, knowing that to speak would send the tears rushing from me. I was tired of crying. I'd spent years doing it.

He sat there for a few more minutes, just looking at Reid as if he was memorizing him. As he stood, he scooped Reid up like he weighed no more than a feather, and I followed him into Reid's room, pulling the sheets back and letting Gabe tuck him in. It was such a small act, but it had pressure building in my chest. And I suddenly wanted to be past this, to have my happily ever after and to have it with Gabe. To have him there every night, tucking Reid in with me.

"I should go," he said, shoving his hands in his pockets and leaving the room.

Closing Reid's door, I trailed Gabe. "Thank you."

"For?" He stopped in front of the door. There was so much sadness in his expression that my breath hitched.

"For tonight. For sharing it with Reid. It meant the world to him."

"It meant the same for me," he admitted, his vision on the floor. "This is hard, Tori." His throat bobbed as he looked back up at me. "You're so close, but the distance is still there. I want to hold you, to make love to you, to have you look at me like you used to. Without the shadow of distrust, without the hesitation." He scraped his hands through his hair. "And I don't know how to get back to that. And Reid...I want to claim him as mine. To declare it to the world that he's my son." His voice fractured, and with it, my heart. "If I could take it all back, erase it all from both of you, I would. But I never can."

I bridged the gap between us and pulled his head down, kissing him as his agony merged with mine. We were both scarred, damaged by the circumstances that had shaped our relationship, and neither of us knew how to proceed because we'd carried those wounds for so long.

His hands encompassed me, bringing my body into his, and I let myself revel in the safety of his arms. Home. That's what it felt like with Gabe. Like returning home after trudging blindly through a storm. He was warmth and security, a cozy blanket and a raging fire. He had been my everything until he wasn't, and now he was back, and I didn't want to go through that storm again.

"I can't do it again, Gabe."

He halted our kiss and gazed at me, devastation resting in his eyes.

"You can't leave me in the storm again," I rambled as my tears rushed free. "I don't think I'll survive this time. I barely survived the last time."

"Storm?" he asked, creases lining his eyes.

"The storm you left me in, to find my way out, to clear away the damage. I can't do it again because this time it will kill me." He wiped my tears away as I continued. "I loved you too much, and...I still do, so please don't let me go into the storm again."

His hold on me tightened, and I turned my face into his chest, smelling his scent and letting it strengthen me.

"I will never let you go again, luna mia. Never until the day you tell me to go."

I buried my face further into him. "I won't tell you to go because I can't survive without you, not now that you're back." Raw and honest, the admission stung because I prided myself on being a strong, confident woman.

He pushed me away so that he could see my face. "You survived all those years. Raised our son, built a career. You can survive whatever comes at you."

"But I don't want to if you're not by my side."

He kissed my cheek, kissing every tear until they were dry. "I'll be here, and I'm not going anywhere ever again. Where you go, I go. If you want to leave this life and live in the country, I'm there. Return to Florida, I'm there. Move to Europe, I'll follow. Because I lived my life without you for too long, and every day was like a knife tearing through my flesh. I won't live it without you again."

His declaration soared through me, fortifying the crumbling structures that were only now repairing. Brushing his lips over mine, he said, "Goodnight, Tori."

"Goodnight." I watched him walk to the elevator, casting a glance back at me before it opened and took him from me.

Sleep was a struggle, my mind on Gabe and his words, the emotions gripping my chest, the possibilities and the fear. I rolled to my side, staring at his side of the bed, the side I'd left empty no matter where I slept. I wanted him there, taking up that space again, but fear had me in its grip. As much as his words assured me, they were ones he'd told me before. And even though I knew the truth, the hesitation was still there, the sting of loss still fresh. I'd spent years trying to erase Gabe's hold on me, and I had failed.

I rolled back over and looked at my phone. It was midnight, and I was too awake to sleep. I dialed Cindy's number, knowing she'd be awake since it was only nine in California.

"Tor? Why are you calling me so late? What's wrong? Did that asshole do something else to you? I told you not to take that job." I'd made the mistake of telling her Gabe was my new boss. It was too hard to keep things from her.

"No, he didn't do anything. I'm just...I can't sleep."

"Why can't you sleep?"

I heard her boyfriend's voice then a quick, "It's Tori."

"Noah says hi," she told me. I could hear her walking through their house.

"Tell him hi back." I pulled myself into a sitting position, the light from the phone flickering on the engagement ring I'd been unable to take off. It was on the other hand, but the weight of it was a reminder of the future that seemed so close that it was almost unreal.

"What's wrong, Tor?"

"I...he..." I dropped my head back on the wall.

"No, don't tell me...damn it, Tori, you did not go back to him!"

I scrunched my brows at the ferocity of her voice.

"I still love him. He told me the truth."

"Truth? About what? How he left you pregnant and alone. Ghosted you and never bothered to explain why he left? Never bothered to come back?"

"It's complicated."

She disconnected, and I stared at the phone, too stunned to move until my phone buzzed with an incoming video call. With a relieved exhale escaping me, I answered, seeing her angry face pop up. Her blonde hair was in two braids, and her green eyes were lined with charcoal.

"That's better. Now I can yell at you face to face."

My lips pursed.

"Are you insane? You do not want that man back in your life."

"Cindy, you don't understand."

She rolled her eyes. "Then help me understand why you would

let a man who destroyed you back into your life. Into Reid's life. What if he does the same thing again?"

"I don't think he will."

"You don't think he will, but you don't know it."

I let my head fall back again. "He had no choice but to leave me."

Her laugh was cruel. "Is that what he told you? He had a choice, and he took it."

"It's more than that." And I wondered if I was trying to convince myself or Cindy.

"Like what?"

"He was protecting me and my parents." I explained what Gabe had told me, my belief in him rising again, the swell in my chest returning because I had seen the emotion in him, the anguish he'd suffered along with me.

Cindy's body dropped back in her chair, and she rubbed her hand over her face.

"He didn't know about Reid, and he...he still loves me." He had remained faithful to me through all the years, and I believed him. There was too much truth in his eyes, pain in his voice. "Do you remember the paper flower I wouldn't let you throw out? The one he made for me?" It was in Reid's baby book. The only piece of his father I could offer him.

"Yeah."

"He still has the one I made for him. He's been carrying it in his wallet all this time."

She sighed, and I could see the change in her. "This sounds like something out of a movie, Tor. This stuff doesn't happen."

"But it is."

"And the other woman? The one who answered his phone? How many women has he been with while he's been in love with you?"

"None. It was his sister. He never knew she talked to me. But, Cindy, he never moved on. Just like I never did."

"Are you trying to convince me or yourself?"

"You. I believe him. If you could talk to him, you'd see it and hear it in his voice."

"God, you're a pain in my ass," she teased. "Did you seriously call me because you're thinking about going back to him?"

"Yes, and we're taking steps."

"Did you kiss him?"

I couldn't fight my smile at the thought of Gabe's kisses. They had ruined me for any other man, and now I had them back.

"Damn it, Tori. You hoe. Did you sleep with him already?"

"No, we're taking it slow. And I'm not a hoe, bitch."

She let out her usual laugh, the one that came from deep in her belly and told me she was considering the same things I was. "What about Reid? Does he know?"

I shook my head. "I'm not ready to tell him. Just in case. I don't want him hurt, but he adores Gabe and..." I thought about Gabe with him, the looks of wonder, pride, and love that were there. "...Gabe adores him. They look and act so much alike. You should see them together."

"Why did you call me, Tor?"

"Because I needed a voice of reason."

She frowned. "You wanted me to give you the answer. I know you, Tor. You fell head over heels for him all those years ago, and you never stopped loving him. I saw it. Even when you were at your worst, you refused to throw that damned flower out. Refused to sell your wedding dress, which is still hanging in the closet at your parents' house. Do I want to ask where you have the bracelet?"

The bracelet Gabe had given me that Christmas. The one I'd held over the trash ready to throw away but couldn't. Instead, I had tucked it into my jewelry box, where it remained buried below enough pieces to keep it from my sight.

"No, you don't."

"You never let him go, Tor."

"I couldn't." I'd given up trying to because he had taken up too much space, and even with the void he'd left, I knew no one could ever fill it. Reid had taken up some of it, but the rest remained a hollow core that no man could reach.

"Do you really believe him?"

"Yes."

She was quiet for a minute, and I could see her thinking about something. "You're going home this weekend, right?"

It had been my plan. My parents wanted to give Reid his birthday present, and my father's birthday was the following week. We'd planned to celebrate. Even Cash and Brandi were coming.

"Yes. Are you and Noah able to make it?"

She shook her head. "No, Noah has a gig. I need to be there to fend the groupies off."

This time I laughed. Noah was in a local band that was earning a loyal following. Their shows sold out, and Cindy always teased him about the groupies. But Noah worshipped her, so there was no chance another woman was a threat. Still, she insisted on attending every show.

"Bring Gabe with you," she said.

My mouth fell open. "What? I can't do that. It's too early."

"And your family hates him. Especially Cash. Shoot, maybe I should go so I can watch the fireworks."

"Cindy, I can't throw Gabe into that."

"Why not? If he really does still love you, he'll go. Let him defend his actions to your family. If he goes, you'll know he's sincere and willing to do whatever it takes to win you back. If he refuses, then you have your answer."

Noah's head popped over hers. "She's right. Any man worth his salt will face the fire if he really loves his woman. If he really gave you up to protect you, he'll do this to keep you."

"When did you become so philosophical?" I asked him.

"Who cares?" Cindy said, tugging him to her. "I think it's sexy."

I rolled my eyes. "You two are gross. I'm hanging up now."

"Bye, Tor. Text me with all the scoop!"

Shaking my head, I hung up before I had to witness more than I wanted. Throwing my phone onto my bedside table, I laid back down, smoothing my hand over the empty side of the bed. The engagement ring glittered in the dim light from the moon, a reminder of what I stood to gain if this worked out. Would Gabe accept an invitation to be crucified by my family? He had hired me, knowing the wrath he faced from me and the pain it would cause him. Was I worth what he would go through with my family? I closed my eyes, intent on finding out because this would flush out any remaining doubt I had about him. And I wanted it gone so that the empty side of my bed was no longer empty.

CHAPTER 29

GABE

The lobby was quiet this early, so when the elevator doors opened, I knew exactly who it carried. Tori walked out with Reid's hand in hers. She wore a long pink coat that came just above her knees, where her skirt ended. The heels of her knee-high black boots clicked on the marble, and my eyes followed their path until I met her eyes. Vibrant blue, they sparkled with the sunlight that filtered in through the hotel windows.

"Gabe!" Reid freed himself from his mother's hand and ran toward me. I wanted to squat down and scoop him up, but I refrained, still tenuous with where Tori had set my boundaries. He stopped in front of me, his hazel eyes dusted with amber and excitement.

"Good morning, buddy. Did you have something sweet for breakfast?"

He nodded enthusiastically. "A donut. How did you know?"

I dusted the powder from his cheek and from where it landed on his navy coat. "Just a lucky guess."

"Good morning," Tori greeted me, and the air stuck in my lungs when I met her cerulean irises. She had her hair tucked behind her ears, a pink hat the match of her coat covering most of it.

"Morning." Every part of me wanted to lean over and kiss her, but again, there were boundaries with Reid that she had set, and I didn't want to test them.

"Thank you for offering to share the ride. Reid was very excited when he heard."

Reid took my hand and led me toward the doors, immediately asking me about my opinion of the movie. He continued to dominate the conversation during the ride, talking excitedly about his favorite characters and scenes. All the while, I peeked over at Tori, savoring the smile that adorned her face. When she would catch my eyes on her, a blush would climb her cheeks, and she would look away.

"Is there a second movie?" I asked Reid, looking for an excuse to see them again. "Maybe one we can watch this weekend?"

"Oh, there is. Can we, Mommy? Maybe we can make popcorn. I love popcorn."

She frowned, shaking her head. "We can't. Remember, we're going to see Grandma and Grandpa this weekend. They want to give you your birthday present."

My spirit dropped.

"Can Gabe come with us?"

Tori froze, as did I. "I don't think that would be a good idea," I told him, knowing how her family felt about me. There was a high probability they would never talk to me again, even with Tori accepting me back into her life.

"Maybe another night," she told him.

"When are you leaving?" I asked, trying to hide my disappointment.

"Tomorrow. I was planning to leave work early since the drive will be so long. Cash and his wife are leaving today with their daughter. Otherwise, I would have gotten a ride with them."

Definitely not an event that would offer me welcome. "Take the company plane," I blurted.

"Oh, no. I couldn't. It's nothing I haven't driven before. We'll be fine."

Reid's head was moving from Tori to me as we talked.

"I insist. I'll have it fueled and ready with a car to take you to the house. It's a perk of the job, take it."

"Gabe, I couldn't." Her eyes creased as she chewed her lip.

"Take it. Otherwise, I'll worry about you the entire time you're on the road. Besides, I'm sure Reid hasn't been on a private plane before. He'll have fun."

"Please, Mommy."

She gave me a sour look that told me she didn't like how I'd gotten Reid on my side, but I didn't care. I didn't want her driving for so many hours, and the weather was turning as winter moved in.

"Fine," she relented.

I texted my pilot and gave him the details as I waited for Tori to drop Reid off. The sound of her heels coincided with my last text. She stayed quiet as we waited for the elevators, and I wasn't sure if she was mad at me for my insistence or if it was something else. Squeezing the bridge of my nose, I tried to calm the nerves that were drilling into me with the thought that I'd screwed this up.

She stepped into the elevator, and I followed, the silence remaining until the door closed.

"Tori, I..." I started, but she stopped my words with a kiss that seared away the doubt. Hands wrapping around her waist and bringing her further into me, I deepened the kiss.

The ring of the elevator informed me we'd arrived, and she untangled herself from my arms, smoothing her coat down just as the doors opened. With a glance back, she threw me a mischievous grin and walked off.

Shaking my head, I didn't bother hiding my smile when I followed her. She swiped us into the office space, giving Paula a bubbly hello before heading to her office. I stopped to get my messages, saying good morning to Paula and attempting to get the heat of that kiss from my mind so I could function the rest of the morning.

Liv hadn't arrived yet, but that wasn't abnormal. She was usually the last one in, making her own hours. I honestly wasn't sure if she'd worked more than two hours a day since my father had left.

Logging in, I stood over my desk, rolling out the tension in my neck. The sound of my door closing had me lifting my head to see Tori strolling into my office. I gave her a sheepish grin, still reeling from her kiss.

"Come with us," she said, and my grin faltered.

"Where?"

She swallowed, and I followed the movement of her hand as it nervously brushed a hair from her cheek. A tremor, barely noticeable, accompanied it. "To my parents' place."

The floor dropped from under me like another nightmare stretching to engulf me. I was certain her family hated me. Fully expected her brother would punch me if he could get a good hit off before I countered it. There was no prospect that me going with her would have a good outcome. But she was there, asking me, nervously awaiting my response, and I didn't want to let her down again. Not ever again.

I walked around the desk and over to her. Taking her hands in mine and seeing the shake in them, I asked, "Is it important to you that I be there?"

She nodded, her eyes tinged with emotion.

"Then I'll go." And suffer the consequences of my decisions... again. I didn't think I would ever stop facing them. It was my punishment for leaving her, and if accepting it kept her by my side, then I would gladly welcome it.

Relief splashed across her features. "Are you sure?"

"Isn't that what I should ask you?" I smoothed my finger over her thumb. "I'm sure I'm the last person your family wants to see."

"I want you there. And I want you to tell them what you told me. All of it."

My hold tightened on her hand. "Tori, I can't."

"You can, because they need to know, just like I did. Then they can judge you themselves."

"And if they still hate me?"

She shrugged. "It won't matter because I don't."

"You really don't?"

"Not anymore. I did. For a very long time, but the love was still there, like an annoying gnat I couldn't kill."

Narrowing my eyes at her, I said, "That's not very nice."

"But it's the truth. I tried not to love you, Gabe, but I couldn't. You embedded yourself too far into my soul, and I couldn't free myself of you."

"And now?"

"Now...I don't know. I still love you. The hate is gone, but the hurt isn't, and that's why we need to take this in steps."

I nodded, understanding and knowing I'd give her as much time as she needed. "With kisses like the one you gave me in the elevator, slow is going to be tough," I teased.

"I never said it would be easy to win me back."

"It shouldn't be," I admitted. "I left too much damage in my wake."

She took my hand, and as I dropped my eyes to it, I saw the ring on her finger. A sign that she had faith in where this was going. Faith again in me. I rubbed my thumb over it, looking forward to the day I could move it to the correct finger and add a band to it.

"I suppose we were both damaged," she mumbled, and my eyes jumped to hers. "And now we can heal together."

Lush strands of ebony encased my fingers as I drew her to me. Our mouths met in a kiss that had a torrent of wings flapping in my stomach. Her hands on my chest sent them rising so that it almost felt like this was our first kiss, a sensation I experienced every time I kissed Tori. Like we were young and in love, experiencing all our firsts and treasuring each one.

A knock on my door had us jumping apart, and I hated that we had to keep what we had a secret. I still wasn't sure what kind of conflict the CEO involved with his CFO presented, but I was certain it wasn't a good one.

The door opened just as Tori was smoothing her hand over her hair.

Our assistant, Sean, came in but stopped, his eyes darting between us. He shook his head, his grin entirely too large.

"Did you need something, Sean?" I asked, having worked with him long enough to read that look.

"Just bringing notes for your ten o'clock." He brought them to my desk.

"I should go," Tori said. "I'll have that report to you by end of day."

"No need to go on my account," Sean said. "It's about time you two dealt with that tension. It's enough to burn the floor down."

He gave us a wink, and I tried not to react, scowling at him.

"We were discussing the restructure," I snapped. "Not that it makes a difference."

"Whatever you want to call it, boss. Just as long as it doesn't heat this place up anymore."

"Leave, Sean."

He laughed on his way out, mumbling about turning the air conditioner on. I pinched my brow, peeking at Tori, who wore an amused smile.

"I let him get away with too much."

"Nah, he's perfect for dealing with you." She straightened my tie, easing her hand down to follow its path. "Do you want to watch the second movie with us tonight? I'm sure Reid will spend the entire plane trip telling you about every car in it."

"I'd love to. Should I bring the popcorn?"

Her smile warmed me to my core. "Definitely." She gave me a peck on the cheek, her hand drifting over mine as she walked to the door. "Seven o'clock, Mr. Icinda. Don't be late."

"Wouldn't dream of it."

I rested against the desk as excitement danced with nerves, making it difficult to move. Another night with Tori and Reid. A full weekend with them. It sounded like heaven, save for the fact that I would have to face her family. There was no way that would go well, and I suspected I wouldn't be welcome enough to do more than drop them off and pick them up.

Reid opened the door, his eyes growing large at the tub of movie theater popcorn in my hand.

"Whoa, is that for me?" he asked, his hands reaching up for it.

"Yup. Only the good stuff for movie two."

I handed it to him and entered the suite. "Where's your mom?"

"Right here." Tori's head popped up from behind the counter in the kitchen. Her black hair was piled on her head, messy strands sticking out in different directions. She had a band T-shirt on that was splashed with globs of strawberry.

I walked over to her and wiped a pink splotch from her cheek. "Rough night?" I asked, glancing at the mess on the floor.

"Something like that." She grabbed more paper towels and returned to the floor. Taking a handful, I joined her. "I was trying to make strawberry milkshakes, but the blender went wonky on me."

I picked up the lid that must have flown off during the incident, studying it. "Is this the same blender I bought you?"

Her eyes leaped to mine. "Yes."

My smile was quick. "No wonder. I'll get you a new one."

"But I like this one." And I could see the emotion in the subtle creases that formed around her eyes. I had bought it for her when we decided on milkshakes and a movie night, running to the store to buy it when she realized she didn't have one.

"I don't think it's working properly, luna mia." The nickname flowed like it always had, and I dropped my sight back to the mess.

She pressed her hands to my cheeks and forced my head up. "I missed that." Her face morphed, and she cringed, bringing her hands back down. "Oops."

Swiping my finger where her hand had left a sticky strawberry residue on my cheek, I brought it to my mouth and tasted it. "Would have been a good milkshake."

Her laughter bounced through me, and I tried to capture it for fear of being without it again.

"Can we start the movie?" Reid yelled from the couch.

"Give me five minutes," she replied, returning to cleaning up.

I stopped her hand and took my phone out.

"Housekeeping, Sheila speaking."

"Hi Sheila, this is Mr. Icinda. There's been a strawberry milkshake mishap in Miss Heck's suite. Can you kindly send someone up to clean it? She's not as adept at the skill as your team is."

Tori threw a wad of paper towels at me, and I ducked it.

"No problem, Mr. Icinda. I'll have someone there in a few minutes."

I thanked her and disconnected.

"I could have handled this," Tori said, standing and walking out of the kitchen.

"Perks of owning the hotel. Besides, housekeeping expects extra duties with the executive suites. I don't bother them often, nor does Liv."

I followed her through the suite, tussling Reid's hair as I

walked by. He peeked up from his game and smiled at me. Not thinking, I continued to trail Tori.

"I'm quite capable of cleaning up my messes." She took her shirt off and threw it into her hamper, walking into her closet.

"And I'm quite capable of spoiling you. Let me."

Not once did it occur to me that we hadn't been doing this for years, that we weren't like every other couple. It seemed natural until she turned, her eyes wide, and my heart thundered at the sight of her in her bra.

I wiped my face, cursing. "I'm sorry. It just...we were...I didn't think."

"Neither did I," she said.

I tried to keep my eyes from devouring her, but it was difficult. "I really want to kiss you right now," I muttered, causing her frown to turn.

"Then you should," she breathed.

In two steps, I closed the distance and had her in my arms. She smelled of strawberry cream and tasted like a summer day. Her skin against my hands sent rivulets of desire careening through me, and I let them explore, soaking in the softness. I walked her into the door frame, pressing into her as she tugged at my shirt, and all awareness fled so that only Tori filled it. The promise to take things slow rushed away, a mere whisper in the back of my mind. I unhooked her bra, cupping her breast and relishing her moan, my own joining hers when she pushed my shirt up higher.

Only the knock and Reid's call that someone was at the door stopped the inevitable. Reality slammed back into me—the risk that our son could have walked in on us, that I had pushed Tori too fast. I moved from her, an apology on my lips until she stopped it with another kiss.

"It's okay, Gabe," she said. "Middle, right?"

I dropped my head to hers, trying to control the raspy breaths that were clawing at my throat. "Middle."

She adjusted her bra and pulled my shirt down just as another knock came.

"Mommy!"

With a laugh, I tucked my shirt back in, thinking of anything but how sexy she was.

"I'll deal with it. You get changed. And..." I kissed a spot of strawberry from her cheek. "...wash up."

Walking to the door was difficult because my body's reaction to Tori was still uncomfortable. I let the staff in and sat with Reid while the two cleaned up. Tori joined us not long after, and we listened to Reid's explanation of the game he was playing. After tipping the staff and thanking them, I saw them out just as room service came up to the door.

"Your shakes, Mr. Icinda." I exchanged the drinks for a tip and turned to find Tori's stunned eyes.

With a shrug, I passed the shakes out, saying, "I may have made a quick call while you were changing."

"Strawberry! My favorite," Reid exclaimed, slurping on his.

Tori shook her head, but her grin told me everything.

"Like I said, I plan to spoil you in every possible way."

Her blush was my reward, and as I sat back to watch the movie, it dawned on me that with everything I'd strived for—revenge, wealth, power—only now did I have everything I needed.

Chapter 30

Tori

I held the phone away from my ear as Cash berated me once more. My father had already left my ear bleeding from his lecture. Neither gave me a chance to explain, but then again, it wasn't up to me to explain. Gabe would need to do that. Opening the door, I gestured for Gabe to come in. Reid was in his room deciding which cars he wanted to bring with us. Our suitcases were packed and in the living area waiting for Reid's decision.

"I'm not going through this again, Cash." I gave Gabe an apologetic look as he shut the door.

Brows scrunched, he contemplated me, his hazel irises dimming.

"I'm not spending the weekend with that man, and I don't know how you could even suggest it after all he put you through," Cash argued.

"You will, and you'll listen to what he has to say."

"Damn it, Tori, how could you let him back into your life? I knew going to work for him was a mistake."

I sighed, squeezing my temple. "Just hear him out, please."

He was quiet. I hated arguing with him, but I knew he was just trying to protect me, like he always had.

"Fine, but that's all I'll do, and only for you. Not to ease his conscience. If I don't like what he has to say, he can sleep at the lodge. I won't allow him in the house."

"It's not your house," I argued.

"I'm sure Dad will be glad to throw him out."

"I'll see you soon," I said, hearing the disappointment in my voice. What had I thought? They had been there for the wreckage, seeing me at my lowest, and now I was asking them to invite the man who had destroyed me back in. To any sane person, it sounded like madness. Even to me it sounded insane, but looking at Gabe and seeing the guilt that marred his handsome face, I knew it wasn't.

Cash didn't bother saying goodbye, and I knew this would be a fight.

"I take it that went over well?" Gabe asked as I tucked my phone into my back pocket.

"As well as I thought it would. No, worse actually." At least Cindy had been supportive when I'd texted her about Gabe's quick acceptance of my offer.

"They hate me." It was a statement spoken with the confidence of a man who understood the damage he had sown.

My mouth twisted as I tried to soften the blow. When I couldn't find a way, I said, "Hate is an understatement. Loathe? Detest? I'm not sure if there are worse ones, but if there are, they would fit."

Hands plunging into his pockets, he gave me a guilt-ridden look. It would have been adorable if it hadn't been so painful. "I deserve it, Tori. To them, I'm the man who broke your heart and left you to clean up the mess. To raise Reid on your own. I deserve nothing more than their hate."

Threading my fingers through his thick locks, I pulled his face to mine. "You don't deserve their hate. Not after all you gave up. Sure, they were there to pick up my pieces, but who was there to pick up yours, Gabe?"

The sadness that flashed through those amber irises almost broke me because I knew he'd suffered silently. I'd had my family and Cindy, but Gabe had no one to turn to.

"Is it plane time?"

I jumped back from Gabe, seeing the hurt that slipped through his eyes. No matter what I felt about him, I wasn't ready to expose Reid to what was happening to us until I knew for sure he wouldn't end up hurt. With Gabe's acceptance of my invitation to face my family, I was closer but needed to get through the weekend first.

"It is," Gabe said, recovering quickly.

I bundled Reid up and grabbed my coat as Gabe took my bag and led us out of the suite.

"Where's your bag?" I asked him as Reid dragged his suitcase behind him.

"In the car. I went down to make sure the car was here earlier."

He stepped into the elevator, holding the door for us, and I couldn't help but notice how good he looked. His beige coat cut his figure perfectly and gave him an air of sophistication he hadn't had when we were younger. This was the version of him that had only come out on rare occasions, and I now realized it was the side he'd hidden from me because it belonged in this world.

Power, money, respect. Those were the things his presence demanded. Heads turned when he walked through a room, and I had to stop my sting of jealousy when women were among the onlookers. There was no reason for it because he'd admitted there had been no one but me even when we were apart. It had been the same for me because no one could fill his shoes. He had been the criteria I based every man on, and so the few dates I'd forced myself to go on had all ended with the reminder that I would never erase Gabe's hold on me.

"Changing your mind?" he asked, giving me a coy grin.

"No," I replied, waking from my none too subtle gawking. "Just thinking."

I stepped onto the elevator, and Reid looked up at me, his eyes filled with excitement. He was clutching the car Gabe had bought him. The same one he'd been attached to since his birthday. With him standing next to Gabe, there was no question he was Gabe's son. Every time I saw them together, it sent my stomach into somersaults.

Once we were in the car, Reid held Gabe's attention, chatting about the movie again before moving onto candy flavors. It continued until we boarded the plane. I had been on private jets before, traveling with Carl Bradman and the other executives to a handful of meetings, but Reid had never been. His joy spilled over, and I peered up at Gabe to see his smile lighting his eyes to a rich hue.

I sat across from Gabe upon Reid's insistence that he sit next to him. When Reid pulled out his tablet, I reached over to Gabe and took his hand. I could see the nerves, even if he was trying to hide them. He was such a powerful presence, had been my rock, my security blanket for the months we'd been together that it was hard to see him so rattled. It reminded me of the day he'd proposed to me, and a surge of emotion swept through me. We were so close to being back to that place, but the distance was still there. His guilt and my wounds causing the divide.

His eyes lifted to mine, and I gave him a slight smile. "It'll be okay," I said. "And even if it isn't, I'm not going anywhere as long as you aren't."

Covering my hand with his, Gabe said, "Never again." His finger brushed over the ring, the constant reminder of what could be.

Soon, I thought. The future I had once dreamed of, the one that circumstance had demolished, would resurface. We just needed to be patient while we picked our pieces up and sealed them back into place.

The front door opened just as Gabe helped me out of the car.

"Uncle Cash!" Reid called, running up to him and not reading the lethal expression in his eyes.

"Hey kiddo." He ruffled his hair. "Go inside and find Shelby. I'll be in soon."

Reid ran in, slamming the door behind him, and my heart thundered. The few times I'd seen my brother this angry had all involved Gabe. He was level tempered but when it came to me, Brandi, or his daughter, he was a beast. And that beast was tearing down the sidewalk toward us. Gabe moved in front of me, his hands clenched but not drawn. The punch hit him square in his jaw, and I screamed, trying to rush around him to stop Cash. Gabe's hand careened into my waist, holding me in place as Cash drew another punch. This one Gabe stopped.

"I think you made your point," he said with a calm that seemed out of place until I thought of that cool, calculating side of him. The side that had torn his father's empire apart.

"Not even close."

"Cash." My father's voice held the authority I remembered from our youth. "Let him be. We promised Victoria we would hear him out."

Cash dropped his fist, his blue eyes dark with vengeance. They flicked to me. "If I don't like what he has to say, I won't hesitate to throw him out."

He turned his back on us and stalked away. Gabe rubbed his jaw, and I saw the tension when he rolled his shoulders. He glanced down at me, his irises a muted earthy tone with shades of gold. I swallowed back the gutted sensation that had me in its grip and said, "You sure you still want to do this?"

I was giving him an out and praying he wouldn't take it even though I didn't want to see him suffer any more. Just like I didn't want to suffer any more.

Taking my hand, he said, "Certain."

My father held the door open, his eyes unreadable as he gave me a kiss on the cheek. There was no greeting for Gabe, not even formalities. I squeezed Gabe's hand, knowing this was the ultimate test. He'd reclaimed my heart. Now he needed to convince my family to forgive him. If they didn't, I wasn't sure how I could survive because I didn't want to give Gabe up.

Everyone had gathered in the family room. So, we were doing this first thing. Nerves tumbled through me. My father stood, his arms crossed, my mother next to Cash and Brandi on the couch. I looked around for the kids, not wanting Reid to witness this.

"They're upstairs with Cindy. In your old room," my father said.

"Cindy came? I thought she couldn't make it."

"She flew in this morning," Cash said. "Start talking."

Glancing at Gabe, I saw the determination there. His strength calmed the colliding nerves that were pulverizing me. His eyes met mine.

"Everything," I told him.

His brows creased. "I can't do that, Tori."

"You will if you really love me." Hurt flashed in those rich orbs, but I could do nothing to soothe it. He needed to do this on his own. I tore my eyes from him and looked at my family. "There are things he's about to tell you that could do damage to his family and business. Nothing goes beyond this room. Understood?"

"Fine," Cash grumbled as the others nodded.

My mother gestured to the loveseat. "Sit, both of you."

I pulled Gabe to it, sitting next to him. Leaning forward, I picked up the glass of scotch that sat on the coffee table and handed it to him. It had been my only ask of them aside from having them listen. He looked at it, then at me, a sad smile forming. He had told me how he'd turned to it when he'd left me, using it as his crutch to get by, and something told me he would need it today.

He took a swig, then leaned forward, elbows on his knees, looking down at the scotch as it swirled in his glass.

"Everything?" he asked again, peeking back at me. And I saw something in him he never showed. Fear. He didn't want to go back to the memories, but they were the foundation of everything that had touched my life.

"The truth," my father said. "And then I'll decide if I want you anywhere near my daughter and my grandson."

Anguish slashed Gabe's face, and my heart ached at the same time it danced in the knowledge that his love for me and Reid was real. Strong enough to crush him if he had to leave us.

He dragged his hand through his hair and talked. Starting from the beginning, the abuse, the devastating suicide, the pact with Liv, her insistence that he block me and erase his ties to me the day she had answered the phone, all the way to the day in the lobby. The same day he'd taken down his father, and I had stepped back into his life.

By the time he finished, his glass was empty, my cheeks were wet, and silence hung over the room. His story was a powerful one, and my family needed to hear it if this was ever going to work.

Cash leaned forward, rubbing his hand down his face. I knew he'd expected excuses and nothing like what Gabe had just given him.

"I remember when your father checked in that week," my father said, finally breaking the silence. "And you."

Gabe's sight slipped to my father.

"You went into the sitting room where Tori was coloring." I couldn't stop my gasp. "He was pissed when he realized you had moved. It's his reaction that always stuck with me. I had known the name the minute I saw it and figured he was checking us out to propose a buyout."

"I remember that day," my mother agreed, taking his hand. "We were nervous for months because he had a reputation for being hostile when he wanted a property."

"My mother loved it there, but he would never let her come back." He rubbed his neck, and I rested my hand on his forearm.

"He dragged you out of that room where you were with Tori and smacked you so hard as he walked you down that hall that I said something to him." My father's eyes grew sad. "I'd forgotten all about it until just now. I'd never seen a father treat his child like that. You hear stories and see the news but...to see it." He wiped his eyes. "I told him if I saw him do it again, he could find someplace else to stay. Your mother was with him. I knew it wasn't my business, but you were so young, and Tori was so upset by it. She cried all night."

My head was spinning. Gabe and I had met when we were children, and I'd never known, the memory lost like a melting snowflake.

"No wonder your father didn't want you marrying me," I mumbled.

Cash sat back, his focus intent on Gabe, as Brandi rubbed his shoulder.

"So," Cash said, "you left to protect my sister and my family. And if you hadn't..."

"He would have had the excuse to take the resort that he'd been waiting for. A reason to break his promise to my mother."

"A promise she had him make because she knew he would turn his anger on me for standing up for you," my father added.

The pieces of a puzzle I hadn't known existed fell into place.

I rose, leaving everyone in the silence that settled over them, and grabbed the scotch from the kitchen. Returning, I filled Gabe's cup and took a long drink, trying not to cough since I wasn't a hard liquor drinker.

"God, how do you stand this stuff?" I said, wiping my mouth with the back of my hand.

"Years of practice," he said, snatching the glass from me and finishing it.

"So...," said Brandi. "Does that mean he's staying?"

She was so sweet it was hard not to smile. The complete opposite of my brother with his overbearing temperament.

"Yeah," my father answered, and the anxiety that had been building since Cindy put the idea in my head and Gabe accepted fled my body. "Gabe, I'd like a few minutes with you."

He nodded and rose as my father gestured for him to follow. Cash stood and stepped into his path. The two had a moment that caused my tension to return before Cash held his hand out. "I still hate how you hurt her, and I hope she's making you work to get her back, but if that's her choice, I'll stand by her." Gabe took his hand. "But don't think I won't make you work for it, too. You weren't there to pick up the pieces and put her back together."

"Neither were you," I heard Cindy say. "I was the one who was there in the beginning, wiping her snotty nose and telling her she still looked pretty even though she has a really ugly crying face."

"Shut up, Cindy," I said as she sauntered over to me and gave me a big hug.

"The kids are playing dress-up in your room. Hope you don't mind. Your prom dress has seen better days." She cringed, then walked over to Gabe. Holding her arms out, she said, "Hey. If anyone had asked me last night if I'd be happy to see you, I would have punched them."

"Don't worry, Cash has already done that for you," Gabe said, rubbing his jaw.

She gave him a hug, which he returned with some hesitation. "You hurt her again, and they'll never find your body."

"Warning noted," he said, clawing his hand through his hair.

"Come on, Gabe. Let's talk." My father gestured for him to follow. After giving me another glance, Gabe trailed him.

"When you said he had a story, I thought it would be a bunch of bullshit excuses," Cash said.

"So did I," added Cindy.

My mother came behind me and gave my shoulders a squeeze. "Our Tori is smarter than that. I knew it had to be something big to get her to take him back."

"Thanks, Mom."

"Mommy, what does this say?" Reid and Shelby came running down the hall, a slip of paper in Reid's hand.

I took it from him and unfolded the note. My hand flew to my mouth, tears flooding my eyes. "Where did you find this?" I managed.

"In the big white fluffy wedding dress," Shelby said.

A sob came out as I stared at Gabe's writing. *I'm sorry. I never meant to hurt you, but if I stay, I will. Ti amerò sempre, luna mia.*

Cindy took the note from me as the tears continued. He had left me something, and I'd never known, locking it away with my heart and my wedding dress all this time.

"Is that Italian?" she asked.

I nodded.

"What does it say, Tor?"

"I will always love you, my moon."

"Luna mia," said Reid, taking my hand. "That's what Gabe calls you."

I stooped down to him. "My moon." I sniffed as his tiny hand wiped away my tears.

"Don't be sad, Mommy."

I took his hand and kissed it. "I'm not. These are happy tears."

"Because Gabe is with us."

I laughed, hearing my brother's chuckle behind me. "Exactly."

"Why does he call you that?"

I pulled him into my arms and kissed his head, my heart healing more as I said, "Because I'm his light in the darkness."

Chapter 31

Gabe

Nothing I'd done had left me this nervous aside from leaving Tori and admitting the truth to her. She was the only one who knew the real me, and now I had shared that truth with her family. There were reasons no one knew my past aside from the news it would cause. I didn't want pity, didn't need sad looks. It was in the past, even if it had shaped me to be the man I was today.

I rubbed my arms at the cold as we stepped onto the deck. Tori's father had grabbed a coat, but mine was still in the house. He leaned over the railing and looked out at the yard that was covered with a light dusting of snow.

"Do you love my daughter?"

Blunt and to the point. This was a man who could have given my father a run for his money, and now I saw why he had dared scold my father on his parenting skills.

"I never stopped loving her. The hardest thing I've ever done was leave her, but living without her these past years has been just as hard."

"And Reid?"

"Is amazing, and I hate that he grew up without me, that she had to go through that without me by her side. If I'd known...if my sister hadn't been such a bitch that day, I would have given it all up. I've thought about the what-ifs a million times since I found out he's my son, and I would have fought my father, sold off my holdings if necessary to keep your business and Tori out of his crosshairs."

"It wouldn't have stopped him."

I sighed, tucking my hands under my arms to keep them warm. "No, it wouldn't have, and Tori would have been miserable. Either way, she would have ended up hurt."

"So you took the blame."

Shrugging, I stared at a spot on the deck. "It made sense at the time. And...it still does. She's thriving. Smart, talented, capable, and Reid is a reflection of that."

"She pretends to thrive, but she was never the same after you left her. Reid helped. I guess he took away some of the pain, but the damage you left never healed."

He leaned over the railing, rubbing his hands together.

"I know." Because the damage had left gashes inside me that were only now healing with her back in my life.

"It takes a lot to sacrifice what you did and to admit the truth like you did. I don't forgive the hurt you caused my daughter, but I understand your reasoning, and I will forgive when you prove yourself to her."

"I'll spend every day of my life proving it to her and to Reid."

He looked over at me. "Then show us. You have the weekend, and this time, you can sleep in the guest room."

"Understood." Not that we were at the point of sharing a bed yet, but he didn't need to know that.

"If you put her back together, make her whole again, I'll walk her down the aisle and hand her off to you. If you don't, I'll support Cindy's plan."

Great, two threats to end my life in one day. I was beginning to suspect there was something I didn't know about Tori's family.

It took a while for the awkwardness to dissipate, but by the end of the night, I almost felt like I had the first time I'd met Tori's family: welcome. There were still a few side glances from her brother, but they lessened through the night. His wife reminded me a lot of Tori, sweet, smart, and strong enough to keep him in line.

As everyone slowly filtered out of the living room, it left me alone with Tori. She and Brandi had tucked the kids in earlier, leaving me with her family, but Cindy's chatter filled the void. As annoying as I'd found her when I'd first met her, I was thankful for her presence this time.

"Is your family in the mob?" I asked Tori, my fingers running through her hair. She was leaning on my chest, flipping channels on the television.

"No," she said with a laugh. "Why?"

"Eh, just the few threats to my life I've received today."

Her eyes popped up from under her tangle of hair. "They get a little dramatic, especially Cindy."

"A little," I scoffed.

She nestled her head back into my chest and returned to channel surfing.

"I remember that day," I said as she landed on a cooking show. "At your parents' resort."

Blue irises peeked back up at me. "You do?"

"I do. I remembered when you first told me they owned it."

She pushed herself up and folded her legs in front of her.

"You must have been four since I was about seven. Sprawled out in front of this enormous fireplace, you were intent on coloring your princess. Staying within the lines, of course."

Her head tipped as she listened.

"You had pigtails and a pair of overalls on. I only remember because I'd never seen them before. My father only allowed my sister to wear dresses, and I don't think I owned a pair of jeans until I was old enough to buy them myself." I scratched my ear, remembering how curious I'd been about her. "You looked up at me and gave me a smile before offering a crayon to me. We colored for a few minutes, and you asked me questions with no filter until my father dragged me away for acting like a child."

"I don't remember that," she said, sadness stressing her words.

"You wouldn't. You were too young." I looked over at the television, where someone was preparing risotto.

The couch shifted, and Tori's hand turned my face back to her. "It's almost like our paths were meant to cross."

My sight fell to her hands, and I took one, rubbing my thumb over her fingers.

"Maybe that's what brought me back to you," she continued. "So this isn't really our second chance. It's our third."

My eyes lifted, meeting cornfield blue that knocked the air from my chest. "We were a little young that first time," I teased.

"But what if your father hadn't taken you away..."

Chuckling, I said, "We lived in different states and were just kids."

Finger against my lip, she shushed me. "Don't destroy my romanticized version of us with your reasoning. Just let me think this was meant to be."

I took her hand and kissed her palm before pulling her into my arms. "Fine, you can keep thinking that, but this is still our second chance."

Adjusting herself so she was straddling me, she took my face in her hands and kissed me. "Killjoy," she murmured as I pulled her further into me.

My fingers tangled in her hair while my other hand ran the length of her body, stopping on her hip.

"Tori," I groaned when she pressed down, grinding into me. "You're making this very difficult."

"I know," she breathed.

Hand slipping below her shirt, I followed the curve of her

waist. Her hands played in my hair, and I deepened our kiss, pushing her mouth closer. There was no way I could take this slow, no way I would honor her father's rule that I sleep in another room if I didn't stop this. But my body had craved her for so long that it seemed an impossible feat.

"Tori," I tried again, forcing my hands from her skin and taking her waist. Pushing her back, I tried to ignore the pout of her swollen lips. "We can't. Slow, remember? I promised you, and I'll never break another promise to you."

She nodded, smoothing my shirt out as her eyes followed the path of her hands. "Middle never seemed so far."

I drew her head down and kissed it. "It won't be forever."

"No, it won't, but maybe the middle wasn't the right place to start."

Lifting her head, I said, "I told you, Tori. There is no starting at the beginning with you. It's impossible."

Her fingers draped over my jaw. "I'm not asking for the beginning."

My heart raced, but I tempered it. "If there's any chance of losing you again, then I'm sticking to the middle."

I drew a lock of her hair forward and ran it through my fingers, relishing the soft texture. Scooting from my hold, she stood and turned off the television before extending her hand to me.

"I need to show you something."

The arch of my brow had her giggling. "Not that."

I let her lead us up the stairs to her room, hating how clammy my hands were growing. Nerves were fighting for dominance as they careened through me for the second time this day. Dresses lay in disheveled piles around the room, streaming from the closet.

"Is there a prom dress fetish I should know about?"

She laughed and picked up a particularly sexy floor-length one with a slit down the leg. "This is the prom dress. The rest are from homecomings and college events."

Imagining her in the dress was a mistake. "Damn, I'm glad we didn't go to school together because I would have fought off every other guy in that school to have you on my arm." A blush climbed her cheeks, and I had the urge to kiss them. "I think I need to attend those black-tie charity events I always make Liv go to. Seeing you in something like that would make them tolerable."

"Taking your CFO as your date might raise some eyebrows," she said, hanging the dress in her closet.

"Not if she's my girlfriend."

She froze, her head slowly turning to me. My chest tightened. Had I moved too fast when I'd just told her we needed to slow down? A tug at the corner of her mouth had me relaxing, especially when it formed a complete smile.

"Is that still middle ground?" she asked.

Shrugging, I replied, "Closer to the end, but somewhere in the middle."

"I like being back in that spot," she said, hanging the dress.

My smile relieved the rest of my tension, and I felt like I'd moved one step closer to finally having her completely. She gestured for me to come into the closet, and memories of the day I'd made love to her in our Jacksonville closet returned. I paused my step, seeing recognition in her eyes accompanied by another flush of her cheeks.

"I want to show you something."

I remained where I was, afraid that if I walked any further, I wouldn't be able to control myself. "That's not convincing me any better."

With the shake of her head, she turned and dug behind the few dresses that remained in her closet.

"How many formals did you attend?" I asked, a streak of unreasonable jealousy striking me.

"I was popular in school," she said.

And that hadn't helped either, but then again, I hadn't been a wallflower. Looking over at me, she grinned. "Just get in here and stop thinking about my past boyfriends. You're included on that list, you know."

With my lips pursed, I tried to give her one of my glares, but she softened me too much when I was with her, and so my look only caused her to giggle. Walking into the closet, my step faltered when I saw what she wanted me to see. Her wedding dress. Someone, most likely the kids, had pulled the zipper of the bag down, and the bottom half of the dress cascaded out of it.

I swallowed, unsure of the emotions that were barraging me. She had kept it just like I'd kept her ring.

"I couldn't bring myself to give it up," she admitted as if she had heard my thoughts. "Cindy told me to sell it, but I couldn't open it. I never wanted to look at it again because I knew it would re-open the wounds. But I couldn't let it go. I almost donated it, but after sitting in the parking lot of the donation center and crying for thirty minutes, I drove it back home." She sniffled, and I hated that she was crying again because of me. "It was one of the last pieces I had of you. That and Reid...and that stupid paper flower."

My eyes flew from the dress to her. "You kept that?"

"I... Yes, it's in Reid's baby book."

I moved closer to her, remembering the night I'd opened the bag, picturing how stunning she would have looked in it. How I was giving up any chance of happiness because I was leaving her that morning.

"I never opened the bag, Gabe." She took something from her pocket. "Shelby likes to play dress up, and Reid pretends he's her judge. I didn't think they'd get this far into my closet." I saw the desk chair pushed to the side, thinking it was a precarious way to reach it. "I never found it."

My eyes flicked to her, then to her hand, where the note sat between her fingers. The one attempt to make what I'd done better. To give her something so I wouldn't leave her so devastated. As if that had even been possible.

"It wouldn't have helped," I said. "Not like I wanted it to."

"It might have, just a little. I wanted to believe you still loved me, but it was so hard, especially after that phone call."

Damn Liv for her interference. "You still would have doubted it, even with the note." My sister had ensured that.

She moved closer to me, her blue orbs misty. "Let's make a deal."

I cocked my head to the side. "I'm listening."

"We leave the past, the mistakes, the assumptions, the pain behind us."

"Can you?" Because I didn't think it was that easy for either of us.

"You've carried your guilt, suffered in silence for too long, and I've carried the pain for too long. We both have wounds that won't heal if we don't let go." Her hand rested on my chest as she crossed the remaining steps between us. "I don't want to live with it anymore. I'm tired of being sad, of being hurt." Tears glimmered in her eyes, and it killed me because I was always the cause. "I love you, Gabe. It never went away. Maybe it faded some behind the pain, but it was always there, and I knew it would never cease the day I saw you in the lobby. You are my soulmate, and I can't live without you because it's like there's a hollowness that never fills, a piece of me I can't find because you own it. I don't want to experience that emptiness anymore."

Reaching my hand around her neck, I brought her mouth to mine, the kiss burning through me like wildfire that destroyed the echoes of pain and turned them to ash.

"I love you, luna mia. I always will." My words were a murmur between kisses, the thrumming of my pulse making them distant as my heart healed completely.

CHAPTER 32

TORI

Gabe stayed true to his word to my father and slept in the guest room. I was ready to have him in my bed again if only to feel his secure hold on me. To wake in his arms and experience the thrill of seeing his lazy smile when my eyes opened.

The tension eased even more the next day, and I could see he had won my family and Cindy over. We spent the morning with Reid opening the belated birthday presents from my parents and celebrating my father's upcoming birthday at lunch. Gabe surprised me again by adding his present to mine. He hadn't mentioned it, and I wondered if he'd been waiting to see if he was welcome. My father loved the UConn engraved pen set he gave him, and I elbowed him when my gift got pushed aside.

"This is where you were," Gabe said, bringing me from my thoughts. We were standing in the main sitting area of the lodge, the fireplace flickering and warming the air. My father had suggested I give him a tour, but it seemed Gabe's memory was sharp enough to remember.

He dropped to Reid's level. "I saw your mommy there when she was your age," he told Reid, pointing to the spot.

"You did?" Reid's eyes were large as he stared at the rug.

"Yup. She was coloring on the floor."

"And did you love her then?"

My mouth dropped open, and Gabe nearly lost his balance.

"Why would you say that?" I asked him.

"Because he loves you now. Ti amerò sempre, luna mia."

Gabe glanced back at me, but I was too stunned to say anything. He cleared his throat. "We were just children, and we didn't know each other then."

A simple answer that I hadn't been able to form.

"But you do now."

"Yes, we do. We have for a long time."

Reid's keen eyes evaluated Gabe. "Are you going to marry my mommy?"

"Yes." Confident, bold, powerful, with no hesitation. My heart flipped, my stomach twisting into nervous knots.

"So, you'll be my daddy?"

Oh God, this was moving too fast, and I should have known because that was how Reid moved. His thoughts came out with the same unwavering confidence as his father. Gabe peered back at me, his brows knitted. I hadn't prepared myself for this conversation, thinking we'd have it after Gabe and I had gotten through more dates. As if we could go back to the beginning. We couldn't, just like he'd said. I knew his touch, craved it, had imagined it for years, and he knew every detail of my body and how to break it. I had insisted we go slow, and I didn't know if it was for my protection or Reid's.

"Maybe. Let's get a snack and look around more." Gabe's answer was an easy one with redirection that had Reid talking about the chocolate chip cookies my mother insisted on having fresh for guests.

Gabe took my hand while Reid held his other and led me away, but my mind was still on the conversation, still fighting internally through what to do. Was I being fair to Reid by not telling him the truth? Or was I protecting him because the fear was still there? And maybe that was it. As much as I had confessed my love, asked to move faster, wanted Gabe back, I was still scared. Because this was how we'd been before my world came crumbling down around me. Happy and in love. My hands shook, and I tucked them into the pockets of my coat.

Reid and Gabe were chatting to Kate, our front desk clerk, and Gabe glanced at me, reading me too easily.

"Kate, would it be okay for Reid to hang out with you for a few minutes?" he asked.

Kate, who was like the mother hen of the resort, beamed. "I'd love that. Wanna help me get another batch of cookies, Reid?"

Reid was pulling her back to the kitchen within seconds.

"We've got him," John, the other front desk clerk, said, shooing us off.

Gabe took my hand and led me out of the resort. There were several hiking paths that led from the main entrance, and he followed one, keeping my hand tight in his until we were far enough for privacy. Halting his steps, he turned to me, pushing my hair back and tucking it behind my ear.

"What's wrong? Was it my answer to Reid? I went too fast, didn't I?"

"Stop," I told him. "You did nothing wrong."

His eyes creased, the hazel a rich mossy color. "Then what is it?"

I sat against the rock that jutted into the path. "It's.." My sight drifted ahead of us, watching a bird flutter in a tree. "He needs to know the truth. To know you're his father."

"But?"

Eyes flitting back to his, I saw the anguish reflected in them. I wanted to leave the pain and the past behind us, but saying it was so much easier than doing it. "I'm scared, Gabe."

His expression dropped, his shoulders with it.

"Everything was so perfect, just like it seems now and then

everything fell apart, and I know I can't handle that again, but Reid...I never want him to experience that pain. He's already so attached to you, and I fear him getting hurt."

He lowered to his knee and took my hands in his. My chest hammered at the move and the emotion in his eyes. "All I can do is promise you I will never hurt him, and I won't ever hurt you again. I will give everything up to keep that promise. I can't take away your fear, and I know that promise is the one I made you the day I asked you to marry me, but I mean it, Tori. I would die before I hurt you again, and if I had any doubt in my ability to keep that promise, I would have turned my back on you that day in the hotel and never let you into my life for fear of hurting you again."

A tear slipped down my cheek.

"Please don't cry, luna mia. I don't want to be the cause of your tears anymore. If this is too hard, if your fear is too great for Reid, I'll walk away."

My inhale was like a knife slicing my throat. "Could you?"

"No, but for you...for him, I would."

My belief in him was pure, not desperate or blind, but complete and unreserved. It drowned the fear, sending it far from my consciousness to an abyss where my pain and hurt were finding space.

I wiped my tears and stood. "Stay here," I told him when he rose.

"Tori?"

"Just stay here, please, Gabe. I trust you. Trust me and let me do this."

Determination guided my steps. Years of excuses, of avoiding the questions, of crying after every lie had built to this moment. My life had been a series of safe moves since Gabe had left me, when before it had been adventurous and thrilling. Running in rainstorms, making love in the kitchen, sneaking kisses at the zoo. Moments I'd taken with abandon and not rationalized. And I wanted that back. I wanted to be free and alive again. Needed the veil of our past to lift and let me live.

Reid had chocolate smeared on his fingers and his mouth when I found him.

"Where's Gabe?" he asked with a mouthful of cookie.

"Outside waiting for us. We're going to take a walk around the property."

Kate handed me a paper towel, and I cleaned him up. "Can you say thank you to Kate and John?"

"Thank you, Kate and John."

"We'll be back after our walk," I told them. I knew Gabe wanted a tour of the resort. His ideas for restructuring hinged on turning some of his properties into ones closer to the family feel that made my parents' so unique.

Reid ran in front of me, racing down the path to Gabe, and I knew I was making the right choice. I couldn't let my fear hurt my chance at a happy ending or Reid's. He rushed into Gabe's arms, and a swell like a rogue wave constricted my chest. Gabe picked Reid up and placed him on the rock where I'd perched only minutes before. They were talking about chocolate chip cookies by the time I reached them.

"Gabe's favorite cookie is chocolate chip, too!"

"I know," I replied, giving them a smile.

Gabe returned my smile, but there was hesitation behind it. He was still waiting for my move, trying to determine what I was up to. "Are we taking a walk?"

"We can," I answered. "But first, we need to talk."

"Boring," Reid said, picking a piece of chocolate from his fingernail and sucking on it. I pushed his hand down and gave him a scolding look.

"Talk about what?" Tension lined Gabe's features, and I stopped it, bringing my hand to his cheek and giving him a kiss.

Reid's giggle had me laughing.

"Don't worry. It's all good stuff," I told Gabe.

The tightness in his jaw didn't fade. Turning to Reid, I tipped his chin up so he would look at me. The words froze in my throat, and with them the fear returned. This was more difficult than I had imagined. But Reid deserved to know the truth.

"Do you know why your hair is brown and mine is black?" I asked him.

He shook his head.

"Because you have your daddy's hair."

Gabe went stiff beside me.

"And why your eyes are so special?"

He shook his head again.

"Because they come from your daddy."

"Tori..." Gabe warned.

"Shush, he deserves to know the truth."

Reid scrunched his eyes as he waited for me to say more.

"Do you know someone else who has brown hair like yours and eyes like yours?" I wasn't so sure he was at the age where he could piece things together like this, but my son was sharp, just like his father.

He peeked around me at Gabe.

"Gabe?" he asked, his eyes inquisitive.

"Yes. Before you were born, I met the most wonderful man. He was handsome and funny and sweet, and he swept me off my feet. I loved him so much that it hurt to be without him. But he had to leave for reasons he can explain to you one day."

"When I'm older?"

I laughed, squeezing his hands. "Yes, when you're older."

"But that man loved your mommy," Gabe said, putting his arms around my waist and resting his head next to mine. "She was the light in his darkness, the smile to his sadness, the salve to his pain. She was everything."

"Then why did he leave?"

"Because he loved her too much, and to stay with her would

have hurt her. So he made the worst mistake of his life, but one he would never take back. He left to keep her safe."

I leaned into his hold, feeling my tears pushing for recognition again. "I was devastated, but then I had you, and you brought light back into my life."

"But not back into his? If you were the light in his life, how did he survive?" He was too smart, too aware for someone his age.

"I didn't," Gabe said. "I went through life with a hole in my chest that never went away. The darkness swallowed me, and it wasn't until she came back into my life and told me about you that the darkness lifted again."

Reid's eyes bounced between us before he hopped from the rock. He took Gabe's hand and pulled him down, his hands going to his cheeks. After turning Gabe's face back and forth, he squinted his eyes at Gabe. Looking back up at me, he said, "So the stocking belongs to Gabe?"

I laughed, the anxiety holding my muscles hostage slipping away. "Yes," I replied, nodding.

"We need to get glitter, and I'll show you how to add your name." He took Gabe's hand and dragged him up.

"What stocking?" Gabe asked, his brows knitted in confusion.

"Your stocking. Mommy puts one out every year, and Santa never fills it. This year, he knows who it belongs to."

Gabe took my hand when I looked away. Meeting his eyes, I saw the understanding there. The truth that I'd told him, and Reid had just admitted. That I'd never stopped loving him, never allowed room for anyone else because Gabe took too much.

If our confession to Reid had any effect on him, he didn't show it. He acted just like he had, and it made me curious if he'd known, if he'd subconsciously recognized that Gabe was his father.

As we rode back to the house, he fell asleep between me and Gabe, his body leaning into Gabe's hold. The look of adoration in Gabe's eyes when he looked at Reid let me know I'd made the right choice.

"So, I have a stocking?" he asked, his fingers drifting through Reid's hair. Hazel orbs took my breath away when they turned to me.

"I was alone in Boston the Christmas after you left. It was horrible and lonely. Gabe was only a baby, and I was on maternity leave. My family wanted me to move home, but I knew I needed to keep working and maintain my independence. I didn't think I would heal if I did." I looked out the window. "Not that it helped. To keep my mind quiet, I decorated, only all my decorations were ones we bought together. I wasn't in my right mind, and somehow having those up comforted me. It was almost like you were there, and as much as I hated you, I wanted you there."

Scratching my nose, I turned back to him, meeting his guilt-stricken eyes. Sadness shadowed them, and I wondered if we could ever truly heal. "I put my stocking up and the one for Reid, but it didn't look right. Maybe it was the hormones still running rampant, but I packed Reid up and went out that night to buy one more stocking. No name, no decorations, just a plain red and white stocking. I hung it next to Reid's that year and every year after until he was old enough to hang it himself."

My eyes dropped to my lap. "I never had an answer for him when he would ask whose stocking it was."

His fingers pushed my hair back from my face, and I lifted it to him. "I'll be there this Christmas and every one that follows."

I leaned into his touch. "I know, and you can replace it with your own stocking."

Head shaking, he said, "No, that's the one I'll use. Besides, I don't have one. I haven't decorated for a holiday since the one with you. I never could bring myself to because it reminded me too much of you, and I wasn't as strong as you are, Tori. Holidays are nothing but reminders of what I lost, so I avoid them."

All the pain I had suffered, the times I had cursed him because I was so sure he was enjoying life without me, leaving me too wrecked to move on, and he was suffering his own hell.

I pulled his face to mine. "From now on, we celebrate every holiday together."

His smile lit his eyes, turning them a beautiful golden hue. "That sounds perfect."

I kissed him as certainty washed through me. This was real, and it wouldn't disappear this time. We wouldn't let it because there was no coming back from the damage a second time. It would devastate us both.

Reid rushed into the house, kicked his boots off and threw his coat on the floor.

"Reid!" I called after him, frowning as I picked up his coat.

"I have a daddy," I heard him tell my father, who was sitting in the living room watching football.

My sight jumped to Gabe, nerves striking me, but it wasn't tension I found in his face. It was awe. How long since discovering he had a son had he been waiting to hear that? I hadn't given it thought, only wanting to keep Reid safe and not thinking about Gabe's emotions.

Taking his hand, I moved into the main room, seeing my father's surprised look as Reid told him all about it. Cash was on the couch, a beer in his hand, his eyes intently focused on me.

"That's great, Reid. Why don't you go find Shelby and tell her all about it? She's in the basement watching a movie with her mom and Grandma."

"Okay." He ran off just as Cindy came into the room, giving me the same look Cash was, and I knew she'd heard it all.

"I told him," I said, the need to defend Gabe rising in me.

Cash leaned forward, rolling his beer between his hands. "Do you think that's wise?"

"He deserves to know."

"But with his track record." He pointed to Gabe, and the tension returned to Gabe's body.

"Shut up, Cash," Cindy said, flopping on the couch next to him and putting her feet on the coffee table. "She's right. He needs to know, and we said we were giving Gabe a second chance, just like Tori is."

"I won't hurt him," Gabe said. "If I thought there was a chance, I would have left Tori to hate me and never put myself back into her life. I would have refused the interview and sent them both home." He rubbed his neck, looking over at me. "The only reason I ever pursued her in Jacksonville was that I thought I could find a way to keep her. I was certain because I knew she was special, that she was the one. If I'd known..."

"You still would have asked her out," Cindy said, taking Cash's beer and drinking it.

"Hey!" He snatched it back. I swore sometimes they were the brother and sister. Cindy had been my best friend since kindergarten, and Cash was as much her older brother as he was mine.

"You two are inevitable," she continued, jabbing an elbow in Cash's side. "I saw it when I visited you in Florida, saw it when I scraped her from the depths of depression, saw it every time she tried to move on and couldn't, and I see it now. There was no avoiding it, which is why you asked her out in the first place."

Leave it to Cindy to sum the two of us so simply. Inevitable. It seemed the perfect word for us. Gabe's finger brushed over mine, and I glanced up at him. For a moment it was just the two of us, and we were back to the beginning, that first day when his hazel eyes met mine, when his attention had only been on me and had remained on me. When he had been my world.

"See, that's what I'm talking about. Inevitable."

Gabe broke the contact, but heat swarmed in my stomach and stung my cheeks.

"That's not what you told me when I called you," I told her, dragging Gabe into the room and pulling him down on the loveseat.

"Eh, that's because I was still pissed at him."

"And you're not anymore?" he asked her.

"It comes and goes," she said with a big grin.

"Great."

Cash rose and handed Cindy his beer. "Finish it. I'm getting a fresh one since you infected this one."

She took it and stuck her tongue out at him.

"Scotch, Gabe?" he asked.

Gabe twisted his fingers in his hands. "Nah, a beer sounds good."

Cash waved for him to follow. "Come pick your poison."

Hand draping over mine as he walked away, Gabe followed, and the emptiness that had claimed a spot in my life for years returned. My father's heavy gaze had me turning my attention to him.

"Was it your decision or Gabe's to tell him?"

"Mine. I didn't tell Gabe. It just...felt right."

He nodded, leaning forward and clasping his hands together. "Let Gabe talk to him alone. I think he needs it and probably needed to tell him in his own way."

Standing, he came over and kissed my head. "I know you meant well, and you're putting your trust back in Gabe, but I suspect he needs to take these steps himself in order to do his own healing."

Doubt seeped in, crushing my spirit. In my overzealous need to make this work, to get to the end when I had specifically drawn the line in the middle, I had let my emotions dictate the moment, never thinking it might not be the right moment for Gabe or even Reid.

I looked up to see Cindy's understanding eyes surveying me.

"Did I mess up?" I asked her.

She scooted from her seat and sat down next to me. "You were never one to keep a secret, Tor. You get too excited, and it just spills out. I know why you told him, and I agree with you. Reid needs to know Gabe is his father. But maybe it should have been a mutual decision between the two of you to tell him. You've been running on your own for so long I think you forget what it's like with a partner."

And that's what Gabe was. No longer was I a single parent. There were two of us in this now, and I needed to remember to include Gabe when I'd never had another voice to help guide me on my parenting journey.

She rested her head on my shoulder. "It's still early, Tor. You'll get the hang of it. Just take it slow. You two rushed in headfirst when you were younger. Take your time so there's no chance anything will come between you again."

I laid my head on hers, thinking she was right. Slow. It had been Gabe's motto when we'd first started dating, and he was willing to let me direct the speed this time. Had allowed me to speed it up after I'd insisted on slowing it down. As much as I wanted to leave the past behind, I needed to keep it present so I would remain hesitant. Otherwise, there was a chance I would blindly rush back in and not savor the moments that built to our inevitable.

CHAPTER 33

Tori seemed off, almost distant, for the rest of the trip. I noticed the change when I returned to the living room with her brother, and it hadn't faded. She sat across from me with Reid, who was fixated on a movie on his tablet, his headphones on as the plane took us home.

"What's wrong?" I asked, causing her head to swivel from where she was absently staring out the window.

Azure blue struck my chest like the snap of a rubber band.

"Nothing. Why do you ask?" She gave me a smile, but it seemed forced.

"Because you've been off since yesterday. Did I do something?"

Her expression faltering, she replied, "No." She rubbed her arms, and I could see the nerves. My stomach plummeted, and the urge to vomit churned within it. "It's something I did."

Eyes narrowing as I tried to figure out what she'd done, I waited for more.

"I said I needed us to take it slow, but when I'm with you, that's so hard to do. I want us to be back to where we were so badly that it's making my thinking irrational."

Scooting forward in my seat, I took her hands in mine. "I want us back there, too, but I won't sacrifice that chance by pushing you. Is that what I'm doing?"

I had thought I was taking my time. After all, she was the one who had suggested this trip, who seemed to fluctuate between middle ground and end. I tilted my head and only then saw the conflict she was describing. The hesitation was still there, and I didn't resent it even if I hated it. She was trying to put it aside, and when she was with me, she could, but it wasn't right, and she knew it.

"I've been an idiot," I said. "If this is too fast, you need to tell me, Tori. I can't read your mind."

"No, Gabe. It's not you, and you haven't done anything wrong." She let out a fractured sigh that gutted me. I had done this to her, and I despised myself for it. "I'm sorry I told Reid. I should have let you have that conversation."

Scrunching my brows, I said, "He's been your son all this time. It wasn't my right to make that decision. It was yours."

She glanced at him, but he was still in his own world, paying us no attention.

"But I need to stop thinking that way. I've done this by myself for so long, it's hard to think of someone else as part of our life. As someone to make decisions with." Taking her hands from mine, she sat back and pulled her knees into her chest. "I'm afraid of messing this up." The confession was a mere whisper, with the power of a scream.

I rose and sat in the seat beside her, turning her body toward mine. "That burden should be mine, not yours. I'm the one who needs to prove myself. Who needs to earn your trust back and show you I'm worth your love. Not you, Tori. You didn't mess this up in the first place. I did, and it's mine to fix. If we're moving too fast, if you want me to back off, just tell me."

She dropped her head onto the seat. "I think we should slow down."

"Then that's what we do. The last thing I want is to push you away." I hid the tremble in my hands, the nerves that threatened to turn me from the powerful man I was to a shriveling mess of emotion—terrified, hurt, sad, anxious.

"Okay. But I want you and Reid to spend time together. Alone, just the two of you, so you can talk to him. He knows now, so it's too late for me to take that impulsive decision back, but he needs to hear it from you, not me. That wasn't my right."

Reid spread out across my seat, resting his tablet on the wall.

"It was only ever your right, Tori. I haven't earned any rights with regards to him."

She turned my face back to hers. "You are and you have."

Slow was going to be difficult because there wasn't a second that passed when I didn't want to kiss her. She turned in her seat and rested her head on my shoulder. Repositioning so she could snuggle into my hold, I wrapped my arm around her, unsure of how many steps backward we'd taken but knowing I would take as many as necessary to have her back.

The weight of my phone seemed to double as I waited for my call to go through.

"I'm surprised it took you so long to call," my father's voice answered.

I rested my elbow on my desk and rubbed my head. Sleep had been minimal. I'd kissed Tori goodnight when we got back and given Reid a hug, but I'd kept my distance today, going in early to work out. I wanted to give her space, to let her lead at her pace.

"Tell me what you have on Bradman."

He chuckled. "You are more like me than you think, William."

My teeth ground at the name and the accusation.

"Just tell me. I know you have something, or you wouldn't have dropped the hint about him."

"Your lawyers still working on breaking that NDA?"

"How do you know about that?" I asked, standing and walking to the window.

"Bradman is infamous for them. He has a hard time keeping women on his staff. I'm surprised she lasted as long as she did, and her departure didn't surprise me."

The clenching of my fist did nothing to ease my anger.

"What do you have on him that I can use?"

He was quiet for a moment. "What's in it for me?"

Just like my father to offer something with conditions.

"What do you want?"

"To meet my grandson."

If I hadn't been standing, I would have fallen out of my chair. As it was, my jaw almost hit the ground.

"No."

"Then you can use your resources to find what you need."

"You can't possibly think I would let you anywhere near him after all you did to me."

He snorted, which only caused my grip on the phone to tighten. "I made you the man you are. Built character and resilience in a boy who clutched at his mother's skirts and cried at a scraped knee."

"Normal things children do, yet you seemed to find them repulsive enough to beat me for them. I'm not letting you within ten feet of my son, and I can guarantee Victoria won't."

"Good luck with Bradman." The phone disconnected before I could say more.

I shoved the phone back in my pocket just as Liv peeked her head into the office.

"Oh, I know that look. Did you talk to Dad?"

Hands scraping through my hair, I motioned for her to close the door. "Unfortunately."

"What's the asshole up to now?"

I crossed my arms over my chest. Her brow arched, and she sat in a chair, waiting for me to answer.

"He's traveling. Something about Greece."

"But that's not what the conversation was about."

"No, it wasn't. He's such a bastard. I knew I shouldn't have called him." I sat on the edge of the desk, running my hand over my face.

"Wait. You called him?" Interest piqued, she sat forward in the chair. "Why would you do that?"

"I needed information."

"On?" Damn, she was too smart and persistent.

"Carl Bradman."

"Why?"

"Let it go, Liv." I walked around my desk, removing my phone from my pocket and dropping it on the desk, unsure of what else to do with my hands. I was a frenzy of nervous energy.

"What are you up to, little brother?"

"Nothing."

She let out a loud laugh. "Don't give me that. You're up to something. Talk."

"I need information on Bradman to take him down."

Her eyes lit, understanding crossing them. "This is about Tori. Did he do something to her?"

"I can't say. There's an NDA."

"That tells me enough."

"Let it go and get back to work."

She leaned back in the chair, folding her hands. "No. Does Tori know you're scheming to take Bradman down? As much as I love a good takeover, Bradman's not one to go after."

"I've got it handled."

"Without telling her?"

"She doesn't need to know."

And I didn't want her to know. She needed to be out of anything unscrupulous I did. Besides, this was my revenge for what he had done to her. She didn't need to be involved.

Liv's laughter was even more annoying this time. "I was all for keeping secrets when we were going after Dad. That was necessary, but this?" She stood, putting her hands on her hips. "You'll lose her again if you do this."

A vise constricted the blood flow to my chest, and I stared at her, speechless.

"She forgave you the first time, but you lie to her again and she'll leave, Gabe." She moved closer to me, her eyes concerned and unusually soft. "You have a second chance. Don't screw it up for some vendetta." She picked my phone up and handed it to me. "If you really want Bradman, tell her what you're planning. Let her be a part of it."

I tilted my head, trying to figure her out. "Why are you being so nice?"

"You have a chance for something some of us will never have. I don't want you to blow it. She's too perfect for you, and there's that whole nephew thing." She waved her hand like she was untangling cobwebs from it.

"It's a good thing you never had kids, Liv. I don't think you'd ever survive."

"Let's not find out. No leaving me on babysitter duty again." She gave me a wink and shoved the phone toward me. "Call her in. Tell her what you're thinking."

"I'm not thinking anything now because Dad wouldn't give me the information."

"What did he want in return?"

I scratched my cheek, forgetting she'd had years to learn our father's ways while I'd been in Florida and at school.

"To see Reid."

Her lips made an exaggerated *oh*. "No wonder you looked so pissed when I walked in."

She took the phone from me and, before I could stop her, texted Tori.

"What the hell?" I said, snatching it from her. "How do you know my password?"

The roll of her eyes emphasized her annoyance with my question. "Because it's the same one you've used for years. I saw you put it in after you blocked me from your phone." Her eyes went wide. "Wait, isn't Tori's birthday in March?"

"Shut up." I didn't like how she knew my password or how she'd deduced it was Tori's birthday.

A gentle knock had my eyes flying to the door. Tori peeked in, her blue eyes bright.

"Oh, an impromptu meeting? Do I need to get Sean?" she asked, walking in. I couldn't stop my eyes from perusing her. She looked sexy, and jealousy stabbed at me. The shirt she wore brought out the blue in her eyes. It cut in a square across her chest, leaving the hint of cleavage but it was the curve hugging skirt with the slit up the side paired with the heels emphasizing her amazing legs that had me wanting to lock her in my office so no one else could look at her.

"No, Gabe has something to share."

I swung my sight to Liv, glaring at her as she gave me a cocky grin.

"What's up?"

"Go on, little brother. Tell her what you're up to."

"Remind me to bury your body in a remote wooded area when I'm done killing you," I snapped.

"You have that on record, Tori. Just in case I disappear."

Tori looked between the two of us, her brows cinching. "What's going on, Gabe?"

I cleared my throat and walked around to the front of the desk, my eyes flicking to the bottle of scotch on my bar. She trailed the action, frowning. I shoved my hands in my pockets to stave off the craving to pour myself a glass. The crutch had been there too long, and I no longer needed it.

"Nothing you need to concern yourself with."

Liv huffed as Tori's confusion grew.

"It's like she's your kryptonite. You get all sappy and soft when she's around. Tell her the truth before I do."

Tori's arms folded over her chest, and I knew the look that now sat in her eyes. Distrust.

"I'm planning on taking Bradman down," I admitted, palming my neck.

The shock that warped her eyes to a darker hue made me regret telling her. "Are you mad? And why..." Her lips thinned, anger staining her features. "You weren't planning to tell me, were you?" When I didn't answer, she looked crushed. "Damn it, Gabe. You promised no more secrets."

She turned to leave, but I ran after her, inserting myself between her and the door.

"I'm telling you," I blurted, feeling completely out of control.

With a glance back at Liv, she said, "Because Liv convinced you to. You promised me, Gabe."

I dropped my eyes, hating that I had hurt her again without meaning to. "I was only doing it to protect you."

She let out a long sigh, shaking her head. "No more protecting me. Not if it means secrets and lies."

"I promise. I...I didn't think about it until Liv pulled the truth from me and opened my eyes to what would happen if I went through with it behind your back. I'm sorry. I didn't mean to hurt you or to have you doubt me."

She sucked her bottom lip between her teeth, her eyes searching mine before she said, "Tell me what you're planning."

"Oh yay," Liv said, rubbing her hands together. "More scheming. I missed this."

Tori shot Liv a look. "I didn't say I would agree."

"I want to take Bradman down."

"You're mad to think you can go up against Carl Bradman. He's too powerful."

"Every powerful man has a weakness."

Her brow quirked. "Do you?"

"You're my weakness. You always have been."

The exhale that left her mouth was alluring, and it would have been the perfect time to kiss her except for Liv's interruption.

"Don't make me sick."

Tori gave me a smile. Realizing I still had my body pinned against the door to block her escape, I ushered her back to where Liv stood.

"You can't take over his company," said Tori. "He's public and we're not, nor do we plan to be. There's no way you can touch him like you did your father's company."

I thought about how my father had admitted he had caught on to what Liv and I were doing. How he had let it play out, like some test to earn his approval without us even knowing.

"Then we take him down another way."

"What makes you think I'll agree to this?" Tori asked.

"I don't," I admitted, scrunching my hair.

She walked over and sat in the chair next to Liv. "What's your plan? And it better be legal or I'm out of here. I will not be involved in anything that could taint my reputation or this company."

My smile spread at the loyalty she already had for the company. "Nothing illegal. That's not the way we work. Clean paper trails only."

"But you can't touch Bradman," she argued.

"Our father knows a way," Liv added, and I scowled at her.

"Your father?"

Now it was my turn to sigh.

Her forehead creased. "What does he want?"

"This should be fun," Liv mumbled.

"To see Reid."

Tori was up from her seat within seconds. "Absolutely not. How can you even entertain that thought after what he did to you?"

I stepped into her space, taking her arms in my hands. "I told him no. That's as far as I got before Liv came in and coerced me into involving you."

"Well, you can thank her for saving your ass because I would have been out of here if you had deceived me again."

"Damn it, Tori. I'm not deceiving you. I just didn't want you involved in something that could hurt you."

"I'm already involved because of what he did." She looked between me and Liv as I released her arms. "Did you tell her?"

"No. I mentioned the NDA, and she filled in the blanks."

Liv studied her fingernails. "It's not that hard. NDA, beautiful woman, quick departure from a lucrative position."

"It doesn't matter," I said. "It's dead in the water until I can dig up something concrete on him."

"Then what?"

Liv looked up from her nails, excitement shimmering in her eyes. "Well then, my brother strikes like the coiled viper he is."

CHAPTER 34

TORI

My eyes moved between Liv and Gabe. Two siblings raised to compete, to hunt, to defeat. They had spent half their lives plotting revenge and enacting it in a methodical takedown that even the most talented thief would have struggled with. And they'd done it all legally, albeit through questionable means.

I had stepped into a life with Gabe unaware of this side of him, but I could no longer claim innocence. I knew exactly who he was and what he'd done. But did that mean I wanted to be part of it? To bring Carl Bradman down after what he'd done to me, and let Gabe manipulate a master manipulator while I stood by his side?

Resting my palm on my temple, I said, "Call your father back."

"I'm not letting him near Reid," Gabe said. I looked up to see the clench in his jaw. His feelings for his father were still raw, and I didn't blame him. I had already seen what a better father that would make him.

"Neither am I, but that doesn't mean we can't make a bargain."

He squinted at me, trying to figure out what I had planned. I honestly didn't know. I was still struggling to make sense of what was happening between the two of us, and now this.

"Oh, I like her more every day. I'm so glad we hired her," Liv said, sitting further on the edge of her seat.

Gabe took his phone out and called his father, placing him on speakerphone.

"That didn't take long," his father said. "And I'm on speakerphone."

"Hi Dad," Liv said, with no emotion in her voice.

"Victoria's with us," Gabe added.

"Ah, Victoria Abigail Hent, daughter of Thomas and Amy Hent and future heir of The Haven Resort. Graduated summa cum laude with a finance degree from the University of Connecticut, earned your master's from Boston University while raising my grandson, and climbed to a senior position at the same financial firm where you tempted my son. Left the coveted position as CFO at Bradman Holdings after three years at a particularly suspicious time to leave."

"You've done your homework," I said, hating how he knew so much about me and the stab at my relationship with Gabe.

"I needed to know who was distracting my son."

My eyes lifted to Gabe. "Did you go to this extreme with every woman he dated?"

Liv snickered, and Gabe frowned.

"Only you. The others never lasted, but you were persistent and impressive enough to know I needed to vet you."

I tried to stop my jaw from gaping. Gabe took a step back as if his father had reached out and slapped him. Even Liv looked flustered.

"What do you want with my son?" I asked, needing time to process that admission.

"To see him. He is my grandson, after all."

A grinding sound came from Gabe, and I saw the tension in

his jaw. He didn't like the idea of his father near Reid as much as I didn't. Protective, just like he'd been with me.

"No. You can't think I'd be foolish enough to let you walk into his life after what you did to Gabe. You need to earn that trust, and nothing you've done tells me you deserve it."

"Then this conversation is over."

"But I'll compromise," I said before he could hang up.

"What?" Gabe and Liv said at once.

I put my hand up to silence them. "You give Gabe the information he needs, and I'll give you a chance to prove yourself."

"Such as?"

I looked at Gabe and Liv, the two people this man had shaped with abuse but never neglect. They had everything they needed, everything but their father's love. Had wanted for nothing, and in the end after all he'd done, he had given them his fortune and a company he would have handed to them if they hadn't stolen it from him first.

I picked up the phone and took it off speaker, walking out of the office.

"Tori," Gabe called.

"Stay and let me talk to him."

His brows knitted, his eyes questioning.

"Trust me."

I closed the office door and returned to my office, closing the door behind me.

"You repair the relationship with your children, right your wrongs, make amends for the damage you sowed."

"I don't need to repair anything, and I regret nothing I did in raising them."

"You beat him. Pushed him through a glass window. There's a history between the three of you, especially you and Gabe, that needs to be fixed before I will let you step foot in my son's life. He is innocent and naïve about the wickedness of this world. Like I suspect Gabe was before you laid your hand on him. I won't let you hurt him, too."

Silence. Long and nerve-inducing. This wasn't my business, but he had made it mine by demanding to see Reid.

"You really love my son, don't you?"

"Yes, and I hate what you did to him. I hate that he still carries it with him. You prove to Gabe and Liv that you're worth letting back into their lives, and I'll consider letting you into Reid's."

"Until then?"

"You stay away from him. I'll allow a Christmas present if Gabe agrees, but no visits, no phone calls. Not until you show us you're worthy of it."

"I can see why my son loves you. Why he was willing to give so much up for you."

"If you hadn't interfered, he wouldn't have had to."

"But then he wouldn't be the man he is today."

"No, he'd be better. Without the scotch habit, without the guilt he carries, without having missed so many years of his son's life. He'd be happier."

"I don't strive for happiness, Miss Hent. I strive for ambition and power, and that's what he has. Now put me back on speakerphone. We're done talking."

He was frustrating, and I didn't know why I'd offered anything to the man. Why I'd thought Gabe or Liv would care to have any relationship with him. But when I stepped back into the office, their worried hazel eyes met mine, and I knew it had been the right thing.

"I see we're keeping our own secrets now," said Liv, feigning indifference.

I put their father back on speakerphone. "They're here."

"Good. Bradman kept you on board for three years. Longer than any female officer he's had. The rest lasted as long as he kept his dirty hands to himself. He keeps his affairs quiet, and when he's done with them, he slaps an NDA on them. Now, I'm not saying all his advances were unwelcome, like I imagine those made at you were, but he plays the power card with promises of promotions and favors."

"How do you know all this?" Gabe asked.

"Because I've known Carl since he was an aggressive, spoiled brat in college. His parents let him get away with everything and covered up his mistakes with money. There's a reason I was hard on you two, and you turned out nothing like Carl Bradman for that reason."

"Like that makes it all better," Liv griped.

"Get to the point before I end this call." Gabe's voice came out almost like a growl, and my eyes jumped to his. He hated his father, and now I questioned the proposal I'd made.

"The NDAs have been a recurrence in his rise to the head of the company, but his parents handled his early misadventures with payoffs, including the girl he raped at a frat party and got pregnant. Not even his current wife, or any of the prior ones, knows about it."

"But you do?" I asked, uncertain what to do with the information.

"The girl was friends with my girlfriend at the time, William and Olivia's mother."

Gabe and Liv exchanged looks. "What aren't you telling us?" Gabe asked, and I didn't know what else he was looking for.

"Nothing you need to concern yourself with."

Gabe slammed his hands on the desk and hovered over the phone. "Why do you want revenge on Bradman, Dad? Why give me this information?"

"So you can avenge what he did to cause him to slap an NDA on the mother of your child."

"I don't think so. There's more to it. You're not that altruistic." His muscles were tense, the vein in his neck prominent.

"All you need to know is that Carl Bradman and I have not

been friends since that year. He knows not to step into my world, and I make it damn clear he's not welcome in it."

"Well, he stepped into mine," Gabe said, wrenching his hand through his hair.

Silence. Again with the silence, and I took the time to think about Bradman's company and the Icinda's. The holdings were similar. Mostly real estate, hotel chains, resorts. Bradman inherited his company; Icinda built his from the ground up. Beginning in his twenties. He took calculated risks that paid off and made a name for himself that far outshined and outperformed Bradman's. All while keeping his company private. His investments were sound and legitimate, just like Gabe's were.

"Do what you do best, son. Bring him to his knees like you did me."

The phone disconnected, but my mind was still racing.

"Well, that was as helpful as a pair of suede boots on a snowy day." Liv grumbled, standing with a stretch. "I hate to say it, but I agree with Tori. Bradman is too big, his network too extensive and too public. We eat up small companies, Gabe. It's a risk hitting at Bradman, and what Dad gave us isn't enough to make him flinch."

She sashayed from the office, mumbling about needing coffee, and shut the door behind her.

"Were you really planning to keep me in the dark on this?" I asked Gabe.

Hands still resting on the desk, he rolled his neck toward me. "Yes, but I know now it was the wrong move. I didn't think. This stuff has always been mine and Liv's."

"You promised to let me in, Gabe."

"I know, and I will."

I moved over to the desk, sitting next to where he was still leaning. "What's your next move?"

"I really don't know. You and Liv are right, but he has a weakness. It's women, and his track record shows it. My father's story confirms it, but he didn't tell us everything."

"Your parents went to school together?"

"Yes. They were college sweethearts. My mother adored him until..."

"When did the depression start?" I had a theory I wasn't certain I wanted to present. Not wanting to bring any more pain to Gabe.

He straightened and rubbed his eye. "College, I think. I remember her saying something about it once, how her parents almost made her drop out, but my father helped her through it."

"Sounds like he wasn't always a bad guy."

His eyes grew shadowed. "He's always been the bad guy."

I glanced down at my hands. "What if the girl your father mentioned wasn't Bradman's only victim?" The words came out as a mere whisper, my fear of voicing them too high to give power to them.

"What are you implying?" I sensed the change, his mood darkening, his eyes flitting to the bar where his bottle of scotch sat.

"What if something triggered your mother's depression, some trauma, and your father was the only one who could bring her out of it? Until even he could no longer reach her?"

"She grew more depressed because of what he did to me and Liv."

"I'm not saying she didn't, Gabe."

He stormed over to the bar and poured himself a glass. I let out a shallow exhale, hating that this had driven him back to it.

"Then what is it you're saying, Tori?" He took a long sip, swirling the alcohol in the glass.

What was I saying? This wasn't my business, but Gabe had made it my business by bringing some vendetta against Bradman into the picture when I was content to leave him in my past.

"I think he did something to your mother, and your father has been trying to get to him since."

He gaped at me, but I hopped down from the desk.

"Think about it. The business mirrors Bradman's except in

going public. The locations are in spots close enough to worry him but not far enough in his territory to cause a confrontation. Every resort, every hotel. They're better and bigger than Bradman's. Every shopping mall and apartment complex. Your father said they don't get along and haven't since school."

"And you think what? That he raped my mother? How did you even come up with that?"

"Not necessarily, but it could have been something close, and your father stopped it. Whatever it was, it hurt her, so she was never the same, and your father spent his life trying to make it up to her." I slumped back on the desk, seeing it too clearly as an outsider looking in through the window.

He drank the rest of the glass and thumped it on the bar. "Well, he did a shitty job if that's what he was trying to do. He drove her to her death, Tori. Not Carl Bradman. My father. A man who spent his life chasing money and power while she rotted away. His company became his life, and he left the three of us to beg for what scraps of attention he gave us."

Standing, I moved to him, rubbing my hand over his jaw. "I'm not excusing his behavior. I'm just suggesting the past is more convoluted than you thought."

He took my hand, bringing it to his lips and kissing it. The darkness hovered behind his eyes, but it softened as they searched mine. "What do you want me to do? I don't know what happened in my parents' past with Bradman, but I'll bring him to his knees for touching you, just say the word."

My kind, sweet, beautiful man with the instincts of a lethal animal caged within him. "Don't do your father's dirty work for him. He spent his life chasing Bradman, don't follow in his footsteps. What happened in their past isn't your fight. It was his, and maybe he spent the years when he should have been loving the two of you and your mother chasing his need for vengeance instead of seeing what he was losing in his pursuit. Don't be that man. You did what you set out to do. Leave Carl Bradman for someone else."

"But he tried to hurt you."

I smoothed my hand up his chest, leaning closer to him. "Sometimes, we need to leave the hurt in the past."

The words resounded through me, and I saw the understanding in his eyes that matched the one that settled in my chest. His fingers sank into my hair, but hesitation dulled the amber in his irises.

"You can kiss me," I said. "Just because we're slowing down doesn't mean I want to give that up."

He chuckled and brought me to him, his kiss flaming through me and setting me on fire. "From now on, I make every decision with you unless it's a surprise."

"I'd like that," I mumbled against his lips as he swept me into another kiss. How I was going to take it slow with him, I really didn't know, but I knew in the end it would be worth it.

***

The computer screen was blurring when a knock pulled me from it. Reid was sprawled on the couch, playing a game on his tablet. Hopping up from my chair, I stretched my back and made my way to the door.

It opened to Gabe leaning on the frame with a tub of movie theater popcorn and a big grin. "Movie night?" he said.

A week had passed since the Bradman discussion, and true to his word, he was taking it slow. Treating me to dinner, walks in Central Park, impromptu coffee deliveries. It was almost like we were a new couple dating and getting swept away in our blooming love.

I ushered him in, and he looked over at the computer and the folders spread on the table.

"Tell me you're not still working."

"I'm not still working," I lied, averting his gaze.

"Tori, there's nothing important enough to bring home right now."

I walked over to the couch. Reid, too engrossed in his game, hadn't noticed Gabe yet.

"The restructure is a lot of work, and I want to make sure everything's consistent. I was just running through some numbers."

He reached over and pulled the pencil out of my sloppy bun, sending my hair tumbling down. Snatching it from him, I gave him an annoyed look. "That took forever to put up."

"Come on. Put it away and relax."

I looked over at Reid, whose tongue was halfway out of his mouth while he fought some creature.

"Take Reid up to your place. He'd love that, and it would give you time together."

He didn't hesitate to go over to Reid and put the bin of popcorn between him and the game.

"Popcorn! Gabe!"

"Wanna watch a movie with me?" Gabe asked him, and my heart thrummed. He hadn't argued or convinced me to go. He had instantly invited Reid. "Unless you want to sit around and watch your mom do boring work."

Reid was up and running to the door in seconds.

"Put your shoes on, young man," I scolded.

"No need. We're just going upstairs. He'll be fine. Besides pajamas and shoes don't make a good look."

He gave me a quick kiss, and they were gone before I could argue anymore. I dove back into my work. It wasn't that the finances were a mess. In fact, Gabe had been meticulous. He had accounted for everything, and the numbers were healthy and solid. But bringing so many separate entities in and folding their finances into one was the challenge.

After weeding through too many systems and spreadsheets for

my mind to handle, I checked the time. It was after eleven, and Gabe hadn't returned. Needing the blood flow to return to my legs, I grabbed my keycard and headed up to Gabe's floor. A simple rap on the door took longer to answer than I expected. When Gabe's dreary eyes and rumpled hair appeared, I laughed.

"Couldn't make it through the movie?" I asked.

He rubbed his eyes and opened the door further. "This one did me in. Something about robots and cleaning up garbage. That's about as far as I got."

"Oh, that's one of my favorites," I said, giving him a kiss on the cheek and spying Reid curled in a ball on the couch. I stopped, realizing the two had fallen asleep with each other, and the image was a sweet one I wished I'd witnessed.

"He didn't make it either."

"I see that." I brushed Reid's hair back. "He's a lightweight, though. From you, I would have expected more."

"Ouch, that's not fair."

"Time to go, Reid," I told him as his eyes blinked open.

"Can I stay with Gabe?" The words came out in a broken yawn. I peered up at Gabe, who shrugged.

"Fine with me. I can bring him down in the morning."

"Are you sure?" I stood, scratching my arm.

"Certain." He ran into his room and returned a few moments later with two blankets. "We'll camp out here for the night."

He spread a blanket over Reid and dropped the other next to him. Excitement shimmered in his eyes.

"That's not comfortable," I argued.

"But it's fun. You're welcome to join us." His brow arched, and my grin came effortlessly.

"I left my computer and all the lights on."

The arch grew. "I can afford the electricity."

He sat next to Reid and scooped him back into a comfortable position, then patted the seat next to him. I debated for a few seconds before I lost the battle and joined him. Spreading the blanket over us, he turned a cooking show on and scooted me closer. By the time my eyes were closing, I was curled up in his lap, content as a kitten.

CHAPTER 35

There's a loophole," my attorney said. "It's a small one, but it's there."

"Enough for her to have told me?"

"Enough for her to tell anyone. A sloppy mistake, if you ask me. Probably been using the same agreement for decades without updating it to current law."

"Thanks, Doug. I'll let you know if she decides to take it further."

"And I'll have your back and hers if she does."

I tapped my fingers on my desk. Doug and I had been friends since college, and he was one of the best attorneys out there. He'd been working for me since I hired him years ago. If he had a way to break the NDA, then it was a valid one.

Picking my phone back up, I checked my calendar and dialed my pilot, booking a flight to Dulles in two days. I left my office and headed to Tori's. We'd been inseparable since the night she slept on my couch with me, but that had been the only night she'd spent with me. We were still in the slow phase, which was killing me, but I would handle it as long as she wanted. Whatever it took to get her back completely.

Movie nights, dinners, and Thanksgiving with her family. The month of November had come and gone, ending when I'd taken her and Reid to Rockefeller Center to watch the tree lighting. Now we were in December, nearing the time I'd asked her to marry me, and the nostalgia this time of year had always left me burying my emotions in my scotch. Not this year. This year I had every intention of making December as amazing as it had been the year I met her.

She was finishing a call and gestured for me to wait. I closed the door and took a seat, listening to her run through numbers with whoever was on the other line. She never ceased to amaze me. Intelligent, sharp, and determined. How Carl Bradman had ever thought she was only there as eye candy confounded me. Sure, she was beautiful, but there was so much more to her, and it was the many layers of Tori that I'd fallen for.

When the call finished, she sat back in her chair and blew a strand of hair from her face.

"Tough call?" I asked, crossing my ankle over my leg.

"Eh, not that bad. What's up?"

"What are you doing this weekend?"

She eyed me, curiosity in those blue orbs. "Reid and I were going to ask you to decorate for Christmas with us. We need to get a tree."

A constricting sensation enveloped my chest. "I'd love that."

Her smile was contagious as she said, "I thought you would."

That changed my plans, but not terribly. "Friday, I'm taking you both to Virginia. I have a meeting with the manager at the Tyson's Corner location, and I thought we could stay in Crystal City and then take the Metro into DC on Saturday. Take Reid to the museums, see the monuments. We're too early for the tree lighting, but I can always fly us back if you want to see it." I was rambling, unsure of why my nerves were so heightened.

Her smile spread, and my nerves settled. "I would love that. As would Reid."

"I can get us back in time on Sunday to get a tree and decorate." I scratched my ear, trying to hide my excitement.

"That sounds perfect."

"Great. The plane is scheduled for ten. I have a two o'clock meeting, then I'm all yours."

I started to leave, and she stopped me. "Is there another reason for the trip?"

My lips thinned as I remembered what I'd promised her. Clearing my throat, I turned back to her. "No secrets, right?"

"No secrets."

I returned to her desk and picked her phone up, dialing our secretary. "Paula, can you get Carl Bradman on the line for me?"

While she gathered his number, I said to Tori, "Bradman spends every December in Northern Virginia, which I suppose you know. He works from an office he has in one of his Tyson's properties. One of the few cities my father's holdings and his ever crossed over."

"I have Carl Bradman on the line," Paula said.

"Thanks. Put him through." I placed the phone on speaker and set my finger against Tori's mouth to let her know to keep quiet.

"Carl," I greeted him as if I didn't want to rip the man's throat out.

"William. How nice to hear from you. I was hoping we'd have a more cordial relationship than I had with your father." I could hear the undercut in his voice. "After our last meeting, I wasn't certain we would."

Tori rolled her eyes, but I kept my hard mask on. "I have a meeting in Tyson's Corner this Friday afternoon with one of my property managers," I said, ignoring his dig. "I was hoping to stop by and say hello before I leave."

"Let's see Friday...I'm free after four. Stop by. We'll have a drink and start fresh."

"Sounds great."

"I'll let the front know to expect you. Safe travels."

I disconnected, and Tori sat back, crossing her arms. "What are you up to? I thought we agreed to let this lie."

"We did, but I need to remind him that touching and threatening the woman I love is behavior I won't tolerate. I may not be my father, Tori, but I'm very much like him when it comes to asserting my power in this world." I adjusted my jacket and took the three strides back to her door. "I won't go after him, but he needs to know I can, and if he ever steps foot near you again, I'll drag him so far under he'll never emerge."

Wide eyes stared at me with a hint of desire behind them.

"Dinner tonight?" I asked her.

"I...umm...yeah."

I gave her a sideways grin and left her still gaping at me.

My shoes echoed on the marble floor as I walked from the elevator. The top floor of Carl's building was a garish display of money and assumed power. Gold patterns, crystal light fixtures, designer furnishings in bright colors. A stark contrast to the reserved, elegant style my father had always preferred.

I stared out the window at the view while I waited for him. Tori was down there somewhere with Reid, shopping like I'd suggested. She needed a dress for tonight, and Reid needed a suit, both of which I'd forgotten to have her pack.

"William, so nice to see you." Carl extended his hand, and I took it, my skin crawling now that I knew his secrets. It was men like him, with their despicable behavior and expectations that they were above the law, who gave all men a bad reputation.

He walked me to his office, which was the only one on the floor. Surrounded by glass, it offered a view that extended over Tyson's Corner.

"Have a seat. Can I get you a drink?" he asked, heading to his bar and gesturing to the seating area.

"I'm good. This isn't a personal call." My demeanor had changed since greeting him, and his vision snapped to mine. Beady eyes waited for me to explain. I studied my cufflinks as if I didn't have any other cares. "You slapped my CFO with an NDA under the threat of smearing her reputation and ruining her career." The same thing my father had threatened to get me to leave her. That was likely the only thing the two men had in common. As much as I hated my father, I respected him as a businessperson. He had never acted like this man did. While he had his own faults, including misogynist beliefs and ignorant biases, he steered clear of anything that could hurt his reputation or our family's.

"NDAs aren't unusual."

"No, but using them to keep women quiet about your misconduct is." He went pale. "And before you threaten anything, my lawyers have unraveled your precious contract and will bury you in the courts if you dare go after her."

His eyes narrowed as he lowered his glass. "What do you want?"

"Stay away from Victoria. If I find out you've laid a hand on her again, dared to even speak to her, or so much as looked at her wrong, I'll knock you from your pedestal and bring your company down around you."

His laughter filled the room. "You can't touch me. You're a boy playing in a man's world. Grow up and come back to me in twenty years."

He returned to pouring his drink.

"Do you think my father was ready to give me his company? Ready to retire so early? I can be a thorn in your ass just like I was to him, Carl. I have enough on you to send your stock plummeting. A few leaks to the press about how frequently women leave your employment or your history of buying off your unacceptable behavior, and I'm sure you won't be sitting so comfortably."

He stormed over to me, but I stopped him, grabbing him by the lapels. "I wouldn't try it. You'll lose, and my attorneys will have a field day suing your ass for attacking me. I'll make this simple, Carl. Stay away from Victoria. I don't want you anywhere near her or anything of mine for that matter. You're not welcome within ten feet of my properties. In return, I'll maintain a civil business relationship with you when necessary and keep your secrets quiet."

I released him and smoothed his jacket. "Understood?"

Clenched jaw and silence. It was almost like talking to my father. "You don't know what you're doing, William."

"Oh, I know exactly what I'm doing. Removing the scum from my properties and protecting what's mine." I stepped closer to him so that I towered over him. "And Victoria is mine. Don't even dare think otherwise, or you'll feel my wrath."

"So, you're sleeping with your CFO, and you have the nerve to threaten me because you have some claim on her? Childish, just like your father."

My hand shook as I fisted it and held back from punching him. Rolling my neck, I turned my back on him and walked to the door.

"I've had a claim on her since well before she worked for you, Carl." Even if I had given that claim up, and now had to earn it back. "And I can guarantee if I were sleeping with her, I wouldn't treat her like a piece of property who owed me something."

I swung the door open and turned back to him.

"Keep your hands off women who don't want to be touched, or I'll have my attorneys unravel the rest of your NDAs as quickly as they did hers."

His face was beet red. I took a step before glancing over my shoulder at him. "Oh, and I won't fight my father's battles for him, but don't think for a second I don't know what you did back then. I'll keep to my business if you keep to yours and stay far away from Victoria, but I can't promise my father won't strike one of these days." The flinch gave away his guilt that something had happened between the two, and I wondered if Tori was right and my mother had somehow been involved. The thought left a bitter taste in my mouth, but I didn't want a war with Bradman. I would win, but it would tarnish both our family names. He had a son he was grooming to take over, and I had Liv and Reid to protect. If things went my way, Tori would have my name as well.

"You think you can come in here and threaten me? A few months in control of your father's failing company, and you think you scare me?" He should have kept his mouth shut because I'd been digging since he left my building, finding all his other secrets. None enough to do enough damage without my father's information but enough to make him sweat.

Taking the few strides back to him, I kept my composure, knowing this was the play that would put him in his place, as unbelievable as that seemed. "My father's company is still intact. It may be in pieces that I've bought up over the past years and added to my multi-billion-dollar portfolio of holdings, but it's there. All in excellent shape since I cleaned them up." Even if I'd been the one to destroy their value. "Unlike what I've found with your holdings, Carl. Shortcuts in building, failed inspections, bribes to inspectors, code violations that continue to be overlooked, suspicious behavior swept under the rug, customer satisfaction rates that continue to slip, employee benefits that lag far behind the industry averages. Should I go on?"

"Get out and hope our paths never cross again."

I gave him a smirk. "Now, Carl, that's not very nice."

His eyes looked ready to pop out of their sockets, and the vein in his forehead was massive.

"We're done here, William."

I buttoned my suit jacket and adjusted my sleeves. "We are. Stay out of my territory, and I'll stay out of yours. It would be good for you to remember, Carl, you may be nothing like your father, not inheriting his shrewd business skills or his finesse, but I am very much my father's son, and I won't hesitate to strike if provoked."

I didn't bother waiting for a reply and saw myself out.

As I waited outside the car for Tori and Reid, I churned my words around in my head. I had never owned my similarities to my father, refusing to admit I was anything like him. Yet in telling Carl Bradman that I was, I had admitted what I'd always known. No matter how I'd strived to be anything but my father, I had become him. Ruthless, shrewd, calculating, and unrelenting. Driven. They were words I'd always associated with him but that now described me.

I rubbed my forehead. As long as I wasn't like him as a father, I could handle being him in the business world. There was a reason my father's name was respected in circles, why he had built a billion-dollar company that had only suffered when I had sent it crumbling. I looked up, realizing the truth and remembering his words. He had known what Liv and I were doing, and he'd let us. He was too smart not to notice, and here we'd been so certain he didn't know. Yet, he'd sat back and watched me unravel his dynasty and not lifted a finger to stop me.

Because he'd known I would build it back to what it had been and make it better. Because he'd trusted me and my skills. He'd trusted Liv and her abilities. A test to prove we were the children he had raised, to show that I was worthy of taking over the company. Maybe it hadn't been a test he'd designed, nowhere near his original intent, but he had let it ride and watched us become just like him.

The revelation left me shaken.

Tori came around the corner with Reid, her hands filled with bags. The driver took them from her while Reid jumped into the car with an exaggerated huff, complaining about how tiring shopping was.

"That bad?" I asked Tori.

"No," she said, lifting on her toes and giving me a peck on the lips. I wanted to pull her closer, to deepen the kiss and have it ease the strain in my muscles, but this wasn't the place or the time. Her eyes looked between mine as she smoothed her hands down my arms. "Did you..."

"Let's get going. I'll order room service for dinner while we get ready."

She cocked her head, her gaze intense, and I read the look. The worry that I was keeping secrets again. Running my fingers through her hair, I said, "I'll tell you about it on the way to the hotel, and you can tell me all about shopping."

Reid groaned from inside the car. "No more shopping."

Laughing, I helped Tori in and took the seat next to her. I gave her the abridged version of my meeting with Bradman, the weight of her eyes heavy. She was reading me, like she always did, better than anyone else could.

Changing the subject, I said, "So you got a dress?"

A momentary pause, and that heaviness continued until she replied, "Yes. You still won't tell me where we're going?"

I squeezed her hand and pulled it into my lap. "Nope. It's a surprise."

"Stubborn."

"I know."

My sight drifted out the window, my mind still on the meeting. Silence fell over the car, and I embraced it, lost in my thoughts.

"You're not him, Gabe." Head swiveling to her, I saw the understanding in her eyes. "You're not your father. You may have his traits, his mind, his skills, but you're not him, and you never will be."

I looked down at our hands. "But what if I become him?" It was a fear that had followed me through life. That, as much as I fought to be different, I would succumb to the inevitable.

She lifted my chin. "You won't."

"You don't know that, Tori."

"I don't? I see you with Reid. See the softness, the love you have for him that would never allow you to hurt him. You are not your father, and you won't become him."

She caressed her hand over my jaw and drew my face to hers. "You love us too much to ever be him."

"But..."

Her lips were on mine before I could argue more. "No more," she said. "Now tell me where you're taking us tonight."

Her kiss muffled my laugh. "Good try."

The stress lifted from me the longer she was with me so that by the time we were at the hotel, I'd left the thoughts behind. It didn't matter if I was like my father. I would never *be* him, and if I ever came close, Tori would be there to stop me from falling over that ledge. She was my lifeline, my calm, my peace, my everything.

CHAPTER 36

TORI

The reflection in the mirror was that of someone I no longer recognized. I'd lost her so long ago that I had to adjust to seeing her again. Happy and glowing. Dressed in the cocktail dress I'd bought earlier in the day, I touched up my makeup one more time before leaving the bathroom and crossing through the bedroom I was sharing with Reid.

A month had passed since I'd told Gabe I wanted to slow down, and he'd kept good on his promise. Too good. He was the perfect gentleman, just like he'd been when we were first together, respecting my boundaries a little too much. He'd done no more than kiss me since we reconnected, except for that moment in my closet. The heat of his touch lingered, and I missed it. But I had done this to us. Needing to be sure, to understand my emotions and to ensure nothing convoluted them.

As I walked out of the room and Gabe's eyes filled with adoration, that certainty came. I was ready for this, for more, for him and the rest of our journey together.

"You look amazing," he said, wonder emphasizing his words. His eyes glided over me, and he took my hand, twirling me around before he drew me into his arms.

"Mommy, you look so pretty."

I looked down at Reid. Backing out of Gabe's hold, I stooped down and adjusted his tie. In his suit, he looked like a mini version of Gabe. I stood and stepped back, taking them both in. Gabe wore a black suit, designer of course, with silver cufflinks and a black tie. He looked so handsome it was difficult to catch my breath. But seeing the two of them together like that had tears pricking the back of my eyes.

"My boys," I said. "You both look dashing." I stepped back into Gabe's body. "And you, I don't know if I want to let you out of this room because too many women are going to be looking at you."

He threw his head back and laughed. "I think I'm the one who needs to worry with as ravishing as you look. If women look, it will only be because they're jealous of you."

"You two are funny," Reid said, munching on a piece of crust from the pizza Gabe had ordered for him.

Gabe planted a kiss on my nose. "Don't want to mess that lipstick up," he said. His cheek brushed over mine. "Not until I'm ready."

Heat rushed through me, and it warmed my face. This was what he did to me. Constantly destroying me with his words, small comments that left me flustered and rethinking my decision to keep this slow. But he'd always had that effect on me, leaving me a wreck with just a word or two before he completely devastated me with his touches. And I missed those touches.

The ringing of his phone stopped whatever comeback was forming in my addled brain, and he released me.

"Yes," he answered. Terse and confident. Sexy.

I walked away, brushing crumbs from Reid's jacket to calm myself.

"The car's here," Gabe said as his eyes dropped to my wrist.

He lifted it, his finger gently touching the charms that dangled from the bracelet he had bought me for our first Christmas together. I had dug it from under my other jewelry, ready to welcome the firsts it represented for me and Gabe.

"Is that…" His throat bobbed, and I could see the emotion brewing in his eyes.

"I could never convince myself to throw it away," I admitted. "It held too many wonderful memories for me to let it go."

He drew me into his arms and kissed me. The love in that kiss worked its way through my body, cascading from my core to my feet, then rose to encompass the rest of my body.

"I love you, Tori." His words were a murmur that warmed my chest. "I don't deserve you, but I will spend the rest of my life proving that I do."

I lifted my hands to his face, forcing his eyes to mine. "You deserve me, Gabe. You don't have to prove it anymore."

He gave me another kiss that blazed through me, leaving me teetering when his lips separated from mine.

"You need to stop that, or you'll mess my lipstick up too early," I said, touching my lips.

"Then you'll need to reapply in the car to ensure those lips are still gorgeous when I'm ready to kiss you again."

I shook my head as he left me standing in the wake of his words. That was Gabe. Constantly devastating me with words and kisses. Ones he had saved for me because, like Cindy had said, we were inevitable.

Gabe strolled across the room and retrieved our coats. Holding mine out to me, he asked, "Ready?"

I wasn't because my legs were like jelly, but Reid huffed, "Finally," before running over and grabbing his coat.

Gabe helped me put mine on before he bent down and fixed Reid's buttons for him. He slid his arms through his long black coat, and my heart stuttered when he looked back up at me.

His sexy smirk and a shake of his head had my knees weakening even more. "You can tell me what you were just thinking when we're alone later."

I inhaled, hating how easily he read me. He led us out, his hand resting gently on my back as he guided me. Walking through the lobby, I felt the eyes on us, saw the looks. Tucking my arm in his, I let him pull me closer, knowing it was as much a claim of ownership as I'd made in giving him my arm. I was ready for him to be mine again, completely. To stop dragging my feet and let Gabe own me again. Again? He had never stopped owning me. Never relinquished his hold on me, and I had never denied it, even in the worst of times.

The capital was lit up as we drove through. The rush of cars still filled the streets. Reid bounced up and down in his seat, asking Gabe question after question, but still Gabe didn't tell us where we were going. When we pulled up to the National Theater, and I saw the signs for *The Nutcracker*, I froze. He had remembered, even after all these years. The sight brought back memories of our past like a rush of emotions. His love encompassed every cell in my body along with the knowledge that this man was mine and worshipped me the way I'd always dreamed.

"Tori." I looked up to see his hand in front of me, the door open as he and Reid stood waiting for me to exit the car. I tried to fight the tears, knowing I'd look a mess of smeared mascara if I didn't.

Taking his hand, I let him help me out. My legs threatened to give out, and I leaned against him.

"Is this okay?" he asked, concern tingeing his eyes.

I nodded, trying to gather my words. "It's more than okay," I said, my voice a soft whisper. I pulled his face to mine, kissing him and not caring that we were surrounded by people entering the theater. "I love it."

"I figured we could make it our tradition?"

Smiling, I nodded again, those pesky tears stinging this time.

"Come on," Reid said, and I looked down to see him tugging Gabe's hand.

My laugh came out mingled with a sob, and Gabe wiped a tear

from my cheek. He kissed its trail, murmuring, "Please don't cry, luna mia."

Goosebumps pebbled my skin, and a sense of completeness fell over me.

"They're happy tears," I told him as he brushed another one away. "Very happy tears."

He kissed every spot where a tear had fallen. Taking my hand in his and keeping Reid's in his other, he led us up the steps. In a way, it was like returning home, stepping into the past with him and reclaiming what we'd been. Accepting that our pasts had damaged us but that our wounds had healed. That what we'd lost had been a blip in time I knew we would spend every day of the rest of our lives making up for.

Exhaustion hit Reid before we were even out of the theater. Gabe carried him to the car and then to the hotel room, where he laid him in bed. I changed him as much as I could without waking him and closed the door softly.

Gabe was standing at the window, overlooking the city. I wound my arms around his waist and leaned my head against his back, hearing the steady, firm heartbeats below.

"I love you, Tori," he said, bringing my hand to his mouth and kissing it. "And I will continue spoiling you and surprising you even after I've earned you back."

Twisting so that I faced him, I brought my hands to his chest. "You've won me back." His eyes widened. "I love you, William Gabriel Icinda, and I'm ready to reach the end with you."

A sharp inhale accompanied the flitting of his eyes between mine. "The end? No middle?"

With a laugh, I shook my head. "No middle. I want my happy ending."

"I love you so much, Tori."

"I know. Can I sleep with you tonight?" My heart was pounding so hard I thought the whole of DC could hear it.

"Thought you'd never ask," he said, giving me a confident grin and sweeping me into his arms.

His kiss muffled my giggle, and I wrapped my arms around his neck, bringing his mouth further into mine. He bumped us into the door on the way in, muttering an apology as he kicked the door shut.

He lowered me to the bed, hovering over me, his eyes hooded and leaving me breathless with the way they seemed to devour me. I drew him back to me, my fingers struggling with his buttons as he laughed against my mouth. There was no hesitation, no nervousness because this man knew me, every inch of me, just like I knew every inch of him.

His mouth lowered to my neck, dragging over my shoulder as he pushed the strap of my dress down. "You don't know how many times I've pictured this. Pictured your body." His mouth draped down my arm. "Remembered your taste." My stomach trembled. "Heard your cries." His hand slipped my zipper down. "Your moans." Butterflies snapped their wings in my lower body. "I've waited years to touch you again, luna mia." His mouth trailed the dress as he pushed it from my body. Kissing every spot, every curve, every dip, every freckle. Worshipping even the stretch marks that now graced my lower belly. "You're still as perfect as I remember."

My back arched as he kissed my inner thigh, his fingers working my underwear off as his mouth traveled down my legs.

"Gabe," I moaned when he followed their path back up, ending with kisses that burned their way through my body, his fingers and his tongue working magic that left me crumbling within minutes.

He slid his mouth down my leg and rose, standing over me with the look of a starving predator. I bent my leg, watching as he pulled his shirt off the rest of the way. His eyes never left mine, and when he unhooked his belt, he asked, "Are you sure?"

Permission. A question of no regrets, giving me the chance to hesitate. But I didn't. "Positive."

A mischievous grin preceded the dropping of his pants, and as he crawled back over me, his lips tracing the path they'd first made, anticipation hummed through me. Mouth crashing over mine, he wrapped his arm around me and drew me into his chest. I sucked in a breath as he nudged my legs open further and entered me. Slow and paced, letting me feel every inch until he filled me completely. Our bodies moved in tandem, a rhythm that reflected the emotions that cascaded over us.

His touches scored me, branded me, claimed me. Reawakening the parts that recognized that ownership. My body was alive because Gabe had been the only one with the power to wake it. And he was mine again.

"Come for me again, luna mia," he rasped in my ear. His hand moved between us, his mouth draping down my throat until he sucked my nipple into his mouth. Heat blossomed in my core, my climax rising until it crashed through me like waves demolishing the shore. Thrusts increasing, one hand digging into my waist, the other into the bed, Gabe followed my release. Breaths synched, we came down from our ecstasy high, and he brought his other hand up and pushed my hair from my face.

"Just as gorgeous as you were our first time." Caging me in, his eyes now a blend of hues, he asked, "Still okay? No regrets?"

Cupping his cheek, I lifted my head and kissed him. "Not a single one."

"Good, because I was looking forward to satiating my hunger for you a few more times."

"Making up for lost time?" I asked, winding my arms around his neck.

"Damn right I am."

"Then let's not miss another minute." I dragged his head

down, my body coming alive again. He lit every cell on fire, reminding me of why I'd never even considered another man. Because there was no one who rivaled him.

My body hadn't been so satisfied and blissful since the night Gabe had left me. Now that I knew the truth, I understood why he'd seemed so desperate and famished. Gabe's sex drive was demanding, but the two nights before he'd left, it had been endless.

Sitting on the side of the bed, I realized it had been the same way last night. Relentless but in all the perfect ways. I took a robe from the bathroom and tied it closed. Wobbling out of the bedroom, I froze. Reid was awake, sitting with Gabe at the table, telling him all about his teacher at the daycare center. His little hands were gesturing, and Gabe was listening intently.

I observed them like I did any time they were together, marveling at their similarities as pressure built in my chest. This was how it should have been, and now it was happening. Years without feeling complete, with an empty space in our family, and now it was whole.

And now I had to explain why Gabe and I were sleeping in the same room and in the same bed. I drew my robe tighter, contemplating the best way to approach the conversation when Gabe looked up at me. Warmth blazed through my cheeks at the heated gaze he gave me, and my insides jumbled into knots.

"Morning," he said, giving me a cocky grin.

"Morning, Mommy. Gabe said you had a sleepover last night. Can I come next time?"

The snort that came from me was loud, and I covered my mouth, the heat in my cheeks almost scalding.

"Somebody woke up extra early today. Good thing I'm a light sleeper and heard him sneaking up on us." Gabe threw me a wink, and I let out a relieved sigh. "We went out and picked up breakfast. There's coffee for you on the counter."

Planting a kiss on Reid's head, I tussled his hair.

"Can I, Mommy?"

"What, honey?" I gave Gabe a kiss on the cheek, but he didn't let me go so easily. He grabbed my waist and pulled me into a kiss that almost made me forget Reid was even in the room.

"Sleep over next time."

If Gabe's display of affection bothered him, he didn't say, and maybe he had just grown accustomed to us kissing, but this kiss reminded me of the power Gabe held over my body. His kisses were like brands that sizzled through my insides and left a mark too far to ever consider removing.

"Maybe. Why don't you go play until Gabe and I are ready to go? You can watch TV if you'd prefer."

He hopped down and ran to the couch, turning on the television and flicking to a cartoon channel.

"Sleepover, huh?" I teased, rubbing my hand up Gabe's chest.

"Yeah." He pulled me closer, nuzzling my neck, his stubble a gentle scratch on my skin. "I think we should have more of them."

"How often?"

"Very often." Head lifting, he wiped a sleeper from my eye. "I forgot how gorgeous you are in the morning."

Laughing, I replied, "Do you need your eyes checked?"

"No, I'm serious." With his fingers drifting through my knotted hair, he said, "Are you still okay with last night?"

Okay? I was still coming down from my high; my addiction to Gabe's touches was almost overwhelming. Running my hand over his jaw, I nodded. "Absolutely."

His smile returned, lighting his eyes to a golden hue.

"But..." I started, hating how the smile faltered. I inched closer to him, stepping between his legs. "You didn't ask if I was on birth control again." I'd gone off it for years, subconsciously knowing I wouldn't need it. There was no replacing Gabe. But I'd started taking it again after I'd accepted him back into my life, something he didn't know.

"Are you?" he asked, sweeping a strand of my hair back.

"What if I'm not?"

Laying a kiss on my nose, he gave me a grin that had sparks flaring through me. "It doesn't matter." I gaped at him as he stood and tipped my chin up. "I plan to have you in my life until there's no life left in me, Tori. If that includes more children, then it does. I'm not going anywhere, so it shouldn't matter as long as we both agree, and since you didn't ask if I had a condom, that tells me you're on birth control or as willing to make our family bigger as I am."

My chest shouldn't have burned as much as it did. I rubbed it, saying, "Did you have a condom?"

His brow lifted. "I haven't carried one since the day I met you." That burning turned into pressure that made it hard to breathe. "There was no need because there was never anyone but you."

I swallowed, the sound loud enough that his grin turned even more mischievous. "I am," I said. A slight frown had me explaining. "I started back when I let you back in." And the grin returned. "And...I think I should stay on it until..." Until what? I was afraid to say the words because the last time they had dominated my life, I had lost him.

"Until we exchange vows and rings?"

A torrent of flutters raced through me. Excitement, nerves, fear. I nodded. "And we'll talk about it first to make sure we're both ready."

"That sounds like the perfect plan." Thumb brushing over my cheek, he brought my mouth to his. The kiss charged through me like all his kisses did. "Until then, I will take every chance to practice." His mouth raced down my chin and over my neck. "Starting with you joining me in the shower."

This time, my stomach did a series of flips that left me unbalanced. I glanced over to where Reid was watching television.

"I think there's a strong possibility I could partake in that."

A devious gleam sparkled in his eyes as he rose. Pulling me into his arms, he dragged his cheek over mine, his teeth nibbling at my ear. "I'll meet you in there, luna mia."

He lifted his shirt over his head as he walked away, and I watched his tight back muscles, thoughts of what he was about to do to me leaving me grasping for words.

I gave Reid another kiss on the head and told him I was going to use Gabe's shower because the one in our room wasn't as big.

"Is Gabe going to help you?"

I stifled my laugh and heard Gabe yell from the room. "If there's a spot she can't reach, I've got her covered."

"I guess that's a yes," I answered Reid, shaking my head as I looked up to see Gabe's sexy smirk peering around the door.

"Gabe's a good helper, Mommy."

"I know he is. Keep watching your show. I'll be out in..." A few minutes would have been my usual estimate, but Gabe's appetite ensured it would be longer. "...soon."

I hurried after Gabe, closing the bedroom door and hearing the water running. Dropping my robe, I joined him under the water where he pinned me to the tiled wall and reminded me again of all the ways my body belonged to him.

CHAPTER 37

GABE

This is the one." Reid put his hands on his hips as if readying himself for an argument.

I looked over at Tori, who was trying to hide her smile.

"Is that your final decision?" I asked him, giving her a wink.

"Final."

Folding my arms, I walked around the tree, pretending to evaluate it. "Good structure. Sturdy." I bent and peeked through the branches. "Space for plenty of decorations." I rose and eyed the top. "And a nice spot for a topper. I think that decision is a wise one."

"So we can take it home?"

I laughed and gave him a nod. "It's all ours."

He bounced on his toes, grabbing Tori's hand.

"Let me pay and have it loaded onto the car. Then we can shop for decorations."

Tori gnawed at her lip, and my brow creased as I questioned whether I'd said something wrong. I'd had to change the regulations regarding the top floor suites of the hotel to allow for a live tree and was still trying to figure out how to avoid violating any fire codes. Getting it up to the suite was going to be its own feat, but for Tori and Reid, I would make it work.

"What's wrong?" I asked her.

She looked from me to the tree to Reid and back to me. "I have decorations," she said with hesitation. "The ones you bought me in Jacksonville."

The admission left me dumbfounded. I had never considered she would keep them.

"I couldn't part with them. They held too many memories."

Swallowing, I said, "They're not here, though." I was certain she had them stored at her parents' house like her wedding dress.

"I... They're in my closet. When the movers brought our things from my parents' house, I had them include the two bins."

The way my heart jumped was almost painful. She'd brought them here like she had known we would shop for a tree together, and the decorations would no longer remind her of a past that had left her broken. They were reminders of our story.

Reid kicked the snow with his boot, and I knew he was anxious to move, but Tori's admission had me wrapping an arm around her waist and kissing her. "I love you, Victoria Abigail Hent."

She giggled against my mouth, and Reid tugged her hand. "All you do is kiss."

I joined her laugh and kissed her once more before saying, "And you're going to get used to it because I plan to kiss your mother every day that I can."

She stepped out of my hold and took my hand. "Do you think..." That serious expression returned. "Well, the house in the Hamptons is so empty and..." This time my heart expanded three-fold, making it difficult to breathe. "...maybe next Christmas we can have the tree there?"

I loved her more every day.

"If that would be okay. I know it holds unpleasant memories."

I stopped her by pressing my finger to her lips. "I told you. I bought it from my father so we could make new memories and bring joy to it again."

"You couldn't have known we would get back together," she said.

"I always knew that you were mine, luna mia. I had planned to seek you out once we closed the deal with my father. That house is for us. If you hadn't come back to me, it would have sat empty like my heart and my life because it's always been you."

She dragged in a sharp inhale just as Reid pulled on a branch, sending snow splattering over us. Her laughter filled the air, and I pulled her to me.

"Let's bring it back to life," she said as I kissed her again. I drew back and searched her eyes. "If that's okay."

"You mean now?"

Her head bobbed. "Take the tree there and decorate it."

"And then?"

She shrugged. "A house needs love to bring it back to life. Maybe we spend the weekends there and stay in the city during the week."

I had never thought it possible to love her any more than I did, but she kept surprising me.

"That sounds perfect. Ready to decorate this tree, Reid?"

"Finally," he said with an exaggerated eye roll.

We stopped by the hotel and retrieved the bins of decorations, drove to the house, and spent the rest of the day decorating. Reid burned out after three bites of the pizza I ordered.

"Should we just stay here tonight?" Tori asked as I carried him up to my old bedroom. She tugged the covering off as I laid him down, pulling the comforter over him. A cleaning service maintained the house, ensuring there was no dust, so I didn't worry about settling him there.

"There's no bed in my parents' room," I admitted. It was the only room that had no furniture. While I'd had the house renovated and the furniture updated in all the rooms, I had only repainted and updated their room.

"Why not? The entire house is furnished."

"I wanted to wait for you." My eyes fell to the floor, but she forced them back to her.

"You really never gave up the hope that I'd return?"

Shaking my head, I asked, "Did you?"

Her eyes saddened. "No. Although I won't share the number of scenarios that involved me giving you a piece of my mind."

"Deserved," I said, curling my fingers around the back of her neck. "You want to christen a few parts of the house?"

"Marking our territory?" she asked with a sexy arch of her brow.

"Absolutely." I backed her out of the room, closing the door before leading her to my parents' room—our room now—where I pinned her against the wall and worshipped every inch of her until touching her had my release so frenzied that I crashed, spiraling over the cliffs of ecstasy with her. Something I then did in several more rooms until we ended up sprawled on the couch, the cream furniture sheet covering our tangled bodies.

"I missed this," she said, kissing my chest.

"Me, too."

She leaned up on her elbow, her blue eyes a dusty navy. "Did you really wait for me? I mean, you're a man, and I know that's a lot to ask."

I moved my hand behind my head to prop it some. "Why is that a lot to ask?"

"Well, we weren't together, Gabe. There was nothing stopping you."

"There was you, Tori. Always you. Although I didn't want to think about it, I expected you to move on and find someone else." I winced at the thought. "But I wanted no one else. And just because I'm a man, doesn't mean I can't control myself or that I need to have sex all the time. My hand sufficed." I gave her a wink, loving how her cheeks grew an alluring shade of pink. "And plenty of memories of this unforgettable body to get me by."

"It's not the same," she said, curving her hand over my jaw.

"No, it wasn't because it wasn't you, but sleeping with another woman wouldn't have been you either. Every part of me has been yours since the moment we met, and if we had never crossed paths again, it would have remained yours."

Tears made her eyes shimmer, and I brought her mouth to mine, relishing the sensation of having her so close to me, her lips to mine, her skin on mine.

"There was never another, Gabe. I wanted no one else, and the two dates I went on were blind dates, and I hated them because they weren't you."

I kissed her forehead, hating how jealous I was that another man had held her attention for even a few hours but content that she'd never gone beyond that. I'd tormented myself with thoughts of her with another man too many times over the years, almost tempted to give up on my obsessive need to wait until I could find her again. But the thought of touching anyone else, of having their body replace hers, was never tempting enough to give that hope up, and so I'd remained faithful to her all those years.

"I love you, luna mia," I whispered as I brought her head to my chest.

"I love you, Gabe."

I held her until the steady rise and fall of her chest lulled me to sleep, which was disrupted the next morning when small fingers lifted my eyelids. I jerked back, blinking my eyes open to see Reid standing over us.

"Were you having another sleepover?" he asked. "Why are your clothes off?"

"Oh God." Tori groaned. "I'm not ready for this conversation yet." Grogginess muffled her words.

"It's a game your mommy and I were playing."

"Can I play?"

"No!" we said in unison.

"I tell you what, buddy," I said, rubbing my eyes. "That room you were in. That's going to be yours soon."

"It is?" His hazel eyes were large.

"Yup. Why don't you go up and think about how you want to decorate it while your mommy and I find our clothes?"

He was off, running too quickly to say more.

"Good diversion," Tori said, peeking up at me, ebony strands falling over her eyes.

"Years of practice in boardrooms." I kissed her nose just as Reid came running back into the room.

Tori groaned and pulled the sheet up higher. The armful of clothes Reid held dropped on the floor next to us.

"Here you go." He ran off again, and I couldn't hold my laughter in. It shook my entire body and Tori's with it.

"This is not funny," she said, smacking my chest.

I snatched her hand, saying, "It's hysterical."

"We need to be more careful," she hissed. "No more of this."

I yanked her over, so that she was on top of me. Bad move because it only made me more aware of how much I wanted to take her again. "There will be plenty more of this, and we will mark every room in this house."

My hand threaded into her hair, forcing her mouth to mine before she could respond. She moaned as my hand slid down her body.

"Gabe," she murmured. "We can't. Not here."

"Then let's find someplace else because I want you."

I maneuvered her from me and stood, lifting her up. She squeaked and wrapped her legs around me, keeping the sheet around us. As I walked us through the house, passing through the kitchen and considering the pantry, I remembered the office.

"We'll save the pantry for next time."

"You're impossible," she said between kisses. "And insatiable."

"Only for you." I kicked the office door closed and dropped her on the desk.

"But Reid," she argued as I draped my mouth down her neck.

"Will be busy playing in his room. The closet is full of my old toys and model sets."

She pushed me back, her eyes questioning me.

"I told you this house was waiting for you," I said, my fingers twisting into her hair as those on my other hand drove into her. I captured her gasp with my mouth, muttering, "And that room was waiting for our future child. Now, it and everything in it is his."

I worked her body the way I knew only I could until her climax had her clamping down on my fingers. Pushing her legs apart, I grasped her bottom, nudging myself into her warmth and shoving her forward just as I penetrated her. She bit her lip to dampen her cry which I stole with a kiss that had her melting into me. Thrusts and moans. Goosebumps that pebbled her skin and trembles that only encouraged me to go deeper and harder. Until her climax claimed her and mine chased it, cascading through me and depleting me entirely.

I clung to her, riding out the waves that threatened to bury me so deep only she could ever bring me back. Her body shook, her muscles still convulsing as our panting filled the space.

"You're naughty," she said, her voice a broken rasp.

I nuzzled her cheek. "But I'm all yours."

"Thank God, because I'm not a violent person, but I would tear someone apart if there was any competition."

Drawing back, I searched her eyes, seeing the fierce claim in them. "It's a good thing there is no competition then. My lawyers are excellent, but I doubt they could get you off for murder. Or me, for that matter."

"You?" she asked, laying kisses on my cheek as her hands wrapped around my neck.

"Damn right. You're mine, Tori. Don't think for a minute that if someone else had touched you while we were apart, I wouldn't hunt them down and make their lives miserable but if anyone dared touch you now...I would do extremely violent things that my lawyers would have a hard time defending."

Blue irises widened, and I caught her bottom lip between my teeth as her mouth fell open.

Dragging my teeth over her lip, I said, "Get dressed before I devour you again." I dropped my head, luring another moan from her as I pulled her nipple into my mouth. That pantry was looking good, and if I didn't stop, I'd carry her in and shake the foundation as I forced more orgasms from her.

Against my body's cravings, I stepped from her. Picking the sheet up, I wrapped it around my waist, letting my eyes drift over her body before I walked out to retrieve our clothes. Keeping myself restrained was going to be difficult. Tori brought out a hunger in me I couldn't contain. It had been that way in our past, and it hadn't changed. I needed to touch her like an addict needs a fix. The years without her had been excruciating, and no amount of resorting to my hand had satisfied the need for her. Now that I had her again, I wouldn't hesitate to take her. I'd gone too long without her, and I was ready to satiate my hunger.

CHAPTER 38

TORI

My feet made a soft padding sound when I walked into the kitchen. Our kitchen. It seemed surreal that Gabe had bought the house for us without even knowing if I would walk back into his life. His confidence astounded me, and maybe it should have frightened me, but that was Gabe. The mysterious darkness he held that drove that confidence and the man he was in the bedroom...or anyplace else he took me.

I shivered at the thought, my eyes landing on him and taking him in. He was shirtless in just his boxers, and I took in every sexy, defined part of him. Peeking up at me from where he was making us coffee, he gave me a coy grin.

"Good morning, beautiful."

That mouth had brought my body to new heights the prior night, just like his body had this morning before he'd left me too weak to follow him to the kitchen. It had taken me a painfully long time to make myself get out of bed.

He put a mug of coffee on the counter for me, and I reached for it, hoping he didn't notice how my hands were still shaking. He did, and a naughty twinkle lit his eyes.

"Guess it's too soon to ravage you again?" He spread his hands on the counter. "We haven't hit this spot yet."

I whimpered, an unexpected sound that had him chuckling. "Maybe after my coffee," I said, finally finding my voice.

Coffee in hand, I walked to the living room, taking in the view of the shore from the windows. His hands wrapped around my waist, his face burying in my neck. I leaned into it, glad Cash had asked to have Reid for the weekend. He and Brandi were taking Shelby to the Christmas festivities in a nearby town and had asked to take him. That left the weekend for just me and Gabe, who had insisted I help pick out furnishings for the master bedroom the day I told him. By the time we'd arrived on Friday, the room was furnished, and the fridge was stocked with food.

We'd been making our own memories in the house since that night.

"What time is the car picking Reid up?" I asked him. It had taken a lot of convincing, but I'd finally relented when he promised me his driver had been with the family since he was young and would ensure Reid got to Cash's safely. Cash had called me the moment he arrived at the same time the driver had called Gabe.

"Noon. We have plenty of time to squeeze in another movie and maybe a few more positions." Another shiver raced down my spine, and his breath was warm on my neck as he chuckled.

The waves beat against the shore in the distance, the wind making their peaks frothy.

"That sounds perfect."

I wiggled out of his hold and placed my coffee on a table.

"Can we talk first?"

"About what?" he asked, coming over to me.

I'd been putting this off, but Christmas was a week away. A text from his father on Thursday had reminded me of the deal I'd made with him.

"Do you remember when we talked to your father?"

His disposition turned, his eyes darkened, and I sighed. This was why I'd avoided bringing up the subject, but I was hoping with as happy as we were now, the blow would be easier.

"Yes." Clipped and sharp.

"Well, I made a deal with him to get the information."

"Secrets. I was waiting for you to tell me."

Lips pursed, I tried to disregard the sting of his words. "There hasn't been a good time. And you won't like it."

His hands dropped from me, and he backed away. "What did you offer, Tori?"

Great, exactly why I'd waited so long. "He wants to see Reid, but I told him he had to earn the right."

He crossed his arms, waiting for more.

"I told him he needs to mend the relationship with you and Liv, particularly you, first."

His jaw ticked, muscles going rigid. "There is no relationship, and whatever he offers, I don't want it."

"Gabe—"

"No, Tori. I have hated that man for years. There's nothing to salvage and nothing he can do to take back what he did."

"I know that, and that's not what I'm asking."

He tugged his hands through his hair, pacing. "And what is it you're asking?"

"For change. For him to show that he's a better man, that he can do better with Reid than he did with you, for him to own up to his mistakes and show you he loves you."

He froze, his head slowly turning to me. "He doesn't love me or Liv. He loves his money and his power. That's all he's ever loved. I don't want him anywhere near Reid, and after all he did to sabotage what we had, I would think you would want him nowhere near you. I certainly don't."

He stormed away, leaving me in the wake of his anger and hostility. The door to our room slammed, and a few minutes later he stalked down the stairs.

"Gabe, can't we just talk about it?"

I trailed him as he grabbed his coat and put on his shoes. "No."

"Where are you going?" Fear stalked through me. What had I done? It wasn't my business, and I'd gone and stuck my nose in it.

"For a walk." He threw the door open, slamming it behind him and leaving me to regret ruining our wonderful weekend.

After I showered and dressed, I warmed my coffee and sat on the couch, staring out the window and thinking of what I'd done. The more I sat and stewed, the angrier I became because even if Gabe thought it wasn't, this was my business. It affected the man I loved and my son. It had shadowed our relationship from the start, and Gabe wore his trauma like a cloak that billowed around him.

By the time I heard the door open, my anger had grown to the point where I didn't even turn around. He needed to face his past, and if he hated me for interfering, then maybe we weren't ready to move forward with this.

His footsteps scuffed through the silence, but still I didn't turn.

"I won't apologize." I said, my sight on a dune in the distance. "You may think it's not my business, but it is. You are my business, and what hurts you hurts me. The past hurts you, and I don't know how to ease it from your shoulders, but if there's a chance, even the smallest chance, that this does, then I will continue to advocate for it. I'm not doing this for your father, Gabe. I'm doing it for you and for Reid. You deserve something more than he ever gave you, and..." I paused, sucking back the tears.

"Tori." The pain in his voice had me turning, and the sight of him had me jumping from the couch. His shoulders were hunched, his entire demeanor drained. The powerful man I knew was no longer there, and in his place was a wounded boy with tears streaming down his cheeks.

I ran to him and folded him into my arms. He wrapped himself around me, burying his head in my shoulder. I'd never seen him cry. The only signs he ever gave me of being vulnerable were when he would put his hands in his pockets or look away from me, palming his neck. This was the broken boy below the man who took over companies and left men like Bradman shaking in their shoes. The side I suspected he only allowed me to see.

I held him as he clung to me. How long had he held his emotions in? How many years had it been building? Long enough to burrow so far into him that it never escaped. Until now.

Cradling his head, I murmured, "It's okay."

"I just wanted his love," he said, the words fractured by the sputtering sobs. "And my mother back."

My heart splintered, and I hugged him tighter. I couldn't fathom what he'd gone through because my childhood had been ideal. Other than my mother's battle with breast cancer, there had been nothing but happy memories.

My father had been doting and protective, my mother loving and present, their relationship one I'd idolized. They laughed together, joked, and played. There was never tension, never a raised voice unless it was behind closed doors where it didn't affect us.

All things Gabe never had. His mother had loved him, but her depression had stolen her from him. Perhaps his father had played a role in that, or perhaps his father had taken the blame in Gabe's mind. Based on all he had done to Gabe, it was no wonder.

"You don't have to do anything," I told him, soothing my hand over his head. "It's your choice, and I made that clear." I pulled him further into my hold, where he remained, his face hidden in my neck, his arms clinging to me. I lifted his head, seeing the tears as he looked away from me. Rubbing them away with my fingers, I forced his eyes to me. "But maybe it's time for you to heal. Whether it's with him in your life or not. You've held onto this pain for too long, Gabe."

He sniffed, giving me a nod before he released me and wiped his eyes with his arm. "I'm sorry," he said.

"Don't be. I love you, and that means I love every part of you. The wounded boy, the intense man. The strength and the tears. This doesn't make you weak, Gabe."

He glanced away again, but I put my hands on his cheeks and brought his sight back to me. "It doesn't, and that you trust me enough to let me see the pain shows me how much you love me."

"I do. More than anything in the world."

"I know."

He inhaled and let out a ragged breath. "I don't know what to do, Tori. What's my next step?"

"What does your heart say?" I asked, placing my hand on his chest.

"To follow your lead because I trust you, and if you think this is what I need, then I'll try."

"And if you fail, then you walk away. I won't judge you, and I won't look at you any differently."

He brushed a lock of my hair back, the intensity returning to his eyes. "I know you won't."

"I told him he could start with a Christmas present to Reid if and only if you agreed."

He tilted his head and gave me a small smile. "You know how to hit him hard. That man never bought us presents. My mother always did Christmas, and it stopped the year she died. He never gave us anything after that."

But a trust fund and a company he would have handed to Gabe if Gabe hadn't stolen it from his father first. But I said nothing even when I had my suspicions that there was more to his father than he thought. Nothing excused the violence and the abuse, but maybe it would help with reconciliation.

"Then maybe this will be the first test."

"Maybe."

"I'll text him your answer."

A brow lift and, "You have my father's phone number?"

I shrugged. "He texted me to see if you'd decided, so now I have it. I'm not sure where he got mine from."

"My father has his ways."

Amber eyes studied me until he touched his forehead to mine. "I love you, Tori. I'm sorry I walked out. You took me by surprise, and I needed time to think. To contemplate letting that man back into my life. I thought I was done the day I bought the company from him. Washed my hands of him, but it seems I can't escape him or the things he did to me. As much as I hate him, he's my father, and he never let us want for anything but his love."

"The most important thing."

"Yes, but it made me into who I am today. For better or worse."

I pulled his lips to mine. "Better," I said. "You are everything he's not, and you're already a better father. I don't doubt you'll continue to be better."

His kisses heated my core, the emotion in them reaching far into my being and reminding me of his claim on me. They didn't stop until he had me screaming his name and drowning in rapture.

CHAPTER 39

GABE

R eid grabbed his coat and came running to where I stood at the door.

"We won't be long," I told Tori as he buttoned up his coat.

"Have fun," she said, blowing us a kiss.

Three weeks had passed since DC, and we were falling into a comfortable routine, spending every night with each other either at her place or mine. Sleep overs as Reid called them, were our new norm, but I was ready to finalize us. To make it permanent.

Snow was falling in gentle flakes as Reid and I exited the car.

"Put your gloves on," I told him, pulling his hat from my pocket and securing it on his head. "We'll get hot chocolate when we're done."

"I love hot chocolate."

"I know," I said with a laugh. If it was one thing I'd discovered about my son, it was his affection for all things chocolate.

He ran ahead of me, leaving little boot tracks in the snow. When he found a patch of snow he deemed suitable, he dropped to his back and began making a snow angel. "Come on, Gabe."

I dropped next to him and made my own, his laughter infectious. We moved from angels to snowmen until I could see he was getting too cold. Gathering him up, I held his hand while we walked to the closest coffee shop.

With two cups of hot chocolate in my hands, we found a seat.

"I need to ask you something," I told him as we peeled our coats off. I reached over and took his hat off. His cheeks were red, so I rubbed my hands on them to warm them up.

"What?" he asked, wrapping his hands around his hot chocolate.

"Let that cool off before you try it." I'd had them add whipped cream, but the cups had still been hot. "I want your permission."

My insides tumbled as I remembered the last time I'd had this conversation, but with his grandfather.

"My permission?" he asked, the word coming out more like prission than permission.

"Yup." He waited intently as I gathered my words. "I want to ask your mom to marry me."

His eyes were like saucers, and he jumped up and down in his seat. Reaching over to calm him before he spilled his hot chocolate, I continued, "But I want your permission. It's been just the two of you all this time, and I don't want to do this without you. Can I ask your mother to be my wife?"

His smile was everything. "Yes." He bounced more. "Does that mean you'll really be my daddy?"

I gave him a questioning look. "I'm already your father, Reid. That hasn't stopped since the moment I found out you were mine."

I hadn't bothered to talk to him about it again, even though Tori had seemed guilty about telling him before discussing it with me. It had been her right to have that conversation, not mine. But maybe I should have, because Reid seemed confused still.

"Do you know why I wasn't part of your life until now?" I asked, the pain of the past returning.

He shook his head.

"Then it's time you hear the truth, and we can have this conversation again when you get older, but you deserve to know the truth." I gave him an abridged version of the events, keeping it at a level he could understand. When I finished, I sat back and waited.

His eyebrows puckered. "Your daddy's not very nice," he grumbled.

"No, he's not."

"Maybe he just needs a hug."

I doubted a hug could cure my father of his disposition, but I wasn't about to burst his bubble. "Maybe." Tori seemed to think there was something worth redeeming in him, and I had agreed to give it a try.

He scrambled out of his seat and ran to mine, throwing his arms around me. "I'm glad you're my daddy."

Clinging to him, I murmured, "So am I, and I'll spend every moment making up for the time we lost."

"When you marry Mommy?" He squirmed from my hold and put his forehead to mine.

"Yes, but that needs to be a secret. Just you and me because I don't want her to know yet."

He made a gesture like a zipper closing his mouth, and I laughed, giving his hair a tussle. "Drink your hot chocolate, and we'll get something special for Mommy for Christmas."

When we finished, I threw the cups away while he waited at the door for me. "Come on, Daddy, let's go get something pretty for Mommy."

My heart stuttered, my feet almost tripping over themselves. The burning behind my eyes had me blinking the sensation away. I scooped him into my arms and walked us out of the shop. "I love you, buddy."

His arms flew around my neck. "I love you, too, Daddy." And the space in my heart that Tori hadn't reached was healed with those five words.

We spent the next two hours shopping for Tori and her family. I let Reid pick his own present out for Tori, a bracelet with three heart charms on it. One for each of us he had told me as the salesclerk wrapped it and handed him the bag. Every moment I spent with him left my heart fuller, and by the time we returned home, I felt like I was living a blessed life. After years of thinking it a cursed one.

Tori was on the phone when we walked in. I hung our coats and walked over to her, wrapping my arms around her and bringing her back into my chest. Kissing her cheek, I pressed my nose to it. She squealed and wiggled out of my grasp.

"Your nose is cold," she complained. "Sorry, Mom. Gabe and Reid just walked in."

"Tell her I said hello," I added, hearing Reid shout, "Hi, Grandma," from where he had taken a spot on the couch with his tablet.

"Gabe says hi and so does Reid." She was quiet for a moment, then said, "Grandma says hi back to both of you."

Quiet again as I poured myself a glass of water.

"Okay, I'll ask and text you if she does. Love you, Mom. Can't wait to see you and Dad."

She hung up and gave Reid a big hug over the back of the couch. I couldn't help taking in the view, and she snapped her head around. "Stop looking at my butt."

"But it's such a nice butt."

Her cheeks bloomed with the blush I loved to see in them. "So what did you guys do?"

"Just some shopping and some guy time," I told her as she walked into the kitchen, leaning her hip on the counter.

"And if I ask Reid what you bought?"

"My mouth has a zipper, Mommy," he piped up from the couch.

The corner of her mouth rose. "Not even a hint?"

"Nope. My mouth has a zipper, too," I said, caging her in. "Although you can try to unzip it."

"I bet I can," she teased, wrapping her hand around my head and bringing my lips to hers. Kisses from Tori were like precious jewels that I wanted to hoard.

"Reid and I had a talk," I said, nipping her lip.

"About?"

"Us. Our past."

Her eyes scrunched, concern lining them.

"Don't worry. It was the abridged version, but he knows the truth now and why I wasn't there before. Why you looked so sad. His words, not mine." I swept my thumb down her jaw and over her chin. When he'd told me, the guilt had returned. Every reminder of how I'd hurt her brought it hammering back.

"I'm not sad anymore," she told me, giving me one of her smiles that made everything okay. "I'm proud of you. That was hard to do."

"But necessary."

"Necessary."

This time I initiated the kiss, stopping it only when it threatened to have me lifting her onto the counter and doing inappropriate things to her. Things I would do once Reid was in bed.

"What did your mom want you to ask?" It took her a moment to catch her breath as lust danced in her irises. I leaned in and whispered, "I'll finish that later."

Her shiver was intoxicating.

"She wants Liv to join us."

I snorted before I caught myself. "Liv doesn't do family events or holidays."

"That's what I told her, but she pointed out that you didn't either and maybe it was time to give Liv a chance to have a nice Christmas."

I tried not to roll my eyes. Liv's idea of celebrating a holiday was getting her nails done and drinking. Then again, mine had been a bottle of scotch and sitting in the dark with my ghosts, so maybe Tori's mother was right. A little of the Hent family might be good for her.

"I'll ask her, but don't get offended if she says no."

She shrugged. "Eh, I'll wear her down."

"You have two days, and I have no doubt you'll try your best." Giving her a peck, I freed her from my grasp. "I was thinking of making gnocchi for dinner. Sound good?"

"That sounds delicious. Oh, by the way," she motioned me to her bedroom and pointed to the bed, "that came for Reid today."

I looked over at the box on the bed, nervous stings pelting my skin. I didn't have to get closer to know it was from my father. Tori had texted him my agreement to the gift, but I wasn't sure I was ready for it.

Her hand caressed my back, and I glanced over at her.

"Second chances, right?" she said, reaching up and kissing my cheek.

"Right."

I wasn't so sure that was the right term for what I was giving my father, but it was up to him to prove he deserved my time. This was a start. He'd said he would send something, and he had. He had met the first test; the future would show me if he would meet any more.

Snow was falling, making for a white Christmas Eve that would turn into a white Christmas. Reid and his cousin were in the kitchen making cookies for Santa with their grandmother, while Tori was in the basement with Cash, Brandi, Cindy, and her boyfriend Noah. And Liv, who after some coaxing from Tori, had agreed to join us. Although the plethora of complaints she'd spouted on the way there had left me tempted to send her home.

Logs snapped in the fireplace, the only sound as I sat in the living room with Tori's father, waiting for him to speak. I stared out the window, watching the snow accumulate on the deck.

"So, the last time I gave you my approval, you broke my daughter's heart," he finally said, and I could hear the hesitation. I'd expected resistance given my track record.

"And I can't take that back. All I can do is make up for it." I turned to him. "Which I've been doing and will continue to do. I promised you I wouldn't hurt her again, and I won't. She and Reid are my life now, and nothing will make me give them up this time."

His blue eyes evaluated me, and I felt the weight of them. "It's been far too long since I've seen her this happy. Don't make me regret this."

"I won't."

"Good. Now go ask my daughter to marry you so we can celebrate for the rest of your visit."

I shook his hand before putting down my beer and making my way to the basement. Cash was telling Liv a story about Tori and Cindy when they were young and getting in trouble for something involving makeup and Barbie dolls. To my surprise, my sister actually laughed. Not her fake 'I'm annoyed and want to leave' laugh. This was a genuine laugh that had me smiling. She looked relaxed for the first time in years, and I thought perhaps Tori's mother had been right after all. Liv just needed a little of Tori's family to remind her of what Christmas could be.

Walking over to Tori, I gave her a kiss on the head and motioned for her to join me. "Take a walk with me," I told her, holding my hand out to her.

Liv raised her finely manicured brow, and I suspected she knew what I was up to.

"I'm stealing her for a few minutes."

"Have her back in time for the movie," Cindy said. The plan was to watch *Elf* with the kids before we tucked them in to await Santa.

"Will do."

I handed Tori her coat when we got upstairs, telling her I needed some fresh air and alone time with her when she asked me what we were doing. The rings I'd bought her were in my pocket. Two wraps to encase the engagement ring I intended to move to her wedding finger. With each step, their weight had my nerves jittering more.

Moonlight lit the back of the house, illuminating the path that led to the frozen lake where I'd proposed to her years before. It shimmered in the strands of Tori's hair that stuck out from under her pink hat.

"Do you remember the last time we were out here?" Tori asked, her hand in mine. There was a melancholy in her voice I hoped I was about to erase.

"There's no way I could forget," I said, turning her to me. The moonlight struck her eyes, leaving them brilliant cobalt. The words I'd repeated in my mind for days fled me, and I stood, awestruck by how lucky I was to have found her again. She looked out at the pond, sadness casting shadows on her face. Fingers going to her chin, I turned her eyes back to mine. "I promised you I would make new memories to replace the bad ones."

"But that one wasn't bad," she argued.

"No, but what followed was. I want to erase it from your mind and replace it with better."

She brought her fingers to my mouth. "It hurt. It nearly destroyed me, but I wouldn't have you take it from me because there were good parts."

With my eyes searching hers, I tried to understand her reasoning.

"The days before you left were nothing short of amazing. You spoiled me, showered me with affection, did things to my body that left their mark for years. I know now that you were trying to take a piece of me with you, and you did. I don't want to forget those days. Nor do I want to forget what resulted from them." She took my hand. "Our son. If you hadn't left me, hadn't completely enveloped me in your love those two days, I wouldn't have forgotten to take my birth control. I wouldn't have forgotten for the two days I couldn't leave my bed." I grimaced, hating myself again for the pain I had caused her. "It was horrible, and I don't wish it on anyone else, but I would never change it because he was my everything when you weren't there, and you now share that space with him again. Never think I would take that away."

I squeezed her hand, cupping my other around the back of her neck and bringing her to me. "You are the most extraordinary woman I know, and you continuously surprise me with how special you are."

I dropped my hand, reached into my pocket, and lowered to my knee. Her hand went to her mouth.

"Victoria Abigail Hent, I love you more than life itself, and my love for you grows every day when I think I couldn't possibly love you more. I gave you up once, and losing you left me gutted and comatose. But I have a second chance, and I don't want to lose you again. I won't survive. Marry me, and I swear that you and Reid will be my priority. Nothing will come between us, and nothing will come before you. I will give it all up, sell everything, retire, turn my back on everything for you both. You are my life, the blood that keeps my heart pumping, the air that fills my lungs, my very reason for living. And if you choose to be my wife, I will worship you every day for the rest of our lives."

A sob escaped her, and I waited as nerves battered my insides, threatening to topple me.

"Yes," she said. "Yes, again and again and again. It will always be yes, Gabe, because I can't live without you."

I was on my feet, sweeping her into my arms and kissing her before she finished the last word. My heart thudded uncontrollably against my chest, and the air seemed to escape my grasp on it. I lowered her, holding her face and looking into her eyes. She was mine, and she'd said yes, but I knew this was only the next step, and what followed would be the real test for her.

Because we had been here once before and fate had intervened, sending our paths careening from each other. I needed to see her walking down the aisle and hear the words 'I do' before I felt secure, and I was certain the same thought was in the back of her mind. No matter how joyful this moment was, our past continued to hold us prisoner. I was ready to shed it and embrace the future where it no longer held sway.

Chapter 40

Tori

Engaged. The word sent butterflies scurrying through my belly, but a sense of tainted déjà vu sat over the moment. As if he were experiencing the same sensation, Gabe's smile faltered. This was the moment that defined us, that had led to our undoing, but I wouldn't let that happen again, and I knew he wouldn't. He just needed to trust that I trusted him.

I turned my head into his palm and kissed it. "We left the past behind us," I said. "That's where it needs to stay. We will make it down the aisle this time. I will be your wife, and you will be my husband."

He rested his head on mine.

"Do you trust me, Gabe?"

"With my life."

I smiled at the power of that statement. "Then believe me when I say that wedding dress is getting worn this time."

He chuckled, and I shifted my face, sending my mouth crashing into his.

"Are you forgetting something?" I asked through our kisses.

"It's a little cold out here to make love to you."

My laugh caused our lips to part. Holding my hand out, I gestured to the ring on my finger.

"Oh that. Shoot, yes."

He pulled the ring from my finger and opened his hand. Two rings sat in it, and I creased my brows, reaching out to touch them.

"Needed to improve on the original," he said, wrapping the two bands around my ring so they formed a circle of diamonds around the one.

As he slipped them on my ring finger, nerves tingled along my spine. Never had I imagined I would find him again, and we would be at this point. I'd dreamed of finding him and telling him off when I stopped crying, but once Reid was born, the emotions cleared, and I couldn't free myself of him. Reid was a constant reminder of him, and the hollow space in my chest was another. But never had I dreamed this moment would happen.

"Did she say yes?"

I looked up to see everyone looking out at us from the deck.

"They all knew?" I asked him.

He gave me a shrug, then cupped his hands around his mouth and shouted, "Yes!"

A cheer rang out, and within moments, I saw a small bundle come running toward us. Reid ran to Gabe, who picked him up and spun him around just like he had me.

"We're going to be a family," he squealed, and Gabe laughed.

"We already were," he said, nuzzling Reid's nose.

Tears sprang, flowing too easily, and Reid reached for me. I took him from Gabe and gave him a big hug.

"Mommy and Daddy." It still left me speechless how he called Gabe that so easily, as if he'd been saying it his entire life. The change had come after Gabe took him out for the day, and I had cried the first time I heard him say it.

"And Reid," Gabe added.

He giggled. "And me."

We walked back to the house. There were hugs and tears and

threats from Cash before he patted Gabe on the back and pulled him into a hug. Even Liv seemed unusually happy. I thought it might be the glasses of wine, but when she gave me an awkward hug, I suspected it wasn't. She wasn't much for showing affection, I'd been around her enough to see that, so I took that hug and catalogued it with the image of Reid sitting between her and Gabe while we watched the movie. I exchanged looks with Gabe every time Reid called her Auntie Liv, and her lips twitched while she tried to maintain her scowl.

The sound of Reid bursting into our room had my eyes flying open and Gabe tugging the sheets up over us. My parents had let us share a room this time, and Gabe had taken full advantage of that hospitality by making me into putty as he repeatedly brought rapture to my body. Celebrating, he had called it, but whatever it was, I wasn't so sure the exhaustion that followed would make for a functional Christmas morning.

As Reid jumped on the bed, and Gabe grumbled, I was certain he hadn't expected the childlike wonder that came with Christmas morning nor the early morning hours that accompanied it.

"Why do you never have your clothes on for sleepovers?" Reid asked, jumping on the bed so that I had to sit up and grab him before he went toppling.

"Because this is a grown-up sleepover," Gabe explained, wiping his eyes. He reached over and looked at his phone. "Why are you up so early?"

"Santa came!"

"Welcome to parenthood," I told Gabe, giving him a kiss on the cheek and pulling the blanket around me so I could stand. "Did you wake Grandma and Grandpa?"

"Shelby is."

"Why don't you go wake your Auntie Liv while we get dressed?" Gabe said with a sly grin.

"Okay." He scooted off the bed and ran out the door, leaving it wide open.

I walked over and closed it just as Gabe's hand yanked my blanket from me. "There's no time for that," I scolded him.

"There's always time for that. Besides, Liv sleeps like a rock. It'll take him a while to get her up."

"That's not nice, sending our son in to wake her. She's just warming up to this, and you're tormenting her."

"She deserves it. I have plenty of paybacks from when we were little." He yanked me to him, and I heard Liv's shriek from down the hall.

"I think you're going to have to wait, Mr. Icinda. Santa came, and those kids will not wait for you to get your fill of me." I maneuvered out of his hold and headed to the bathroom.

"Damn, I might have to rethink this holiday thing."

He'd had fun the night before setting all the gifts under the tree and stuffing the stockings. It was almost like he was a kid, and seeing the joy in his eyes had made my heart even fuller.

Gabe came in while I was brushing my teeth. His hair was messy, and he looked incredibly adorable. It tempted me to make Reid wait an extra half hour to take advantage of Gabe, but there was no way I'd convince my son to wait for Christmas.

After we'd both dressed, me in my Christmas pajamas that Gabe promptly teased me for and him in a pair of sweatpants and a T-shirt that made me regret not stealing a few minutes because now he was just sexy as hell, we headed down the hall. Reid and Shelby were eagerly waiting at the top of the stairs, both knowing the rules that they had to wait for the adults—not that I thought they hadn't peeked at the tree while we were dressing. Cash and Brandi were standing guard, keeping them from wandering, and the others were congregating as we joined them. Liv gave Gabe a glare that had me relieved that he would have to deal with her wrath and not me.

"Why in God's name are we up this early?" she grumbled.

"Because it's Christmas morning, and this is what we do," Brandi explained.

"Can we go down now?" my niece asked.

Cash stood aside, and she and Reid bolted. I took Gabe's hand as we followed. "This makes it all worth it."

Instead of watching the kids, I watched Gabe. It was his first Christmas with Reid, and emotions played on his face. Wonder, excitement, awe. This moment was one I would remember along with the other significant ones that were slowly healing the painful ones.

When wrapping paper sufficiently covered the floor, Gabe took my hand and pulled me into his side, kissing my head. I peered up at him and saw that his eyes had grown misty.

"Can we go play?" Reid asked, gathering a handful of presents while his cousin did the same.

"There's one more present for you," I said, looking at Gabe to make sure he was still okay with this.

"For me?" Reid asked, dropping back to the floor. The move sent his presents tumbling from his hand.

Gabe rose and went to our room, returning with the box his father had sent. Neither of us had opened it. He placed it in front of Reid, and Liv shifted in her seat, her hands clenched. This was a big step for them, and I knew she was just as uncomfortable as Gabe was. Anxiety sent my nerves tumbling through my stomach like falling blocks.

"From Santa?" Reid asked, putting his hand on the box as my mother handed Gabe a pair of scissors.

"No," Gabe said, and a collective tension ran through the room.

My parents hadn't been happy about the gift either, my father taking on a protective stance regarding Gabe and even Liv when we'd told them. As much as this had been my suggestion, however, it was Gabe's decision, and I was proud of him for making it. I would have backed him either way, but I knew there were too many raw wounds remaining in him.

As he cut the tape on the box, the image of him tear-soaked and vulnerable returned, and I found myself moving closer to Liv. She had her hands bunched in her lap, and I reached over and placed mine on hers. Gaze flying to me then to our hands, she tensed, and I thought she would pull away. She was anything but touchy-feely. But she gave me a small smile and left it there, relaxing some.

Gabe removed a wrapped present from the box and pushed the empty box over to me. He sat on the floor next to Reid, staring at the present for a moment, and the emotion I witnessed pass over his face had me tightening my grip on Liv's hand. She put her other hand over mine, encasing it between hers, and we both held our breath.

"We should let them have a moment," my mother said, but Gabe shook his head.

"No, it's okay."

Reid looked between them before scooting closer to Gabe, whose focus remained on the present. He kneeled and put his hands on Gabe's face, lifting it. The prick of tears burned my eyes.

"Are you okay, Daddy?"

Gabe sniffed and cleared his throat, rubbing his eye before taking Reid's hand and kissing it. "I'm fine. This is from my father for you."

Reid's eyes grew large, and in a hushed voice he said, "Your daddy? The not nice one?"

Gabe chuckled, and Liv moved her hand from mine and cleared her throat. I leaned closer to her, knowing Gabe had Reid in this moment, but Liv needed someone, too.

"Yes, he's your other grandfather, and he's trying to be nice. I guess."

Reid sat back, contemplating his words. Silence fell over us, only the clink of Shelby's building set she had opened making any sound. Reid scratched his nose and tilted his head as he studied the present.

"Why does that make you sad?"

I inhaled, a sound that shattered the silence, and I glanced up to see my father holding my mother, who was wiping her eyes.

"Because he doesn't give presents," Liv said for Gabe.

Reid looked up at her, his eyes darting between her and Gabe. "He's your daddy, too?"

A simple question, but with so much weight that I felt it settle over her.

"Yes."

Reid took the present from Gabe and set it down. He got to his feet and gave Gabe a hug that nearly knocked him over, then ran to Liv and tackled her with a hug that left her frozen.

"She doesn't do hugs, buddy," Gabe said with a laugh that eased the tension in the room.

But Liv accepted the hug, holding him tight until she peeled him from her. "Don't wrinkle me," she said, humor in her voice.

"You're in pajamas," Gabe observed.

She shot him a look as Reid sat down with the present. "It's good that he's trying to be nice," he said. There were times he reminded me of a tiny adult. It was the side of him he got from Gabe because in those moments he sounded and looked the most like him.

"I think so, too," I said.

He gave me a big smile before he tore into the present.

"Is that a briefcase?" my brother asked.

"Leave it to my father to give a child a briefcase for Christmas. No wonder Mama bought all the gifts," Liv muttered.

Gabe ran a hand through his hair as Reid excitedly took the child-sized briefcase from its box. Fingers tracing the engraved initials, he read them, "R. N. I. Reid Nathaniel. What's the I for?"

My heart stopped, blood freezing in my veins. I'd never stopped to think about his last name, giving him mine on his birth certificate since Gabe was no longer in the picture. But I had listed Gabe as his father with the only name I knew him by: Gabriel Hughes.

Gabe seemed as speechless as I was because we hadn't discussed this yet, and we'd only just gotten engaged.

"Icinda," I said, finally finding my words. "It's Gabe's last name and will be mine when we marry."

"And that means it's mine, too?"

Gabe looked over at me, and I nodded.

"Yes," he said. "It will be."

That was the end of the conversation for Reid, who opened the case, his excitement growing at the things inside: a miniature legal pad, a pen, a play phone, and a clip-on tie.

"Can we go play?" he asked.

"Of course you can," I told him.

He stood, keeping the briefcase in his hand as he gathered a few other toys and ran off with his cousin. My mother said something about starting lunch as we picked up the discarded wrapping paper.

Grabbing the box to stuff it into, I said, "Gabe, there are other presents in here."

His head snapped up, and everyone froze. I pulled the three small packages out.

"For Reid?" he asked, and I shook my head.

I handed the one with Liv's name to her, the one with his name to him, and kept the third one with my name on it.

"Why don't we help your mom with lunch?" Brandi said, dragging Cash from his seat.

"That sounds like a good idea," my father added, following them from the room.

I sat back on the couch next to Liv and clutched the box, waiting to see what Gabe wanted to do.

"He really is an asshole," Liv muttered. "All these years, and now he wants to give gifts? Do you know how many years I gave him presents only to hear him grumble about hating holidays?"

"Was he always like that?" I asked as she tore the paper off her box.

"No. When Gabe was small, he would celebrate with us. It really wasn't until Mom's mental health slipped further that he started having business trips at Christmas."

"Was he cheating on her?" I didn't know where it had come from, but the thought was there.

"Nah," she said. "He just didn't want to be around us. I think we ruined things for him."

Gabe stayed quiet, his eyes still on the gift.

Liv opened the box, her jaw dropping. Hand shaking, she pulled a diamond necklace from the box. Her eyes went to Gabe.

"He said he got rid of everything." Her words were so low they came out as a whisper. "Two days after the funeral, every trace of her was gone." She ran her finger over the necklace. "I used to play dress-up in her jewelry box. She had so many beautiful pieces, and she would do my makeup and let me try on her gowns. I wanted her jewelry, and he told me he had given it all away."

She pulled other pieces from the box—earrings, bracelets. A collection of jewels and a curt note. *She would have wanted you to have these, and it's time I let her go.*

"What the hell does that mean?" she asked, but the picture that was slowly forming of their father was a more complex one than I thought they knew. "Open yours, Gabe." She shoved the jewelry back in and slammed the lid over it.

His throat bobbed when he looked up at us.

"Go on," she said. Every day, she revealed more of the commanding big sister and helped me see what torment Gabe had gone through when he'd let himself fall in love with me that first time.

With more finesse, he removed the wrapping paper. While

Liv's box had been a long rectangle, his was a larger square shape. The lid popped off, and his hand trembled when he dropped it.

He looked up at me, so vulnerable, with emotion splayed across his face, his hazel eyes a myriad of shades. Handing me the note, he said, "You read it."

I opened it. "This was my favorite picture of the two of you with her," I read. "The others are ones I could never share."

When I looked up, I saw the photo in his hand. Tears welled in his eyes, and he swallowed them back.

"That's Mama," Liv said, leaning over to see the picture. "I think that's in Italy. Remember, we would go every year to visit her family?"

She looked at me, and a reflection of the young girl she must have been before her father's verbal abuse and having to witness his physical abuse against her little brother had hardened her. Her eyes were vibrant with the memories. "We would go every summer. There was so much family, so many people and the food and laughter. And my mother was happy. It was the happiest I remember her."

She took the picture from Gabe and handed it to me. "That's Mom. She was the most beautiful woman, elegant almost regal."

The woman in the photo was indeed beautiful. With long auburn hair in curls that cascaded down the front of her dress. Her smile lit the photo, and her hazel eyes were identical to Gabe and Liv's. It was obvious they had taken after her. In her arms was a baby with a head of brown curls, the spitting image of Reid when he'd been a baby. Gabe. And at her skirts was a little girl who looked like a miniature copy of her mother. The photo was creased; the edges frayed.

"Like he kept it in his wallet," I said, not realizing I'd spoken out loud. My eyes jumped to Gabe's, thinking about the flower he'd kept all this time.

This man had held onto his past so much that he'd let it damage his present.

Gabe rifled through the other pictures, mumbling about how his father had told them he'd burned them all. Almost like he'd wanted his children free of the past that haunted him, never knowing how much he was hurting them.

"What did he give you?" Gabe asked, stuffing the pictures back in the box.

I handed the picture back to him and looked at my box. The smallest of the three. Fear crept up my spine. My chest was already aching for them. I didn't want to bring them anymore pain.

"Open it, Tori," Liv told me.

With a sigh, I removed the paper, finding a ring box. I glanced up at Gabe. Tension sat in his shoulders, his muscles taut under his T-shirt. Opening the box, I stared at the ring. A cluster of diamonds surrounding a sapphire gem set in a white gold band. No note accompanied it, so I picked it up and showed them.

"Mom's ring," Gabe said, his brows cinching.

"Yes, but it was Dad's mom's first. He gave it to her on their wedding day. I remember her telling me the story of how it passed down to the firstborn son of every generation. If there wasn't a son, it would pass to the firstborn male cousin, following that part of the family's line."

"I can't accept this," I said, handing it to Liv, who put her hand up and pushed it back to me.

"It's yours. Gabe is the firstborn son. He'll pass it to Reid when you're both ready."

Gabe rose, stretching his back before coming over to me and pulling me from where I was sitting. He took the ring, spinning it in his fingers before picking my hand up and slipping it on my finger where it fit surprisingly well. "It's yours. There's little we have of our family except the bad, but this was always part of the good. My mother never took this ring off, and she would want you to have it. My father knows that, just like we do."

"I need a drink," said Liv. "Scotch, little brother?"

He waited for my reaction.

"I think this is a scotch kind of day," I told him, ruffling his hair with my fingers.

"Scotch it is, big sister."

She strolled out of the room, leaving us alone.

"You all right?" I asked him. The morning had been emotion packed.

"I think so. Knowing you're here with me helps." He picked my hand up and kissed my engagement ring. "Knowing you'll be my wife soon makes it even better."

"Should we get that glass of scotch and start discussing dates? I already have the dress."

He drew me against him. "I was thinking April," he said, his mouth coursing down my neck. "And I have just the location."

Chapter 41

Gabe

The weather had turned. Spring was here, and in another two weeks Tori would be my wife. It had seemed a lifetime ago when I'd first asked her, and now it was finally here. I watched the people walk by, enjoying a stroll in the warm weather. Birds ran in front of them, snatching crumbs from the ground.

"I always hated this park," my father said, taking a seat next to me.

I kept my sight on the path. "Is there anything you don't hate?"

"Not much."

Silence fell over us, and I glanced at him. He looked relaxed and tanned. Khaki had never been a color my father wore, granted it was rare to see him out of a suit, but he wore it today with a polo shirt, something I'd only seen him wear when he had last visited me at the office.

"Retired life seems to be treating you well," I said, turning my focus back to the birds.

"It's surprising, but I'm enjoying it."

"Look," I started, unsure of what I wanted to say to him.

"Let me start," he interjected. I peered over to see him lean forward, his hands clasped. "I was hard on you."

I snorted. "That's an understatement."

"And maybe I didn't make the best decisions."

"You think?"

"You called me, William. Not the other way around. I put it in your hands, and you made the first move."

"Because I wanted to hear your excuses. Hear what could possibly make you think I'd forgive you for laying a hand on me, for hurting me so badly that I still carry the scars."

"My father."

I snapped my gaze to him. Creases lined his brown eyes, his age clearer now than I'd ever noticed.

He let out a sigh, rubbing his hands together. "It's not an excuse. I know, but he would take his belt to me, his fist, sometimes whatever he could find when he was drunk. I left when I was eighteen and never looked back. A scholarship to Harvard I'd earned by throwing myself into my schoolwork was my way out. I worked every part-time job and accepted every internship, and when I met your mother, I swore I would never treat her like my father had treated my mother. That I would never raise a hand to my children."

He lowered his head, running his fingers through his hair. "I made the same promise when Olivia was born and when you were born. Promised I wouldn't be my father. But your mother's depression continued to haunt her."

"Bradman?" I asked.

"Yes." He looked up at me, sitting back. "She witnessed everything, and he'd been set to do the same thing to her when I found her. I beat the shit out of him and took her roommate to the hospital. His parents hushed it up, and the girl dropped out when she found out she was pregnant. Your mother was never the same. It would come in waves. I know now she was bipolar, but back then, we didn't know that.

"I didn't kill your mother, William. Depression did. But I was a weak man, and I left her to deal with it on her own. I didn't know how to help her, and when I was home, it just reminded me of how weak I was, how helpless it made me."

"So you decided beating me would make you a man?" I snarled, my anger surfacing.

"Yes. I didn't mean it to happen, and the first time I hit you, I left for a week, telling your mother I had a business trip and sleeping in the office instead. It scared me, but then the anger at the situation returned when I stepped into the house again, and...I became my father. I never hit your mother, never hurt your sister—"

"Not with your hands, but you still hurt her."

"I was tough on her."

"Tough?" I laughed. "That's your idea of tough? Telling her she'll never make it in a man's world? How dumb she was? That she needed to give up her fight and stay in the kitchen?"

"It shaped her into the woman she is today. She fought everything I told her, proving me wrong at every turn. She's not some spoiled rich girl. She's strong, smart, and can hold her own against any man."

This was the first time I'd ever heard my father compliment my sister, and it left me stunned. My jaw went slack as I stared at him. "Did you ever think of telling her that?"

"No." He bent forward again. "Maybe I should have."

"Yeah, you should have."

"I made mistakes, William. Too many to take back, but it made you both into adults who are formidable."

I didn't know how formidable Liv was with her manicures and spa days, but I didn't argue.

"You could have done the same without the abuse."

"Maybe, but I can't and won't take it back. It's too late. All I can do now is try to mend things."

I stood, straightening my jacket. "That's a difficult thing to do, and I'm not sure I want to mend anything."

"Your fiancé thinks you do. She's smart and impressive."

"I know, and she left the decision in my hands. I'm just uncertain about what I want to do with it. Mending fences with a man who used me as a punching bag instead of getting help for his anger issues seems a waste of my time." I pulled the invitation from my pocket, weighing it in my hands. "This is as far as I'll go right now."

I handed it to him and walked away.

"William."

I stopped and turned back to him.

"Ask Victoria how she found out about the CFO position. I'm not the monster you think I am."

My brow creased as his words knocked around in my mind. Turning from him, I continued my path, leaving his puzzling words and excuses behind. When I returned to the office, I went straight to Tori's office.

She looked up from her computer, her smile filling her face. "How did it go?"

"Not the way you wanted," I admitted, closing the door behind me. I walked over to her and dragged her from her chair, needing her touch to calm my spirit.

"That bad?" she asked as my hands climbed up her sides.

My mouth was on hers, stealing kisses. "I gave him the invitation."

"That's a start," she murmured, her head falling back as I scraped my mouth over her cheek and down her neck. The dress she wore wrapped around her body, and I had the urge to untie it and let it fall open.

Remembering my father's words, I asked, "How did you hear about this position?"

"A recruiter called me two days after I left Bradman."

I halted my attempts to seduce her and met her eyes. "I didn't use a recruiter."

She squinted at me. "Of course you did. She said she saw my resume...which I hadn't put up yet. I didn't even question it."

"What was the name of the company?"

"WPI Recruiting."

I pinched the space between my eyes, hating that my father had yet another hand in my life. "Damn him. My father owned that company. He sold it right before I took him down, and I thought he was trying to find money in a last-ditch effort to avoid selling the larger holdings."

"What are you saying, Gabe?"

What was I saying? That my father had brought us back together? But that made no sense. He was the one who had torn us apart. But the visit, running into Tori in the building, none of it had been coincidence. The candidates he had turned down, the excuses that they weren't the right fit. He hadn't been planning to give me back the CFO position. He'd known what Liv and I had planned and was waiting for the right moment to woo Tori from Bradman. I leaned against the desk trying to stay upright. All this time I thought I'd been in control, yet he'd been manipulating all the strings.

"Gabe?"

"My father wanted you here. He wanted us to reunite. He had the recruiter call you because he wanted you here." I squeezed the bridge of my nose. "Why did you check in that day we bumped into each other?"

"The recruiter told me to check in at ten."

Exactly when my father was signing the papers. My world fell from under my feet, and I held onto the desk.

"Gabe, what's going on?" Tori stepped up to me, and I dragged her between my legs, burying my face in her chest.

"I thought I had him, and all this time, it was just a series of tests. He knew everything. He already told me he knew we were scheming. But he knew I was taking him down, knew I'd be waiting in the lobby that day at that time. Knew you'd be checking in and would likely bring Reid with you."

She lifted my head, her blue eyes darkening with worry. "He brought us back together?"

"He tested me. All of it was a test, and when I was where he wanted me, where he thought I was strongest, he set it up to reward me. Let me buy the company, let me think Liv and I had beaten him, let me have every holding I bought from him over the years, and put you back in my path."

"Making up for what he did to us?"

"Maybe."

Cobalt orbs searched mine as her fingers draped over my jawline. "You still did all of it, Gabe. He didn't let you do anything. You proved yourself by taking it from him. That was the test. He didn't hand it to you. You took it just like he wanted you to."

"But what if you'd married someone else? How could he have known you would return to me?"

"You said he knew about Reid, right?" A nod of affirmation. "He was watching me just like he was watching you. He knew we were both still in love with each other, and if we weren't, then he would never have let our paths cross again."

"That's a lot of credit to give my father."

"As much as you just gave him." She brought her face closer to mine. "Stop overthinking it. We're here. We're together, and we're getting married in two weeks. Nothing will come between us again, and if you sit around and think only about what-ifs, you'll miss all we can truly be."

I wrapped my arms around her waist and stood. "You're right."

Arms coming around my neck, she kissed me, saying, "I know I am. You'll get used to that."

I chuckled and untied her dress.

"Gabe!"

"Hush. I want you to show me what we are, luna mia." I

picked her up and planted her on the desk. "Show me what awaits me when you're Mrs. Icinda."

Her dress fell open, exposing the matching bra and panties I'd watched her pull on that morning. "You already know what awaits," she argued as I cupped her breast.

"I need reminding."

She let out a moan as I pressed into her so she would know how desperately I wanted her. Within seconds, we both forgot the unlocked door, and as she fell apart for me, I didn't care who walked in because there was no way I was stopping. In fact, I didn't stop until she'd come undone a second time with me following not far behind.

Three days before our wedding, I awoke to find Tori's side of the bed empty. Unusual since I was typically up before her. Yawning, I rose, pulling a pair of boxers and sweats on. Searching the house, I scratched my head, wondering where she and Reid were. I grabbed some orange juice from the fridge and after pouring myself a glass, I walked over to the windows, seeing neither of them on the deck or the beach. We'd moved Tori out of her hotel suite, setting up home in the house instead but keeping my penthouse suite for nights we didn't want to commute.

The front door opened, and Reid came running in. He came to a halt, looking mischievous as Tori closed the door behind them.

"You're up," she said, coming to me and kissing my cheek.

"What are you two up to?" I asked, squeezing her waist and giving Reid a wink.

"We have a surprise," she said, and Reid looked like he was ready to explode. "Come sit down."

I looked between them and let her lead me to the couch. She seemed nervous, and Reid seemed way too excited.

"You two would not make good poker players."

She ran over to her purse and took out a manila envelope. Handing it to Reid, she put her hand on his back. "You give it to him."

"Give me what?" My curiosity was on overdrive.

Reid handed me the envelope, and I questioned them both with my eyes.

"I had a meeting with our attorney this morning," said Tori. "He pulled some strings when I gave him a copy of our marriage certificate." My brow rose as my curiosity hit its peak. We'd gone to the courthouse to get our marriage license a few days before, making us officially married. A day we'd celebrated in bed, after taking the day off and dropping Reid off at the childcare center. "Just open it."

I unhooked the metal tabs and reached in, pulling out the papers. The envelope fell from my hands as I stared at the birth certificate listing Victoria Abigail Icinda and William Gabriel Icinda as Reid's parents. Pressure built in my eyes.

"There's more," Reid said excitedly.

My fingers slipped as I pulled the second document from behind it. A court order recognizing a name change. Changing Reid's last name to mine.

"It's official," Tori said, and I heard the tears in her voice.

I couldn't talk. All I could do was pull Reid into my arms and hold on to him. He was officially mine now, and nothing had felt better than that moment except the moment Tori and I had signed the marriage certificate.

I held him tight, tears stinging my eyes. When I looked up at Tori, I saw tears streaming down her cheeks. We had made it. After everything we'd suffered, every mistake, every agonizing step. We had gotten to our happy ending, and I would never let us lose it again.

Chapter 42

Tori

My hands were trembling, my bouquet moving uncontrollably in my hand.

"Calm breaths," my father told me, putting his hand over my wrist.

"I don't know why I'm so nervous," I said, blinking back the building tears, fearful of looking like a mess of mascara streaks by the time I got to Gabe.

"Because the two of you have been through a lot, and this moment once seemed impossible."

I thought about his words and all Gabe and I had weathered to get to this step. The breeze picked my veil up, scattering cherry blossoms over it. Two of them danced in front of me before the wind pulled them apart. I watched them float away, meeting up again when they landed. Like me and Gabe, our lives intersecting then separating only to come crashing back together.

My father reached up and adjusted my veil. "You look like a princess," he said, giving my cheek a kiss before he pulled the veil down.

"Thanks, Dad."

The music started, causing my heart to beat erratically.

"That's your cue," the wedding planner said, gesturing toward the path. She straightened the train of my dress as my father took my arm in his.

"Ready?"

"I've been ready," I said, realizing I'd been waiting for this moment since the day I met Gabe. Even through the devastation and lowest points, I'd secretly waited for it, knowing he was my soulmate and he was still out there. Never knowing he was waiting for me but dreaming he was, that there was a happy ending for us, one that explained why he'd left me.

"Then let's get you to your husband."

A current of nerves sparked through me at the word. Gabe would be my husband, and I would be his wife. We'd finally be a family.

My father led me around the edge of the path toward where the guests were seated. Pausing, I took a moment to watch the blossoms from the trees spread through the air like magical beacons. In my periphery, I saw the outline of a man and turned my sight to see Gabe's father standing in the shadows. Not part of the festivities but still there, present and standing witness to our joyful moment. His eye caught mine, and he gave me a curt nod, which I returned, feeling my father's grip on me tighten.

"Still not happy about that," he muttered.

"I'm sure he won't stay. But he's here, and that says something."

I returned to my path toward the aisle, seeing Gabe's narrowed gaze slip from his father to me. Hazel orbs danced with awe and love, and my heart sputtered. He looked so handsome in his tux, and the smile that filled his face had me quickening my pace.

His three friends from school, including our attorney, stood next to him along with my brother and Reid with his tiny tux, looking just like his father. Cindy, my cousin Anna, Brandi, Shelby, and Liv stood across from him in their pink dresses, ones I insisted

I wanted even after Liv complained it wasn't her color. She looked spectacular, so I really didn't know what she was talking about.

My eyes stayed on Gabe, every step leading me to him, and when my father handed me to him, I thought my smile would fracture the muscles in my cheeks.

"Mommy looks beautiful," Reid said, causing everyone to laugh.

"Yes, she does," Gabe agreed.

As the ceremony progressed, the world faded away so that there was only me and Gabe, locking eyes in the waiting room as he entered that day for training. Confident and sexy.

The vows fell from my lips, following his. The rings slipped onto our fingers, and the day that had never been finally became real.

"You may now kiss the bride."

Gabe lifted my veil, his eyes moist. He brushed a tear from my cheek and kissed me. The kiss, like all his others, reached far into my depths and awakened his claim on me. And I knew it would always be like this with him. Alive, adventurous, passionate. With him, I had everything and more than I could ever have dreamed. It had taken us years to get to this point—heartache, anguish, pain, and pleasure—but we had made it, and I knew in my heart neither of us would ever sway from the path. We would always be because we always had been. Like the paper flowers we had once made, our love would never fade.

EPILOGUE

GABE

Fourteen years, two months, ten days later

I juggled the coffee as I kicked the door closed, eyeing the two suitcases next to the door. That there were only two confirmed my suspicion that today would test my patience. After placing the coffee on the kitchen counter, I jogged up the stairs.

"Stay out of my bathroom, Reid!"

"I wasn't in your bathroom," came a grumbled reply, muffled behind Reid's bedroom door.

I opened it to find him buried in blankets, a pillow over his head, his long leg hanging off the bed.

"Why are you still in bed, and what did you do to your sister this time?"

The pillow lifted, and groggy hazel eyes squinted at me. "Because I'm on summer break."

Rubbing my temples, I waited for the rest.

He gave me a devious grin, his messy curls flopping on his forehead as he lifted his upper body and stretched. The same grin he'd been giving me since he was five, but at nineteen, it meant I had an annoyed pre-teen daughter to contend with.

"I may have reorganized her lip glosses. But to be fair, Dad, she has like twenty of them. Who needs twenty tubes of lip gloss?"

Nobody, and I had my sister to blame for how obsessed her niece was with fashion and make-up.

I pinched the bridge of my nose. "Get up and leave your sister alone." My eyes fell to the open suitcase with a balled-up pair of socks and two T-shirts hanging haphazardly from it. "Tell me that's not the suitcase you're planning on taking with us?"

"Yeah."

My patience frayed further. "The car will be here in thirty minutes. Get up, get ready, and pack, or I'll change your seat, so you're stuck next to your sister the entire trip."

His mouth fell open, and I shook my head, turning from his room and running smack into the cause of his annoyance.

"Daddy, he messed them all up." Blue eyes that could break even the coldest heart and that matched Tori's looked up at me.

"It's lip gloss, Ariella, not the end of the world. Pack two and get your suitcase downstairs."

She gaped at me. "Two? But I need one for every day."

I almost didn't want to ask, but I did. "Why?"

"Because a lady always changes her shade to keep them guessing."

Strangling Liv had been a natural urge since she had taken our daughter under her wing. "And who would a twelve-year-old girl need to keep guessing?"

"Her imaginary boyfriends," Reid chimed in from behind me.

"Pack, Reid. Now." I said, shutting his door and moving Ariella back before she went feral on him. I could see it in her eyes, that same look her mother had when she was ready to sink her fangs in.

"He's so mean to me."

"Are you packed?" I asked her, ignoring the constant friction between the two. Reid loved his sister, but he also knew how to push her buttons. I was glad he was in college because as much as I missed him while he was gone, I didn't have to deal with this.

"Yes. Is Auntie Liv here yet?"

"They're meeting us at the plane."

She bounced on her toes, gave me a quick peck on the cheek, and ran back to her room. Another shake of my head and I peeked in our room, looking for Tori. The bed was made, the curtains open, but no Tori.

Heading back downstairs, I checked outside, seeing her figure in the distance on the beach. The waves were crashing against the surf when I reached her. Folding my arms around her waist, I kissed her cheek. Just having her in my arms soothed the tension the kids had caused. A sigh came from her, and she placed her hands over mine, leaning into me.

"Escaping the chaos?" I asked, inhaling the salt air and the scent of vanilla and cherry blossoms on her skin.

"Something like that."

"Just think, in ten hours we'll be in Italy, the kids will be busy with their cousins, and we can sneak away."

She chuckled, turning to face me. "How many years have we been making this trip?"

Since the year we'd married. Tori had arranged the first trip, somehow convincing my father to give her the information on my mother's family. That first year had been a reunion too long in the making, and it had been like returning home to see the family who had always welcomed us when my mother was alive. We'd been taking the trip every year since, Liv in tow.

"Fourteen years," I said, knowing the number because it was the number of years we'd been married. Each one as wonderful as the first.

"And you think we'll have time to slip away?" Cornfield blue shimmered with humor.

I pushed a strand of hair from her cheek and tugged her closer to me. "I do. In fact, I plan on keeping you and this body to myself the entire trip. We'll say our hellos, sneak off, and lock ourselves in our room until it's time to return home."

Her smile lit her eyes, and I marveled at how even after all these years she was still the most beautiful woman in the world.

"I like that plan," she murmured as I threaded my hand through her hair and brought her mouth to mine. Kissing her still set the crevices of my soul ablaze, and I drew her as close to me as I could.

"Mom, have you seen my phone?" Reid's shout broke the magic of the moment, and I dropped my head to Tori's neck.

"It's in the basement," she called to him, her laughter at my predicament not unusual.

Picking my head up, she asked me, "How much time do we have until the car comes?"

I looked at my watch. "Twenty minutes."

"I think that's plenty of time." She wiggled out of my arms, and I quirked my brow, wondering what she was up to. "There's a spot in the pantry I think we neglected to christen." There was mischief in her blue eyes that sent my pulse racing.

"Is that so, luna mia?"

"Mm hm." She backed away, giving me that gorgeous smile that still broke me. "But only if you can catch me first." She turned on her heel, her bare feet sending sand splashing behind her.

I watched her, wondering how I'd gotten so lucky to have her in my life. I had found her, then lost her, and somehow found her again. A second chance that had never ended and never would because Tori was my life, my essence, my reason for everything. The light in my darkness.

Letting out a laugh that came from deep inside of me, free and complete, I ran after her, catching up to her. The squeal she made as I swept her into my arms and carried her into the house was almost as rewarding as sneaking into the pantry and destroying it with our unrelenting need for each other.

Almost.

About the Author

J. L. Jackola is a writer of love stories with morally gray men and the feisty women they adore. She's an admitted sugar addict with a penchant for anything with salted caramel. When she's not weaving tales, snacking on sweets, or downing her morning cup of tea, you can find her logging miles in her running shoes, watching movies with her family, or curled up with a book.

She resides in Delaware with her husband and three children.

To learn more, visit her website at www.jljackola.com and be sure to sign up for J L's newsletter to keep up with all the latest release news.